A Walk to the River

A Walk to the River

WILLIAM HOFFMAN

Doubleday & Company, Inc.
Garden City, New York
1970

*All of the characters in this book
are fictitious, and any resemblance
to actual persons, living or dead,
is purely coincidental.*

LIBRARY OF CONGRESS CATALOG CARD NUMBER 71–103756
COPYRIGHT © 1970 BY WILLIAM HOFFMAN
ALL RIGHTS RESERVED
PRINTED IN THE UNITED STATES OF AMERICA
FIRST EDITION

For
Ruth Beckley and Margaret Kay

Book One

[1]

I, Jackson LeJohn, a dead man, sat in the office of my dusty, aging hardware store and listened to the slow tick of an old clock on the tongue-and-groove wall. Up the street in the heat of the day I heard noise from the Progress Store. They were having a sale. They were always having a sale, and the windows were ablaze with red and yellow posters shaped like tulips. Loudspeakers played hillbilly music, and a machine tapped a metal mallet against glass, making a sound like a telegraph key. On display was a small ferris wheel with cans of cheap paint in the seats. Colored lights flashed. The Progress Store was enough to make a man sick—if a man cared.

It was hot in Virginia. Heat had burned off the morning dew. Thick, muggy air slowed time until the golden pendulum of my old clock ticked like a drum at an execution. I slapped at a fly that moved casually out of the way, as if he weren't concerned whether I squashed him or not.

The bell on the spiral spring over my front door rang for the first time since I'd opened the store at eight thirty. I turned in my swivel chair to see Sutter listing toward me down a dusty aisle of paint cans and plow handles. Sutter was in his late sixties, a slight and rumpled man who looked as if he'd just come from a grave. He wore a creaseless gray suit, a straw hat, and brown-and-white shoes with perforations in them. Across his vest was a golden chain with an Elk's tooth on it.

I'd never seen Sutter when he didn't appear tired. Even early in the morning or relaxing at a movie, he seemed on the point of falling over. A stranger's impulse was to hurry forward and assist him by taking an elbow.

Like me, he was a mournful man. He'd patched up too many bones and sewed too much flesh. He knew mortality and death the way some men knew their wives, and it'd killed the spirit in him.

He walked into my office and sat down by my roll-top desk. He settled his straw hat into his lap. He kicked shut the door.

"Hot," he said. "Too hot for mess."

I watched him warily. If it were mess, I wasn't going to let him put it on me. I narrowed my eyes and set myself to resist.

He pulled out a ball of a handkerchief and dabbed at his face. His skin was puffy, as if it had bubbles of air under it. Sutter drank—not to the place where he was sloppy, but often in the loneliness of his work he pulled out a pint and sucked it. I'd seen him do it right in front of the state police the time he gathered up the bloody scraps of four high-school Negroes who'd smashed into the center pillar of an underpass and shredded themselves through the jagged steel and windshield like black cabbage.

"A lot of people are going to be sick today," Sutter said. "They don't feel bad on good days, but when the snow's falling or Hell has busted open they all get sick."

I didn't speak. I opened the door for air, but again he kicked it shut.

"You're not talking much," he said.

"So far I haven't heard anything that needed talking."

"You remind me of a setter I used to have. Every time I'd take out my pipe he'd curve away from me because I once blew smoke in his face. All I had to do was show him the pipe, and he'd curve away."

"That setter had good sense."

"More sense than people," Sutter said. He focused on me. His brown eyes were moist and bloodshot. His glasses made them loom. He sighed. "You got real mess."

"I decline," I said. It was so hot in the office with the door closed that my sweat was sweating. Given half a chance I could stay dry even on a day like this, but sweating depended on inside coolness, and lately I'd been nervous. Now Sutter was at me. His bony fingers drummed against the hard crown of his straw hat.

"You're the man," he said. "Chairman, Board of Officers."

So it was church mess. The Board of Officers was the governing body of our congregation. I was chairman not because I was a religious man—I had lost that—but because there were people who were trying to trap me back into life.

"We can discuss church business on Sunday," I said and stood. I opened the door.

"Sit down," Sutter said. He kicked the door shut. "You're going to do your job even if I have to shame you."

I sat slowly. Why couldn't they just let a man be dead? Sutter was staring at me. His fingers stopped drumming. He spread his palm flat on his hat.

"I don't know how to say it." He sagged in the chair. The office heat seemed to be melting him away so that in another minute he would slide off and become a puddle on the floor.

"Try plain English," I said.

He cleared his throat, adjusted his glasses, and resettled his hat in his lap.

"A member of the congregation claims his wife was lechered."

I sat up. I'd expected something about reseeding the lawn or a fund drive for air conditioning. We had a small church, less than two hundred members, and about nine-tenths of us were kin to each other. Nobody had ever pinched a choir girl or short-changed the collection plate—much less lechered.

"Who?" I asked.

"Lou Gaines is all."

I wiped sweat off my face. Lou was the kind of man people made way for, and he was crazy in love with his wife. I thought of her, the elegant Caroline who walked down streets on those slim, beautifully formed legs, her heels clicking against the concrete, her head held imperially, that girlish body always stylishly

13

dressed, so that you never saw her in the same clothes twice. She was haughty, and when she passed, men squared their shoulders and removed their hats, though none would have dared whistle at her, not even the hoi polloi of the pool parlor who colored hairs on the calendar pictures nailed to walls.

"Who?" I asked a second time, sitting tense in my chair now, braced as if against a wind.

"That's the best part," Sutter said and looked sadder than ever. He looked as if tears might spill from his eyes. His shoulders seemed to sink into his waist. I expected Sutter's legs to shorten and draw his dusty shoes right up off the floor. "It's the cream on the strawberries."

He spoke the name as if it were a holy word and rubbed his nose. I leaned toward him.

"My ears must be going bad," I said.

"You heard," he said.

"Who?"

"Our shepherd," he said and threw his hat on the floor. "Our good pastor—Preacher Paul."

The old clock ticked above me. It had been given out to dealers in the early 1900's by a firm that sold harness and wagons. The clock had a yellow face, Roman numerals, and a lazy golden pendulum which swung inside a cherry case. Now the ticking was so loud that I wanted to stand and still that pendulum. It was as if the clock had listened and were protesting.

There might have been something more Sutter could have done to shock me. He could have drawn a revolver, pointed it at my face, and pulled the trigger. That act would have affected me more, but not a whole lot more than to say that our preacher had put his hands on a beautiful, icy woman most of us were afraid even to glance at because of Lou Gaines' jealousy.

Yet while I was shocked, in the depths of me I was not greatly surprised. I had lost faith in man. I expected the ugly, the perverse, and the evil from him. Why should it be different with preachers?

14

The clock ticked great slow ticks. Sweat slid down me, along the creases of my skin. My hands were shaky on the arms of my chair. I thought of Paul Elgin, minister, who charged down the aisles of our church and wrestled the Devil to three falls.

"What am I supposed to do?" I asked. I fanned the door to cool the office.

"You know the rules," Sutter said. He picked up his hat.

"You want me to call a meeting of the board?"

"I don't want anything."

I was becoming wetter by the second. Sweat seeped into my clothes. I watched Sutter. Damp gray hair lay flat against his skull. He pouted.

"The question is what you should do," he said. He fanned himself with his hat. "My advice would be to calm the waters."

"Who knows about it?" I asked and wiped my face.

"Just a few of us now, but general knowing won't take long." We sat, hearing the clock.

"Are you sure about everything?" I asked.

"I'm not sure of anything," Sutter said, pouting. "Lou came to me. He was pounding on my door at three this morning."

"Give me the details," I said, not wanting them, afraid of them.

"Lou returned from Richmond late last night. When he put his car away and went in his house, he heard Caroline yell. He ran through the house to the porch—the screened-in porch at the back. She was protecting herself from Paul."

"Lou saw it?"

"He saw it."

I rubbed my face and tried to focus on Sutter's words, but the picture was all blurred. I couldn't imagine Caroline yelling or showing emotion. I couldn't visualize our Hell-charging minister grabbing her and thrusting under her dress.

"Lou jumped him," Sutter said. "He knocked Paul down and chased him out of the house."

I thought how awkward it must have been—how ugly.

15

I tried to think of some way to keep it quiet, but I could not. Life in Black Leaf was too connected. When a person lifted his hand, he jostled his neighbor. Moreover the town—any town—had antennae for scandal, as a butterfly does for the lily and rose.

"Goddamn!" I said and stood. I was angry at Sutter's hooking me into this. "I'm chairman by accident. I'm no churchman."

"Maybe you'll be lucky," he said. He fanned himself. "Maybe Lou's cooled off and our pastor's already gone."

He stood, put on his hat, and left my office. I followed him. Sutter walked lopsidedly. He'd carried his black doctoring bag for so long that he pulled down along his right arm and hand.

He went out the front door. He tipped his hat to a lady. When he put the straw hat back on his head, he smacked it down as if trying to drive himself into the hot concrete sidewalk.

[2]

I was a man holding a rattlesnake: no way to let go without being bit.

I went to my office, sat in my squeaky chair, and tried to think. I believed in never doing anything hurriedly. Time was the great healer, my father had used to tell me. I was counting on time.

I had one picture very clearly in mind—of Lou Gaines roaming the streets with his shotgun and blasting the preacher to eternity. I imagined the whole town blowing up—the buildings and people, cats and dogs, everything flying up through the air and tumbling end over end.

The telephone on my desk rang. It had to be trouble. I pushed away.

Suppose, however, the call were business. God knew I needed that. At the other end of the line the school superintendent could be waiting for me to quote him a bid on a hundred gallons of roof paint.

Trapped by money, I moved my shaky hand to the telephone and lifted it. Immediately I was sorry.

"I'm waiting for you," Lou said.

"I'll come right over."

"You better," he said and hung up.

A lot of people didn't like Lou. He was aggressive, and while drive might be a virtue in New York or Chicago, our people were suspicious of anybody who tried too hard. There was a belief such a person couldn't be genteel.

Occasionally I had to remind myself Lou was my friend. We'd smoked nickel packs of Sunshine cigarettes in the woods when we were boys, and I'd fought him a couple of times until we were both bloody. We'd bought our first liquor together, a Mason jar of white lightning which we drank with orange pop. We'd gotten so sick we lay on the grass moaning and puking.

I had to remember that at this moment Lou had every right in the world to be rude. How would I have acted had any man touched my Kitt?

I locked up, got in my car, and drove through Black Leaf. The brick of small stores and buildings had been browned by smoke which coiled from the foundry chimney in spring and fall when plowpoints were being cast. Now the foundry was closed for good, victim to Sears Roebuck and the catalogue. Starlings roosted in the rafters and sat on the smokestack to gossip.

There were two locally-owned department stores, a bus station, a fertilizer and feed store, a movie, a co-op, the Progress Store, an Oliver farm equipment dealer, a drugstore, the electric company office, an ABC store, a bank, a ten-cent store, and three cafes, one of which sold beer and provided pool tables. There was an old hotel where men sat on the porch, hoisted their feet, and spat into the petunias. At the end of the street was a small, muddy river where the laundry and grinding mill were.

17

You drove over the river to reach Lou's. He had nine hundred acres of land, most of it open and under scientific cultivation. The land was groomed like a fine horse. Miles of white plank fence— oak sawed right out of his own woods—bordered the fields. In the summers he hired schoolboys to paint the fences. They squatted in the heat of the sun, competing against each other to take home the most money.

I turned in at the iron gate hung between white brick posts. The drive led up under maple trees to a stone house with a slate roof. Sprinklers twirled, throwing water in long, sparkling arcs.

I left my car in the courtyard at the rear of the house. A paddock and stone stable were just beyond the garage. Caroline's black stallion stood at the paddock fence, watching me. I thought of her, slim and proud in her canary pants and black boots.

At the side entrance, I raised my hand to the heavy lion's-head knocker. Before I touched the brass, Lou opened the door.

He wasn't tall, about five eight or nine, yet he gave the impression of strength—bulldog strength. He seemed to have no waist. His expensive suits hung straight down on him, as if draped over a block of stone. His tailor must have wept at the impossibility of bringing grace to Mr. Gaines' stubborn body.

"You took your time," he said.

He was florid, with curly red hair and reddish-brown eyes that probed as if cutting for your heart. He was aggressive to the point of being jumpy. I couldn't imagine him merely sitting or sleeping —or when he did sleep, it must have been with a clenching of fists and grinding of teeth at the squandering of time.

I followed him through the stilled house. It was air-conditioned, not because Lou bothered about heat or showing off his money, but because coolness was necessary for Caroline who never allowed herself to be seen unless she was groomed and crisp.

I was unsure how to act. Maybe I should tell him I was sorry and become solemn as if in the presence of death. Or perhaps I should be indignant for him and storm against Paul.

"You think I'd let you wait around at a time like this?" he asked as we walked.

"No, you wouldn't," I said. If I were in trouble, Lou would have been on top of me.

We were walking toward the rear of the house. Before Caroline came, the place had lacked style—big and expensive all right, but furnished like the rooms in a resort hotel. Caroline sold the furniture and brought in antiques, the really good ones made of walnut and cherry, and in her house I could believe I'd entered an era where people with powdered wigs and buckle shoes would come floating down the curving stairway.

Our feet were hushed by Persian carpets. I wondered whether I would see her. I felt her in the house—as if the thick walls had absorbed her and gave out her femininity like a faint cologne. To touch anything—a chair, a lamp, a table—would be like touching her.

I guessed she was upstairs, in a pink bedroom, among satin and ruffles, perfume and mirrors. I attempted to imagine her weeping or even distraught. I couldn't. She was too controlled. She was silk over marble.

Lou led me to his office, a large room at the back of the house. The room was masculine, but she still dominated the dark paneling and the stone fireplace by means of photographs on the walls and mantel. There must have been twenty pictures, each of her alone—standing by a rail fence, sitting under a colored umbrella at a beach, astride her black stallion. You could turn nowhere in the room without seeing her. There were also pictures of Lou's two golden daughters.

"I can't believe it yet," Lou said. He shut the door and crossed to his desk. He never moved easily, slowly, but always as if attacking.

"Who could believe it would happen to him?" he asked. He circled the desk. He looked confused and weary.

Out of photographs Caroline watched us.

"Just try to imagine," he said.

We in the town had never expected him to marry. There were men who didn't belong to women. Those men went to outposts in the Arctic or built dams in South America. They were too undomesticated for a nest.

"I was in Richmond." He leaned against the side of his desk. His thick legs were bent as if to spring. "I went to see about the auxiliary power supply for the pumps." Lou raised his hands and let them fall against his thighs. His face was confounded, as if unsure how to set its features. Putting thoughts into words seemed to burn him. "I intended to spend the night. When I finished dinner, I went back to the hotel. I've never been able to sleep in a hotel room. I decided to come home."

He prowled around the desk and me. I had to keep turning to watch him. He shook his head at the wonder of it. I felt the weight of him on the floor as he passed.

"It was after eleven thirty," he said. "I put the car in the garage and walked into the house."

He stopped talking, puzzled. He shook his head as if he could not assemble his thoughts. Then he rubbed his heavy hand over his mouth.

"I heard talking. Out on the porch." He looked in the direction of the porch. "Before I got there, I heard—" He raised his hands as if holding a ball. "I heard Caroline yell."

His reddish-brown eyes widened in astonishment. He couldn't believe his own words.

"I ran to the porch," he said. "She was backed against the glider. She had her hands up, and that sonofabitch was about to grab her."

Hearing it from Lou was different than from Sutter. Sutter had been clinical. Lou was living it.

"Suppose I hadn't come," he said, staring in the direction of the porch. He was pale and kept shaking his head. "That's what I think of. Suppose I'd stayed in Richmond."

He was awed and outraged by the thought.

"I should have killed him." He paced, and his big hands clenched as if he had Paul's neck in them. "I should've torn his head off." In spite of the coolness of the house, he was sweating. His collar was turned up at the tips, and his blue tie off center. He stopped in front of me.

"A minister," he said. "Can you imagine any man doing it—but a minister!"

He circled the desk and came back to me. He held out his hand as if asking for money.

"Why shouldn't he be in jail?" he asked. "Why shouldn't I get a warrant and put him under the jail?"

"You don't want that."

"Why not?" he said. He meant to shout but remembered in time and bit the words down to softness. "I know what you'll tell me—that I'd be hurting Caroline and the town more than him. God knows she's been hurt enough. If it weren't for her, I swear I'd kill him."

He breathed like a man who'd been running. Sweat slid down his nose and dropped to a lapel of his tan suit.

"A preacher," he said. "A man of God. It's terrible enough with ordinary people, but he's supposed to be a man of God."

His face was agonized—as if the thought were too much for the circuitry of his brain to carry. He touched me on the arm.

"I want him out," Lou said. "You get him out."

"I hope he's already gone," I said. If not gone, surely Paul would be frantically making arrangements to leave.

"You make sure," Lou said, his face mottled. He trembled. He was Black Leaf's most powerful citizen, but he looked as if he might break down and weep.

"How's Caroline?" I asked.

"She's resting," he said, and his voice softened. He couldn't speak her name without gentling. "Sutter gave her pills."

He turned from me, crossed to his desk chair, and sat. For a moment all the muscles in that hard, chunky body went soft, and he appeared plump and aging.

"Maybe I'll wake in a second," he said. "Maybe this'll be a dream."

He stood, opened the door, and walked with me through the house. I felt Caroline, and as I passed the curving steps I glanced up, half expecting to see her, but nobody was there.

"Help me," Lou said. He opened the front door.

"I'll try." I went down the porch steps and around the house to my car. As I started the engine, I looked up to a window on the second story. I saw movement—a shifting of curtain and the drawing back of a lovely, tragic face into shadows.

[3]

The maple-shaded street ended at the church—a basilica of dark brick with a portico and steeple.

I stopped my car in front of the manse. It was a story-and-a-half frame house, painted yellow. There was a picket fence. A small boy walked past the fence and held a stick against it, causing the pales to go bap-bap-bap.

I looked for signs of retreat but saw none. The gate was open, and children played in the yard—boys and girls, crawling in and out of a large cardboard box. They kicked it and swarmed over it.

Some were Paul's children. I didn't like seeing them. I was reminded he had to feed those mouths. I wasn't sorry for him but for Helen. She was the one who would really be suffering.

I left my car and walked through the gate. Termites had eaten pales in the fence. There were patches of red dirt in the yard,

and children's toys were scattered on the ground. Right in the middle of the lawn was a hole three or four feet deep. A child with blue eyes was in the hole and peered at me.

The house seemed knocked off center, as if the rollicking of children were too much for it. The walls needed paint. The TV antenna was askew. There were rocks on the roof. It was an austere house which had been betrayed into the hands of a family man. It was a house near a nervous breakdown.

I went up the walk. If they were my children I'd have put them to work cleaning up the place. As I passed the cardboard box, a dirty-faced boy saw me and became motionless. The other children sensed an adult presence and became still. They watched me with great swallowing eyes.

I climbed the porch steps. Just let it be simple, I thought. I raised my hand and knocked softly on the screen door.

The screen had a hole in it. I bent forward to look inside but could see only a few feet into the dimness. I made out a yellow oak hatrack and a red picture on a yellowed wall—a crude oil painting of the Crucifixion, modern, unframed, with a bewildered Christ nailed to a cross of stone.

Out of the dimness a young girl took shape. She was pale and had long black hair. She wore a ruffled white dress.

"Please come in," she said, her voice louder than I expected. She pushed open the door for me and took my hat.

It was a tiny house, the walls close together and flimsy. The rooms were furnished with pieces people in the congregation had donated—castoff items. In the parlor was a horsehair sofa, a marble-top table, and curtains with tassels. The red rug had been walked across so often that the milky underside showed through. A black upright piano grinned its yellow keys. A mahogany wardrobe had a cluster of grapes carved into it.

"Please sit down," the girl said and indicated a cheap blue leatherette armchair which had a matching ottoman. It was the company chair. She glided away.

I sat hot and uncomfortable. The room bothered me. It was not the smallness or lack of style, but the fact nothing seemed permanent. A lot of preachers had passed through, yet there was no comfortable mark here of the living they had done. This house absorbed people and remained unloving.

A door opened and closed in the rear of the house. Helen came out through the dining room. She pushed at a strand of hair and offered me her hand.

She must have been pretty years ago, but she'd become heavy and rounded with childbearing. She had lifeless brown hair which would not stay in place. Her expression was distracted, as if she had grown addled trying to keep up with her children. She appeared buffeted.

She sat in the center of the horsehair sofa, her knees pressed together, her hands folded tightly in her lap. She was tensed, prepared to jump.

"It's humid," she said and fanned her fingers in front of her moist face. The touch of her hand was still in mine—rough and burning, as if she'd just pulled it from a sink of hot water. She wore a summer dress so faded that the flower pattern had almost disappeared. I couldn't tell whether she'd been crying or not. She was a woman who looked as if she were always attempting to remember. "Let me fix you a glass of tea."

"No thanks," I said quickly. She was on the point of springing up. She stared at me—or through me, as though I were a rain or fog. "If I could just speak to Paul."

Before she could answer, a voice in the rear of the house howled like a wolf. A small boy came galloping out of the dimness and spread himself across his mother's lap. He rubbed himself against her and wept. She stroked the back of his neck with her trembling fingers. He turned his face into her stomach.

"Charlesbitkickthumbwhack," the boy wailed.

"You tell him to be good," Helen said, her eyes coming into focus for an instant to inspect the thumb. There was no sign of injury, but she kissed it.

24

"Iwasn'tdidnothimkickthump."

"Don't fret," she said and stroked him. His wailing subsided to a sniffle. She raised him from her lap and sent him out with a soft push on his behind.

"He cries at anything," she said, rubbing her palms on her dress. "He saw the moon last night and thought the man in the moon was angry at him. He cried and cried."

"Yes'm," I said. I thought, *The sins of the father shall be visited onto the children, yea unto the third generation.* It was a terrible line. Perhaps when children saw a mean face in the moon, the sin visiting had already started. "I'd like to speak to Paul if he's about."

"He's gone to Richmond," she said.

Slowly, silently, I let out my breath. He'd run. There would be no confrontation, no further unpleasantness.

"When do you expect him back?" I asked, hating to do it but having to make certain.

"I don't know exactly when." Her hands fluttered in her lap. "Shall I have him telephone you?"

"I'd appreciate it," I said and stood. I felt like wiping my brow, only I was sorry for her too, and the three generations.

As she rose, she pushed against her knees. Her shoes were low-heel and scuffed, and her ankles thick. I wanted to offer help, yet an offer would not have been sincere. As sorry as I was for her, I intended to shun further involvement.

At the screen door we again shook hands. She pushed nervously at her hair and flinched at the sound of scuffling upstairs. There was a crash. Two young boys tumbled down the steps. They punched and kicked all the way.

"If you're going to roughhouse, you'll have to stay outside," Helen told them, not raising her voice. Gently, resigned, she pulled them apart. "You hear me? Outside."

They glared at each other, and she looked as if there were something she should be remembering.

25

I sat at my desk to call Lou. He always sounded as if he were going to come right through the telephone and grab you by the throat.

"You're positive?" he asked.

"I just came from there. He's definitely gone."

"He better be."

"I understand how you feel."

"No you don't understand how I feel. Nobody understands unless it happens to him. I can't think of it without being sick." He was silent a moment. "Anyway, thanks."

I worked the rest of the afternoon. At least I sat in my office and waited. Because of the sale at the Progress Store, I had few customers.

When it was five o'clock precisely, I locked my store and drove home. I lived in the country on a hundred and eighty acres, most of which I'd planted in loblolly pines. The house, two-story white frame with a porch on three sides, had belonged to my grandfather.

Injun wasn't around. I fed the dogs—two English setters and a Labrador, a bitch, yellow and glossy. There was also a redbone hound, gaunt and forlorn, who lay panting in the dust. He raised his head only when he heard the rattle of pans. He was so tired he ate lying down.

It was a sad time of day for me, the time I thought of Kitt and my empty house. She used to keep everything alive. She was small and moved quickly. Every year we'd made wine, standing right in the crocks, she holding up her skirt and laughing, blue-red to her knees.

I fixed myself a little food and would not look at it as I put it into my mouth. Afterwards I cleaned the kitchen, took a bath, and shaved. In the mirror I told myself I didn't look old.

I drove back into town to fetch Val. She'd been working all summer on her master's degree at the State Normal School in Farmville. I stopped my car in front of Miss Minnie Meekens' genteel rooming house. Miss Minnie sat on the porch, rocking and knitting. She set her glasses down on her nose so that she could watch everybody who passed. I was certain that in her eyes I appeared a fool.

"Jackson," she said as I stepped onto the porch and rang the bell. Her knitting needles quickened. I removed my hat. At forty-two, I was too old to be going through the ritual of courtship.

"What will you do?" she asked. I was never sure whether she smirked or not. I knew I wanted to be away as fast as possible. I listened for Val's footsteps.

"Do?" I asked, holding my hat. What happened between Val and me was none of her business.

"At the church," she said.

I stared.

"Has he gone?" she asked.

"He?"

"Our pastor."

"Yes, he's gone."

She waited for more, but I held my jaw rigid.

"I never thought I'd live to see the day," she said, clacking her needles. "A *mini*ster doing a thing like that."

I heard Val coming down the steps inside, and I opened the screen door. She wore a yellow dress with black trim on the sleeves and neck. The dress fitted snugly around her hips. She had on black high heels which made her appear six feet tall and also a big black hat with a sombrero-like brim which flopped as she walked.

She was twenty-four years old and had an angular, impatient

face. Her lips were large and sulking. Her hair was the blackest I'd ever seen on a woman—shiny black like hot tar. She moved with long strides, her shoulders squared, her arms swinging free.

"You don't have to open doors for me," she said, sweeping past clean and perfumed. She was both athletic and feminine. She could serve a tennis ball as hard as a man, yet go so soft she flowed.

"I might like to open doors for you," I told her. I tried not to notice the grin on Miss Minnie's face. She was happy to see a woman humble a man—any man.

"Southern chivalry," Val said, sarcastic, contemptuous. She was from Ohio and had studied sociology at Columbia where they had taught her to feel superior to everything southern.

"Good manners," I said. I was patient with her. She was wrong about many things, but she was pretty enough not to have to be right. "They have those some places even in the North."

She smiled, showing just the tips of her teeth between those heavy lips. She had large dark eyes.

"Oh the southern gentleman's polite," she said, spreading her feet so she'd be solid upon her high heels. "He always takes off his hat and lights my cigarettes. I can't stand that he doesn't, too. He's a perfect cavalier to a maiden, but let him lead her to the altar and ever afterwards he lets her wash his clothes in a tub and slop hogs and sucker tobacco, while he sits on the veranda with his feet cocked to the railing. He allows her to kill herself for him."

"You do think kindly of us," I said, uncomfortable at the show she was putting on for Miss Minnie. Miss Minnie would have it on the telephone before we were out of sight.

"Chattel," Val said. "That's what women are down here, chattel."

I got her by the elbow and steered her off the porch. Behind us, Miss Minnie snickered, and those knitting needles clacked victoriously.

I started not to open the car door for Val, but my father had broken me to be polite. Ten years after I married Kitt, I was still lighting her cigarettes, mixing her drinks, and sleeping on the outside of the bed.

"Hypocrite," Val said as she bent to slip into the car. Though a big woman, she had good balance and didn't lurch into the seat. I watched her dress draw over her pretty knees. She pushed the dress down and raised her dark, plucked brows at me. She reached out and pulled the door shut.

I drove up the street. Val stacked her long hands in her lap. She wore no jewelry, not even a ring or bracelet, because she believed jewelry was symbolic of woman's subordinate status in life.

"I suppose if I told you I'm glad you're back, you'd consider me hypocritical," I said.

"I'd think you were sweet-talking me," she said and crossed her legs. She was careful to keep her skirt down. I heard the rasp of nylons.

I had no right to her. I was a dead man who was warming his cold bones in the heat of her youth. I conspired against her because I needed a good woman to rear my son.

I dreamed too of again bringing my house alive. I imagined it ablaze, the beams of light shooting out windows and doors. I thought of it clean, the cobwebs down and the cracks in the plaster fixed. I conjured up the feel of cool sheets on my bed and carpets ungritty underfoot. I saw us entertaining among the boxwoods, with lanterns hung on oak trees and punch served from silver bowls.

She moved her long tan arms to reach into her black pocketbook for a cigarette. I punched a knob on the dashboard. She pushed my hand back to the wheel.

"I'll fire my own cigarettes," she said.

I turned in between brick gateposts and drove up the winding road to the club. Until Val came to town, I hadn't used the club for years. Now it was where I stalked her.

We crossed the grass to the small, one-story building with a screened-in porch overlooking a swimming pool and dusty pines beyond. While I fixed drinks, she sat on the porch. She arranged her yellow dress over her lap.

I carried the drinks to the porch. We watched the high-school boys showing off—flipping and contorting for the girls who sat prettily and passively on the side of the pool.

I glanced at Val. Her tan skin was covered by a delicate dark down. She would make a fine mother for Injun. She was strong enough to break him. She would also bring comfort to a man on long bleak nights. Yet at the very instant I eyed her, I pictured my Kitt—small, sad, and loving.

"What's happening at the church?" Val asked, facing me. "Miss Minnie's been on the telephone all afternoon."

"It's finished," I said.

"Then he did—I mean really?"

"He apparently tried."

"Well," she said and thought about it as a woman must, seeing herself standing against a wall and the bulk of a man coming at her.

It was growing dark. The swimmers were walking up from the pool. They were milky shapes. They changed their clothes and put on records. A clarinet played in a low register.

I'd never told Val about myself—how at eighteen I'd seen death and putrefaction piled high as my gullet. I'd eaten my K rations on a table while the owner, a dead German shot in the mouth, lay under it. I'd put out my Camel on one of his glazed eyeballs.

I'd been killed, but I'd been resurrected in my wife Kitt. She'd laid her hands on me and created hope and belief. But only for a time, because the awful flower was abloom in her, and she'd died slowly as I watched. In a few months she'd become old and ugly and stank. And I'd died with her.

Now in the darkness I reached for Val's cool hand. She let me hold it. I intended to cheat her. If I couldn't have life of my own, I would borrow hers.

30

[5]

In the morning I stopped for gas at a ramshackle filling station owned by a colored friend named King Soloman Bates. Solomon was near ninety, and he sat on the shady side of his unpainted frame shed in a wicker chair, a cane held between his legs, a straw hat on his head. He spat tobacco juice at chickens who pecked too close to his splayed feet. They squawked and flounced away.

"Hot," I said as I filled my own tank. Solomon never waited on anybody. He sat like royalty, scorning the world, and you expected him to have a voice like a man speaking from deep within a cave, but actually he was squeaky.

"It's hot if you're a dog and cool if you're a lizard," he said. "It's hot if you're a mule and cool if you're an egg."

"Well, I'm a man and I'm hot," I told him as I hung the nozzle on the pump.

"The outside of you can be hot and the inside of you cold," he said and pointed his cane at me. "Man's a fool." He poked the cane at me. "He can sit in the shade of his own tree, but he's going to the moon. He's shooting himself out into space where the fuzzies will get him."

"What are fuzzies?" I asked.

Solomon sat straight and banged his cane into the dust. He looked at me as if I were ignorant. "They're little folk who got red fuzz on them. When they catch you, they bite." He lowered his voice. "They're sharpening their teeth and waiting."

I paid for the gas and drove to the store. Before I had my key in the lock, I heard the telephone. I walked into my office to answer it.

"He's back," Lou said. "The sonofabitch is right there at the manse."

I sat down slowly.

"He probably has to help with the packing," I said.

"You make sure," Lou said. His voice was an accusation. "Get him out!"

I didn't hurry. I opened the mail first. It was my way of proving that Lou didn't own me.

I locked up. Down the street hillbilly music pounded from the Progress Store. I got into my car and drove to the manse. In front I recognized Paul's old Dodge. There were dents in the fender, and one bumper hung lower than the other. Nobody criticized him for having an old car—we expected our preachers to be poor—but some of the ladies believed he could have washed the Dodge occasionally.

I heard voices and shouting around back. Instead of going to the door, I followed a path at the side of the house. Paul was on the grass, near a broken sandbox. He was playing with children, at least a dozen of them, and they swarmed over him as if he were a piece of sugar. He tossed them off gently. He rolled and tickled their stomachs. They howled and flew through the air as if in slow motion.

Red-faced and gleeful, they dived back into the squirming pile. A little boy exploded up five or six feet. As he came down, he seemed certain to smash himself but two large hands reached out and caught him inches above the ground.

Children lay on the grass laughing. Their eyes were wet. They crawled, their heads hanging. I saw parts of Paul—a foot, his arm, a hand stretching out. Children kept flying up like popcorn.

I spoke his name. The boiling of flesh subsided, and as children moved off they revealed him in patches—his khaki pants, his stained T-shirt, the flash of his pale belly. He set children aside as if they were delicate vases.

I didn't like seeing him with them. After what he did, he

32

shouldn't be allowed to touch a child. I wondered whether there was something perverse about it, something sexual in inviting children to climb over him and rub against him.

Moreover I was upset he was here. He ought to have cleared out. He had no right to smile or play.

"Brother LeJohn," he called to me as he pushed up from the grass. He dusted his hands and came toward me. Children still tried to wrestle him. They charged at his legs and jumped at his back. He loosened their grips and set them away—like a picker working through a field of lettuce.

"Quit now," he said, laughing. He had to stop to loosen a foot. He was a big man who'd once been muscled and strong, but in the ministry he'd started to go soft, and his flesh no longer fitted him tightly. He'd had a head of black hair, thick like a horse's mane, but now that hair was thinning on top, allowing his pale scalp to shine through. Streaks of gray spread upward from his temples.

His face was squarish, rough-cut, with outswept jaw and jowls which quivered when he spoke. He walked with his arms drawn up slightly and his feet spread as if carrying a load—great draft-horse feet that left the grass flat under them.

"Brother LeJohn," he said again, his hand stretched to me, the palm big as a cleaver. I didn't want to touch him, but his fingers captured mine. He dropped his left hand on my shoulder and squeezed. He laughed in his deep, loud voice, grinning and peering at me, his eyes—light, just verging on blue—bugging as if they would pop out in enthusiasm at seeing me. On the center of his forehead was a strip of flesh-colored adhesive tape.

"You want to be treated like company?" he asked, still holding me. His khaki pants were grass-stained, and curly black hair stuck up over the neck of his T-shirt. "If you do we'll go to the parlor."

"We'll go to your study," I said. I freed myself and started across the back yard toward the church.

"Wait, friend," Paul called.

33

I heard him hurrying after me, but I kept on to the church. Dry grass crackled under my feet. I went down steps which led into the Sunday-school end of the building. On the creamy walls were crayon drawings of Jesus. All the pictures had Jesus smiling and happy except one where He stood alone on a brown field and cried—great big tears which fell from His eyes like links in a chain.

I walked along the dusky, warm corridor to the minister's study. Paul was behind me. He was switching on lights.

"Where's the race?" he asked and opened the study door. He walked to his desk to snap on a lamp. He unfastened a window which overlooked a small flower garden. The flowers, planted by Women of the Church, had been killed by the heat. A squirrel ran across a stone bench under an apple tree. Around the garden was a wall.

Dust motes spun in the hot light and settled on the leather sofa and chairs. Already the new furniture appeared battered. He allowed his children to play here.

On the walls were a framed diploma, a picture of the Last Supper, and a yellowed photograph of the Colosseum.

Around the sides of the room were bookshelves, though I guessed Paul had read few volumes among them. He was no intellectual preacher like Mr. Gwaltney, his predecessor, who'd quoted Greek in his sermons and dwelt on the etymological and epistemological. Paul seemed to believe that if he talked fast and loud enough, he could pound religion in like a carpenter hammering nails.

"Rest yourself," he said, motioning me to the leather chair at the side of his desk. He sat behind the desk. Wood creaked under him. He leaned back and stretched his arms. "I like to see a man up early, enjoying the freshness of God's morn."

I resented his pretending this was just another day. As I stared at him, I thought he was essentially a fleshy man, a Rabelaisian who'd somehow become entangled with religion. I'd always been wary of noisily spiritual people—suspicious that their zeal came from the dark places, the swamps and bogs of the soul.

34

"Though you don't look as if you're enjoying it," he said and bobbed his black brows. "In fact you look sick."

He was spinning words, trying to tie me up in them. I stared past him to the bookshelf where a golden figure of a Greek athlete stood—a trophy Paul had received in his football days. The fact he'd been a star impressed the men on the pulpit committee who chose him to come to Black Leaf. They believed he would work particularly well with the youth of the church.

"I'd like to hear what you intend to do," I said. I was still looking at the trophy. It sparkled in the light. The Greek stood on his toes and held a golden wreath over his head.

"Do?"

"Don't act innocent," I said. There was no place for kindness, not after what he attempted with Caroline.

"I'm not acting anything," he said. "I don't know what you're talking about."

"Oh no," I said. I pointed at the tape on his forehead. "And I suppose that's a stigma."

"This?" he asked and raised a thick finger to the tape.

"Don't tell me you've forgotten who gave you that."

He lowered his hand and watched me. He frowned, stood, and moved around the desk toward me. When aroused, he gave the impression of power. I thought how frightened Caroline must have been.

"Are you here on an official visit?" he asked, stopping in front of me.

"I am," I told him. I felt small in the shadow of his bulk.

"Ah," he said. He moved around me. He had a rolling gait. His thick shoulders slumped, and his hands hung low. He turned. "It was an unfortunate incident."

"I don't call it an incident."

His face creased, but he didn't appear ashamed. There was no sign of guilt or contrition. I could have been bothering him with a trifle.

"I don't know what Lou told you," he said. "I think, however, that the less we talk about this, the better off everybody will be."

"You don't seem to understand," I said. My hands were clenched. "Unless you leave, he's going to press charges."

Paul walked to the desk and leaned over it toward me. His fingers touched the blotter.

"You expect me to leave?"

"Yes."

He nodded, rubbed his nose, and stood straighter.

"You're judging me without facts," he said.

"If you have facts, let's hear them."

He sighed as if he'd put down a heavy weight.

"Suppose, just suppose, everybody went on as if nothing had happened."

"Not a chance," I told him.

He watched me, his light blue eyes closed slightly, like a man calculating percentages.

"I suggest that after Lou cools off, he'll listen to reason," Paul said. "I suggest further he'll understand that to attack me can only hurt this community and our church."

"Now wait a minute," I said, and I leaned over the desk. "You attacked his wife."

"We'll get nowhere discussing that."

"We're going to have to discuss it," I said.

He sat slowly and ran a big hand over his hair. His face firmed, and I saw the ghost of what he must have been once—a ruggedly handsome man with bold, muscular features.

"For the good of the community and our church, we ought to work toward reconciliation."

"Impossible."

"You, for example, could go to the aggrieved parties and attempt to talk. You could explain calmly that this is the sort of situation where many people will be hurt."

"No," I told him, and I was angry. "For the good of the community and church, I'd like you to pack up as quickly as possible and get out."

He sat passively in the chair, his face expressionless. He didn't seem to have heard me. Gradually, slowly, he shook his head. He kept shaking it as if answering a hundred questions.

"No," he said.

I felt as if the red fuzzies had their teeth in me.

[6]

He showed me to the door. I was so furious I was shaky. I got into my car and drove through town. The sun burned on metal, and the steering wheel was hot in my hand.

At the corner by the bank I stopped for a red light. Hot sun came straight down between the old buildings, cooking the street and sidewalk. Heat shimmered off cars, causing the air to appear wavy. The town seemed on the verge of melting and flowing away in its own gutters—like dirty candle wax.

When the light changed, I drove to the hospital, a brick building with columns in front. I walked through the basement to Sutter's office.

His receptionist, Miss Tobin, told me he was on the wards. She'd been a young lady when she first started working for Sutter and had grown old with him. Now she was proprietary about him—like a wife.

"He's very busy," she said. She tried to protect him from all people who wanted his time. She was a mousy woman, white-haired and shrunken, but she was strong too—strong enough to have lived alone most of her life and to have seen and withstood the procession of pain which came through this office.

Instead of waiting for the elevator, I climbed the steps to the

37

first floor. Starched nurses hurried along the corridors, their perfume blending with floor wax, Lysol, and ether.

I found Sutter on the East Wing. His white smock was too large for him, his shoes were worn at the heels, and his trouser cuffs dragged the corridor. His brown tie had got pushed out of place so that the knot was half hidden under his collar.

I felt sorry for Sutter because in all the years I'd known him I doubt that he'd been able to lie down and sleep eight hours the way ordinary people do. He couldn't sit to a chicken dinner without the telephone ringing or somebody pounding on his door. As a result, his watery brown eyes were stark and unblinking behind his glasses. Nurses had to take him by the hand and aim him in the direction he should go.

"Don't bring me problems," he said, moving away.

"You brought this one to me," I said, walking after him. "And I need advice."

"I don't give advice. I give medication, and I charge for that."

"We'll go to your office."

He came along, his shoulders slumped, his feet dragging. He muttered and glanced about, hoping the nurses would rescue him. They smiled at him as one might at a pretty child.

We went down on the elevator and into his office. I closed the door so Miss Tobin couldn't hear. She was already checking on me through her intelligence apparatus which had strands through the nurses and orderlies to the hospital kitchen and as far as the drugstore.

Sutter dropped into his chair. He was resentful of a system that put so much on him. He was one of the people who had responsibility in his bones. He could no more stop noblesse oblige than he could the beating of his heart.

"He calls it an incident," I said.

Sutter's eyes widened, and he grasped the arms of his chair.

"And he thinks Lou will listen to reason."

"No," Sutter said and pushed back in his chair as if trying to retreat.

"It's a very interesting attitude for a minister to take after what he's done."

"He just looked you in the face and called it an incident, did he?"

"Pretty much."

"Maybe you should have pointed out that there are some members of the congregation who don't approve of having their wives lechered even by a preacher."

"Why don't we use the right word?" I asked.

"What is the right word?"

"Rape."

"It's a terrible word. With lechered, you don't have to see it."

The office was hot. Outside, an ambulance sped by, its siren shrill. Below the hospital, a N&W locomotive sounded its horn. Pigeons flew up.

"Does his calling it an incident mean he's not leaving?" Sutter asked.

"Worse than that. He doesn't even act ashamed."

Sutter looked unbelieving, and his hands flopped on the desk. The desk was so covered with papers, books, bottles, and drug samples that he had to write out prescriptions on his knee. Behind him, nailed to the wall, was a colored anatomy chart which laid open the body in slices.

"What you going to do?" Sutter asked.

"We have to see Lou."

"Not me," he said and stood.

"It has to be you," I said. Sutter was the only one who could handle Lou. He could do it through the debt of healing. He had assuaged too much suffering for Lou to turn on him.

"You dropped the ball," Sutter charged. "He should be gone."

"You think I don't want him gone?"

We glared at each other. Pigeons pecked past the basement window, their feathers smudged. Sutter reached into his smock pocket and brought out a crushed pack of cigarettes. His yellowed fingers trembled.

"You're using me as a shield," he said and threw the pack to his desk.

"I admit it," I said and reached for his hat.

"Don't I have enough holes in my hide?"

[7]   •

We drove toward the mill. Rumpled and weary beside me, Sutter wouldn't speak. He slouched in the seat and smoked one cigarette after the other. He ordered all his patients to stop smoking, and if they asked why he didn't quit, he answered that he was so puny that a cancer couldn't live on him anyway. It would shrivel up and die of malnutrition.

"You're going pretty slow," he said.

"I don't hurry for trouble."

We saw the mill on the flat land that had once been pasture— low, modern buildings with no windows in them. The buildings lay alongside the river. Around the property was a high wire fence. A silver water tank stuck up like a great tulip.

I turned in at the gate and drove to the parking lot in front of the office. I opened the car door for Sutter. He walked as if his joints had stiffened on him. It was a defensive measure. The idea was to make himself so pitiful that Lou couldn't jump him.

We went up the steps of the building. Just inside glass doors a long window displayed colored yarns. We entered a second door. A battery of secretaries clattered away at their desks.

I prodded Sutter. He hobbled. We approached Lou's secretary, a brunette named Nancy who taught in the Sunday school. She stopped typing to smile at us.

"If he's busy, we can come back," Sutter said.

But through his open door, Lou had seen us. He came from his

40

office and gestured us in. He shut the door. Though it was cool in the air-conditioned office, he worked in his shirt-sleeves.

"Well?" he asked and looked at me.

I looked at Sutter. He had his eyes lowered, and he held on to the back of a chair.

"Can't either of you talk?" Lou asked. He moved to get in front of us.

"Paul's here all right," I said.

Lou seemed to swell. He gave the impression he would burst through his clothes. He walked to his desk and punched a button. We heard Nancy's voice over the intercom box.

"Get me the Commonwealth Attorney's office," Lou told her.

"Wait a second," I said. All we needed was to get Billy Barnes, our crusading Commonwealth Attorney, involved. He'd put on a circus for the town and county.

Lou scowled. Blood came up through his thick neck into his face. He flipped the switch on the intercom and told Nancy to hold the call.

"I'm listening," Lou said.

"You don't want scandal."

"I want that sonofabitch out or in jail," Lou said. His florid face was mottled, and the muscles in his neck had pulled taut.

"Could there be any misunderstanding?" Sutter asked. Bent and haggard, he held to the chair. I knew what was bothering him. Paul should be running. He was not acting like a guilty man.

"You mean could Caroline have made a mistake?" Lou asked, and he spoke softly, almost in a whisper, but it sounded very loud.

"We're capable of great misinterpretations," Sutter said. "I see it every day."

"You think she could be mistaken about a thing like this?" Lou asked.

Sutter looked trapped. He glanced toward me for help.

Lou scowled at him—at us. He came around his desk rolling down his sleeves. He reached for his jacket.

"Come on," he said.

41

Sutter and I followed Lou's dusty car as he drove fast back through town. Lou was not an ostentatious person, but he always bought Cadillacs and used them hard even when he wasn't hurried. It wasn't a disregard for the law as much as his belief that automobiles were built to go fast and you weren't receiving your money's worth unless you pushed them to their limit.

I pressed my foot hard on the accelerator. Sutter held to the seat. I could just keep Lou in sight. As he turned in at his gate, a colored tenant drove a John Deere tractor into a ditch to keep from being hit.

Lou was parked and waiting by the time Sutter and I reached the house. Lou opened the door. Sutter limped as Lou led us into the parlor.

"Wait here," he said and left us to go up the steps.

The parlor was a large room with a stone fireplace big enough for a man to lie in. The glass in arched windows cooled the hot yellow light and made it paler. Around the windows were heavy, gold-colored curtains. The chairs, sofas, and tables were white. It was Caroline's room.

Over the fireplace, in a heavy gilt frame, was a portrait of her great-grandfather, Augustus Van Meissen. He was a tall, imperial man with a small mouth and a drooping mustache. He wore the uniform of a Confederate colonel. His aristocratic hands rested on the hilt of a sword large enough to hack off a head.

There was another painting, smaller, this one of Caroline in her Melton and stock. She was mounted on Lord Force, the stallion she'd bought in Kentucky. Holding a whip with one hand and reins with the other, she looked out with the haughty gray eyes of the colonel. Though the stallion was strong and huge, she seemed stronger.

Sutter lowered himself into one of the delicate white chairs. He groaned softly and allowed his head to loll forward.

"Don't leave it all to me," I whispered.

"I'm too old for contention," he said.

We heard Caroline and Lou coming. Sutter stood, and we faced the steps. At parties she made her entrances down those steps—white gloves up to her elbows and jewelry sparkling on her long neck. It was like royalty descending, and I felt my own back wanting to bend.

I saw her foot first, then a leg, and the sweep of her dark silk skirt. Lou walked beside her, not touching her, but hovering, ready to reach to her if she faltered. Her long hands were folded at her waist.

She was not a tall woman even in high heels, but people thought of her as tall because of the erect way she carried herself. She was in her middle thirties, a blonde whose skin stretched so tautly across the bones of her face that she appeared impassive and severe. Yet her mouth was full and startlingly red.

She crossed to Sutter and shook his hand. She wore a white blouse. She came to me. Her hand was dry and cool in mine. She was fragrant.

"Shouldn't we all sit down?" she asked. She walked to a settee. She never moved fast. She carried her body as if it were a jewel on velvet. As she sat, she swept a hand under her thighs.

I tried not to see her legs. Like all men in Black Leaf I was attracted to her. Once at a summer dance when I was drinking heavily, I'd watched her rhumba with Wayland Counts, and she'd moved her hips not to the music but slowly, voluptuously, as if hearing her own beat. She'd worn a tight red dress that split into a small diamond over her stomach. As I watched, I'd had an impulse to kiss that patch of skin. The impulse had frightened me so badly that I left and went across the grass to my car to drive home.

43

"Would you like a drink?" She slowly pushed down her skirt. The silk rustled as it settled. She smiled ruefully.

"They don't need a drink," Lou said. His face was flushed, and his red hair messed. He stood at her side as if he believed we'd hurt her. "Just tell them."

We'd never believed he would marry. Even with money and position, he was too brusque for a woman. He'd amazed us by coming back from the Navy with Caroline. What astonished us most of all was not her beauty and breeding, but the fact she called forth a loving consideration in Lou none of us had ever seen. He had become uxorious.

"Tell them?" she asked, raising her face to him. She blinked, but carefully in order not to disturb her lashes.

"They don't realize," Lou said, his normally blustering voice apologetic.

"No?" she asked and looked at us. Sutter sank deeper into his chair. I felt I'd been rebuked.

"It has to be done," Lou said. He walked behind the settee and touched her shoulders.

"I don't know how," she said. She folded her hands into her lap and gazed at them. I again tried to picture what Paul had done. She was so clean and cool I couldn't imagine any man disheveling her. Yet under the powder and cosmetics lay suffering. When she wasn't smiling, her face appeared gaunt.

"Try," Lou told her.

"Isn't there any way to let this die?" she asked. Her gray eyes lifted to me.

"You see how she is?" Lou asked us. "She's too damn good." He leaned over her. "They have to know."

She changed the position of her hands in her lap. When she spoke, her voice was very quiet. I had to bend forward to hear.

"Men sometimes become excited," she said. "They misinterpret a woman's intentions."

44

"He couldn't have misinterpreted that much," Lou said. "You're not helping anybody by trying to protect him."

Caroline looked at her hands. We waited for her to speak.

"You see how terrible it is for her," Lou said. "She can't even talk about it. Honey, will you at least answer their questions?"

"Yes," she said, not raising her eyes. She didn't really say it. She moved her lips, but there was no sound.

"All right," Lou said. "Go on and ask."

Sutter and I glanced at each other. We didn't want to question her. We would have preferred to leave. Lou, however, gestured at us. Sutter cleared his throat.

"How did Paul get here in the house?" he asked, his voice a whine.

"I brought him," Caroline answered. She kept her eyes down. "I was driving home from a bridge party."

"She was just being hospitable," Lou explained. He again crossed to the rear of her. "Paul was walking by the river. She recognized him and picked him up."

Sutter didn't ask the next question, the one I wondered about myself, but she must have known we were thinking it. She unclasped her hands.

"When we reached the house, I offered to take him to the manse. He told me he wanted to walk. We got out of my car. I had to ask him in."

"You naturally have to ask a minister in," Lou said. "Everybody does that."

Sutter and I nodded. Even a married woman whose husband was away would invite a preacher in.

"They sat on the porch," Lou said, too impatient to wait for her to explain. "Caroline was tired and wanted to go to bed, but she sat up to listen to him."

"Listen to what?" I asked. I hadn't meant to speak, but the question was off my tongue before I could capture it.

45

"Nothing really," Caroline said. She was pale. She appeared spiritual and sexy at the same time. "He wanted my advice on new curtains for the Sunday school. That sort of thing."

We waited for her to go on, but she sat staring at her hands.

"Tell them all of it," Lou said softly. His thick fingers massaged her ladylike shoulders.

"I'd rather not," she said, her face strained.

"Okay," Lou said and came around the settee. "She was tired. She'd been shopping all day and played bridge for three hours. She wanted a drink."

He looked at her. Caroline watched her hands.

"When she fixed herself a Scotch, she offered him one," Lou said. "She never thought he'd take it."

"He was drunk?" Sutter asked.

"He didn't act drunk," Caroline answered.

I studied the angles of her face and tried to picture Paul with too much liquor. Maybe it made him believe he was irresistible. Caroline, in spite of her haughtiness, gave a man the impression of caring. Paul, not used to liquor, could have been set off by the sweetness of that perfumed, pampered body.

"How many drinks did he have?" Sutter asked. He couldn't stop himself from being analytical. He had worked too long manipulating symptoms in the play against death. Instinctively he sifted and pigeonholed.

"How many?" Caroline asked. For an instant she raised her gray eyes. "I didn't keep count. He had several."

"You kept offering them to him?" Sutter asked.

"I shouldn't have after the first one," she said. "I realize that now. I didn't use the best judgment."

She folded one long hand over the other and bowed her head. I'd heard enough. As far as I was concerned, everything hung together, and we ought to leave. Sutter, however, was caught up in analysis.

"Then what happened?" he asked, and I thought only he could

get away with it. Lou would have resented cross-examination from anyone except this sniveling old wreck of a doctor.

"You know what happened," Lou said. "I already told you."

"Paul just stood and attacked you?" Sutter asked Caroline. He had the dumb look. Caroline raised her eyes to him. Sutter pushed back in his chair.

"Goddamn, Sut," Lou said, provoked now.

"I just want to get it straight in my feeble mind," Sutter said.

"He tried to neck her first," Lou said. "When she wouldn't, he got rough."

He stood in front of Caroline to shield her.

"You fought him off?" Sutter asked, his voice whining, but his eyes shrewd, and his mind clicking away at the facts.

"She fought," Lou said. His voice became hushed. "He pushed her down and tore her blouse."

I attempted to see the lovely and elegant Caroline struggling against a drunken bull. Those long white fingers with red nails would have turned into claws. She would have bared her small white teeth. I thought of Paul's rough hand tearing a blouse to reveal a silken brassiere and perhaps spilling a coddled breast.

"Terrible," Sutter said. He slumped in the chair. His eyes watered, and he sniffled.

"You satisfied?" Lou asked him. "Because if you're not, I can show you more."

"No," Caroline told him.

"Show them," Lou ordered her.

"No, please."

"I want them to know."

He crossed to the rear of her and put his thick fingers to the collar of her blouse. He unbuttoned it and revealed the base of her long neck.

On the right side, where the neck joined the shoulder, two marks were sunk into her skin—two semicircles not quite joined: the impression of ardent teeth which had bit hard.

47

[9]

Sutter and I left Lou's. I drove so slowly the car bucked. Heat wilted us after the coolness of Lou's house.

Seeing those teeth marks on Caroline's neck made us feel the struggle and the awfulness of force. We were stunned by reality.

Rather than go to the hospital, I turned onto a dirt road between a stand of pines. I parked in a fringe of dusty shade. A hawk sailed over us and screeched. All other birds were silent.

"Don't ask me," Sutter said before I opened my mouth. His old hands scratched at his knees. His voice trembled. "Don't I have enough? Everyday people put troubles on me."

I let him complain. He had done ten times more than any man in the community, and he carried the weight of grief and death. His hands flapped on the seat.

"You're the one who has to decide," he said. "You're the chairman."

"He has to go," I said. "How do I make him?"

"Total depravity," Sutter said. He believed in Calvin. He saw the secret sins of the people he served. They came to him with their syphilis, beaten children, and daughters who'd taken lye for abortion. Like me, he saw a world of filthy, desperate little men, each drowning in corruption.

I put the car in gear, backed onto the highway, and drove into town. Sutter would not look at me. At the hospital, he left me without a word.

I drove to the store. I sat at my desk and dialed the manse.

Helen answered the phone. Her voice sounded faint, distracted.

"Paul's playing tennis. Though goodness knows I think it's too hot to be hitting balls."

48

I thanked her, locked up, and went to my car. I was gaining momentum. The fact he could play tennis after what he did to Caroline was making my job easier. I wanted to step on him.

I drove along hot streets toward the town tennis courts. At the end of the war, the civic clubs had built a community park. The idea was the park would help attract industry. One industry had come, a small garment plant trying to escape the unions. It had stayed nine months and closed, leaving a lot of unpaid bills. Enthusiasm for the park withered. Now weeds grew out of the asphalt, the basketball hoops were broken, and shattered pop bottles glistened in the sun.

There were three tennis courts. Only one was usable and that because Peter Legge, who was on the team at Carolina, maintained it.

I stopped my car in the shade of a cork elm and walked to the rusty fence. Honeysuckle wound through the links. Paul raised his racket in greeting.

"I need to talk to you," I called to him.

"Can you wait a second?" he asked and collected balls to serve.

I wanted to tell him, Damn you no I can't wait, but he'd already turned from me. Unlike Pete who was dressed for tennis in white shorts, white shirt, and white shoes, Paul wore khaki pants spotted with paint, no shirt, and high-top sneakers.

He looked too heavy and awkward to maneuver, yet he won points from Pete. Pete, slim and hard, was a skilled, thinking player who used his racket like a scalpel, but Paul didn't know when he was beaten. He tried for everything. He lunged and swatted at the ball. His big feet slapped loudly against the black surface.

Paul lost his serve, and I expected him to come to me, but they started another game. I paced and kicked the dust. I would have walked onto the court and confronted him except I didn't want to embarrass Pete. I thought how pleasurable booting Paul out was going to be.

49

They were playing hard tennis. Pete had a beautiful slow stroke only good coaching could produce. Paul swung crudely but fiercely at the ball. At times he grabbed the racket with both hands and used it like a bat. He fell, rolled, and got up laughing.

I was surprised at his staying power. He was so overweight the flesh bounced on him. He shone slickly with sweat.

Pete won the game by arching a lob over Paul who jumped high enough to tip the ball with the edge of his racket. The ball sliced into the fence.

Laughing, Paul shook hands with Pete, and they crossed toward me. Pete appeared thin and delicate next to Paul whose thick legs were slightly bowed.

"He scared me," Pete said, smiling. He wiped his hands and face on a white towel stuck into the fence.

"College boys think they know everything," Paul said. His racket was old and battered-looking. A string unraveled. Sweat soaked his khaki pants, turning them dark. He reached for his T-shirt, which hung from the fence. "Let's have a coke."

"I want to talk to you now," I said.

Both he and Pete looked at me.

"You go on," he said to Pete. "I'll take you next week."

Pete nodded. He walked off, swinging his racket in slow back-hand strokes.

Paul eyed me. He rubbed his face and neck with his T-shirt.

"A man has to be crazy to play tennis in this heat," he said. "Course I have an angle." He glanced toward Pete, who crossed the field. "I hope to win him for the ministry."

"You're not winning anybody," I said. "You're out."

He stopped smiling and dabbed at his wet, hairy chest with the shirt.

"Well," he said.

"Either go or we send you."

He sighed, walked to the base of the cork elm, and sat on a rickety bench. His arms rested on his legs. He looked across the playground. Old newspapers had blown against a fence.

"I suppose you've thought this through," he said. He watched a group of children who were throwing a ball near the fence. He spun his racket.

"No thinking required."

He frowned and raised his chin. It was square as a brick and had mule in it.

"You expect me to give up my life in the church?" he asked.

"I expect you to get out of this town."

"If I leave, the church will know why. I'll never be able to find another pulpit."

"You don't deserve another pulpit."

"You're very quick to condemn."

"I just came from Lou's house. I talked to Caroline."

The racket was motionless in his hand. He turned his light blue eyes on me.

"What did she tell you?" he asked.

"I saw marks on her neck."

He was startled and let his racket droop to the ground. He slowly wiped the palm of a hand against his khaki pants.

"Has the Board of Officers met?" he asked.

"I'm trying to save you that."

"That's nice of you."

"I'll also try to get you severance pay," I said. I doubted that I could, and God knew he didn't deserve it, but there were his wife and children.

"You're too kind to me," he said.

"I don't have to listen to your sarcasm," I told him. I started away.

"There's a verse which sustains ministers," he said. He wiped his face with his forearm. The strip of flesh-colored tape was still on his head. " 'All things work toward good for those who love God.' "

I could have told him a few things about Paul's letter to the Romans. I had remembered it when I was in the Army, in Germany, and had come across a stone barn where a hundred and eight men, women, and children were piled on top of each other like saw wood, splashed with gasoline, and set on fire. I'd felt something break in me that day. I'd stopped believing in good because of that heap of agony where a little life still remained and bodies writhed like blackened worms.

"All I have is the ministry," Paul said. He watched the children chase the ball. "Leaving it would be like leaving my life."

"We'll make you go," I said.

He worked his mouth as if it were dry.

"I'll resist."

"You don't have a chance."

"Being a minister of the Lord, I have every chance in the world."

"I don't believe the Lord allies himself with your kind," I said. I wanted to rub his nose in it. I wanted to see contrition.

"On the contrary, the Lord allies himself with the dregs. 'The first shall be last, and the last shall be first.' I'm surprised you don't see that's elemental."

"I'm not discussing theology," I said. "What you did goes past that."

"Nothing goes past theology." He watched the children. A larger boy had taken the ball. He threw it up and caught it. Smaller boys gathered around him.

"Don't you feel any shame?" I asked. I didn't understand how he could sit there and act holy after what he did.

"Maybe there are things you don't know," he said and smiled.

"What things?"

He didn't answer. He lifted his racket. He tapped it against the dusty ground and looked toward the children. The large boy pushed a small one down.

"If you have an explanation, I'll listen," I told him.

He stood slowly, ponderously.

"I have no explanation," he said. "But I have faith in you, Jackson. I know you'll do the right thing."

He walked away from me. He crossed through weeds to the

yellowed grass where the children were fighting. He worked in among them and set them aside. The large boy tried to run. Paul caught him and held him by the elbows.

Paul talked and joked with them. In a moment he had them all smiling. He gave the ball to the younger children. He started a game and made the large boy the umpire.

I stood in the shade of the cork elm, but Paul never looked my way.

[10]

I was not a man who let himself become overly excited. I had, acting from anger, done too many things I was sorry for. I thought of my Kitt and the terrible, drunken infighting we'd been through. The experience had seared me, and what was left of me her dying had taken.

As I left the park, however, I felt hot blood pumping through my chest. It wasn't Paul's refusal to leave or the fact he quoted Scriptures—though those were bad enough—but rather his patronizing, self-righteous remark about my doing the right thing. He'd attempted to put me into the position of his defender.

I returned to the store, sat down at my telephone, and called the church officers to a meeting.

At five o'clock I drove home. I fixed Injun and me a plate of cold chicken. Injun was my twelve-year-old son—a skinny deadpan boy. Even as a baby he'd been deadpan, and my Kitt, thinking he was sick, had paced around his crib until she wore a circle on the floor. She'd picked him up and petted him like a puppy, but he'd never changed his expression.

He ate quietly. He was small and wiry like me, with the same tow hair and long face. He had hazel eyes like his mother, but his nose was short and sharp. He could have poked holes in a tin can with his nose.

"You go to your Aunt Delia's," I told him when he finished eating.

"Yes, sir," he said, and from the front porch I watched him walk through a parched alfalfa field, climb a rail fence, and cross a pasture. He became a pale dot in the dusk.

I was not a good father to my son. Being a dead man, my acts toward him were automatic and without passion. I went through the ritual of fatherhood without the love. He, therefore, did not bloom as a child should but was quiet, somber, and ghostly.

I sought out a surrogate. If I could not give him love myself, I might borrow it for him through Val. I would marry her, and he too could nourish himself in the quickness of her young life.

Just at dark I heard a car turn from the highway onto my drive. Headlights splashed against oak trees. The car came across the gravel and stopped by a line of boxwoods my grandfather had planted.

Wayland Counts got out of the car. He was our banker, a dapper man who used tie clasps and collar pins. He wore pointed, two-tone shoes. I stood at the top of the steps to shake his hand.

"Jackson, boy," he said and held my hand tightly. He was hearty not by nature but because he believed it was expected of a man in finance. Like me, he'd had a drinking problem.

"Hot," he said and sank into a chair. He crossed his legs but was careful of the creases in his suit. "It's so dry the ground's cracking open and tobacco's coming up like dandelion weeds."

I heard a rattling pickup truck turn into my drive. It belonged to Harvey Boyle who operated a small store and gas station out in the county. Harvey was a stingy man. He never owned more than one pair of shoes and two shirts at a time. He was too tight to marry. He had a terror of turning a woman loose in his bank accounts which he'd built up out of nickels and dimes.

"Howdy, howdy," he said, climbing the steps. He wore the same suit summer or winter—a faded gray fabric with two pearl buttons on the jacket. A plump man, he put his feet on the steps as if afraid they might give way under him.

An old Packard nosed toward my house. The Packard was hosed daily in the summer, and the radiator chrome was kept polished. Archie LeBuck came up the steps—a courtly, straight-backed man who carried a cane as if it were a saber.

Archie was in his seventies, but still vigorous. He didn't need the cane. Rather it was as if the LeBuck hand had been too long trained to the hilt of a sword to go empty.

Archie wasn't as rich as Lou Gaines, but Archie's money came off the land. It was old money, mellowed by the soil, and it seemed to spend better.

We heard Sutter coming. His Buick bucked and snorted. He walked through the lightning bugs on the lawn. Out of habit, he carried his black bag.

"Nobody's sick here yet," Wayland called to him.

Sutter used the railing to come up the steps. He wheezed and made for a chair like a dying man. His head lolled about.

"If anybody would care for refreshment," I offered and stood near the screen door, ready to go inside.

"I'm not sure it's appropriate at a time like this," Wayland said. It sounded almost funny coming from him. He used to drink so much he wandered around his back yard at three in the morning wearing his undershorts. His face had been puffy, and he'd powdered it to hide the dissipation. Like most reformed boozers, he'd become righteous.

"What do you mean at a time like this?" Harvey asked.

"Everybody knows why we're here," Wayland said, impatient. Lou had a substantial interest in the bank, and thus Wayland was Lou's man.

"I don't," Harvey insisted.

"Don't tell me you haven't heard talk at your place," Wayland said. "You could write the newspaper out there."

"I haven't been told anything officially," Harvey said. He didn't care for Wayland—at least that part of Wayland that had no consideration for doing a job slowly and thoroughly.

They glanced at me. I sat down and tried to think of the best way to get it done.

I talked carefully. I told them of Sutter's first coming to see me and of my going to Paul, Lou, and Caroline. I said I'd seen the teeth marks on her neck.

I finished and sat waiting. Even in darkness I could make out the men's faces. Their expressions battled between astonishment and outrage. They moved restlessly.

"Godalmighty!" Harvey said, and though he meant it strong, the word was a whisper.

"He has to go," Wayland said. He leaned forward in his chair.

"He refuses," I said.

"How can he refuse?" Wayland asked.

They stared at me. They were growing, filling with resentment and anger.

"Who can believe it?" Harvey asked.

I waited for them to stop toothing and to bite down, but they kept watching me as if I had answers. I looked out past them, toward the dark, hot fields. The pines were still. Deep in the woods a lone whippoorwill started a halfhearted call and gave up in the middle of the phrase.

"What do you suggest?" Archie asked finally. He had both hands on his cane.

"I'm just the chairman," I said.

"I move we dismiss him," Wayland said.

"Does that mean you'll do it?" I asked Wayland.

"It's not my place to do it," Wayland said.

"It's not mine either," I said.

They sat quietly, watching me.

"We never had anything like this in the church," Harvey said. He wiped his face.

"The sooner we get it over with, the better," Wayland said.

"I don't feel it's my place," I said.

"Who if not yours?" Wayland asked.

"Am I supposed to throw him out?"

"Cut off his money," Wayland said. "He'll leave."

"Wait a minute," Sutter said.

He surprised us. He'd been so quiet we'd forgotten he was with us. He didn't raise his head. He looked asleep, and his voice sounded as if it came from far away.

"Wait for what?" Wayland asked.

"I'm dumb," Sutter said. "I'm the most ignorant man in the world. So you have to explain things to me."

"Explain what?" Archie asked. His cane tapped the floor.

"I'm just trying to put everything in place," Sutter said. "On the one hand we have a lady, a prominent member of our congregation, who claims she's been attacked."

"Claims?" Wayland asked.

"On the other hand we have a minister who denies he did the attacking."

"He denies it?" Archie asked, turning to me.

"He avoids it," I said. "As if it really isn't important."

"Is he sane?" Archie asked, leaning toward Sutter.

"He's plenty sane," Wayland said. "The quicker we throw him out, the better."

"It would be a terrible thing to be wrong," Sutter said. He spoke softly, his head lolling forward.

"How can we be wrong?" Archie asked.

"I'm stupid, and I know it, but it seems to me a guilty man would run," Sutter said. "He'd be gone."

He looked up slowly—as if his chin were heavy and a great straining of muscles were required to lift it.

"You're going to disbelieve Caroline?" Wayland asked. He dropped a foot to the floor.

"In the stress of the moment people are often mistaken in judgment," Sutter answered.

"What is it you want?" Archie asked.

I shook my head warningly. We needed to be rid of this thing, not let Sutter lead us into one of his mental contortions. Sutter believed everything could be explained if a person pushed deeply enough into understanding.

"I've seen people in cracks," Sutter said, his voice slow and weary. "I've seen cowardice, courage, lying, and nobility—the storms and stresses of the human spirit. I've found everybody thinks he possesses the truth, even when the truth lies elsewhere or there is no basis for the kind of truth being put to the test."

Wayland squirmed. Harvey's lips were puckered. Archie's cane had stopped tapping. They were wary. Like me, they knew Sutter was a man who long ago had traveled past the practical. He had become a person who could not put his foot on any path because he saw too many.

"Will you get to the point, Sut?" Harvey asked. "What is it you want us to do?"

"I hold a certain respect for a man's life and work," Sutter said. "It doesn't last long and is not of much consequence, but I find it glorious that man lives at all with the horrors that are arrayed against him."

"Don't go poetic on us," Wayland said.

"Especially a preaching man," Sutter said. "Of all the people in this land of plenty the preachers are the bravest. So before we consign this one to Hell, I think we should be very sure."

"How much surer can we be?" Wayland asked. He looked around for support.

"Facts are like dead ground hogs," Sutter said. "They have to be dug up."

"Will you tell us what you want?" Archie asked, and tapped his cane impatiently against the floor.

"What do we know?" Sutter asked. He sat a little straighter. "What do we really know?"

"Plenty," Wayland said and nodded as if he were doing it for all of us. "We know more than plenty."

"We're hurrying too much," Sutter said. "Hurrying kills the truth."

"How can you even doubt it?" Wayland asked, his voice rising. We were silent. I thought of Caroline—haughty and cold. There were some things you couldn't allow yourself to doubt.

"I'd like a closer look," Sutter said stubbornly.

"Who's going to do the looking?" I asked. I saw the trap Sutter was setting.

"I'm against stalling," Wayland said. "Let's finish it off tonight."

"I'm with Wayland," I said. Sutter stared at me.

"How about you, Archie?" Wayland asked.

"I'm not certain," Archie said. He respected Sutter. Moreover, Archie came off the land and had learned patience. "Who will be hurt by a little more time?"

Wayland turned to Harvey, on whom the vote depended. He fidgeted. He wiped his hands on his pants and pushed out his lips as if he were going to kiss a girl. Harvey hated to take sides. He was a merchant, accustomed to fitting himself to customers.

"Goddamnit!" he said.

"Is that a vote?" Wayland asked, alarmed. He feared if we didn't act, Lou would blame him.

"I'm in a bind," Harvey said.

"Well, get out of it and do something," Wayland said.

"I can't think under all this pressure," Harvey said.

"You have to break the tie," Wayland told him.

"I don't have to do anything," Harvey said. He crossed his arms.

"I'm not taking the responsibility for this," Wayland said and stood. He walked toward the steps.

"But what is it we're supposed to do?" Archie asked Sutter. "Let's get down to specifics."

"I want to know more," Sutter answered.

"You mean an investigation?"

"I'm leaving," Wayland said. He went down the steps.

"Investigation is a fancy way of putting it," Sutter said. "What we need is more facts."

"But who's going to do the investigating?" Archie asked.

Though he spoke toward Sutter, the question was to me, and I pressed back in my chair. I was silent and unmoving in the dark. Slowly the faces turned toward me. Wayland came back up the steps.

"Not me," I said finally. "I'm out of it, and I don't care."

"You," Sutter said. "You because you have something else in your blood besides corpuscles."

"What's that?" I asked, seeing the trap swing shut on me.

"Honor," Sutter said.

And nobody laughed.

Book Two

[11]

I drove to Richmond. All the windows of my Ford were open, as well as the two ventilators under the hood, yet I sweated. The drive required ninety minutes, and with each mile I grew hotter. Pines and runty corn drooped like soldiers after battle.

I crossed the James River. The water was low, and large white rocks humped out of it and were dusty. Ahead was the city. A bluish haze hung over it—industrial fumes clamped down by heat. People on sidewalks bent with the weight of the sun.

At a filling station, I asked directions for the seminary. It was across town, and I drove past the entrance before I saw it. I wanted to back up, but drivers glared and blew their horns. They looked as if they wanted to run me down. I had to go around the block a second time.

On the campus, locust trees shaded dry grass. Pigeon droppings splotched Victorian brick buildings. I followed the road until I saw a sign shaped like a pointing finger and marked Administration Building.

I parked in the graveled lot. I had yet to see a student or a living soul. I went up steps and inside the building, which I expected to be dark and churchlike, but which was brightly lighted by fluorescent tubes along the ceiling. In offices secretaries typed, cooled by air conditioning.

I walked to a desk in the corridor. A gray-haired lady had her hand inside an open drawer. She smiled at me. I told her my name and that I'd like to see a school official.

"May I ask the nature of your business?"

"It's a confidential matter."

"Wait a minute please," she said and stood. She walked to a door behind her desk, opened it, and went through.

I looked about me. I saw no evidence of religion. There were no pictures of Christ, no busts of Calvin or Knox, not even a cross. The place could have belonged to the Internal Revenue Service.

The secretary came out and motioned to me. She stood aside for me to enter. I walked into a large office which had mullioned windows. The walls were covered by books from floor to ceiling.

At a shiny wooden desk sat a handsome, sandy-haired man who wore glasses with thick black rims. He had on a dark suit and vest. He stood, smiled, and shook my hand vigorously.

"Powers is the name," he said. "Rest your feet."

"Are you the dean?" I asked. I had seen no title on the door.

"I'm not that lucky, Mr. LeJohn. I'm the head factotum of what some people describe as this preacher factory. My students call me the chief."

He offered me a chair and sat. He folded his hands over his stomach. He appeared a well-fed, happy man, and I had to get it out of my mind that preachers should be gaunt and suffering. There were few John the Baptists left to eat locusts and wild honey in the wilderness. Ministers could now wear sport jackets, drive red convertibles, and shoot golf at country clubs.

"It's good of you to see me," I said. I hadn't expected to be talking to the president. I wasn't certain how to proceed.

"I'm delighted you stopped by. I don't suppose you're a prospective student, though we have many a good bit older than you are."

"No."

"Then how can I help you, Mr. LeJohn."

"I need information about a minister, a former student here," I said.

"What right have you to information?" he asked, still smiling.

"I'm Chairman of the Board of Officers in the Black Leaf church."

"And you want precisely what?"

"Your files."

"An irregular request," he said, his face tightening to seriousness. Light glittered off his glasses. "Our files are confidential."

"I'm on an official mission of the church."

He frowned and removed his glasses.

"Unfortunately lines of jurisdiction in our faith are hazily drawn." He pulled out his handkerchief to polish his lenses. "If you tell me what you're after, I might be able to help."

"I'd rather not."

He put on his glasses, stared at me, and sat forward in his chair to press a plastic button on his telephone. He lifted the receiver. "Janet, ask Rob to come by, will you?" He put down the receiver. "Do you have credentials?"

"None that proves I'm a church officer," I said. "If you want to call Black Leaf, I can give you numbers."

"You ought to have some sort of identification," he said, looking petulant. "You could be from one of the finance companies."

I took out my wallet and handed him the celluloid folder that held my cards. As he glanced through them, there was a knock at the door, and an elderly man entered. He was bald except for fringes of white hair just above his ears. He had a thin, austere mouth.

"Mr. LeJohn, Dean MacKensie," Powers said.

I shook hands with the dean. His fingers were bones.

"I'd like a file, Rob," Powers said. It seemed presumptuous for the younger man to be calling this grave, dignified ascetic Rob. "One of our former students by the name of—" Powers turned to me.

"Elgin," I said. "Paul Elgin. He would have graduated here after the war."

Dean MacKensie glanced at me, nodded, and left the office.

"I don't intend to turn the file over to you," Powers said, handing me my wallet. His chair had a high back, and he leaned his head against it. "I want to refresh my own mind. Then I may or may not answer certain questions."

"Do you remember him?" I asked.

"Frankly I don't. He was undoubtedly here before my time."

Dean MacKensie returned. Sunlight reflected the sheen of his dark suit. He carried a folder which he handed to Powers. Powers adjusted his glasses and opened the folder.

"Thank you, Rob," he said to MacKensie.

"Do you need me?" MacKensie asked.

"If you have a moment, rest your feet."

MacKensie sat but not on one of the comfortable leather chairs. Rather he chose a straight, uncushioned chair with no arms. It was the action of a man who would believe it sinful to be comfortable. It was easy to imagine him a monk, living in a cell with skulls.

"Okay," Powers said as he turned pages within the folder. "You can fire away. I'm not saying I'll answer everything, but I'll listen."

"I want his full name, his place of birth, and his parents," I said. I took out my pencil and a small notebook.

"Paul Armisted Elgin, born Dusty Cross, North Carolina, son of Mr. and Mrs. Virgil Beardly Elgin." He whipped off his glasses and turned to Dean MacKensie. "I don't see any harm in giving this information, do you?"

"No," MacKensie answered. He sat quietly, a white hand on each black knee.

"Where'd he do his undergraduate work?" I asked. I didn't feel it was necessarily important, but I wanted to probe gently.

"Beauregard-Marion College," President Powers said and smiled. "Known more for its tennis and azaleas than its academics. He majored in"—Powers glanced at Dean MacKensie—"Physical Education." Powers pulled off his glasses and leaned toward Mac-Kensie. "I'm rather surprised."

"He was given special dispensation by your predecessor," MacKensie said, his voice toneless.

"I knew Rob would remember," Powers said. "He remembers

66

everybody." He again leaned toward MacKensie. "What sort of dispensation?"

"Because of his academic background, the Admissions Committee turned him down. He went to President Emery with a story."

I watched Dean MacKensie. His severe face showed nothing, but I believed I heard something.

"There's no record of it here," Powers said. He tapped the folder with his glasses and faced me. "What else?"

"What sort of student was he?"

"I'm not sure I should answer that," Powers said, frowning. "What do you think, Rob?"

"It depends on the use," the dean said.

"Exactly," Powers said. "How do we know you aren't trying to undermine Mr. Elgin?"

"You have my word I'll keep the information confidential," I said. "Only church officers will be told."

"Still a man's past is his past," Powers said. He bit an earpiece of his glasses. "You can be sure anyone who graduates from this seminary is qualified to stand in the pulpit."

I didn't press it. The question wasn't that important.

"What did he do before he came to the ministry?" I asked.

"Before?" Powers asked.

"If he was older, he must have worked somewhere after he finished his undergraduate degree."

"Let's have a look," the president said, leafing through pages. He adjusted his glasses. "Here we are. Mr. Elgin was a salesman, and a very successful one at that. He made a great deal of money."

"Who employed him?"

Powers started to speak but hesitated. He glanced at Dean MacKensie. "I don't think I'll give you that information," he said. "I just don't believe it's necessary."

"Is it something that needs to be hidden?" I asked. The dean turned his head and stared. Powers was irritated.

"I am not hiding anything," he said. "I can see, however, that taken out of context the information might hurt him. I don't want anyone hurt."

"I'd like to know what his parents were in Dusty Cross," I said.

"Farmers."

"Military experience?" I asked.

"Mr. Elgin was in the Army during World War II."

"What branch?"

"The Quartermaster Corps. He served in England and Europe."

"But never saw combat," Dean MacKensie said.

Powers and I looked at him, surprised that he'd volunteered information.

"Is that a criticism, Rob?" Powers asked.

"No."

"It sounded like one," Powers said. He faced me. "The fact is Mr. Elgin served his country honorably."

Dean MacKensie sat motionless, his hands on his knees, his expression severe, unbending. Powers turned pages in the folder.

"He was not only a successful man before he made his decision for the ministry, he also gave quite a bit of money to the church."

I thought I saw a change in Dean MacKensie—a gathering around the mouth that broke the discipline of his face.

"Can you tell me anything else?" I asked Powers.

"Sorry," Powers said and closed the folder. "He graduated here after meeting full degree requirements and thus passed from these doors with our imprimatur."

"May I respectfully suggest that as an officer of the church this gentleman is entitled to further information," Dean MacKensie said, his voice toneless but firm.

Powers was startled. He resented the intrusion of opinion. They were two entirely different men—one slick, rounded, oiled, the other built of flint, angular, and all rough edges.

"I don't agree, Rob," Powers said. "We don't undercut our graduates." He opened the folder. "The fact is Mr. Elgin was one of our best speakers. He won the Boscoe-Shook silver medal for his student sermons."

"He was other things too," Dean MacKensie said, his face set.

"There's nothing here which would be of further interest to you," Powers said to me. He closed the folder and slapped his immaculate hand on top of it. He was angry at Dean MacKensie.

"I'd still like to look through it," I said.

"I feel I'd be violating the ethics of the seminary if I allowed you to."

Powers transformed his displeasure into a professional smile, a money-raising smile, and walked me to the door. The dean didn't speak. He sat on the straight chair and stared toward a mullioned window. As I left, Powers presented me with a color brochure which described the seminary and made an appeal for contributions to build a new gymnasium.

[12]

I didn't return to Black Leaf. Instead I removed my coat, loosened my tie, and drove off campus to a drugstore where I ate a sandwich. I bought a newspaper and sat in front of a fan to read the sports page.

At five fifteen, I drove back to the seminary, stopped a colored man who had a red hose coiled around his arm, and asked where Dean MacKensie lived. The colored man pointed across the yellowed grass to an isolated grove of locust trees.

Under them was a small stucco house with green blinds. I parked my car, went up the brick walk, and knocked. There was no bell.

Dean MacKensie answered the door. He wore his loafing clothes —tennis shoes, shapeless cotton pants, and a Hawaiian sport shirt which was faded and patched. The shirt appeared particularly frivolous and bizarre over his pale, ascetic flesh. In his hand he carried a book. His index finger was stuck into the pages to keep his place.

"I hope you can spare me a moment," I said.

"For what reason?"

"I'd like to get out of the heat."

Reluctantly he pushed open the screen door, stepped back, and let me pass into the dimness of the hall.

We hadn't had rain since early June, yet the house smelled damp. Perhaps it was built over a spring. I was sure the walls would be moist.

He led me through a corridor. I glimpsed a parlor where furniture was covered with sheets. In a small dining room was a table and only one chair. There were no pictures or curtains. The floors were bare of carpets.

We went to his study, a small room so filled with books and papers that he had to shift them around to find a place for me to sit. His own dark chair was of dry, peeling leather. It held his imprint.

"Excuse the clutter," he said. He wasn't really apologizing. I would bet he never apologized in his life except to God. "My wife brought order into my slovenly existence, and she's been dead these years."

So, I thought, we have a bond, a slender line of understanding, the companionship of lonely men who have suffered through the death of love.

"I lost my wife," I told him.

"It flays one," he said, the severity of his face softening. "I sometimes wander through the house as if I've lost my eyes."

For a moment we sat in silence, two husks, reaching out to comfort one another. He then coughed, as if ashamed he had exposed himself to emotion.

"Why is it you come to me, Mr. LeJohn?" he asked. His pale hands rested on the arms of his chair.

"Duty," I said, because I was certain he was a man who believed in duty above all else. I was also certain he had information about Paul. "As a church officer, I was sent here to find out about our minister."

"You heard the president."

"I have the impression you remember Paul Elgin well."

"Do you also have the impression the president doesn't want me to open my mouth?"

"This isn't an office. I'm in your house asking you personally."

"I'm not a disloyal man, Mr. LeJohn."

"I'm not either, but I feel my highest loyalty is to the church." I was lying. I had long since lost all feeling for the church. I could not forgive God for taking my Kitt from me.

MacKensie stared. The white hair above his ears was ruffled. His bony hands gripped at the arms of his chair.

"Is your minister in trouble?"

"He is."

MacKensie sighed and nodded.

"They should have seen it," he said. "They should have seen it from the first day." His lips worked against his teeth. "I was on the Admissions Committee. I advised against him."

MacKensie stood and paced the narrow aisle between his books.

"First, he didn't have the qualifications. How can we send superior men into the field unless they're properly prepared? I've always believed that we should ask more of ministers than other men. The seminary's stand all along the line should be higher."

No longer seeing me, he prowled among his dusty books.

"I've spent most of my life here," he said. "Almost forty years. Through that time I've fought for the principle that we should accept only the best men. Above all we should not become a refuge for misfits and howlers—the spiritual freaks."

As he paced, his hands struck out angrily.

"The ministry is man's highest calling, and each time a misfit is allowed to wear the cloth, the whole fabric of God is weakened."

He stopped in front of the window and touched fingertips to the streaked panes.

"There are pressures," he said. "In administration you learn that. There is always the desperate need for money. There are the cries of the churches for more graduates. There is"—he turned and made a face—"public relations. Imagine a seminary with a public relations department."

He came back toward me, but his eyes were looking inward.

"I fought," he said. "For years I've fought." He grimaced. "I was once considered for the presidency here. Conservative elements of the church put me forward, but conservatives are no longer fashionable, not even in the ministry."

The wound, I thought, the lash. He had been passed over for a round, slick type who could smile professionally and hand out brochures.

"I'm not a fanatic," he said. He crossed to his chair and sat in it. "Rather it's my belief that God is better served with one good man than ten thousand mediocre ones."

He lowered his voice and leaned toward me.

"That's the reason I opposed your pastor's matriculation in this seminary. He came without qualification. His degree was in Physical Education. He was a salesman with no history of religious experience. It's my belief he was running."

Again he stood and paced slowly among the books.

"For his own good I attempted to keep him out. When he was admitted anyway, I tried to keep him from graduating. In the faculty meetings I recommended we request him to leave. 'We can't,' they said. 'He's given so much money.' He bought his way in, and I knew he was destined for trouble."

"What sort of trouble?"

"I have a daughter," he said. "She's married now, to a medical missionary in Brazil. She's a good girl—at least as good as a girl can be. When he was a student here, your pastor came to see her. He attempted to use her. He knew I was against him—he was failing my Ethics—and he hoped to win favor for himself through her."

72

He paused in front of me, and his hands worked.

"It's the feeling I had the entire time he was here—that he would use me, my daughters, or anybody to further himself in the ministry. He was a religious hustler."

He breathed loudly, and his mouth was pulled so tight against his teeth that his lips were bloodless. He put his hands behind him and flapped them.

"That's all I have to tell you, Mr. LeJohn," he said. He squared his shoulders.

"Answer me one more thing," I said.

He squinted, and his hands beat softly against each other behind his back.

"I believe I've already said too much."

"You mentioned you believed he was running. From what?"

His hands broke free and fluttered at his lean shanks. When he spoke, his teeth bit into the words.

"From guilt," he said.

[13]

I hoped for more, but he turned away my questions. He was anxious for me to leave. He walked me to the door and shook my hand. I went out under the locust trees to my Ford.

I drove home. What sort of guilt? I asked myself. I was in a line of hot traffic which stained the air blue with exhaust fumes.

At the house I took a quick bath and put on a clean shirt. I checked the kitchen to see whether Injun had eaten. There were no plates in the sink. That meant he was bumming his food from his Aunt Delia.

I drove to Val's. I walked up to the porch of Miss Minnie's

house. She wasn't in her wicker chair, though her knitting bag was on it. I was happy I didn't have to run the gantlet of her tongue.

I rang the bell. I heard Val's heels tapping against the pine floor. She swept out of the shadows in the old house. She wore a white blouse, a white skirt, and white shoes. She looked as if there were no heat in the world hot enough to wilt her.

"It's been a lousy day," she said as I walked her to the car.

"Lousy how?" I asked. I breathed in her perfume.

"Southern history. Why I picked anything southern to do my thesis on I don't know. None of it makes sense."

I held the car door open for her and went around to the other side.

"Take Robert E. Lee," she said. "He loved the United States. He was against slavery and secession. Yet he resigned his commission and fought for the South."

I drove through town. Street lights were just coming on. Val talked beside me. I listened to her voice and not the words. All that youth, energy, and conviction. I was stealing it from her.

"Take Stonewall Jackson," she said. "Take that mean old hillbilly who prayed for the souls of the men he slaughtered. He couldn't do anything right except kill. He was inadequate, ridiculous, a freak until he found battle, and then he slew like Joshua. He was a righteous killer."

I would have smiled except that I'd have hurt her feelings. She was attempting to bring order into history, as if it could be straightened like a messy room. She hadn't learned yet that history wasn't logical, that nothing was logical. She hadn't made the acquaintance of the grand jester—death.

"But Lee," she said. "He knew better. He could have turned Virginia, which still had to secede. If Lee had held firm, thousands of men need not have died."

"Lee stuck with his friends," I said, marveling that she could care so much.

"He failed to live up to his principles," she flared. She turned in the seat toward me.

"But he lived up to his friends."

"I suppose you think it's admirable to choose friends over principle," she said. When she argued, her mouth became small and prim.

"I think there's some virtue in choosing flesh and blood over the abstract," I said.

"You're all sick," she said. She turned away and slapped her hands into her lap.

I took her to Cliff's—a shingled roadhouse with a red neon beer sign which lighted up the gravel parking lot. In the long dark room the jukebox blazed like an altar.

I ordered beer from a waitress and put a quarter into the jukebox. I was aware of teen-agers watching and talking about me. Robbing the cradle, they might be saying. The music thumped.

"The South was bound to lose because it was fighting for something it really didn't believe in," Val said when I returned to the table.

"Let's dance," I said.

"You're all hedonist," she said, but she slid from the booth. She held her big body stiffly and aggressively, unlike my Kitt who had snuggled in and seemed to know each movement of my feet before I made it. Because I had to be so careful of Val, I realized I must appear awkward to the teen-agers. They were smiling about me.

"It's stubbornness, not honor," Val said as we returned to the booth.

"What is?" I asked. I looked into her dark eyes and tried not to think of Kitt who sat invisibly beside me.

"What southern people have. They act as if it's honor and pride, but it's just plain stubbornness." She ordered a steak.

As she finished eating, she glanced toward the door. The young doctor, my competition, had come in. He wore white slacks and a blue jacket. His blond hair was cut short. He had pale, hospital skin, but he was so terribly young.

He saw Val and came to our booth. She gave him a big loving smile, and I thought it was on my steak and beer he was getting it.

"Hello, hello," he said and as if he had a right slid into the booth next to Val.

"We were just leaving," I said.

Val's eyes widened.

"Where you going?" he asked. He smiled those pretty teeth his mother had spent a fortune on. He asked the question as if I were obligated to answer.

"That's a secret," I whispered.

Val glared. What made me mad was that he acted amused. It was as if I were the boy and he the man.

"A dance first?" he asked, turning from me to her. Val smiled at him.

"If Jack doesn't mind," she said.

She glanced at me, and the glance was a warning I'd better not mind. He was already out of the booth. He held a hand to her.

They danced differently. With me Val stood straight and held her back as if she were royalty. With him she did the jungle stuff, which distorted the body. She swung her hips and thrust out her breasts as if attempting to bust them from her brassiere. Top-heavy on her high heels, she slipped off balance and reached to him to steady herself.

I tried not to look, but I had to. She was having a better time than she ever did with me. I pressed back into the corner of the booth. I didn't want the teen-agers to see me. I felt abandoned and shriveled.

[14]

First thing in the morning I went to see Archie LeBuck. His house was eight miles south of town. A hard-packed dirt road lay red under cedars. Green land sloped to the river.

We sat on the porch. Archie was freshly shaven. He wore a cattleman's hat. He pushed it back, and a strip of his silver hair was uncovered.

I told him about my trip to Richmond. I described my talks with President Powers and Dean MacKensie at the seminary.

"It's not enough," he said.

"I know it's not enough. I don't know what to do next."

"You have the end of a thread," he said. "Follow it."

"What thread?"

"You found out he was a salesman. That means Paul was involved with people—lots of people."

"I don't even know what he sold."

"Find out."

"How'm I supposed to do that?" I flared.

"Salesmen are a fraternity, aren't they? Ask around in the right places."

"I don't know the right places."

"Put your mind to it. You'll think of something."

I drove to town. Up the street hillbilly music pounded from metal loudspeakers at the Progress Store. The redcoats were having another sale, and windows were ablaze with red and yellow signs shaped like firecrackers sizzling. People hurried in and out of modern glass doors.

At my place I walked between linoleum tubes and bins of nails to my office. I sat listening to the slow tick of the clock. I turned on no lights. In the dimness I stared at the wall.

I thought about Ed Lopes, a salesman who carried a bulging sample case and sold stoves. Ed was gregarious. He would hear talk of the trade. I opened a desk drawer to look for his card. I had a stack of salesmen's cards bound by a rubber band. They were filed alphabetically.

I put through a person-to-person call to Charlottesville. The operator talked to Ed's wife who gave us another number. The operator tracked him.

"Jackson LeJohn?" Ed asked. "You buying stoves in the summertime?"

"I need help, Ed."

"Is it going to cost me money?"

"Not unless you let me down. Did you ever hear of a man named Paul Elgin?"

"Elgin? Why should I hear of him?"

"He used to be a salesman."

"What line?"

"I don't know."

"Jack, there are a lot of salesmen in the world."

"You could ask around."

"I'll be glad to do that. You sure you don't want some stoves?"

When I hung up, I picked several more cards—salesmen in paint, sporting goods, and appliances. I called and told them the same thing I had Ed. I pretty well covered all sections of the state, and if Paul worked any territory in it, one of the salesmen ought to have crossed his trail.

I heard sooner than I expected. As I was dusting shelves that afternoon, the telephone rang. Pete Potter, in sporting goods, called me from Norfolk. He had, he said, eaten lunch with a friend who knew Paul Elgin years ago.

"Tell me one more time," I said, sitting very quietly, my eyes closed. I heard the slow tick of the old clock.

"Liquor," Pete said. "Elgin waltzed the booze."

[16]

I put on my hat, locked up, and walked the steamy street to the ABC store, which had a glass-brick facade and was built next to the bank.

The manager of the store was Phil Butterwood. During the 1920's he had supposedly made a million dollars in the stock market and lost it by going long on RCA just a few hours before the break. He then tried to recoup by joining a syndicate drilling for oil in New Jersey. He was picked clean.

When Phil lost his money, he lost his nerve. Craving security, he entered the womb of the state as a clerk. He still looked afraid —as if listening for sounds of the world coming apart.

"Have a cup of coffee with me," I said.

A balding man, he wore a starched beige jacket with his nameplate pinned to it. He eyed me and told the other clerks to mind the store. We crossed the street to the Planters Cafe where we sat in a booth.

"You never bought me coffee before," Phil said. He stirred milk into his white mug and watched me as if he expected me to solicit him for a contribution.

"I never needed information before," I said.

"What sort of information?"

"Do salesmen ever call at your store?"

"All the buying's done in Richmond."

"Who does it?"

"The commissioner—by the hundreds of cases to save you citizens money."

"I want to talk with him."

"About what?" He put down his mug.

"Just telephone and make an appointment for me."

"You paying for the call?"

"Charge it to my number."

"Okay," he said and finished his coffee. "Just don't shoot me down."

We recrossed the street and went to his office in the rear of the store. While I sat on a straight metal chair, he dialed Richmond. He talked to the commissioner's secretary.

"Ten thirty tomorrow suit you?" he asked me, holding his palm over the receiver.

I nodded. He confirmed the time with the secretary and hung up.

"It's set," he said.

[17]

When I drove home after work, I was thinking of Paul and didn't see the radar until I was through it at sixty-four miles an hour. That brought Jay Boney, a state trooper, after me with his red light flashing and his siren howling. I'd gone to high school with Jay, and he was apologetic about the ticket.

"There's no way I can keep from writing you up," he said. Sweat stained his heavy gray uniform, and sun reflected from his handcuffs.

He gave me the ticket, and I drove down the road. This time I crawled, and cars stacked up behind me. The more they honked, the slower I went. I had to use first gear to keep my Ford from bucking. On straight stretches people roared around me and glared.

One car kept blowing its horn. I didn't look. I slowed even more. The car came up beside me. The driver continued to sound the horn. I still would not look. I heard a voice. I glanced at the dusty Cadillac. It was Lou Gaines.

"Pull over!" he shouted. He thrust out his hand as if to push me aside.

I curved in to the grassy shoulder of the road. I got out of my car. Lou was already walking toward me.

"What were you doing?" he asked. He wore a wrinkled gray suit, and his dark tie was off-center. Sweat glistened through his red hair.

"I didn't know it was you."

"But hell," he said.

He was worn and harried. He could have just come off a drunk.

He pulled out his handkerchief to wipe his ruddy face. He peered at me over the handkerchief.

"You been avoiding me?" he asked.

"No, Lou."

"He's still here, isn't he?"

"It's being taken care of, but we need a few days."

"How can he have the gall?" Lou asked. He flapped his short, thick arms.

There was no answer I could give. I waited for him to berate me but he sagged against my car and searched out my eyes.

"You're on my side, aren't you, Jack?" he asked. There was a lost, sad quality about his confusion.

"Nobody could be more on your side than I am."

"Okay," he said. He straightened and stood away. "I know I can count on you."

He walked to his Cadillac and drove off without another word. His dust settled in the hot light.

[18]

I was up early next morning and fixed breakfast for Injun. He stood in the drive and watched me leave. He wore khaki shorts and no shoes or shirt. I felt him longing after me.

I avoided my son. I believed I had nothing to give him. I saw Kitt in him too, looking out at me disapprovingly. I could not face his eyes.

For the second time I drove to Richmond—downtown where the air tasted acrid and used. I left my car in a public lot and walked to Capital Square. Iron palings were too hot to touch.

I entered the state building. It was not air-conditioned, and workers moved dreamily through the corridors. Men were in their shirt-sleeves, and women fanned themselves and dabbed at sweat. It was a place of sighs.

I found General Dempsey's name on the register and took the elevator to the third floor. I walked into his office.

A secretary turned to me. She must have been close to forty, a heavy woman with blond hair and pale blue eyelids. Her cheeks were rouged. There was a blowsy quality about her, like an aging burlesque queen.

"Yes?" she asked. She sounded impatient. She touched her powdered forehead with a Kleenex.

"I have an appointment with the commissioner." I stood in front of her desk.

"You're Mr.—?"

"LeJohn," I said.

She ran her finger down a list. The nail was long and fire-engine red. On a chrome-leatherette sofa sat a man. He grinned at me.

"General Dempsey will see you momentarily," the secretary told me and with a languid hand indicated I was to wait on the sofa.

I settled myself beside the man. He was young, his hair crew cut, and he wore one of those gray synthetic suits which have a metallic sheen. He glanced at me, winked, and eyed the secretary. His lips pursed to a silent whistle.

As she typed, the secretary's heavy bosoms trembled above the keys. Their weight had pulled her white blouse loose from the rear of her checkered skirt. The skirt was pulled drum tight across her thighs.

A salesman came from the commissioner's office. The secretary picked up her telephone, spoke softly into it, and sent the man next to me inside. The salesman who'd come out stood by her desk. He too was young and carried an attaché case. He smiled at the secretary. She pushed a yellow pencil into the tangle of her blond hair.

"He's benign today," the salesman said. He was sun-darkened. "Didn't snarl at me more than a couple of times."

"He's got a raise coming," she said. "Legislature put it through. So he's practically kindly."

"Well, it's been nice seeing you again, Flo," the salesman said. He glanced at me and lowered his voice to her. "Maybe we can go to the ball game some afternoon."

"Your wife doesn't like baseball?" she asked.

"She's not much of a fan—not like you."

"I tell you, Eddy, I've given up baseball."

"Too bad. You were great at it."

"Many thanks," she said, and her face grew hard and accusing.

"See you," he said. He backed off and felt for the knob.

"You know it," she answered, and after he was gone, she sat still a minute, her hands in her big lap, her eyes fixed on the door. She then turned to see whether I was watching. I swerved my eyes.

The man who'd sat beside me came from the commissioner's office, hurriedly, as if to escape a foot in his rear. The door slammed. He wiped his forehead, blew out his cheeks, and flipped a hand as if to fling sweat.

"Corpsman!" he whispered and held a palm over his chest as if wounded. He went out the door. He stuck his head back to wink at the secretary.

She ignored him. She had already picked up her telephone and was speaking my name into it. She nodded to me.

I crossed to the door, pushed it open, and stepped into General Dempsey's office. It was a Spartan room. The walls were mustard brown and bare. In the center of the room was a metal desk and two wooden chairs—one behind the desk and one in front of it. On the desk was a cardboard sign which read, "Wine is a mocker; strong drink is raging, and whoever is deceived thereby is not wise."

General Dempsey himself sat at the desk. He was a tall, hairless man with a long, outraged face. His skin shone with washing. He wore a black preaching suit. His hands were spraddled palms down against the desk—as if he expected to spring up.

84

"Come on, come on," he said and thumped a hand against the desk.

Holding my hat, I crossed to the chair and started to sit. His fingers snaked to a riding crop which he pointed at me.

"There's no need to roost if we have business that can be dispensed with quickly," he said. "Every minute I save accrues to the benefit of the state and its taxpayers." He sniffed. "I assume you're after a job."

"No."

"Isn't that why Butterwood made this appointment? I further assume you're related to him."

"No, sir."

"No, sir, which?"

"I'm not related to him and don't want a job."

"Well," he said and looked surprised. He had no eyebrows, and his face seemed an expanse of shiny skin that stretched from his chin over the top of his head. "Are you selling anything?"

"No."

"In that case I'll ask you to sit," he said. "Mr. LeJohn, is it? I expect you're thinking I'm not the soul of courtesy. It may interest you to know that by nature I'm not discourteous. Rather I feel it's my duty to give my best to the state. That means not wasting time."

He eyed me, and with the leather crop he tapped the cardboard sign on the desk. "Perhaps you find it strange that such sentiments are expressed in this office. A lot of people do."

"Well," I said.

"I like to make my position clear to all who enter." He slapped the crop on the desk. "I am not a drinking man. I spent thirty-four years of my life in the United States Army, but I never had liquor in my mouth except once—a shot of tequila which I spat on the ground without swallowing. I was nineteen years old."

He beat the crop against the desk.

"People assume that because I work for the Alcohol Beverage Control Board that I approve of liquor. The fact is I abhor John

Barleycorn, and if I had my way no intoxicating spirits would be sold in Virginia or anywhere else in the world."

He scowled as if he expected me to take issue with him. I sat quietly, my hat in my lap.

"But I believe in law," he continued. "If our legislature sees fit to say liquor will be sold, I will obey that law and enforce it. I'd rather have state control of dissipation than no control at all. And if you find it peculiar that a person such as I sit in this chair, you might remember there are terrible temptations in this office and that I'm not a man susceptible to influence or pressure, which is the reason the governor put forward my appointment."

He smacked the crop across the desk, leaned back, and smiled. The smile was like seeing stone crumble.

"Now I've made my little speech. What is it you want, Mr. LeJohn?"

"It's about a salesman," I said.

"You're shilling for a salesman?" he asked and sat forward as if I'd tricked him.

"A former salesman," I said quickly. "I need information."

"This isn't the Information Office," he said and eyed me suspiciously. His long face was pinched and moral. He was the avenger who would take all the enjoyment he could out of liquor drinking so that the stink of sin would not be too offensive to the nostrils of the Lord. "I suggest you go downstairs and consult the directory."

"General Dempsey, I'm Chairman of the Board of Officers in my church, and this is official business."

"Allow me to shake your hand, sir," he said and stood. He reached across his desk. His grip was hard. "I don't get many churchmen in this office." He returned to his chair. "Fire with all your guns."

"Did you know a salesman named Paul Elgin?"

"Very few of them call on me," he said and sounded pleased. "They've found it does them little good."

"You never heard of him?"

"I didn't say that. Did I say I'd never heard of him?"

"No, you didn't."

"He was one of the few I could stand," General Dempsey said and rested his hands on his stomach. "Most are clowns, put on the road to entertain. Elgin was different."

"Different how?" I asked. I was on the edge of my chair.

"He didn't perform," General Dempsey said. "He never slapped my back or tried to bribe me with dinner or a ham at Christmas. He maintained his dignity."

I was disappointed. I hadn't expected approval from this Puritan. I didn't want approval.

"He didn't belong in the liquor business," General Dempsey said. "He was a straight shooter."

"Can you tell me anything else?"

"No."

"About his background, say."

"I never allow myself to become intimate with salesmen. I keep my distance so that my judgment is not swayed."

"Can you refer me to anybody who knew Mr. Elgin?" I asked, trying to salvage something.

He leaned forward like a judge about to rap his gavel, picked up his telephone, and spoke into it. The door opened, and the blond secretary entered—not fast, with no urge to please, but in an arrogant glide, her heavy thighs pushing against her checkered skirt.

"Bring my appointment list," he told her.

She turned and moved back through the door, her girdled hips rising and falling. From her desk she lifted a paper which she carried to General Dempsey. While Dempsey read, she stood at his side and examined her red nails. She glanced at me as if I were vermin.

"Boone of South Seas Distilleries is due here at eleven in the morning," General Dempsey said.

"He knows Paul Elgin?" I asked.

The blond secretary lowered her hand and looked hard at me.

"They all know each other," General Dempsey said. "It's a den of thieves and Boone is the senior member."

The secretary dropped the hand to her hip and watched me.

"Boone stays at the Hotel Jefferson," General Dempsey said. "You could leave word for him."

"Thanks very much," I said. I stood and shook General Dempsey's hand. I had an impulse to salute—a vestige of the Army.

I left his office. I was aware of his secretary right behind me. She shut General Dempsey's door. Her heels hit heavily on the uncarpeted floor.

"I couldn't help hearing you ask about Paul Elgin," she said. Her voice was so low she sounded like a man. She touched at the yellow pencil in her hair. The movement raised her right bosom. "I wonder whether he's the same Paul Elgin who worked this office."

"Yes," I said and thought that if this woman knew him, it could be in only one way.

"Do you see him?" she asked. She tucked in her blouse.

"I'm a member of his congregation."

"Well," she said and smiled. The smile was startling on such a contemptuous face. She had large teeth and showed just the tip of her pink tongue. "Tell him hello for me. Tell him Flo Legere sends her regards."

"I'll be glad to," I said. I was holding my hat. I still had a hand on the doorknob.

"I haven't seen him for years," she said. She was wistful and again she touched the pencil in her hair. "I have difficulty thinking of him as a minister. I mean his conversion was so sudden. I hope he's getting along all right."

"He's making quite a name for himself."

"He used to come here and was nicer than most. Respectful, if you know what I mean."

I nodded, though I had no idea what she meant. Perhaps he ravished her perfumed flesh with delicacy.

88

"We miss him," she said, and there was no doubt she meant it. Her green eyes were alight, and her voice was husky.

"I'm sure he'll be glad to hear from you," I said.

"We sometimes went out," she said. "Before he entered the ministry."

"Well, I'll be happy to give him your regards," I said. I opened the door.

"Tell him to stop by if he gets a chance. The General would love to see him." She smiled. "Paul was the only salesman who could get on the good side of General Dempsey."

She touched her blond hair, turned, and crossed to her desk. As she sat, she smoothed her checkered skirt across her thighs. She squared her shoulders and drew up her bosom. Yet her expression was still dreamy—not for me because she no longer noticed me, but for her memory of Paul.

[19]

Down on the street I went into a drugstore and telephoned the Jefferson Hotel. I asked the clerk for Mr. Boone of South Seas Distilleries. The clerk said Mr. Boone wasn't expected until late. I gave my Black Leaf number and told the clerk to have Mr. Boone call me long-distance collect when he arrived.

I drove home. The hot traffic moved slowly. I smelled the sourness of my sweat. When I reached the house, I took off my shirt and sat on the back porch steps.

I was tempted to get out the bottle of bourbon under the kitchen sink. Instead I went to the telephone and called Val.

"How about a swim and dinner?" I asked her.

"Pick me up in thirty minutes," she said.

I undressed and filled the claw-foot bathtub. I lay back in the bubbly water. Don't think of Paul Elgin, I told myself. For a little while, erase him.

I put on a fresh shirt and a summer suit which had just come from the cleaners. I dabbed myself with after-shave lotion and slicked my thin hair with Vitalis.

Injun walked silently down the hall. Startled, he glanced at me and hurried past.

I drove him to Aunt Delia's, my father's sister. The family considered she had married beneath her by going off to Baltimore with a piano player. She was a delicate, otherworldly woman with white hair and a way of drawing back as if afraid. She lived alone on a piece of land my father had given her. She had planted a thousand flowers around her small white bungalow, and they gave out fragrances the wind carried across fields to my place.

She was in her garden. She wore a large hat to shade her face, a green smock, and canvas gloves with cuffs. She had her sprinkler turned on and held a galvanized watering can.

"Just send him home when he pains you," I said to her of Injun. He walked to the sprinkler and through the cooling water. Looping around him, water struck and glistened on his brown skin. I told myself there was no reason I should feel guilty for not taking him with me to the river.

"Which will be never," Aunt Delia answered and smiled fondly at him. "Would you like flowers for Valerie?"

"How'd you know I'm going to see Val?"

"You look almost respectable when you're on your way to her," Delia said and pulled scissors from her smock. She cut a bouquet of pinks, wrapped the stems in wax paper, and fastened a rubber band around the paper. I put the bouquet beside me on the seat. I thanked her and started to drive off.

"The poor man," she said, frowning.

"What poor man?" I asked.

"At the church."

I was surprised she'd heard about the trouble at the church. She'd given up going out and had no telephone.

"Lou's tough," I told her. "He'll be okay."

"Not Lou," she said, and her lavender eyes swung to me in reproof. "Our minister."

"Don't waste your time feeling sorry for him," I said.

"Ministers have such a terrible time," she said. "More than anybody—even the poets."

"I don't know about that," I said and thought she would never understand what'd happened to Caroline. Who could tell her?

"You must help him," Delia said and touched my wrist lightly, apologetically. "Don't let them butcher him like—"

She stopped speaking and rubbed her arms as if cold. She trembled with memories of her husband, a man who'd stepped off an iron bridge into eternity. She believed he'd been a great musician. She'd made him that in her mind because otherwise the anguish and pain she'd suffered for him were meaningless.

"I'm doing all I can," I told her.

"We must always be kind," she said, still rubbing her arms.

[20]

As I drove off, I looked in my rearview mirror to see her turning on the water harder for Injun who danced in loops from the sprinkler. There were, I thought, people too gentle to live. Delia was one of them. She should have been a nun. Life, after all, was the breaking down of man—a prolonged and precise kind of butchery. She would never accept that truth.

I drove to Miss Minnie's and parked. Miss Minnie sat on the shaded porch, knitting and rocking. I hesitated to take the bouquet but figured I had more to win than lose.

"Those posies for me?" Miss Minnie asked and tee-heed.

Her knitting needles clacked. As I rang, she kept giggling. She

91

made me realize how ridiculous I must look—a grown man standing there like an awkward, red-faced schoolboy.

I rang a second time and straightened my tie. The tempo of Miss Minnie's needles changed. Their clacking became soft and calculating. She rocked in short, fast pumps of her stubby feet.

"When you going to act?" she asked.

"Act how?" I said, peering into the house shadows for Val.

"You officers," she said. "People are expecting you to act."

"It's being done," I said. I thought of telephone lines smoking and knitting needles being worn out.

"Some people claim you're dilatory," Miss Minnie said, rocking and clacking.

"Do they?" I asked. God, couldn't I get away from Paul Elgin even for a minute?

"Preacher walks around as if nothing'd happened," Miss Minnie said and crinkled her potato-like nose. "It's time somebody did something."

Before I had to answer, Val pushed out. She had her black hair twisted high on her head and a blue scarf wrapped around it. She wore a white shift with large red buttons down the front and cork shoes which tied around her ankles. She carried a small canvas bag with her swimming things in it.

"Aren't you being sweet tonight?" she asked when she saw the bouquet. She took the pinks from me and held them under her nose. She put her arm through mine and started me off the porch. A strong girl, she moved me faster than I normally walked.

"What time will you be in?" Miss Minnie called after us.

"In the bye and bye," Val called and squeezed my arm.

Instead of the club, I intended to take her to the river where we'd be alone and no young doctor could interrupt us. I passed the street where I usually turned. Val looked at me.

"You know where you're going?" she asked.

"River swimming's better," I answered.

I didn't even glance at her. She continued to look at me as I steered the car out of town and down the highway.

I slowed for a red dirt road that ran crooked through the pines. Behind me a rooster tail of dust exploded up from under the tires. I was nervous about the river, even without Val.

When Kitt and I were first married, I'd built the cabin. We'd wanted a place where we could shuck off the world. In those early years we'd lived out here in the summers.

We wore our bathing suits and ate out of the river—big steel-colored catfish fried in so much country butter the meat floated. We popped hot chunks of white meat in our mouths and had to work the meat to keep from burning our tongues. I had a little garden where I grew snaps, corn, and potatoes. I put in melons on a sunny bank where they swelled fat and sweet.

Then Kitt and I started arguing. I didn't understand she was sick, and she didn't understand it either. I had the LeJohn stubbornness and wouldn't give in. We drank too much, and to my shame I hit her one evening and knocked her against the wall.

We stopped coming to the cabin. We could fight just as well at home. We didn't speak unless it was to gut-rip each other—as if words were knives. It was the worst part of my life because I loved her, and when I found she was eaten up, I wanted to die too.

Now I was driving up to our place with another woman. The yard was in weeds, but the cabin didn't look so bad. A little paint and some tin on the roof would do a whole lot.

"I didn't know you even had this," Val said.

"We can change inside if you don't mind the dust," I told her.

The door wasn't locked, but I had to throw my shoulder against it to get it open. Val followed me into the kitchen where a rotted fishing net and a bait can lay in front of the rusty refrigerator. I led her to one of the bedrooms. The mattresses had been stolen.

I went to another bedroom to change. As I put on my bathing suit, I heard the sound of the river flowing, touching the bank and dragging willow limbs, a quiet, whispering sound.

I walked to the dock and tested it. The pilings were firm. As I stood on the end of the dock, Val came out. She wore a yellow two-piece bathing suit which fitted her so tightly the pants cut in around her legs. Unlike Kitt who was slender, Val had big hips and strong shoulders.

"It's beautiful here," she said and stuck a foot in the water. She put out her hands to keep her balance. Her stomach firmed into ripples.

I had not allowed myself really to look at the river yet. I raised my eyes. It flowed wide and deep between willows and maples which threw shadows on the water. There was a trail of green pollen floating down and curling in against the bank.

Val came to the end of the dock. She tucked her black hair into a yellow bathing cap, set her feet, and dived into the water. I watched the air bubbles hiss away.

When she didn't come up, I peered into the river. She could have hit a log or be stuck in the mud. Frightened, I dived after her. Frantically I felt along the bottom. The water was warm and murky. I could see only a foot or two beyond my waving hands.

I thrashed about, yelling under water, desperate to see the whiteness of her body. I shot to the surface, gasped for air, and again went under. I kicked to the bottom and threw up mud.

I swallowed water, coughed, and fought toward the surface. I broke through to air. My eyes blurred. I moaned. I couldn't endure more death.

I heard her laugh. I looked upstream. She was on her back, kicking and splashing. She raised one pretty leg and sank slowly.

Shakily I swam after her. One thing I could do was swim. I'd spent my boyhood on this river, and though I'd learned no country-club stroke, my choppy style was suited to the relentless current. I caught her easily.

I didn't mean for it to become a race. I suppose I wanted to show off a little, to prove to her that, like the young doctor, I was sound. When she saw me coming, however, she took it as a challenge and reached upriver in a graceful Australian crawl, her flutter kick precise, her face turning up with the rise of her wet shoulder.

She was good. It was her nature to believe nobody could beat her at anything. She went ahead of me. I didn't like competing, but I couldn't see any way out. If I beat her, I wasn't a gentleman, and if I let her beat me, she'd compare me to the young doctor and think I was over the hill.

She poured it on against the current. Her long arms swept glistening out of the river. I caught her but didn't try to get ahead. I kept smiling in her direction so she'd see it was all in fun.

She wouldn't quit. She'd slow for a minute or two and then start off in that beautiful crawl. Her face was determined and petulant.

I was becoming tired. She understood her age advantage and attempted to wear me out.

I allowed my body to sink lower in the water. I opened and closed my mouth on pollen. My strokes became lazy, casual. Even so I was breathing hard.

She was tired too. She was not raising her arms as high. She began to sidestroke and let her head slide under the water. She pushed at hair that had escaped her yellow bathing cap and was pasted across her forehead.

"Why don't we rest?" I suggested. I'd let her go a little way ahead so she could stop with honor.

"You give up?" she asked, heaving for breath.

"There's nothing to give up."

"Admit you're beat," she said. She swallowed water and coughed.

"Why's beating me important?" I asked.

"You started it." Her mouth was at the surface, and her words bubbled through water.

"Let's swim to shore," I said.

"Ha!" she said and struck out. She held about even against the current. Her skin had a greenish cast from the pollen.

"Give up?" she sputtered. Her mouth slipped under water.

"If it'll make you feel better."

"That's not really giving up," she said, swimming on.

95

On the bank cows watched us. They appeared bemused.

"I'll quit . . . if . . . you . . . will," I called to Val.

"You . . . first," she answered, treading water.

"Same . . . time," I said.

"I—" She went under water and came up. "I . . . win."

She tried to swim. She couldn't raise her arms. She bent her face into the river and floated down with the current. I dog-paddled to her.

"Don't touch me!" she said. She kicked away.

The current moved us in toward the bank at a bend of the river. We reached shallow water and crawled out, our heads hanging, our hands and knees throwing up mud. Mud splotched her skin and yellow bathing suit. We were at the edge of a pasture, and we crawled into orchard grass and lay belly down on it. She let her forehead sink to her arm.

All the coolness of the river was gone. Flies buzzed around us. Her body, like mine, heaved with the struggle to breathe. Rough edges of orchard grass cut at us. Mud crusted our skin. She rolled over and slapped her stomach. She cried and kept slapping. Ants were biting her.

"Damn you!" she said. Flies swarmed on her back, and she was too tired and helpless to reach them. "Oh damn you!"

I crawled to her. On my knees behind her, I shooed them off.

"Take your hands off me!" she said, still out of breath. "I don't know why I ever bothered with you." She tilted and almost fell. "It's what I get feeling sorry for people."

I jerked my hands away. She crawled slowly to the shade of a willow oak and settled against it. Her head lolled, and her legs spread ungracefully. She peeled off her yellow bathing cap.

I stood and started across the pasture.

"Are you abandoning me?" she called.

"I should abandon you."

As I walked I had to be careful of burrs and thistle in the orchard grass, yet I hardly felt their sting for the hurt Val had caused by telling me she was sorry for me.

I crossed the field and climbed fences to reach Henry Baker's place—a white frame house with a red tin roof and flowers planted along the front porch. Chickens pecked in the hard red dirt.

On the porch at the side of the house Henry's wife Lavinia churned butter. When she saw me, she let go of the churn stick and made a movement with her mouth as if she were going to blow a soap bubble. To her I must have appeared an escaped lunatic—half naked, splotched with mud, my hair hanging into my sweaty face.

"Jackson LeJohn," I said to reassure her. "I swam a little farther upstream than I intended."

She was an old woman, weathered, in a white cotton dress which hung to her ankles and heavy black shoes that could have been homemade. She stared.

"Where's Henry?" I asked.

"At the barn," she said, edging toward the kitchen door.

I backed away. I started to tip my hat but remembered I didn't have a hat on. She kept staring at me.

I hurried to the barn lot. At the gate I hollered for Henry. He stepped from a stall. He held a manure fork and leveled the prongs at me as if I might attack him.

"Jackson LeJohn," I said. "Can I use your truck?"

"Your car broke down?" he asked, coming a little closer but still holding the manure fork ready. He wore a red cap, bib overalls, and rubber boots.

"I don't have my car."

"How'd you get up here?"

"I swam," I said and realized how ridiculous it sounded. "I'll pay to borrow your truck for a few minutes."

"Broken," he said. He kept looking me up and down. He wouldn't come too close.

"Your tractor."

"The clutch link snapped."

I held to the gate. I thought of Val and me trying to walk to the highway. Whoever picked us up would spread the story—as would Henry and his wife. When I turned, I saw two black inner-tubes hanging in his equipment shed. I walked to the shed, stood on the rusty hitch of a hay baler, and lifted the tubes from a spike.

"What you going to do with my tubes?" Henry asked. He still held the manure fork like a weapon.

"I'll rent them if you'll just get me a pump."

He had an old hand pump, the kind supplied with Model T Fords, and I filled the tubes three-quarters full of air. I hooked a tube over each arm.

"I'll return them tomorrow with a new pump," I told Henry. I walked off without waiting for him to agree.

"What's he doing with the tubes?" his wife called to him.

"He's aborrowing them," Henry answered.

He and his wife followed me. They came in line, Henry first, swinging his boots in long country steps, his wife after him, her face shaded by a blue bonnet. They stayed twenty yards behind me. Henry carried the manure fork. I stopped to let them catch up with me, but they stopped too. I continued on across the pasture.

When Val saw us coming, she stood under the willow oak. She was embarrassed because Henry gawked and his wife glared. Val fluttered her hands and bent her shoulders and knees as if to draw in and hide behind herself.

I led her down to the water and helped her sit in a tube. I gave her a little shove which sent her spinning into the stream. I pushed off to follow her. Henry and his wife stood on the bank and watched us until we were round the bend.

"I feel like a chippy," Val said. "I've never had anybody look at me that way before."

I didn't speak. I didn't even turn my head to her. Hurt lay deep in me. I was thinking that all this time I'd been courting her I must have appeared pitiful. She felt sorry for me. God.

"Is him angry?" she asked. She'd washed mud off herself, and she paddled her tube around in front of me. She tried to peep into my face. "He is angry. Val very sorry. Val apologizes."

She lapped water over her fine legs and scrubbed at a spot in the pants of her yellow bathing suit. Her hair was down, and her yellow cap set on her head with the ear flaps turned up.

"Val likes him," she said. "Val wants him smile at her."

She kept paddling around me. When I still wouldn't speak, she did the thing that broke me down. She came to me and washed the mud off. She held to my tube with one hand, and with the other she cupped up water and rubbed it against my skin.

"That's better," she said, and she held her tube against mine. "Him smile."

It became good going down the river. We moved slowly, and the lowering sun shot thick yellow streaks through willow trees. Occasionally a fish rolled in the warm water, causing ripples to break the film of greenish golden pollen.

We spun and watched shadows grow long on the water. Val splashed and kicked her painted toes. A beaver slapped his tail so loudly it scared her, and for an instant she held to me. Her hand was warm against my back.

We became drunk with the sun and flow of the river. My eyes no longer focused, and we seemed to be living in a green-gold haze. I had the sensation we'd been floating forever among the pollen, with the sun touching us and the deepening shadows passing over our skins like lace.

When we reached my landing, it was night. I helped her out of the water to the bank. I was going to take the tubes up to the car but she held my wrist and drew me back. She put her wet arms around my neck and lay her warm body against mine. She drew my head down.

"That was nice," she said. She smelled of river.

I kissed her, and for a moment she held to me. She then stepped away, smiled, and walked toward the darkness of the cabin. She moved slowly, as if yet bound by the rhythm of the river. Her bathing suit was a yellow blur in the dark.

I stood trembling—not with yearning or lust, but with the realization and the fear that I was very close to life.

The next day I was in Richmond by noon. I waited in the musty, marble lobby which had once held a pond with alligators in it. The alligators had lived there so long they became mossy.

Mr. Asa Boone of South Seas Distilleries had called me last night. The telephone had been ringing as I entered my house after taking Val home. He'd agreed to see me.

Now I sat in a chair and spread a newspaper across my lap. I had already rung his room. There'd been no answer. I asked the clerk to let me know when Mr. Boone came in.

Boone was seven minutes late. The clerk raised a finger to alert me, but before I was out of the deep chair Boone crossed to me, shook my hand, and apologized.

"I was detained," he said. "Unavoidably detained."

He was a clean, plump man with a beautiful set of false teeth. He wore a double-breasted blue suit and a pearl-colored hat, which he swept off to reveal black hair. The hair had to be dyed because he was at least in his late fifties. On the little finger of his left hand was a stud diamond.

"Traffic conditions," he said. His face was pale and rubbery, and each word from his soft mouth quivered his jowls. His voice was deep, and he sounded as if he were crooning bass instead of talking. "Simply awful. Let's go to my suite."

He put his plump hand in the small of my back and prodded me to the elevator. As we went up, he fanned himself with the floppy pearl hat.

"It's thirsty weather," he said and winked. "Thank God for little favors."

We walked down a carpeted corridor, and he unlocked the door to his suite—a kitchenette, parlor, and bedroom. In the parlor was a bar. On top of it lay a yellow leather suitcase with golden clasps. He crossed to the suitcase and rubbed his hands over it.

"Mr. LeJohn, I believe in putting cards on the table," he said and fingered the clasps. "I am not a teetotaler." The clasps sprang up with loud clicks. "I'm in the habit of having a small liquid refreshment before dining." He raised the top of the suitcase. It was lined with velvet pockets, and each pocket was cut so that bottle labels were displayed: reds, yellows, sunbursts. Boone held his hands over the bottles like a pianist about to touch the keyboard. "I hope you'll do me the honor of joining me."

"Bourbon," I told him.

"The Virginian's liquor," he said. "Though a Kentuckian would fight you for it."

He selected a bottle and set it on the bar. He walked behind the bar and tore the paper off two sanitized glasses. He inspected them against the light. He gave the impression that if he found a smear he would hurl the glasses against the wall.

He brought a silver bucket from a shelf under the bar. With tongs he chose large cubes and dropped them into the exact center of each glass so as not to splinter the ice. He raised a jigger and measured two ounces of bourbon as precisely as a scientist in a laboratory.

Behind the bar he had a gallon jug of water. The label said the water was from the limestone region of Kentucky. He poured the water carefully, stopping two-thirds of the way up the glass. He wrapped my drink in a linen napkin, came around to me, and presented it as if it were a treasure.

"Never ask a Virginian what he takes with his bourbon," Boone said. He gestured me to a comfortable chair near the window air-conditioner and went for his drink. "If he doesn't want branch water, he'll tell you."

He sat across from me, on a sofa which sunk under him. Smiling, he held out his glass to me. We sipped. It was fine whisky which slid easily over the tongue and into the throat. The heat spread slowly in the stomach.

"They take more pains making this stuff than Michelangelo did painting the Sistine Chapel," Boone said. He watched me drink while pretending not to. His living would depend on his being able to size a man up quickly and accurately. "And one hell of a lot longer." He held his glass against the light. "It's a quality product the company loses money on and makes only for love."

He selected his words as if looking over each of them before allowing it to leave his mouth. There was a theatrical quality about his deep, musical voice, and it wouldn't have surprised me had he started to declaim Shakespeare.

"Now that we're comfortable and cooling off from the fires of Hell, just how may I accommodate you, sir?" he asked, leaning back to fit the sofa to his spine.

"General Dempsey recommended you to me."

"Ah?"

"He intimated you knew everybody in the liquor business."

"After twenty-seven years of waltzing the goods, I know their children and grandchildren. Twice I've been president of the Spirit Wholesalers of North America. I estimate I've sold more than three million gallons of absolutely first quality liquor in my life."

He shifted his weight and crossed a plump leg.

"There are misinformed people who believe shame and whisky are handmaidens. While it's true occasional men, and ladies, have problems with overindulgence, nobody has ever calculated the number of lives liquor has saved. Think of the thousands, yea millions of human beings who come home after a crushing day and are able to become civilized through the magic of a highball. Think of our elder citizens whose appetites are increased and whose blood is quickened by drink. Consider the unhappiness that has been routed and the pain that has been surceased by the use of Nature's most magical and most maligned gift—the grape."

He sounded Biblical, but it was a spiel he'd used so many times he didn't have to think about it. As his mouth moved loosely, he sat cool and undisturbed.

"The ancients, wisest of men, considered alcohol godly," he said. "They worshiped the killing of pain. In this vale of tears, in the midst of this travail, what in God's name is wrong with man asking to share a moment of blessedness and joy that only good clean liquor can supply? I tell you the world is upside down."

He leaned forward to set his drink on a leather-covered coffee table. He offered me a cigar. I shook my head. He lighted up, his lips settling around the cigar and caressing it.

"Who is it you want to ask me about?" he said, eyeing me through the smoke.

"A former salesman named Paul Elgin."

His face did not change, but he held the match an instant before dropping it into the ashtray. He picked up his drink. He was careful, not ready yet to reveal or deny.

"Why yes," he said. "Everybody knew Paul."

"Tell me about him."

"Tell you what?" He was still affable, but ready to parry.

"Anything you can."

"Well," Boone said and shifted his weight. The weight didn't lift as much as it flowed from one side of him to the other. "That's a big order. And I think I'd better know why before I talk about an old friend."

"I'm an officer of his church. I've been directed to gather information."

"I wouldn't want to hurt Paul," Boone said. "I'm sure you can understand that."

"I haven't asked you to hurt him."

Boone frowned, considered, and recrossed his legs. He hooked a hand under a knee to do it.

"You ask the questions," he said, his mouth firming. "I'll look them over."

"What sort of salesman was he?" I asked. It wasn't what I really wanted to know, but it was a start.

"He was one of the greatest," Boone said. "He sold more liquor than water has flowed down the Nile. He's the only man I ever acknowledged as my better romancing booze."

"You competed directly?"

"Oho, let me tell you how I met him," Boone said. He put down his cigar. "I was on a golf course in South Carolina. I had two members of the liquor commission with me. Nothing shady—just public relations. Our fourth didn't show. I didn't know then Paul had fixed it by faking a long-distance call that the game was called off."

Boone laughed, the laughter starting low in his swelling belly and rising full and rich. He slapped a thigh.

"Paul appeared to be just standing around the first tee. Out of desperation I asked him to join us. I was glad to have him fill in when I saw how beautifully he hit the ball. He was a perfect athlete and made the rest of us feel like clumsy old men, yet without envy. That was his greatest asset—he caused no envy. And before I realized he was even in the business, he took a hundred thousand dollar account right from under my nose."

Boone touched his reddening nose and laughed again. He patted his shaking stomach as one would a pet he was fond of.

"I was the hotshot then," Boone said. "I sold more liquor than water rolls down the Mississippi. When I went to the home office, the president of the company stood to shake my hand. Then Paul came along, and suddenly nobody, not even district managers, were standing for me."

Boone reached to the coffee table for his cigar. He puffed on it vigorously until it was well stoked.

"Paul and I worked the Southeast," he explained. "That means we dealt with state-controlled liquor authorities where the whim of a commissioner is life or death for a salesman. If he likes you, you're able to put your line in the stores. If not, you blow out your brains."

He spun the cigar in his mouth and blew a smoke ring which settled heavily and broke over the toe of his shoe.

"Paul had a new technique," Boone said. "He didn't make a direct pitch. He acted dumb and helpless. He played beautiful golf, of course, and almost always there was a bunch of good-looking women swarming around him, but he'd stammer and act embarrassed if he had to talk about business. The commissioners would have their hackles up, waiting for him to pressure them, but he walked out of their offices without even mentioning the name of the distillery he represented. They were so sorry for him and concerned he wasn't doing his job properly that they'd call him back in and sell themselves."

Boone rose and lifted the glass from my hand without asking. At the bar he went through the same precise ritual of mixing the drink. He examined each ice cube as if it were a diamond.

"I did plenty of sweating because of Paul Elgin," Boone said. "My commissions dropped twenty-eight percent in less than two years. I wondered how I was going to pay for my swimming pool."

He laughed, carried me my drink, and returned to the sofa. His face shone with the fondness of memories he savored.

"Yet, and here's the important thing and the truth if I ever told it, Paul Elgin throughout the whole period was a friend. Never was there a man I liked better."

I didn't want a testimonial. I needed dirt and ugliness.

"I heard he was wild," I said. It was a chance shot. I was thinking of good-looking women swarming about him and of Flo Legere, General Dempsey's fleshy secretary.

Boone smiled at me around his cigar. His eyes crinkled as if to let me know he wasn't deceived. He removed the cigar from his mouth and examined the ash.

"The liquor business isn't for children," he said. "You can't expect Sunday-school conduct." He returned the cigar to his mouth. "By the standards of our profession—and we have them just as any endeavour does—he was an honorable man. If he sold more liquor, he worked harder and with greater imagination."

He allowed the ash to fall gently from his cigar into the ashtray.

"He made one of the great moves in the business," Boone said.

"It was a summer very much like this one—hot, oppressive. We were in Charleston, West Virginia, attempting to romance the new commissioners who had come into office with a change of administration. They were a hungry lot—one's still in prison. They welcomed favors and didn't bother to duck under tables."

He laughed, not in disapproval or disgust, but as if the greed of man were a wonder to behold.

"I gave a little party. I had a suite of rooms in the best hotel and a colored waiter to serve champagne. I had some charming ladies—beautiful in their colored silk dresses."

He narrowed his eyes at me and mouthed the cigar.

"You strike me as a sensible man, Mr. LeJohn. You drink like one. I hope, therefore, you aren't offended or quick to condemn the fact that there were often women. After all, business is conducted with them as catalyst everywhere, including the courts of Europe, or what are left of the courts of Europe. In fact the first girl I ever kissed was sent to me at a dance by fraternity men who were attempting to get me to join their organization."

He laughed, leaned back, and recrossed his legs. Dreamily he rolled the cigar in his mouth.

"At my party for the commissioners, the ladies brightened up the suite like freshly cut flowers. They added grace and beauty. They were demure, and when I slipped a new hundred-dollar bill into each of their small, moist hands, like Japanese maidens they lowered their eyes."

He put down his cigar to sip his drink.

"I'd had a little talk with the chef at the hotel, a surly man from Austria, but capable of decent cooking if his ego was sufficiently nurtured. He sent waiters with a feast. They set up a buffet which would have made Nero gasp."

Boone nodded, and his mouth worked as if it were again tasting ambrosia. For a moment the aroma of food rose in the room.

"I had the commissioners mellowed," he said. "I'd wined and dined them, and my ladies cradled their heads. The men purred like cats. They believed they were young and irresistible. I dreamed of my rising sales curve and the glory that would wait me at the home office."

He laughed, set down his drink, and picked up the cigar.

"At the very moment of my victory, the incredible happened. First there was a tap at my window." He looked at the window and so did I. "We were on the seventh story of the hotel, where I was certain I was safe from any intrusion, yet we all heard this tap-tap-tapping on the glass. We blinked. At the window was a man. It was Paul. He knelt on a stone ledge and pressed his nose against the pane the way a child will do to make a funny face.

"Before I could react, he was in the room. The ladies hurried to open the window for him, and the commissioners laughed and slapped his back. They gathered around him and asked questions, treating him as if he were the center of things instead of me who had given the party and spent up a month's expense account."

Boone laughed and shook his head. He reached for his drink.

"Paul was dressed in evening clothes, and there was never a better-looking man in black tie. When he passed, people turned to stare, believing him a celebrity. To the ladies he was irresistible. They clustered around him and lifted their eager faces.

"The commissioners should have been angry at his taking the girls, but they weren't. He spoke softly to the men, touching them on the elbow or shoulder, and they acted as pleased as if he were bestowing alms.

"Everybody was talking at once. They wanted to know how he got out on the ledge. He explained he'd rented a room down the hall and merely stepped out the window for a stroll. Somebody, he said, had forgotten to send him an invitation to the party. They all looked at me and howled."

Boone shook his head and laughed. It was as if he couldn't believe it even now.

"I tried to keep myself between him and the commissioners," he said. "It was like attempting to stop a puddle of water with a finger. Paul flowed around me to them. I spoke in a whisper to the ladies, reminding them of their duty. They tried to recapture their beaus, but the commissioners ignored the ladies for him. It was a strange thing, and I've often tried to analyze it—this attraction he had for men and women. I think it's that Smooth gave out an effluvium of joy they thirsted for."

"Who?" I asked.

"What?" Boone asked, startled.

"You said 'Smooth.' "

"That's what we called him—Big Smooth. He was silk on velvet. That night, however, I believed he was making a tactical error. He and the commissioners started flipping coins—dimes, quarters, half dollars. I didn't interfere. Smooth was winning. Let him take their money and make them sore."

Boone leaned forward as if pulled by the memory. He put his drink on the coffee table and rubbed his pudgy hands.

"When all the change was in his pockets, they started playing high card. They'd throw a dollar into the pot and turn up against each other. Again Paul won. I winked at the girls. They stood behind the commissioners, egging them on. The pot went up to five and ten dollars a play. Paul's pockets were soon bulging with money, and he stuck bills between his fingers. The commissioners began to sulk."

Boone leaned back, and his face was benignly puzzled—as if he were sorting the memory in an attempt to understand it.

"Even yet I don't know exactly how he did it, but he maneuvered them into playing double or nothing against their losses. There was suddenly sweat in the room. The ladies were quiet. Over a thousand dollars was on the table.

"The three commissioners drew first, and the highest card among them was the eight of spades. Paul smirked as if he'd already won. For a moment they really hated him. He reached to the deck and fingered the cards as if his skin could read spots. He slipped a card from the deck fanned across the table, let it lie to build up tension, and then flipped it with a flourish. The card was the four of clubs, and he'd lost."

Boone laughed quietly, his eyes almost closed.

"Of course he never meant to win," Boone said. "It was a bribe pure and simple—a way of slicking them with their own money. It hadn't cost him a cent."

He chuckled and rattled the ice in his glass.

"The commissioners would realize they hadn't really won anything once they got home and started thinking logically. He hadn't arranged a prepaid trip to Bermuda, say, or lent them Chryslers they would never be asked to return."

He stopped abruptly, worried that he'd revealed too much. He stared at me hard, the cigar motionless in his mouth. He rattled the ice in his glass.

"I'm afraid I'm shocking you," he said.

"I'm not shocked." There was always ugliness.

"I repeat that we played by the rules of the business. Liquor is very competitive. Millions of dollars are involved. Whenever you have that kind of money, the fight is without quarter. It isn't the best way, but it's the way the game's evolved, and as a salesman you have to play it."

He stood to take my glass. I shook my head. I'd had my fight with whisky. I never drank more than two drinks now. Moreover, I needed to listen.

He mixed himself another. Liquor seemed to give him a gloss— as if he'd been waxed. Sunlight glittered on him.

"I figured I still had Paul beat on the account," he said, talking of the party. "He was slippery, but after all I had the girls, the ladies, who would have the last—I don't mean to be vulgar— crack at the commissioners."

Boone smiled.

"Paul, however, wasn't finished. He hadn't really made the big move yet. He'd just laid the bait."

Boone returned to the sofa, sat heavily, and crossed his legs.

"He acted resentful, sullen. He wanted to bet some more. The commissioners were wary. Now they had those dollars in their pockets, their fingers stuck to them. He argued for one last bet —with all the chips on the table."

"'What kind of bet?' they wanted to know. He acted as if the idea just came to him. He crossed to the window, the same one he'd come in. He opened it and had the commissioners look out. Down below were lights and a statue of a horseman in the park of the YMCA across the street. A Salvation Army band played."

Boone leaned to his left to draw a handkerchief from his hip pocket. He wiped his hands.

"The ledge outside the window was hardly a foot wide, and at intervals were concrete decorations—keystones and cornucopias —which narrowed the ledge to mere inches."

Boone stood and crossed to a window. I joined him. He opened it. We were on the fifth floor of the hotel, and outside was no ledge, but I felt the pull of space.

"He wanted a bet—not money this time—but his line of hooch against mine that he could go all the way around the hotel on the ledge in less than three minutes."

Hot air pushed into the room and noise rose from the street.

"The ladies fluttered about him, and the commissioners looked at me. Everybody was fascinated at the gamble because over the play was the biggest pot of all—danger."

He pushed the window down and turned to me.

"I was as fascinated as the rest of them. I also sensed opportunity. The ledge was so small and the hotel so large that it seemed a foolish gamble on his part. Not that I could have refused the bet. The commissioners wanted me to take it, which meant if I didn't, I would probably lose the account anyway."

We again sat. Boone picked up his drink.

"Smooth methodically removed his coat and shoes. He handed them to the ladies who surrounded him as if he were a knight going to battle. He rolled up his pants and shirt-sleeves. He tightened his belt. He asked me to keep time and to signal when the secondhand was at the top of my watch."

Boone took out his watch, large and golden, and rested it in his palm.

"Smooth didn't hurry. He smiled at the ladies and climbed into the window. When I lowered my arm, he swung out. His chest rubbed bricks. There were pigeons out there, and they fluttered into darkness. We crowded into the window and watched him go to the corner of the hotel and around it—that is, we all did except one commissioner. He went to the bathroom and closed the door."

Boone fingered his watch.

"I never believed Smooth would make it," he said. "It required almost a minute for him to reach the corner. He had three more sides of the hotel to get around.

"Down below, the Salvation Army band played. We stood looking at our watches. The secondhand on mine passed two minutes. I thought he could have already fallen from the rear of the hotel —onto one of the dirty garage roofs or into an alley.

"The commissioners were becoming nervous. They were thinking that if Paul did fall, there would be police and scandal. Their fingers trembled on the window sill. The one commissioner remained in the bathroom with the door shut."

Boone wound his watch.

"At two minutes thirty-one seconds—when I believed he couldn't possibly make it even if he were still on the ledge— Smooth rounded the opposite corner of the hotel. His shirt was dirty from brushing against the building, and his hair hung in his face. I was relieved to see him, yet furious at him too. The ladies, my ladies, cheered, and the commissioners called to him. The one commissioner peeked from the bathroom.

"Just as the secondhand of my watch touched three minutes, Smooth climbed down through the window. While I stood glumly, he kissed the ladies and hugged the commissioners. He removed his clothes and walked in his underwear to the bathroom where he had a shower. The ladies giggled around the door, and the commissioners laughed and poured drinks. I knew I was beaten. I slipped away without being noticed."

Boone laughed, softly, the way an older man will when trying to conserve himself. He put the watch back into his pocket.

"I didn't learn for almost a year how he tricked me," Boone said. He kept laughing. "You see, he rented rooms at both ends of that hotel. Soon as he was around the corner where we couldn't see him, he went into the window of one room. He then ran down the corridor to the other room where he climbed on the ledge again. He never had to go all the way around the hotel. He was able to light up a cigarette while he waited. It was a beautiful move, and he made his company a million dollars."

He laughed and dabbed at his eyes as if he'd weep with the joy of it.

"I should have hated him, but I couldn't," Boone said. "Nobody could. He was a man you'd bear-hunt with. He was a beautiful person."

[22]

When I drove back to Black Leaf, I went to my store and tried to telephone Sutter. He wasn't at the hospital. I left word for him to call.

I waited an hour. I dusted the merchandise and went through the mail. I listened to the clock tick and heard the sound of hillbilly music from the Progress Store. Not a single customer came in.

I telephoned the hospital a second time. The desk told me they had given Sutter my message but that he'd again gone out.

I reached for my hat and drove to his home. It was a three-story Victorian house that had belonged to his father, also a doctor. For years the house had gleamed white, and blue flowers had grown in cast-iron pots set on the porch steps.

Sutter had never married, and the house had become swaybacked with neglect. He had put off painting until the boards were weathered and the scrollwork on the porch was warped and falling. At the windows hung ancient, yellowed curtains that came to pieces in the rare hand that touched them.

He did have his grass cut occasionally but never fertilized, and the result was the yard had become mostly dandelions, with brown patches in them burned out by the sun. There was a dead locust tree at the side of the house, yet he wouldn't have it sawed down because he believed Nature did her own pruning with wind, ice, and snow.

At the rear of the house was a small porch almost hidden by boxwoods and shrubbery which had grown up and pressed into the screening. In hot weather Sutter rested there.

I parted a boxwood to peer in. He was on his cot, lying with his thin arms over the edges, his legs spread. His mouth was open. He was barefooted, and his shirttail was pulled out. On the floor around the cot were newspapers and mail he'd never opened. Near the door was his black doctoring bag.

I went up wooden steps which flexed under my feet. Sutter blinked and raised his head.

"That you, Jack?" he asked.

"You get my message?" I asked. I went in the door. I picked up a pile of old medical journals from a lawn chair and sat in it.

"You call me, did you?" he asked. His watery brown eyes swerved, and he lowered his head.

"I've been on the road," I said, deciding not to chide him. It was no use. He simply became more evasive, slipping in and out of words as if he had grease on him.

"Have you?" he asked. He turned on his side and put his hands under his cheek the way a child will do. The bottoms of his feet were dusty.

"Listen," I said and told him about my conversation with Boone. I made it look as bad for Paul as I could. I talked about his selling liquor. I told of his gambling, the women, and his being out on the ledge. I admitted Boone had spoken well of Paul but likened it to praise from a whore. I wanted to arouse Sutter enough to take him with me to Archie LeBuck. I would then have the votes to throw Paul out.

Sutter listened with closed eyes. I wasn't sure whether he was dozing or not. I bumped the cot with my foot. He opened his eyes and stared at the ceiling.

When I finished speaking, Sutter didn't react immediately. He rubbed his face and wheezed. Slowly he pushed himself up. His feet thumped to the floor.

"What's the difference between selling liquor and anything else?" he asked. He scratched his puny chest.

"It's not lawn mowers or fertilizer."

"Even if I admit that, it's all before the fact."

"What fact?"

"Before he became a preacher. It's not relevant to now."

"What do you want me to do?" I asked. The liquor Boone had served me had burned out, and I was tired. I wanted to lie on that cot myself.

"It's my training," Sutter said. "I had a very great man teach me pathology. He was a German Jew, and he believed in being skeptical. He taught skepticism like religion."

Sutter reached for his socks and began to pull them on.

"I had a case once," he said. "It looked simple enough. A woman, age twenty-eight, had a breaking out on her skin. Like hives. I sent her to an allergist in Richmond, and he mailed me a report that she was sensitive to corn, tomatoes, and strawberries. I told her to avoid corn, tomatoes, and strawberries in her diet, and the rash went away."

He lay back on the cot, his hands behind his head. He stared at the ceiling, which was splotched with mud dauber nests.

"The fly in the ointment was that they didn't look one hundred percent like hives to me. The pattern was wrong. I should have been more skeptical and considered human nature. The woman was a high-bred society type, a young wife of the horsey set. So it never occurred to me those hives weren't caused by corn, tomatoes, and strawberries, but by a screw worm called spirochetes. A simple blood test even on a society woman would have found them instead of crippling a child she bore and making me feel like a killer."

Sutter looked stricken. I thought that all doctors, if they live long enough, have nothing but failures. He rubbed his nose.

"Let's put the lid on so there's no way it can come off," he said.

"How?"

"It's the character defect we're after, the pattern of conduct." He sat up. "A man his age just doesn't start molesting women. There has to be a design."

"I have a business to run and a boy to bring up," I said.

He scratched his stomach and spoke as if he hadn't heard me.

"You always have to find the design," he said. "And then you'll have to drive the nails."

"What nails?"

"After you skin him," Sutter said. "You nail him to the barn door."

[23]

On Sunday morning I told Injun to take a bath and get in the car. Clean as cracked corn, he wore the brown summer suit I'd bought him for his birthday. He sat in the back seat, as far away from me as he could push.

I drove to Miss Minnie's. Val waited on the porch. She came clicking down the brick walk.

I opened the car door for her. Her yellow dress rustled as she sat, and she controlled her skirt with a sweep of her white gloves. She glanced at me to see whether or not I was eyeing her legs. She could approve and disapprove of me at the same time—wanting me to look at her and yet acting as if I were nasty in doing so.

"Hello," she said to Injun.

He stared at his feet.

"Answer the lady," I said as I started the engine. I intended to use Injun. Through him I meant to get at Val. She would see his need for a mother. That need was the big advantage I had over the young doctor.

"Hello," Injun said, his small mouth twisting as if the word were bitter on his tongue.

I drove toward church. Val, fresh and crisp beside me, filled the Ford with perfume. I thought of us as married. She would rear Injun for me, and I would borrow her life.

"Are you sure there's even going to be a service this morning?" she asked. She spoke softly, not wanting Injun to hear.

I wasn't certain nor was anyone else. Some people said Paul wouldn't dare enter the pulpit. Others believed he'd arranged for a replacement.

"We might sing a few hymns and go home," I said.

"Miss Bonner has music," Val said. Miss Bonner was our organist.

"We'll know in a minute," I said.

Curiosity was bringing people to church. Cars were parked on both sides of the street—under strips of shade laid down by maples. I found a space around the corner.

I was careful to walk on the outside of Val as we approached the church. Injun trailed us. I felt eyes on me. Men stood on the grass, and their lips were caught up at the corners. I tipped my hat to ladies whose eyes were brightly devouring. The telephone lines would be hot. A man didn't bring a woman to church unless he was serious. It was a public proclamation.

We passed the young doctor. Val smiled at him. Unlike Sutter, his face was unmarked. He hadn't learned yet about failure.

I took Val inside, to the LeJohn pew. I made Injun go first. He would be penned by the wall on one side and Val on the other. She was trying to be friendly. He didn't look at her.

The church had stained-glass windows—three of them, depicting Christ breaking fishes, healing a blind man, and giving up the ghost on the cross. The windows lay red and green checks on the pews and dark carpet.

At the front of the church was a small altar table, the pulpit, and behind the pulpit the golden barrels of the pipe organ.

The sanctuary was filling up. Older members sat toward the center. The closer to death a man drew, the more forward he sat. That being the case, I thought, I ought to be on the front row.

There were people I hadn't seen since Easter—John Bartow, a contractor who was making himself a fortune building interstate highways; Priscilla Bennet, the only girl in Black Leaf who'd ever gone to Vassar; and Tommy Tines, our benign alcoholic whose father had left him enough money to drink his way through life gracefully. He sat tilted, smiling as if he knew the secret of eternity.

Though the church was full, one pew was not being used. It belonged to Caroline and Lou Gaines, who always sat flanked by their daughters. The emptiness of the pew was an accusation.

Bernice Bonner finished the organ prelude and was undecided what to do next. The congregation became silent. We watched the door to the right of the pulpit.

Paul didn't come. We glanced at each other. Some were disappointed. They wanted a show. I was glad. He's given up, I thought. He's run.

The congregation grew restless. Bernice didn't know whether to play the organ or not. Men stood, ready to go back to the shade of pecan trees at the side of the church. Women adjusted their clothes and reached for their pocketbooks.

The door to the right of the pulpit opened, and Paul appeared. Unhurriedly he walked to the thronelike oak chairs behind the pulpit. He carried a Bible and wore a black vestment.

He sat in the middle oak chair, crossed his heavy legs, and nodded to Bernice to play the processional.

117

The choir, which usually formed up in the vestibule and came in white robes down the aisle, had not met. Bernice was nervous, and her brittle fingers jammed keys, causing a discordance that made people draw in their shoulders.

Paul held his Bible in his lap and looked out at us. He didn't appear intimidated by the glares we fixed on him. His expression was bland, and it seemed inconceivable that he'd ever frenziedly torn a blouse or bitten a neck.

"Don't," Val whispered to me.

"Don't what?"

"You look as if you'd like to kill him."

When Bernice finished the processional, Paul stood and walked to the pulpit. He raised his eyes and spread his arms. "The Lord is in His Holy Temple. Let us come, bow down, and worship the Lord."

He had a fine voice, one of the best I'd ever heard from a preacher—rich and deep, like a basso. It made the commonplace seem unusual, and the profound vibrant. It was, I thought, a voice that had been honed on salesmanship.

The voice was his strength, and he knew it. He rolled the words from his mouth, shaping them almost sensually with his large lips. He could coax and threaten, plead and terrify. His voice touched and manipulated us as if it were a hand forming clay.

At least it had before this morning. Now it seemed too loud, too firm. He led us in the Lord's Prayer, and he enunciated in a manner that was false. He pronounced even the silent syllables of words. He made two syllables out of *bread* and stressed the *or* sound of *debtor* as if he were reading Poe. The congregation followed him sullenly, lagging behind his rhythm.

"We'll sing," he said, after the prayer. In the pulpit he had a mannerism of smiling slightly, as if everything were amusing, even doom. "The purpose of our hymning is to glorify the Lord. It is worship that carries the same burden as prayer. Therefore open your hearts and mouths."

Not many people sang. They held hymnbooks but pursed their lips. They scowled, resentful of his piety, outraged that he should have the nerve to stand in the pulpit.

He on the other hand sang as if he were enjoying himself. He let out with his great voice, *I come to the garden alone,* and speeded Bernice's playing. It was old-fashioned revival singing, stirring and pounding, and the song could just as easily have been "Hail, Hail, the Gang's All Here."

"He's got nerve," Val whispered to me.

When the hymn was finished, Paul prayed. "Lord," he said, dropping his voice even lower, "we walk in darkness here. We are lost men groping for light. Give us the hand of love and lead us into the brightness of Thy truth. Amen."

Older members of the congregation had never liked Paul's short prayers. They didn't feel a minister had prayed over them unless they became aware of the hardness of their seats. They associated piousness with pain.

I thought all religion was a refinement of superstition practiced in shadows of wood and jungle. I went to church because church was possibly of some use to my son and might help me find him a mother.

Paul called for the offering. Bernice played, and deacons moved up the aisles with golden platters. Colored lights from the stained-glass window of the breaking of the fishes fell upon Paul as he sat in the oak chair and opened his Bible.

"They won't get much today," Val whispered. The velvet bottom of the platter was barely covered.

The deacons carried the offering to the table in front of the pulpit. We sang the doxology, and Paul raised his arms: "For Thy gifts to us, Lord, we return a small portion. Amen."

The deacons sat. Paul laid his small Bible on the large pulpit one, the golden-edged pages of which were stiff and heavy. Yet he didn't have to read. His light blue eyes moved across us. "'Let him who is without sin cast the first stone.'"

God, I thought, not that, not today.

"Let him who is without sin cast the first stone," he said a second time and his eyes sought out the balconies and far corners.

"Is there a man here without sin?" he asked. He looked at us as if he expected an answer. "Is there a person in the entire world without sin? Even the sweetest, nicest, prettiest white-haired lady lives in sin. The child, beloved of Christ, beautiful and close to God, stirs with sin."

He had the automatic smile on his face. We sat stiffly and set our feet against him.

"Sin is the most powerful and pervading force in the world," he said. "It's stronger than dynamite or the hydrogen bomb. It has all the power of rivers running and planets turning. Sin drags the strongest man down to loss, pain, and despair."

We knew what he was doing. He was using the sermon to justify himself. I felt the smirk on my own lips.

"What is sin?" he asked. He pronounced each word carefully and with fullness of tone.

"Sin is the refusal to accept God's love and forgiveness. No man is denied that love, and no man can open his being to it and not be changed in the direction of good. There is only one power in the universe stronger than sin, and that is the huge power and force of God's love."

He wasn't using notes. He had, I thought, spent some time preparing this one.

"In the light of God's love, sin becomes an itch, a mite, a nothing. It is as the worm to the lion."

The strip of flesh-covered tape was gone from his forehead— the place where Lou had hit him. I saw no bruise. Perhaps Paul had used a dab of his wife's powder to hide it.

"How do we show we accept God's love?" he asked. "Is it by making donations to the church or coming to Sunday school? Is it by kneeling at our beds and reaching out in prayer?"

He shook his head. I glanced at Val. She was intent on his words. Even Injun was listening.

"All of those things are good and important, but they are not *the* way we show acceptance. *The* way we prove we accept God's love is by being like God."

He leaned across the pulpit as he spoke, his voice soft, deep, confidential.

"I know that sounds presumptuous," he said. "How can miserable little bugs like us be godly? Why that's pride. Satan was thrown from Heaven for aspiring to Godhead. It's sacrilege."

Paul stepped to the side of the pulpit.

"I'm not talking about trying to be God," he said, smiling. "I'm not advising anybody to go into competition with the Lord. It would indeed be sinful and destructive to aspire to His glory."

His eyes stopped on me. At least I thought they did. Perhaps it was training from the seminary, a trick to make each member of the congregation believe he was being addressed personally.

"How, you say, can anybody be like God if he doesn't try to be God? It's so simple and so profound. He has one quality we can and should aspire to. It is the greatest part of God—the most beautiful, the most powerful, and yet the gentlest. That quality is forgiveness. God forgives."

He paused, letting the words settle around us.

"We can, therefore, all be like God in His most sublime aspect. We can forgive. And oh, my brethren, what a divine privilege it is to forgive a person who has wronged us. It is man at his highest and noblest moment. We ascend into Heaven and in this life sit at the right hand of God, who in the last instant of recorded time will Himself judge—and forgive—us."

Paul prayed and announced the last hymn. He held his hands toward us as he pronounced the benediction.

"Now may the peace, love, and mercy of God go with you and be with you now and forevermore. Amen."

As Bernice played the organ postlude, he walked to the rear of the church. At the entrance were three doorways, and he stood in the center one. Nobody went out that door because no one wanted to shake his hand. Paul clasped his Bible at his waist and smiled.

I drove Val home. She sat frowning and chewing at her lips.

"I don't believe it of him," she said, speaking so quietly that Injun couldn't hear.

It was a woman's reaction, strong in emotion. She was still caught up in his words. She hadn't heard Caroline's account of that night or seen the bite of teeth into white, pampered flesh.

I stopped the car in front of Miss Minnie's and walked around to open the door for her. We went up the brick walk to the porch. Val was still frowning.

"I had the strangest feeling during the sermon," she said as I opened the screen door too.

"What kind of feeling?"

She pinched at the fingers of her white gloves and watched me out of dark, moist eyes.

"All during the sermon," she said. "I felt he was preaching at you."

[24]

On Monday morning Sutter came to see me at the store. He had an Esso road map which he lay on my desk. There was an inked circle around Dusty Cross, North Carolina—the town President Powers at the seminary had told me Paul was born in.

"He'll have kin who can fill in chinks," Sutter said. "The church will pay your expenses."

He walked out of my office. I threw the Esso map into the wastebasket.

That afternoon Archie LeBuck stopped by. He carried his cane and wore his cattleman's hat. He purchased a fishing reel and said he was sorry he couldn't make the trip south with me.

That evening Wayland Counts called. He said he'd be glad to

go to North Carolina with me, but it was impossible for him to get away from the bank because the auditors were in town.

Harvey Boyle was at my store Tuesday morning. He had a truck loaded with watermelons. Harvey explained he'd like to help me, but that he was on his way to Baltimore.

"I have a business to run," I said.

"We're all on your side," he told me and drove off.

Even then I might not have fished the Esso road map from the trash had I not seen Lou Gaines. He didn't see me. I stood at the front of the store, and he passed in his dusty Cadillac.

He glanced at the store, and his expression wasn't indignant or angry. Rather he appeared betrayed. His features seemed to say he would have fought for me. I walked to my office and pushed my hand down into the wastebasket. I came up with the map.

I left early Wednesday morning, before the sun burned the land. The roads were secondary ones which twisted and dipped through the piney piedmont. It was country desolated, the red earth turned up like wounds.

By ten o'clock I was so hot my skin stuck to my clothes, which in turn stuck to the car seat. I'd stopped half a dozen times to check the map.

I reached Dusty Cross in midafternoon. I almost went through without noticing and would have if I hadn't seen the name on a Big Orange sign—rusting, bent, askew in a patch of weeds.

There were a couple of stores, a shed, and a fire tower. To the west a hot haze lay over the indistinct bulk of mountains. I saw nobody, and on the narrow cracked highway not a car moved except my own.

I stopped at an unpainted store with a yellow gas pump in front. A limp flag hung over the door. A crudely-lettered sign painted on the wood of the building said this was the post office. The screen door had an Honest Snuff advertisement nailed to the frame.

"Can you tell me where the Elgin place is?" I asked the old

man who sat in the wooden cage of the post-office window. He wore an eyeshade.

"You go down the road two miles and turn right at a live oak," he said, pointing. "Then bear right until you find the mailbox."

I thanked him and drove south. I found the turn by the live oak, but from there on the road was curving and dusty. I went five miles without passing a dwelling. The red dust flew up behind my car and seeped into joints and cracks. I coughed, spat, and fanned the air in front of my eyes.

The road turned hard left. In the angle was a small board-and-batten farmhouse with a well in the front yard. A woman was at the well, her hand still on the chain. She shaded her eyes to see who was driving in.

She was big-boned, like Paul, but older—maybe fifty. She wore a blue work dress which reached almost to her ankles. On her head was an old-fashioned poke bonnet which shaded her creased face.

I crossed to her and told her my name. She must have believed I was a salesman, for when she shook my hand with her hard palm, I felt resistance in it. Her face was brown, her blue eyes set deep. They squinted suspicion.

"I expect you're thirsty," she said, her voice slight for so large a woman. She handed me the dipper. The water was just cool and tasted of the wooden bucket it'd been drawn in.

We went to the shade of the porch. She offered me one of the two unpainted straight chairs. Flies spiraled up and buzzed around us.

"We're near burned out," she said as if too weary to speak words. She dabbed at her forehead and cheeks with a wad of handkerchief taken from her dress pocket.

At a glance I'd seen it was a poor farm, a patch of hard-baked red dirt where a person could live maybe a notch above poverty. There would be a small tobacco allotment, a field of corn growing puny, milkweed pasture, hogs, a cow or two, and a mule for work-

124

ing tobacco rows. It was as if the land had turned red from the blood of men and women who'd struggled to make it grow.

"You Paul's sister?" I asked. I smiled.

"You know Paul?" she asked, his name bringing light to her face.

"I belong to his congregation."

"Well," she said, pleased. "I'm his sister all right. People tell me I favor him."

"You do."

"Well," she said. "It's a real pleasure."

"I'd like to ask you about him."

"Ask what?" she said, her face drawing tight.

"It's church business."

"Can't you ask him?"

"I'm supposed to ask everybody. It's my job."

"I don't mind talking about my little brother," she said and smoothed her dress against her lap. "He's the one of us that went out and made good."

"He grew up here, did he?" I asked, looking around.

"He did," she said. "We all did."

They were a poor family, she said, as if that needed saying. Her father, Henry Elgin, had bought the land with money he'd earned as a section hand on the Southern Railroad. He'd meant to go into the hog business and set up a stand on the highway to sell hams to tourists, but he'd lacked capital and there'd been no tourists during the Depression. In the end the land had become just another scratch farm in the piney woods.

Everybody struggled merely to eat—the father, his wife, the children. The girls helped in the kitchen and with the house and milking. The boys suckered tobacco and chopped the long rows. At harvest time the whole family went into the fields.

"He was always stronger than anybody else," the sister said, shooing a fly from her lap. "Paul was. He once won a dollar for lifting a mule off the ground. Then Papa hit him on the side of the head for betting."

If it weren't for football, she said, Paul would have been there yet. The county built a consolidated high school big enough to hold seven hundred students. For the first time, they had a coach. He came to see the father, but the father said it was a waste of time and labor. Who would do Paul's chores?

The coach, a country boy himself, drew up a schedule whereby Paul got up two hours earlier, which was before daylight. At night Paul carried a lantern out to the barn and even plowed in the light of the moon. Nobody was allowed to help. That was the law the father laid down. If Paul couldn't handle his work, he had to quit football.

"Brother would come home awfully tired," the sister said. She'd drawn her feet to a rung of the chair. "Sometimes he'd get a ride, but he usually had to walk from the paved road, and he was always tired. He'd be hungry, but Papa wouldn't let him eat until the stock was fed. Papa could just never see the sense of it. And he believed playing of any kind was sinful."

During his last year of high school, Paul's name and picture were often in the Sunday paper. His mother cut out the pictures and put them in the Bible. He made All-State, and a congressman presented him with a silver cup at the awards banquet. Though the father was invited to the banquet, he wouldn't go.

Paul never talked about college, not even with his mother who kept his uniforms washed and rubbed his back and legs with hot oil after a game. As the oldest son, the farm would be his to operate. The father was already so bent with labor that Paul had to take over most of the work. College was like central heating and indoor toilets—things only the rich could afford.

"One hot afternoon a man from South Carolina drove up," the sister said. "He brought Papa some new seed corn the Department of Agriculture had developed and a colored picture calendar for the kitchen. He ate dinner with us and sat on the porch afterwards, talking crops and stock. The last thing he did was to bring out a catalogue and show a picture of the dormitory Paul would live in if he came to the college."

"For nothing?" the father kept asking. He was unable to believe. "You going to let him come down there for nothing?"

It wasn't only that he couldn't believe. It was also an insult to his way of life that for running up and down a field with a ball —for playing—a person could be rewarded above a man who labored.

All during the summer the family argued with the father. Especially the mother. Her eyes brightened, and her face became set. She pecked at the father early and late. She rattled the pans and burned his corn bread. She whined at him as he lay weary in the bed.

Finally one evening Paul returned from the fields, his sweaty brown skin covered with wheat chaff, and found his mother packing a new tin suitcase for him. She also had a bus ticket she'd bought with her chicken money. When Paul was washed and dressed, his father would not tell him good-by.

"We didn't understand how good he was," the sister said, shooing flies. "He didn't even play the first year, and Papa thought the college would try to Indian-give the tuition. He believed the man would come and demand the money back. 'I'll run him off the place!' Papa would shout, and his hand twitched toward the shotgun he kept behind the kitchen door.

"But Paul stayed at the college. He didn't come home except summers. He was making new friends, and he was meeting girls, which he never had much chance to do around here. When he did come home, he'd carry a football down to the pasture and kick it. We'd sit here on the porch and listen to him kicking, and Papa would shake his head as if he was still saying no."

In his third year at college Paul made his reputation. His name was not only in the county paper, but also in Charlotte, Columbia, and Richmond dailies.

Early Saturday afternoons the mother and all the family except the father would ride the wagon into Dusty Cross to listen to the radio. They dressed as if for church. They stood by the salt blocks in the store where they ordered one coke each and heard the crowds and the excited voice of the announcer yelling, "Elgin! Elgin! Elgin!"

"He didn't come home after college either," the sister said. She touched her boxlike black shoes to the weathered boards of the porch. She dabbed at herself with the handkerchief and gazed out at the listless pines powdered with dust. "At least for no more than a day or two. He got himself a city job. Maybe you know that."

"Yes," I said.

"He was ashamed of it. He came home for a visit and wouldn't name the company. When Papa found it was selling liquor, he tried to hit Paul. Papa was smaller and weaker, but he punched at Paul, and Paul reached out as if picking apples and guided the blows aside. Papa was furious and ordered him out of the house. Mamma was crying and walked to the car with Paul. He stopped at the gate to wave and drove away."

She stopped talking. She looked tired and sad. She wiped her fingers with the wad of handkerchief.

"Except for funerals Paul didn't come home after that ever," she said. "Papa was first, and when Mamma went I never thought I'd see him again. For almost three years I never even heard from him. Then one night in the winter he knocked on the door and asked to stay. I led him up to his old room, and he just stood looking at things—the brass bed, the mahogany dresser, the wood stove."

"Why'd he come back?" I asked, but she went on as if she hadn't heard me.

"He helped with the hay and stock," she said. "He patched the barn and put in some new fence. He planted melons, which sold well in Charlotte. We had a good tobacco crop."

"But why?" I asked.

"Why what?" she asked, looking at me as if she'd forgotten I was there.

"Did he quit his job?"

She stared at me.

"He gave up that fancy job and all that money to come back here," I said.

"I never asked him why," she said. "He's my brother, and this is his home."

"How long did he stay?"

"Two years." She was still staring at me. "Would you like to see where it happened?"

"What happened?" I asked.

She stood and led me from the porch into the dusty yard. We walked around the house and through a flock of chickens. She didn't swing her arms as she walked, a characteristic which made her appear to be marching. She held a sagging wooden gate for me, and we crossed a field grown up with milkweed and thistle. We reached a barbed-wire fence, beyond which was corn.

The corn was parched and stunted. Cracks zigzagged through red clay. At the end of the field was a withered hackberry tree.

"He was mowing," she said. She pointed across the rusty barbed wire. "He pulled up his mule and stopped under the hackberry yonder."

The tree was dying. During the best of seasons the hackberry's shade was thin, but this one's shadow hardly marked the ground.

"He sat," she said. "He'd been mowing all morning, and he needed to cool. He leaned his head back against the bark and closed his eyes. Then he heard the voice."

I did the staring this time. She held her manlike hands at her waist. She watched the tree.

"He thought somebody had come up behind him," she said. "He stood to look around the tree."

Her voice had become reverent—as if she were in church instead of standing among dusty milkweed. Her folded hands moved up her chest and pulled tight.

"He kept walking around that tree," she said. "He thought somebody was playing a trick. When he found no one, he believed it was too much sun or maybe the caw of a crow.

"He sat again. Across to the southwest he saw a thunderstorm

129

gathering—the first black clouds rolling across the white hot sky. He was thinking he ought to get the mule to the barn. At that instant he heard the voice a second time. He tumbled flat to the ground."

Her face was pale and awed, her voice like a prayer.

"It was Saul on the road to Damascus," she said. Her hands were clasped under her chin.

"What'd the voice say?" I asked.

"His name. It spoke his name twice." She turned to me, her expression rapt. "When God speaks, it only takes one word. His word goes to the heart like fire."

Slowly she turned her head to look across the cornfield to the hackberry tree.

"It was the end of his trouble."

"What kind of trouble?" I asked.

"He'd come home wounded."

"Wounded how?" I asked, knowing I was right on the edge of it.

"It's too hot to stand here in the sun," she said. She reached for the wad of handkerchief and dabbed at her face. She started toward the house. "I'll draw you some cool water."

"What wounded him?" I asked, going after her.

"He's saved," she said.

[25]

It was all she'd tell me. We walked back to the well and sat on the porch. She was as polite and gentle as ever, but she would reveal nothing else about Paul. Her face shone. She believed he was touched by glory.

I thanked her, shook her worn hand, and went to my car. She called to me to wait. She went into the house and came back with a small sack of tomatoes. As I drove off, she stood by the well. The poke bonnet flared around her head and darkened her face.

I didn't for a second believe what she said had happened to Paul in that field. He could have fallen asleep, been touched by the sun, or struck by lightning. His sister was a good and honest woman, but she had the country people's capacity for religious gullibility. She would accept without reservation water's being turned to wine, Jonah's being swallowed by a fish, and Lot's wife being transformed into a pillar of salt.

I drove home in the last heat of the day and into the night. It was eleven thirty when I reached the house. There were no lights. Injun was staying at his Aunt Delia's. I fell on my bed.

I slept poorly. I steered my car through my dreams. In the morning I was sticky and tired.

I went to the store and put in a slow, foot-dragging day during which the ticks of the clock seemed to come at ten-minute intervals. I sold less than twenty dollars' worth of merchandise. Down the street, the banjos pounded at the Progress Store. The redcoats were having another sale.

I called no one about my trip to Dusty Cross. I didn't want to speak to anybody or to think about Paul. He was taking possession of me.

At five o'clock I telephoned Val and asked her to go for a swim. She'd been working all day on her thesis.

"I hope it won't be like last time," she said. "At least I hope it won't be like part of last time."

We swam in the river and were careful not to race. She wore a pink bathing suit with a little skirt. Her cap was covered with rubber hair. We floated, squinting against the sun and allowing the river to carry us downstream.

Injun walked out of the woods, climbed into the jon boat, and crossed the river to check his trotlines. I swam to the dock and went to the cabin for beer. I tried not to see Kitt in any of the dark corners. I carried out cans of beer in a bucketful of ice.

As I'd hoped, Val swam over to Injun. I was counting on Injun to win her for me. Surely she would want to civilize him, to make him wear shoes, to brush back his hair. Through me she could have him.

She reached Injun and held to the end of the jon boat. She pulled herself up to talk to him. Sun glistened on her wet shoulders and arms. I could just hear her voice across the whisper of the river.

Injun turned his back on her as he worked his trotlines. She dropped into the water and swam slowly toward the dock. Her long arms moved lazily, and her hands dipped delicately into the river. Her body left a trail through golden-green pollen. In that rubber-haired bathing cap she could have been a nymph risen out of lilies.

"Do you suppose he'll ever talk to me?" she asked.

"You're a woman," I said, helping her out of the water. She sat and leaned against me. Her skin was warm with the sun and river. She rubbed her wet hands against her tan thighs. She peeled off her cap and shook out her dark hair.

"Then you've noticed?"

She reached for my beer. She didn't turn the can around but put her mouth where mine had been.

"Women are the enemy," I said. I rubbed her back with her towel. She pressed into my hands. Along the edges of her pink bathing suit were white edges of skin that sun had never touched.

"I'll win him over," she said.

"Not with kindness."

"How?"

"Can you shoot a shotgun?"

"Well no."

"Can you skin a catfish?"

"I abhor catfish—ugly whiskered things."

"Can you bait a trotline?"

"All your questions are loaded."

132

I allowed my hands to give way gently so that she fell in toward me. I put my arm around her waist and my cheek against hers. Her hair touched my neck. She covered my hands with her own.

"Save your energy," I said. "You don't have a chance with Injun."

"You'll see," she said, squinting across the river at him. She had taken the bait.

We had another beer, smoked, and watched dusk settle on the river. The air cooled slightly, and in the silvery light, fish rose to patch the water.

Injun rowed to the dock. He'd caught a couple of fair-sized catfish on his trotlines. Val wrinkled her nose, but I decided to grill them—as I had used to do when Kitt and I came here. I had a stone fireplace I'd built in the yard. Behind the cabin I found wood. While it burned, I drove down the road to Harvey's store where I bought butter and hot mustard. I mixed a basting sauce.

"You appear competent," Val said, watching me at work.

She had found forks, spoons, tin plates, and glasses in the cabin. She washed them carefully in water heated over the fire before putting them on the picnic table. One leg of the table was eaten by termites. I propped it with a rock.

While I heated butter in my iron skillet, she winked at me and crossed to Injun who knelt by the river and cleaned the catfish. She squatted by him. His tow hair fitted wet around his skull. He wore khaki shorts and nothing else.

"We had a bear come right into our back yard once," Val said, trying to hook him. "He licked the peanut butter out of our bird feeder."

Injun glanced at her as if she were school. Women meant baths, shoes, and discipline. No matter how pretty they were or how nice they talked, they were not to be trusted.

"You ever seen a bear?" Val asked and smiled.

Injun eyed her suspiciously. He turned and looked at me to find whether I was watching and expecting him to be polite. I nodded.

"No'm," Injun answered.

Val glanced at me as if she'd won a victory. I could have told her "Yes'm" and "No'm" didn't count with Injun. He'd say that to anybody, even a teacher. It was getting a sentence out of him that counted.

"I was disappointed in his size at first," Val said.

As she talked, Injun slit catfish and washed their guts into the river. He ran his finger along the clean white belly. Val tried not to show her distaste.

"I thought bears were supposed to be terribly large, but this one seemed hardly bigger than a pony. Then he heard us whispering and reared. He looked so huge that our dog—a cocker named Jeff—ran under the house yelping. My father called the fire department."

She laughed, but Injun, deadpan, went on cleaning fish. She stopped laughing and studied him. She knew I was watching. She tried to find a chink in him.

"We had big trees around our house," she said. "We used to climb them, but we were always afraid of bears after that. My brother thought they lived up in the trees."

"How high?" Injun asked of the trees.

Again Val glanced at me. Her expression said she was interesting Injun in spite of himself.

"Very, very high," Val said. "You'd hold tight and shiver you'd be so high."

Injun looked at a big sycamore. He considered himself a climber, and the sycamore was his favorite tree. He'd started climbing it before he was six years old. I'd felt Kitt's heart beating against her skin at seeing him so high.

The first year he'd gone only a third of the way up. In the next year he'd worked up to perhaps the second third. When he was eight, Kitt looked out of the cabin one afternoon and screamed because he was in the very top of the tree. The wind was blowing, and Injun bent with the trunk like a sailor on a mast—which he was pretending he was.

thought perhaps it was a joke she and Injun had worked out on me. Or perhaps she was merely sitting on a limb dreaming.

"Val," I called.

She didn't answer, and in the tunnel of leaves it was dark. I climbed faster. The limbs were more difficult to step to. When I stopped for breath, I looked out through a hole in the leaves to the fire below. It was small, and for the first time I had the sensation of height.

"Val," I kept calling. It had to be a trick. I climbed. I was really high, and my hands fitted too easily around the smaller limbs. I carefully placed my feet close to the trunk. I thought she had hidden and allowed me to pass her. I waited to hear her laughter.

I stopped and decided to go back down, but as I lowered my foot, I heard something up there, or thought I did—a sound so small it could have been in me.

"Val?" I called and listened. I went up higher. I saw a patch of milkiness. I took another step. Through leaves hung two feet.

"Nice trick," I said. I was out of breath but choked my puffing in order that she would not think me old and broken.

I expected laughter, but she was quiet. I stared at her dangling feet. They seemed to be trembling.

"Why aren't you talking to me?" I asked and climbed up another limb. I saw her legs through the leaves.

She spoke, but not a word. It was more a sigh—as if she were blowing out a candle.

"What is it?" I asked and went higher. I saw her hips, her breasts, and finally her face.

She was terrified. Her eyes were wide, her mouth drawn in, her head bowed. In the moonlight she appeared bloodless. She sat a foot or two out on a limb, and her hands gripped it. She kept making the sound, not through her mouth, which was clamped, but through her nose.

"Are you sick?" I asked, fearful she might be suffering some sort of attack. I thought what would happen if she fell and crashed down through the dark leaves.

137

She shook her head, just once, and that only an inch or so.

"Here," I said and reached toward her.

She made a whimpering sound—like a rabbit caught in the jaws of a dog. I jerked my hand back.

"Come to me," I said softly. "We'll go down."

"I can't," she answered, not in her voice, not husky and warm, but tiny, as if she were a child. She lifted her face and turned toward me, very slowly, as if delicately balanced.

"Why can't you?" I asked, thinking how crazy it was that she and I were talking up a tree in the moonlight.

"Ac-rob-a," she said. She spoke without moving her lips.

"What?" I asked.

"Acrophobia," she said.

The word made me remember the liquor commissioner, the hotel room, and Paul's race around the ledge.

"You can't move?" I asked.

I was thinking that if she fell, I'd have one short moment to lunge and grab. I tried to decide what part of her I should go for. I decided on her hair.

Instead of answering, she nodded slowly and just once. She looked as if she wished to cry, but she was frightened of crying too. She sniffled.

"Give me your hand," I said.

I edged toward her and extended my fingers. Injun, I thought. He must have suckered her out on the limb and caused her to look down. I felt the space under me.

"I can't," Val said, sniffling.

"I'll come and get you," I said and moved slowly toward her.

"No!" she said and tottered on the limb. Her hands, feet, legs, torso, head—everything was shaking.

"It's all right," I told her quickly, gentling my voice as if training a puppy. My fingers were still out to her. "Just shift a little this way."

"I can't," she said, weeping. On the ground her facial expressions would have gone with bawling, but up here she was almost silent.

"Come on," I said. "You know I'd never let a pretty girl slip away from me."

"No," she said.

"You can do it," I said. I considered taking her by surprise. I'd have to be awfully sure. She was a big woman who could pull us both from the tree.

"Don't come near me!" she cried.

I hugged the tree. I decided I'd have to play against her pride.

"If you could see how ridiculous you look," I said.

She opened her mouth and closed it, but made no sound.

"No wonder Injun's laughing at you," I said. "I think I'll yell down and tell him to get a camera so I can take your picture."

"Oh!" she said as if I'd pinched her.

"Injun!" I shouted. "Bring me the camera and flashbulbs from the dresser drawer of the cabin."

There were no flashbulbs or camera in the dresser drawer. I was counting on Injun not answering, and he didn't.

"Oh!" Val said again, this time louder. Her anger battled her fear of falling.

"I might be able to send the picture to the newspaper and win a contest," I said. "Hurry up, Injun, before she moves."

"You!" she said, and she shifted—not much, about an inch. She was shivering.

"I can't wait to tell people about this," I said. "It'll be all over town, and your students'll hear about it. They may give you a nickname in commemoration."

"Oh, oh, oh!" she said, but she was still moving. She had come in maybe half a foot.

To fool her, I turned away. Then I quickly reached out and caught her by her biceps. I gripped her hard and jerked her toward me. I hooked an arm around her waist and hugged her to me and the tree trunk.

She wept and shook so hard she bumped against me. She was cold with fear. I held her tight and rubbed her back.

I began to work her down, talking to her as if she were a child.

"Now move your left foot. That's it, the left foot. Now your right. I won't let you fall. That's a girl."

I took hold of her legs and guided her feet with them. Her eyes were shut. She moaned. She wouldn't let go of limbs. I pried her fingers loose.

I don't know how long it took us to go down the sycamore. To me it seemed half the night. Muscles in my arms and shoulders ached. My back was sore from crouching.

Toward the lower part of the tree, she became limp so that I carried all her weight. She opened her eyes. She didn't stop shaking, but she occasionally helped me by sticking her feet down for branches and reaching for handholds.

At the bottom of the tree, I wedged her in a fork and dropped to the ground. I held up my hands for her. She lowered herself to me. She hung on to me, her arms around my neck.

"I've never been so embarrassed in my life," she said.

She cried in shame and wouldn't let me see her face. We walked, holding each other, past the fireplace. The catfish had turned black. Injun was gone. I shouted for him, but there was no answer.

I drove her home. She walked quickly into the house. I sat in the car and laughed. The sound startled me. I turned and looked around as if the laughter had come from somebody else.

[26]

Barney Evans was a fraternity brother who'd inherited ownership of a Richmond newspaper from his mother. For a long time Barney hadn't even read the newspaper. He'd married three beautiful women, all of whom divorced him. He'd raced cars and fox-hunted. He'd suffered through his love affair with liquor until doctors told him his liver was shot and that if he wanted to live he'd have to make terms with self-denial. Barney, thirty-five, became an ascetic and went to work.

He walked into his newspaper, commandeered an office, and ordered his name put on the masthead. For several years, the newspaper had bucked and snorted like a lashed stallion. In the end newsmen either quit or surrendered to his authority. He transformed the paper from a provincial gossip sheet into a fine conservative daily. It made him rich.

"What?" he asked, glaring at me across his desk.

Barney resembled a knife. He was all cutting angles, and his nose could have sliced cheese.

"I'm trying to be a detective," I told him. I hadn't seen him in a dozen years, but he neither stood nor offered to shake my hand.

"You a detective?" he asked. His lips curled as if he'd tasted sour milk. He was no older than I, but he'd lost his hair, and his skin was yellowish. He appeared brittle. He never smiled. Maybe it was the pain of austerity or perhaps he had seen too much duplicity in his own newspaper.

"I need to find something on a man," I said.

"How you know there is something?" he asked. His office was small and had no window. There was an ancient electric fan which turned slowly.

"His sister let it slip. She called it 'his trouble.'"

"Everybody comes to the newspaper," he said as if I had no right to interrupt his work.

He led me down a shabby hallway to a narrow room where newspapers had been bound and placed on shelves. Each brown volume was marked in heavy black letters.

"Don't take any volumes from the room," he said. "I'd ask you to lunch but I work for a living."

"Fine, Barney."

He left me. Employees stepped back for him. I remembered the weekend he'd gone on a binge and driven his new red convertible into the swimming pool at the country club. He'd floated up among bubbles, and for a while the horn had blown under water.

I removed my coat, rolled up my sleeves, and switched on a lamp hanging over a table. According to my calculations, Paul had graduated from the seminary seven years ago. He would have had to spend at least four years at the seminary itself. He'd been two years with his sister. Since his trouble had taken place before that, I had a thirteen-year span I didn't need to check into.

I carried the first volume to the table. It was heavy, dusty, unwieldy. I sat before it. Slowly I turned pages and ran my finger up and down the columns.

I sweated, and dust caused me to sneeze. Occasionally a copyboy or pressman would glance in. My eyes blurred from print. My fingers became dark with ink.

As the hours passed, I lost hope. Maybe his trouble was not the sort of thing which got into newspapers. Perhaps it was some private wrestling of the soul.

Moreover, reading about so much suffering brought on my old dejection. Death was everywhere, and blood flowed in gutters. Human life again took on the frailty of a snowflake. I thought of the dead German's eyeball.

I turned pages. Human misery piled up before me. I heard shrieks, wails, and screams. I closed the heavy cover.

I stood and crossed to a window. Panes of glass were grimy.

People walked down streets quite normally, but they were lost—and that loss seemed insignificant.

"You still here?"

Skinny and angled, Barney stood in the doorway, his coat folded over an arm, a newspaper rolled into his fist.

I carried the volumes back to the shelf and reached for my coat.

"You don't look happy," Barney said.

"I'm laughing on the inside."

"Well come on and have supper with me."

"I've lost my appetite."

"You can watch me eat."

I followed him out of town. Surprisingly he had a large new car, a limousine. He was dwarfed by it, like a child playing at driving.

He lived on the south bank of the James River. In the winter months, you could see the water, but in summer, willows grew up to form a green wall. His house—a miniature château built by one of his wives—was made of stone. The doors and windows were arched.

The rooms were all furnished, but everything looked unused except the kitchen. Hanging on a chair at the table was an apron. I supposed Barney wore it.

"I guess you want something to drink," he said.

"I don't need it," I said. Since his love affair with liquor—an embrace that had almost put him under the ground—he never drank.

"Oh Jesus," he said. He brought out a bottle from a cupboard and measured one ounce of cheap bourbon into a fine crystal glass. The bottle appeared old—as if it had been aging in the dark for years.

"You want ice?" he asked, as if he'd be doing me a great favor by getting it.

"If you can spare any."

"Smart ass," he said. It was like college.

We went to the back yard and sat among his rosebushes. Each

bush was pruned and mulched. They were lined up like a platoon on parade. It made me even sadder to think that wild men of the world ended up tending roses and nursing their livers.

"I could sell this piece of land for a hundred and fifty thousand dollars," Barney said, indicating the green flat between his garden and the river. I smelled the river and heard cars crossing the bridge. Their tires thumped and hissed.

"Why don't you?" I asked, sipping.

"What would I do with the money? I can't drink. I'm afraid of women. I can't even eat shrimp."

For supper he fixed potato salad and sliced tomatoes from his garden. On the plate was a square of precooked ham. He used soda crackers rather than bread. Instead of iced tea, he poured water.

"Most people eat too much," he said and didn't offer me seconds, though I wanted none anyway. He hadn't let me have a second bourbon either.

I had to help with the dishes. He put on his apron and did the washing, and I stood beside him and dried. He eyed me to make sure I didn't cheat on wiping.

"Isn't that a dishwasher?" I asked, nodding at a machine next to the sink.

"We haven't dirtied enough to use the dishwasher," he said. "I don't like to waste water."

As soon as the dishes were dry, I handed him the towel and reached for my coat.

"Don't go yet," he said.

"It's a long way home."

"I want you to see something."

He hooked a bony hand around my arm and led me down the steps to the basement. At the bottom was a door with a heavy padlock.

"To keep the maid out," he said, taking a key from his pocket. He unlocked the door, pushed it open, and switched on lights.

In the room, and taking up most of it, was a waist-high platform with more electric trains than I'd ever seen in my life—

trains of every sort, from old-fashioned steam locomotives to sleek diesels. Track spiraled up head high and down through tunnels and around artificial lakes.

There were trestles with warning lights, crossings with bells, hopper cars, tankers, gondolas, and big johns. A coal barge floated beside a loading pier.

Barney cut on the current. Locomotives hummed to life. Red lights flashed. Signals changed color, and arms flew up. The trains pulled out, slowly at first, as if on an uphill drag. Barney adjusted rheostats. The engines moved faster.

They continued to gain speed, at least twenty of them, rushing through tunnels and crossing ahead of each other with split-second precision. They whizzed past one another in frighteningly synchronized patterns Barney had worked out during the lonely nights of his life.

He was at the control panel. He had on a striped engineer's cap and steam driving gloves with cuffs. He punched buttons. All the engines whistled, and bells clanged at crossings. He flipped toggle switches. Headlights flickered across his bladelike face, and a smile fought to emerge onto the sourness of his mouth.

Abruptly, as if he'd revealed too much, he cut off the current. The engines died. He removed his cap and hung it on a peg in the wall. He jerked off his gloves. The air smelled of electric spark and oil. In spite of his embarrassment at showing himself to me, he had to touch each train before he left—as one would children he was putting to bed.

"You see what I've descended to," he said, locking the door. "Have a cup of coffee."

"No thanks," I said. I needed to get home.

"I insist."

I followed him to the kitchen. I didn't want to hurt him, not after he let me see inside him. I sat at the table. He served instant coffee and offered me neither cream nor sugar.

"I hear a lot," he said, sitting across from me. He blew on his coffee before drinking. "I have ears all over the state. I've probably listened to more scandal and smut than any man in Virginia. If I chose to blackmail, I could make half of Richmond run for the hills."

He set his cup down carefully, precisely, and watched me. He had light eyes, almost colorless.

"I hear it all," he said. "The larceny, the fornication, and the adultery. It all comes into my office, not only from Richmond. I even know what goes on in a small puddle like Black Leaf."

I sat alert, my hands still.

"In my profession you have to do childish things like play with trains to keep your sanity," he said. "Because where I sit at the paper I see total depravity in action."

"Are you telling me something?" I asked.

"I had to figure why a rube like you would come snooping down here," Barney said. "It wasn't hard. We had a line from our stringer in Black Leaf. Your preacher's got his ass in a sling."

"He's got mine in it too."

Barney hesitated. His yellowish skin pulled tight over his angular face, and he appeared gloomy—as if he were thinking what was the use since I too would be corrupt. He stood and carried the cups to the sink.

"I might be able to help you," he said.

[27]

While I waited in the kitchen, he went to the front of the house and made a telephone call. We then walked to his car. It was air-conditioned and smelled new.

"I'm not totally without vanity," he said of the limousine. "If I were, I'd long ago have drunk hemlock."

He drove out from under the willows, crossed the bridge over the James, and headed west. In the glow of dashlights, his face was ghoulish.

"You know about Richmond, don't you?" he asked.

"Know what?"

"And most other cities—even towns like Black Leaf. Or maybe I should say especially towns like Black Leaf."

"What?"

"Not everything makes the newspapers. Ninety percent of the garbage which crosses my desk goes into my wastebasket."

"You have garbage for me?"

"Wait," he said.

He bent forward to steer, glaring as if he expected other drivers to bash his new car. He honked his horn unnecessarily and long. He passed everything on the road.

We were away from the city, into the farm country of white plank fences and cattle. Their eyes reflected our headlights.

"I'd like to know what you're doing to me," I said.

"Each day I see the corruption of man—greed, sloth, anger, lust, envy, gluttony, and pride. A newspaper is supposed to print all the news even when it hurts."

"Hurts who?"

"Goodness is a myth."

He slowed, and we turned hard right through a stone gateway. A white gravel drive, pale under the moon, curved between evenly spaced magnolia trees. The drive split around the house—a white brick mansion with a veranda on both the first and second stories.

"Who lives here?" I asked.

"Come on," Barney said.

We walked to the front door. He lifted a heavy brass knocker in the shape of a fox head. The sound banged into the house.

The door opened. A tall, white-haired man in a dinner jacket nodded and shook Barney's hand. Barney introduced me. The man's name was Clinton.

147

"Come out of the heat," he said, his voice quiet and sounding English.

He led up through a hall of marble floors and Greek columns into a darkly paneled library which smelled of leather. On shelves were photographs in silver frames—of Clinton with Roosevelt, with Churchill, with Truman and Eisenhower.

I recognized him. He was heir to a tobacco fortune. He had played polo, owned a race horse which won the Kentucky Derby, and raced his yawl to Bermuda and Mexico. In his later years he had become an ambassador.

He asked us to sit. He and Barney talked about a crusade to clean the James—a beautiful river befouled. Discussing it, Clinton became coldly indignant.

"We would never throw feces onto our floors," he said. He reached for a cigarette in a silver dish. "Yet we pollute the mother of us all—the waters."

As he talked, he eyed me. He held his cigarette with his thumb and forefinger reversed. On others the gesture would have seemed affected. He made it natural and his own.

When at last he turned to me, he was polite and soft-spoken, but under his manners was the hardness of an imperial man.

"Barney tells me you've come about Paul Elgin," Clinton said, speaking smoke with his words.

"Yes, sir," I said, glancing at Barney. He sat in a leather chair, his head hung forward, his hands on his knees.

"His name is filth in this house," Clinton said. His face drew taut, and his pale green eyes narrowed as if he were taking aim. "You are a man of trust or Barney wouldn't have brought you. Certainly you would never abuse information I give you in the privacy of my home."

"No, sir."

Clinton put out his cigarette, stood, and crossed the room in long strides to a desk. He lifted something from it and carried it to me. It was a small picture, painted on ivory and held in a gold frame. The picture was of a young girl, dressed in pale pink that tinted her fair skin. Her hands were folded at her waist, and in them she held a pair of white gloves. Though she appeared as sweet and lovely as a child, she was on the threshold of being a woman.

"My daughter," Clinton said. The words were an accusation. He took the picture from me and returned it to his desk. "The child of my old age. I was forty when she was born, and nothing in my life gave me the pleasure she did."

I again glanced at Barney. He was staring at his hands.

"Many people consider me a hard man," Clinton said. On his desk two ashtrays made of sawed-off shell casing glittered. He picked one up as if testing its heft. "Duty and circumstances at times forced me into hardness, but for my daughter I kept a part of myself as soft as mother love."

Carefully he put the brass ashtray back on his desk and returned to his chair. He crossed his ankles.

"If I told you I lived for her, it wouldn't be true. Other things were important to me, but it was she who gave what I did meaning. I saw accomplishment through her eyes."

As I listened, he talked fondly of her. He sorted through memories as frugally as a miser counting money. He had, he said, taught her how to wing shoot and sit a horse. She'd made her debut in a Grecian gown that had made her look as pure and cold as a goddess. He'd taken her with him to diplomatic posts all over the world. While in Paris, he'd sent her to a school with the daughters of noblemen. She had, he said, become chicly arrogant and spurned the proposal of a marquis.

"Without her I might have been a monster," Clinton said. "With her I developed patience and gentleness. She provided me an understanding of love."

He ran the fingers of one hand slowly over the palm of the

other. The softening of expression that occurred when he spoke of her vanished.

"Now as to your Mr. Elgin," he said, biting at each word as if he would clip it in two. "He killed her."

I sat very still. Clinton placed his hands carefully on the arms of his chair. He leaned back slightly.

"I had no idea they knew each other," he said. "I believed my daughter was going out with the son of a friend who is a prominent attorney in the city. She was home from France for Christmas. She brought this cold house alive. The telephone was always ringing, and her friends came in with snow on their furs. She never looked so pretty or full of life."

He stood and strolled to the fireplace. He clasped his hands behind him. He was speaking no louder, yet I felt I could have heard him anywhere in the house.

"Somehow—" he said and stopped. He cleared his throat and started a second time. "Somehow he and my daughter made an arrangement. Even today I'm not sure of the precise steps. She must have come in with her young man from a Christmas dance and slipped out to meet Elgin. My daughter had just turned nineteen. He was fourteen years older than she—a panderer and notorious manipulator of women."

Clinton closed his eyes and drew his lips so tight they paled.

"I should have been more concerned with her personal life," he said, opening his eyes. "She needed a mother to counsel her. She was so innocent. She must have been a pushover for that suave sonofabitch."

I had never heard a curse spoken more quietly, yet with more force. The word was like the strike of a snake.

"I was in bed," he went on. "The telephone rang at ten minutes after two. I drove to the hospital, but she was already bled out. She'd been cut by the windshield. The car had lain on the bank of the James hours before anyone found it. That night she'd worn a pretty pale blue dress with tulle at the skirt and shoulders. She had come to show me how she looked before she went out. She was unbearably beautiful."

Again he stopped. He raised his head and blinked.

"The dress was in the hospital room, tossed into a corner, the flimsy silk dirty and soaked with blood. It was just a heap of rags in a corner."

His hands behind him, he lowered his head and looked at the floor.

"He was still drunk," Clinton said. "I tried to get at him. I wanted to kill him. I spat on him as he lay in the hospital bed."

Clinton was breathing hard, but his voice never lost control. He could have been teaching a class.

"She was a sweet and innocent young girl whom I loved more than life. I buried her beside her mother."

I realized he was crying. He made no noise nor did it show in his face. The eyes merely grew wet. He did not wipe at them.

"I've had a difficult time living without her," he said. "My house has become a mausoleum and I a ghost."

He stood straighter and allowed his hands to swing forward. He raised his chin slightly. He built his expression into hauteur.

Barney stood and thanked him. Clinton offered us a drink. I told him I had a long way to drive. He walked us to the car. Barney steered us down the white drive. When I glanced back, I saw the porch light go off.

"Everything comes across my desk," Barney said.

"He's beholden because you kept it out of the paper?"

"We put in she was killed."

"What else is there?"

He was driving fast and didn't look at me.

"It wasn't the first time she was out with him. They had a little nest."

"Where?"

"A motel," Barney said. "Called the Paradise."

[28]

I reached Black Leaf late and lay in my bed. The night was hot, and the whippoorwill's song seemed a cry of pain.

I felt I had enough now, yet I wasn't certain I had it all. I wanted Paul tight in his coffin. I tossed and thought where I could find the last nails.

I slipped into the black pit of sleep, but only for a few minutes. The sun came down in shafts through my white oaks—like light penetrating the murkiness of water.

Groaning, I pushed from my bed. One thing was sure—I could no longer neglect my business, or what little of it I had left. I'd been trying to think of somebody to hire as temporary help. The trouble was Black Leaf, which used to have men willing to earn a dollar standing on every corner, had lost its surplus labor to Danville, Roanoke, and Richmond, where even for sweeping out a plant a man could earn more in a couple of months than he could in a year suckering tobacco or clerking in a store.

I attempted to come up with the names of college boys or high-school students who might help me, but they were all at the beach. I wondered that there were enough oceans in the world to take care of them.

I drove into town to open the store. I lowered the green awning over the sidewalk. Down the street banjos at the Progress were already twanging. I sat at my desk. As I started to slit an envelope, I had the idea.

Quickly I picked up the telephone and called the house. There was no answer, and I didn't really expect one. When I came in last night, I'd looked into Injun's room to find him sleeping, but he'd been up and out of the house before me this morning. Moreover, it was unlikely Injun would answer a ringing telephone if he were standing right on top of it.

I penned a sign saying I would be back shortly and taped it to the glass of the front door. I then drove back to the house. I walked around it and shouted for Injun. The dogs barked. I walked to the edge of the woods and hollered.

I drove along a fire trail, hoping to catch a glimpse of him roaming through the pines. I went up and down back roads. I tried the river, but his jon boat was tied to the dock.

I turned in at the ice plant, an old, out-of-plumb building standing in the center of a weed field. When I was a boy, it'd been the best place to loaf on a hot summer day. You could sit on crates next to the ice and with your knife chip off chunks to chew. Often the ice had wooden splinters on it from the floor, but the splinters didn't keep it from being ten times better than anything that came from a refrigerator.

Injun was on the platform with a colored boy named Hoot. Hoot wore a rubber apron and rubber boots. Injun had on shorts. His jaw bulged with ice, but he stopped chewing when he saw me.

"Get in the car," I told him.

He believed I was going to punish him and hunched up on the other side of the seat from me. He was dusty, and his toes splotched and caked with mud. I drove him home.

"Get yourself cleaned up," I said. I ran water in the tub.

"Why?" he asked, wary and ready to duck.

"I want you to look as if you're going to church."

I stood in the doorway of the bathroom to make certain he soaped his neck and ears. He was a small boy, skinny, and without his clothes he looked particularly vulnerable. I could count all his ribs. I felt guilty, even though thinness ran in my family. I ought to have seen he ate better and more regularly.

I ordered him to put on fresh underwear and his summer suit. As he dressed, I sat on the bed. I thought how few hours I'd spent with him these last years. Many times, sunk in my own blackness, I had turned away when he came to me. I hadn't wanted my misery interrupted.

I eyed his room. Around the walls, on shelves, and hanging from hooks screwed in the ceiling were animals he had stuffed. He'd sent away a coupon cut from a comic book to enroll in a correspondence course, and ever since he had been stuffing hawks, herons, ducks, blue jays, cats, coons, and fish with excelsior and coat hangers.

Over his desk was a plaque covered with arrowheads he'd found in a plowed field near the house. There was an old bayonet and two rusty cannonballs. He had pictures of his heroes cut from newspapers and magazines—Daniel Boone, Stonewall Jackson, and Wyatt Earp. Another picture was of a man named Billingpot who lived among Pygmies he'd befriended by saving them from blood fever.

In a corner was Injun's Iver Johnson shotgun. I'd given it to him, but I'd never taken him into the field and taught him to use it. I'd never driven him to Lynchburg or Richmond for the circus. Even on Christmas our house was quiet, and the cedar tree I cut and he decorated burned as a mocking symbol of my failure to give him a proper home.

I picked up his shoes and shined them for him. He slicked his hair with a comb and water. His face gleamed, and his Adam's apple juggled above his starched collar.

We went down to the car. He glanced at me as I drove back to town.

"You sending me somewhere?" he asked. I'd once talked about military school, and he'd gone and hidden in the woods for seven hours.

"No."

I parked behind the store, unlocked it, and took down my sign. He followed me into my office. I sat. He stood waiting, and for a moment Kitt was looking out of his hazel eyes—her face pert and accusing. I had to turn away.

"Have a seat," I said.

"What'd I do wrong?" he asked.

"You haven't done anything wrong. You're starting to work."

I had a little speech prepared. I told him that when I was young, my father had taken me into the store and taught me merchandising. I tried to be businesslike, but I kept seeing Kitt. I wanted to put my hand over Injun's eyes.

"I'll pay you wages like any other man as long as you carry your share of the load," I said. "You won't get paid a whole lot to begin with because you don't know anything. The more you learn, the more the wages."

"I don't care about the money," he said. He turned to look at the store.

"I want you to care about money. Don't get the idea this is a game. I expect hard work, and for it I'm paying you seventy-five cents an hour when I'm in the store and a dollar an hour when I'm out."

His eyes got really big. He calculated that was more money than he'd ever dreamed of. He was thinking of all the taxidermy equipment he could buy.

"Take off your coat," I said. From the storeroom, I got him a cotton jacket I sometimes wore. I draped it over him and rolled up the sleeves. The jacket reached almost to his knees.

I held a mirror up for him, and he was startled at his appearance. He became serious. Then his face changed.

"Who's going to check my trotlines?" he asked.

"You do that in the evening after we close."

"Who's going to—?" he asked but didn't finish.

I knew what he was thinking. Who was going to squat on the bridge and watch the bass or scare the pigeons off the barn or lie in wait for the deer at the salt lick or sit in the cool with Hoot and suck on the sweet ice.

"Any more questions?" I asked.

"Why can't I wait on somebody just as good with my shoes off?" he asked. He held up a foot.

"People think you lack sense without shoes."

"I don't wear them on my head."

"Come on."

I led him through the store to show him where things were. He already knew about the hunting and fishing equipment—the bass plugs, the flyrods, the rifles and ammunition. We passed nails, bolts in bins, and shelves of paint. He watched solemnly.

"The price is always written somewhere," I explained. "It might be on the merchandise or it might be on the shelf."

I took him to the cash register. He wasn't tall enough to reach it, and I got him a box to stand on. I taught him how to punch the buttons and count change. I showed him how to write up charge tickets. We practiced.

"You got to talk to your customers," I said.

I put him to work unpacking a case of insect repellent. I went to my office and sorted the mail. From time to time I peeked at him. He was intent on his job. His hair was already free of its slicking down, and the cotton jacket was smudged. He was building the cans of repellent into a pyramid.

A customer came in—Alec Turns, principal of the high school. Injun, scared, looked at me. I nodded. He went shyly up to Alec.

"I need a strap hinge," Alec said, already at the bins. He wore overalls and a painter's cap.

"What for?" Injun asked.

"I'm rehanging a door on a shed."

"What kind of shed?"

"My toolhouse."

"What happened to the old hinge?"

"It's rusty."

"Put some oil on it."

"It's worn almost through."

"Must have been a pretty poor hinge."

Alec turned and eyed Injun, who had his hands behind him.

"Look, how about selling me what I want," Alec said and poked into the bins.

"You need two hinges to hang a door."

"I got another one left over."

"Left over from what?"

"You sure ask a lot of questions before selling me," Alec said.

"I can't see why you have a hinge left over. You always need two to hang a door."

"I don't know what it's left over from. Now how about helping me."

"You can't lift a hinge?" Injun asked.

Alec stared at him and then dug down into the bins. He found a hinge. With mock politeness he presented it to Injun. Injun carried it to the cash register and stood on his box to ring up the sale. He took Alec's money, dropped it into the drawer, and gave back the hinge. Alec stared at the hinge. He shoved it into his pocket and walked quickly out of the store.

I called to Injun. He came to the office. He held a can of insect repellent.

"The idea is to wait on customers," I said. "Don't make them do it themselves."

"They do it themselves at the Progress Store," he said.

"That's a trashy place. We been here since 1901. And if the purchase will fit, always put it into a paper bag."

"All he wanted was a darn ten-cent hinge."

"Think of it this way: one day he might want a stove or refrigerator, and he'll come here because we treated him right on a ten-cent item."

Injun frowned and nodded slowly. He could see the sense in what I was telling him.

"Now you don't have to question the customers. Give them what they want and let them go. It's not up to you to approve or disapprove."

"Yes, sir."

"You can go back to work."

While I was leafing through invoices, Mrs. Porter Poindexter, a small, prissy woman who'd married a great hulk of a husband, walked in. She'd chipped away at Porter over the years until he was shrunken and bewildered.

"I'm looking at paint," she told Injun. He'd straightened up and was wiping his hands on his cotton jacket.

"What color paint?" Injun asked. So far so good.

"I haven't decided." She had a flouncy way of walking and held her nose up slightly—as if she smelled manure. "I'm having the kitchen done."

"Yes'm," Injun said and looked puzzled. I started to stand and go help, but he remembered what I'd explained about giving the customer a color chart. He handed one to Mrs. Poindexter. He waited politely while she put on her glasses and squinted at the chart.

"Are these all the colors you have?" she asked, sniffing as if to nose out deception.

"There must be fifty," Injun answered.

"I can see how many are here. I'm toying with a certain shade of topaz which is not here."

Injun looked frightened. He didn't know what color topaz was. "Excuse me a moment," he said. He came to the office. He shut the door. "She wants topaz," he said.

"Topaz is a yellow," I said. "You tell her we can mix it."

Dutifully he went back. Mrs. Poindexter waited impatiently.

"We can mix it," Injun said.

"I'm not sure I want it," she said.

"I thought you just said you wanted it."

"I said I was toying with it." She adjusted her glasses. "I rather like this Golden Candlelight." She tapped the chart. "Let me see a sample."

I'd told Injun about samples. He read the number on the color chart and went to the shelves. There he had to climb a ladder to get the can. He carried it down and clamped it in the machine to stir it. He pried off the top with a screwdriver. He selected a stick from a bundle of plywood cut to three-inch lengths and dipped it into the paint. He handed the stick to Mrs. Poindexter.

"I'm not sold," she said as she examined it critically. She shook her head. "Let me see the Jamaican Sunset."

Injun had to put the Golden Candlelight back and move the ladder. He climbed to a top shelf. He made up a sample and gave it to her.

"No," she said. She clucked her tongue. "Let's see the Coral Pink."

She kept sending him up the ladder. He was sweating. He glanced at me for help, but I figured it was a test. If he could please Mrs. Poindexter, he could handle any customer in the world.

He brought her down a can of Velvet Blue. She took the sample from him as if the stick were dirty, touched her chin with a little finger, and shook her head.

"Let's see the Perugian Pearl," she said.

Injun went back up the ladder a dozen more times. He had cans spread along the aisle and on the shelves. Paint spotted his fingers. There was a blob on his jacket. He was breathing through his mouth.

"No," Mrs. Poindexter said on the last can, a Camelot Chartreuse. She shook her head. She crossed toward the door.

"You're not going to buy?" Injun asked, his voice charged with disbelief. He stood among cans of paint he'd opened for her.

"I'm going to see what the Progress Store has," she said. "Their paint's on special."

As she was about to priss through the door, Injun belched. It seemed impossible that such a loud noise could come from so small a boy. He mouthed the sound into a profanity. I shot up out of my chair.

"What did you say?" Mrs. Poindexter asked, astonished and fearful. She backed away with a hand on her breast. She peered about as if she suspected somebody might leap on her.

Before I reached Injun, he belched a second time, even louder. The sound blasted her. She retreated.

"I'm going to report you to the authorities," Mrs. Poindexter said. She put a hand on her hat and fled from the store.

I grabbed Injun by his skinny arm. With my other hand I unbuckled my belt. Injun waited passively. I raised the belt. He shut his eyes and tensed for the blow.

He was fragile in my grip, like a little bird, and he was so reconciled to my hitting him that I slowly lowered the belt. Those hazel eyes opened. It would be like hitting Kitt. I let go of him.

"Don't do anything like that ever again," I told him. "Even if a customer has you between a rock and a hard place."

Amazed I hadn't whipped him, he stood in the aisle and looked after me. I sat at my desk with my back to him. I could have called him into the office, and perhaps it would have been the start of a relationship.

But I did not call. A relationship meant exposing oneself, even to a son, and, as I'd learned, exposure meant pain.

[29]

At three that afternoon I told Injun I was going to have to leave him in charge of the store. I made a check list of things for him to do before closing.

"If you have doubts, tell the customer to come back when I'm here."

He nodded, serious with responsibility.

I went up and down the street alerting merchants to the fact Injun was running the store. I asked them to look in from time to time to see he was getting along all right.

At home I took a bath, changed clothes, and drove to Richmond. I had decided to call upon a woman—Flo Legere, the painted, voluptuous secretary who worked for General Dempsey. She had asked me about Paul. She was the sort who'd know a lot about any man she went out with.

I left my car in a parking garage and entered the state building, which blazed white in the sun. I was nervous. I patted my hair and adjusted my tie. The elevator man glanced at me.

In front of Miss Legere's office door, I stopped and listened. I heard her typewriter clicking. I was unsure how to set my face.

I opened her door and looked in. She was standing from her desk to cross to a file cabinet. She moved heavily, almost clumsily on her large legs. Her heels scuffed the floor.

She turned to me. Her blond hair was piled in a loose spiral on top of her head. She was faded, worn, but she still gave out an invitation to sensuality.

"Yes?" she asked. She didn't remember me. Her expression was contemptuous.

"Excuse me a moment," I said and backed into the corridor. I'd forgotten what I wanted to say to her. Moreover I was shaky. I smoked a cigarette and shook my arms to loosen up.

I opened her door a second time. She was sitting sideways to her desk, and her striped skirt had pulled over her plump knees. With a slow, bored gesture, she pushed her skirt down.

"Do you want to see the General?" she asked. She touched at her hair, and the charm bracelet jingled on her wrist.

"I was in the other day," I said.

"Were you?" she asked. Her heavy hand moved to a switch and clicked off her humming typewriter.

Before I could continue, a tall, tanned salesman came in. He carried an attaché case.

"How's my Flo?" he asked. He was a young man and he smiled.

"I thought maybe you'd fallen in a hole," she said, but she was glad to see him. She chested and touched her hair. She smiled as he leaned over her desk.

"You've been always on my mind," he said.

"Oh sure," she said. "I been losing sleep too."

"There's only one reason for losing sleep," he said, grinning.

"I wouldn't know," she said, and she fluttered her bluish eyelids.

She then remembered me and looked at me inquiringly. The salesman turned.

"May I speak with you privately?" I asked her, because I couldn't talk in front of him.

"Where?" she asked.

"In the corridor."

"You want me to go into the corridor?" she asked and glanced at the salesman. He was amused.

"I was in the other day," I explained.

"I can't leave the office."

I left. I shut the door, went to the elevator, and punched the button. Downstairs, I crossed through the lobby to a public telephone. I looked up the number. She answered.

"You again," she said.

"If you'll just listen a minute."

"I'll call the police," she said. She spoke to the salesman. "It's the man who wanted me to go into the corridor."

"I was in the other day," I explained. "You asked me about Paul Elgin."

"Oh," she said. She was silent a moment. "How's Smooth?"

"If you can spare a few minutes, I'd like to talk about him."

"I don't know you."

"I promise I won't keep you long."

She thought it over.

"Do you belong to a club?" she asked.

"I'm from out of town."

"We could go to mine," she said, but she sounded reluctant. "The Rue Royal on West Franklin. I'll probably have somebody with me, which means I won't have much time for you."

"I'd appreciate even five minutes."

"Five minutes you can have."

I thanked her. She hung up. I leafed through the telephone directory to find the address of the club. I wrote the number down on the back of an envelope.

I walked along West Franklin and looked at the gabled Vic-

162

torian houses that had once known grandeur. They were now commercial property, for doctors mostly. The air smelled of anesthetic.

The Rue Royal was between an obstetrician and a psychiatrist. It occupied the lower floor of a stone townhouse. Flanking the entrance were two gaslights. A red-and-white-striped awning extended to the curb. At the curb was a black iron statue of a Nubian who wore a white turban and held a red scimitar.

I rang the bell. A colored man in a white jacket opened the door a crack.

"I'm meeting Miss Legere," I said.

"Come on," he said, opening the door farther. He held a small tray with empty glasses on it.

He showed me to a room near the door. The room had yellow leatherette seats and scenes from Paris painted on the walls. I glimpsed a dusky corridor with line drawings of Paris taxicabs. I heard a piano playing, ice tinkling, and laughter.

I sat and crossed my legs. I flipped through the pages of a girlie magazine from the table. I smoked.

At five thirty she still hadn't come. Each time the colored man answered the door, he glanced at me. A lot of people were ringing —mostly younger men, a few with women. They were happy to be off work and called to each other.

By six o'clock I believed she wasn't coming. The colored man acted as if I'd lied to him. There was a telephone on the table, and I picked it up.

"No long-distance calls," the colored man said.

I dialed General Dempsey's office. I let the phone ring eight times. There was no answer.

At fourteen minutes after six, Miss Legere came in. She was by herself and appeared aggrieved. It occurred to me she had expected the tanned young salesman in the office to bring her.

"Hello, Jerry," she said to the colored man. She handed him a package and an umbrella. Her striped skirt was tight around her big hips. She smoothed her white blouse so that it pulled against her breasts.

163

"He with you?" Jerry asked, indicating me. I had stood.

"Sort of," she said, looking me over.

I followed her down the narrow, dusky hall painted with French taxis. Our feet were silent on rugs hardly visible in the dimness. The hall opened onto a large room with a circular bar in the center. Bottles were lighted like jewels. The walls had pictures of cancan girls.

All the red leatherette booths were filled. Miss Legere crossed to a small table close to the bar. I hurried to hold her chair.

"You do drink, don't you?" she asked, eyeing me as if she might not let me sit down.

"I drink."

"That's something."

A Negro waiter came to us. He had on a red jacket with gold buttons. Miss Legere ordered vodka and excused herself to walk heavily to a booth with four men in it. They were all younger than she. She laughed and touched her breasts. The men grinned at her.

The waiter brought our drinks, but she stayed over there a long time. I felt exposed sitting alone at the table. I was out of place among youth, gaiety, and laughter.

I sipped my bourbon until she came back. Her spiked heels sank into the red rug. She hailed people and waved. I stood for her. She sat and drank the vodka thirstily. She called to a handsome, rawboned man named Bruce.

"I saw your picture," she said.

"It was lousy," he answered. He wore a bleeding madras jacket and cream slacks. He was on his way out.

"You were beautiful!" she called after him.

She ordered a second vodka. When she saw I was nursing my drink, she pushed at her hair impatiently. A blond ringlet fell back against her cheek.

"You going to be a pooper?" she asked.

"I have to drive."

"I believe you're going to be a pooper," she said.

164

"Just talk to me a minute."

"I don't even remember your name."

I told her my name, but she didn't listen. She drank, leaving lipstick on the glass, and she glanced at people coming into the room. Before I could question her, she was up again, this time to talk to three women who had slid into a booth. She leaned over the table, and they all laughed.

On her way back to our table, she curved to the bar where she stopped by a man and put a hand on his shoulder. He was muscled and swarthy. She fingered his neck, and as they laughed she pressed her breasts into his back.

He wasn't interested, but she nuzzled him. She kept stroking his neck. He finished his drink, excused himself, and left. She looked after him. Women in booths were watching her and whispering.

"Here's the pooper," she said when she returned to me. I'd stood. "Don't you ever do anything but hold chairs?"

She was hurt and attempting to be brave. I felt sorry for her because she once must have been in full bloom and now she was wilted and couldn't attract a man.

She tried once more—an older man this time. Dressed in a dark suit and striped tie, he entered and sat alone at a table near the door. She stood and crossed to him. As she passed, people watched her and smiled. They glanced at me to see whether I realized the game.

The man was polite, held her hand, and talked to her charmingly, but when he emptied his glass, he patted her hand and left. She came across the rug, her walk unsteady, her feet spread to keep her balance.

"You still here?" she asked me. She shook her empty glass at the waiter. I held her chair. She sat on the edge of it and touched her tongue to her upper lip. I believed she was going to cry. Lord, I thought, don't let her break down on me.

The colored waiter brought her drink. She gulped it, stood, and left the room. People glanced at me.

165

Not certain whether she was coming back or not, I paid the waiter. I went down the hall by the French taxis and stood outside the ladies' room. A young redhead opened the door. She was patting her hair.

"Is there a lady in there?" I asked.

"Funny man," she said and cut me off with a fling of a girdled hip.

I went to the front door where the Negro in the white jacket stood. He was smoking.

"Did Miss Legere leave?" I asked.

"In a hurry," he said and opened the door for me.

I went up the steps to the street and looked both ways. I saw her down the block, walking fast. I went quickly to my car. I drove past her, swerved into a no-parking zone, and leaned to the window.

"I'll be glad to ride you home," I said as she approached my car. She stopped and looked at me as if she'd forgotten who I was. Her umbrella hung from a wrist.

"All right," she said and came to the car. She listed slightly. I opened the door for her. She let her body collapse into the seat and drew her feet inside. Her hands slid limply from her package to the seat.

A policeman on a chestnut horse blew his whistle and motioned me out of the no-parking zone.

She sat slumped, her eyes unblinking. Her umbrella fell to the floor.

"I don't know where you live," I said.

"Will you feed me first?" She spoke listlessly. "Even a pooper ought to do that."

I stopped at a place which had a red neon lobster over the doorway. The restaurant was cool with air conditioning. A bored hostess led us to a booth. Miss Legere excused herself and went to the ladies' room.

When she came back, she had a better hold on herself. She'd painted her lips and powdered her face. She allowed me a faint smile. I felt sick at the thought that by refusing her I too would hurt her.

"I haven't been very nice to you," she said. She ordered the most expensive steak on the menu. "Actually you're not so bad."

"About Smooth," I said.

"After we eat," she told me, widening her eyes. Her bluish eyelids were creased—like an old woman's.

She was a dainty eater. She held out her little finger and nibbled. She dabbed at her mouth with her napkin. She cleaned the bone and ordered pecan pie. She drank two cups of coffee. She leaned back in the booth and sighed. I lighted her cigarette for her.

"I may live," she said. She patted her stomach and the sound was like a ripe melon. "What you want to know about Smooth?" Her foot touched mine.

"Let's start with the name," I said.

"Big Smooth," she said. "Everybody called him Big Smooth because he was like velvet."

"As a salesman?"

"Well, not exactly as a salesman," she said. Again she widened her eyes. "For a woman, there's only one way a man can be like velvet."

I imagined a hand of black velvet rubbing itself over her white body.

"So he was very popular with the ladies," she said. She drew on her cigarette and exhaled through her nose. "He liked to take them sailing. His company had a boat, a schooner, and he made trips to Maryland."

Her face softened. She stared across the room as if she were seeing memories on a screen. An ash fell from her cigarette to the table.

"Smooth and wild," I said.

Her face tightened, and she focused on me.

"You trying to shoot him down?" she asked.

"I'm telling you what I've heard."

She crushed out her cigarette.

"He was wild, but nice wild," she said. "He once took a bath in beer. Honestly. He emptied a keg of Schlitz into his hotel tub and lay in it." She smiled. "He had foam on his hair."

I pictured that too—Paul, muscled and hairy, reaching from the suds, like a god of the sea. I didn't ask what he was wearing or what she was doing with him at the time.

"He was wild, but he stayed velvet," she said. "He never lost the velvet touch. And he was never mean."

Again her foot touched mine.

"Of course I couldn't believe he was a preacher," she said. "I heard girls talking, but I thought it was a joke."

Her foot brushed mine.

"I can tell you one thing," she said. "When he left, there were a lot of broken hearts. I shed a tear or two myself."

Instead of gaining information to use against Paul, I was receiving another testimonial. Consider the source, I thought, a blowsy blonde who'd been community property. She would, however, have seen him after the heat of love, when he had nothing to hide.

"Anything else?" I asked.

"You sound peeved."

"I'm not."

"You want something to hurt him."

I stared at her.

"If I had anything to hurt him, I wouldn't give it to you, but I don't," she said. "I liked him. I liked him as much as any man I've known. He was a gentleman and kind."

"Let's go," I said.

"In a hurry, are you?" she asked, and she pushed her knee against mine. She tried to be coy, but the expression on her aging face was both comical and sad.

I didn't want to go home with her, yet I didn't see how I could avoid it. She was smiling as if she knew something naughty about me. She put her hand through the strap of her umbrella and slid her big hips out of the booth.

In the car she sat near me. I smelled her perfume and sweat. I thought of pretending to be sick or telling her the truth—that I was haunted by my Kitt and had never been unfaithful to her—but no matter how I put words, they would be a rejection and cause hurt.

She leaned against me. Her weight was fluid and flowed to the motion of my car. She gave me directions. She pointed and let her hand fall. It touched my thigh.

"For a man in a hurry you're not driving very fast," she said, her face turned to me.

She lived in a neighborhood of old houses, iron fences, and dying elms. The brick sidewalks were moss-encrusted.

"There," she said and pointed at a three-story Victorian mansion with an *Apartment For Rent* sign in the yard. I parked. She was out before I walked around the car. I opened an iron gate. The yard smelled of honeysuckle.

"I expect you want to come in," she said when we reached the porch. She ogled and felt in her pocketbook for a key. She unlocked the door, which had oval glass in it, and smiled coquettishly. I stared past her into a hallway bare except for a globed lamp painted with faded pink flowers.

"Well?" she asked, waiting for me to move.

Behind me I heard rustling. Miss Legere's coy, teasing expression changed to fright. I whirled. A figure jumped from shrubbery. He threw himself at me.

"Erskine!" Miss Legere yelled.

He was on me, choking me and hitting me on the head. Miss Legere grabbed at him. I covered my face and staggered around the porch.

"Erskine, you stop!" Miss Legere said. "You hear? Stop!"

Erskine pulled my hair. He was a small, skinny man, light on my back, but he was hurting. He bit my shoulder. I yelled. Miss Legere tugged at him. She hit him with her umbrella.

I tripped and fell to the porch. Erskine still held on. I bucked. His skinny legs loosened, and I rolled. For an instant he let go. I twisted free, stood, and ran into the yard. Miss Legere was yelling.

He came after me, and Miss Legere chased him. He windmilled ferociously. Miss Legere struck him with her umbrella. I ran around an elm.

Porch lights were flashing on and windows banging up.

"You stop, Erskine!" Miss Legere shouted. She caught him. She put her heavy arms around him and lifted him off the ground. His feet were still running. She talked soothingly to him. She stroked his head and nuzzled his neck. All the while he was yelling.

I edged around the elm.

"He's so jealous," she said as she quieted him. In the light from the house, I saw she was pleased. She still held him. He glared and waved his fists.

"I'll get you!" he yelled at me. "I'll wipe you out!"

"You're so silly," she said, soothing him. "This gentleman was just escorting me home."

"I'll bet," Erskine said. "Just turn me loose and I'll deck him."

"Everything all right down there?" a man called from the house next door. He stood in a window, his body dark against the light bulb behind him.

"Fine," Miss Legere shouted. "Fun and games." She petted Erskine. "You go on up to the porch and let me say good night to this gentleman."

"I'll kill him," Erskine said.

"Do what I tell you now," she said softly, like a mother speaking to a cross child. She released him and gave him a little smack on his skinny behind. Erskine bellied and lurched reluctantly toward the porch. He glared at me.

"He thinks he loves me," Miss Legere whispered. She smiled. In the pale light she was even pretty. "He told me last week he wasn't ever going to see me again, but here he is. You better leave and come back some other time."

"Yes," I said and thought, *Saved.*

"I know you're disappointed, and I'm sorry," she whispered, glancing at Erskine on the porch. "I was just becoming fond of you."

"Florence!" Erskine called petulantly.

"You can telephone anytime," she whispered and started toward Erskine. "Of course he might be around."

I nodded and backed away. Windows were closing and lights going out. I dusted myself.

She walked to the porch where Erskine stood with his fists in front of his chest. He glowered.

"If you think you can come here and hide in my bushes, you got a thing or two to learn," she scolded him. She shook a finger in his face.

I hurried to my Ford. I heard her voice chiding—so softly that it was like love. I drove off and glanced back. She was holding the door for him and shooing him into the house.

[30]

I was on the highway to the beach, not for a vacation, not to stretch out in the sun and listen to the beat of the ocean, but to sniff down the trail of Paul's past.

The morning after I returned from Richmond, I telephoned Miss Legere at General Dempsey's office. Her voice sounded musical—as if she were smiling as she spoke. I asked for the name and address of the distillery where Paul had worked.

She had it in the files—a Louisville company named Bonnert's Golden Industries. She also gave me the telephone number and the information that Smooth had worked directly under the owner's son, a man called Bunny.

"They'll all tell you the same thing I did," she said. "Smooth was velvet."

"How's Erskine?" I asked.

"He proposed last night," she said. She laughed.

I telephoned Bonnert's Golden Industries in Louisville and asked for Mr. Bunny Bonnert. The call clicked through two secretaries. The second one asked the nature of my business. I told her it was personal and very important.

"In the nature of an emergency," I said.

"He's in North Carolina," she said. "He has a summer house on the ocean."

"May I have the address?"

"He doesn't want to be disturbed."

"Surely he doesn't want to cause hardship and suffering," I said.

She hesitated.

"He'll fuss at me if you bother him."

"You can tell him I bullied you."

She gave me the address. Before leaving, I went by the store to see whether Injun was all right. He was standing on his box at the cash register ringing up a sale of kitchen pans to Mrs. Throckmorton. Proudly he showed me the till of the cash register. There was more money than I'd seen for some time. Business had improved because of people who'd stopped by to help him out.

I drove due south from Black Leaf to the North Carolina border and then worked east toward the coast. In midafternoon I reached the tourist beaches with their brightly-painted clapboard cottages. It was dune country, a land shaped by wind. Sea oats leaned away from the ocean.

The road narrowed, and there were warnings to stay off sandy shoulders. I was looking for a place called Osprey. The town was just a faintly scratched word on my Esso map.

I stopped my car in front of a shed that was as gray as driftwood.

Two colored men wearing overalls and straw hats sat on bottle crates in the shade. Behind them, leaning against a live oak, was a rotting boat.

"You know where Osprey is?" I asked.

"This here is Osprey," the older of the men answered. Both had their legs crossed and their hands cupped over their knees.

"Can you tell me where Mr. Bonnert lives?"

They looked at one another and shook their heads as if synchronized.

"We don't know him," the older man answered. "He must be summer people."

"Is there anybody who can give me information?"

"Mrs. Grimstead," the younger man said.

They both pointed down the road to a stand of pines around a house. I thanked them and drove to the house. It was square, frame, and held up off the ground by stones. The walk to it was covered by pine tags. Under a downspout was a galvanized tub to catch rainwater.

I wasn't sure the old porch would hold me. Boards gave under my weight. The door was closed. There was no knocker or bell. I tapped on glass etched with the design of a swan.

A woman opened the door. She had white hair fixed in a bun, and a face as weathered as the outside of the house. She wore a loose cotton dress and was barefooted.

"I'm looking for Mr. Bonnert's place," I explained.

She blinked as if light hurt her eyes and moved from foot to foot. Her lower lip was pulled in tight against her gums. I suspected snuff.

"You another of his friends?" she asked. It sounded like an accusation.

"I'm trying to find his summer house."

She looked me over slowly before answering.

"You go up that way," she said, coming onto the porch. She lifted her arm and pointed at the road. "About two miles until you reach a cutoff between the dunes. Look for crushed shells."

I thanked her. She didn't answer but kept peering at me. It's the native's contempt for the tourist, I thought. The commercial fishing had given way to hot-dog stands, and the strong women who waited for their husbands to come home from sea had been crowded off beaches by the oiled body in the bikini.

I drove down the road. I checked my odometer, and when I had gone a mile and three-quarters, I slowed. Along the shoulders were sea gulls which flew up and circled back after I passed, like crows feeding on carrion. Wisps of sea oats shook with a breeze off the ocean.

I went past the cutoff. I backed up. The road was so narrow that it didn't seem possible a car could drive through without touching dunes. Though it was paved with shells, sand had blown over them.

I let some of the air out of my tires to gain traction and drove carefully. The tires crackled on shells, which flung up under the car and pinged against the frame. At times my fenders did touch dunes, and sand spilled against the car.

Repeatedly the road looked as if it were ending only to curve on. There were no tracks. The only sign of life was an empty pack of Lucky Strikes blowing across the sand.

I began to believe I'd turned in at the wrong place. My tires slipped on sand. I couldn't stop and attempt to back for fear of losing momentum and getting stuck.

The road curved right and straightened to a rise. From the top of the rise I saw a grove of live oaks. Moss hung over a red roof. The yellow house was built on the style of an Italian villa and had a yellow wall around it. At the windows blue shutters were drawn.

The road stopped at a black iron gate. I stood in front of it. A rope hung from a large polished ship's bell. I rang it. It sounded like a call to come to a country church.

I waited. Nobody appeared. I looked in between the black iron bars. I saw a garage and the tail end of a yellow car. I heard water splashing in a pool.

I rang the bell a second time. Sea gulls glided over the house. Moss stirred with a breeze.

I heard a door open and close. Next there were footsteps on shells. A young Negro came toward the gate. He wore a short white jacket, black pants, and shiny black shoes. He had on a black bow tie. He was slim, like a dancer.

"Is Mr. Bonnert in?" I asked.

"Do you have an appointment?"

He was eighteen or nineteen. His words didn't sound country like the men down the road.

"No appointment, but it's important."

"What are you selling?" he asked.

"I'm not selling."

"Give me your name."

"He won't know my name."

He shrugged and started away.

"It's Jackson LeJohn," I said. "Tell him I drove all the way from Virginia to talk to him."

The Negro walked up the drive and across the grass. He took small, careful steps. He was blocked from my sight by a blooming crepe myrtle.

In bending after him, I saw just the tip of a swimming pool. A chrome ladder reflected the sun. I squinted against the glare. I backed into shade made by the gatepost.

The young Negro came back. He shook his head.

"Mr. Bonnert's not in," he said.

"Sure he's in. You just spoke to him."

The Negro didn't answer. He merely turned and started away.

"Tell him one more thing," I called. "Say I came here for Paul Elgin."

He didn't glance back, and I wasn't certain he would go to Mr. Bonnert. I held to the warm iron bars and sagged in the sun.

As I waited I grew angry. I decided to sit in my car and blow the horn until Bonnert had to come out. I jerked open the door and raised my hand to pound it onto the steering wheel.

I heard footsteps on the shells. The Negro was coming back. As he walked, he took a key from his pocket. He unlocked the gate and stepped away for me to enter.

When I was in, he relocked the gate. Without a word he led me over grass and past the turquoise pool. At the edge of the pool striped umbrellas stuck from centers of white tables. Heat shimmered off a brightly-painted shuffleboard court.

He led me to wooden steps built across the dunes. At the platform on top the steps, the ocean breeze struck my face. I looked out to the water. Each wave broke a series of times as it rolled shoreward.

The tide was low. Gulls walked along the fringe of the water or stood on one leg. Down the beach lay the jagged hulk of a wooden ship half buried in the sand.

Midway between the dunes and the ocean was a cabin on stilts. It had a thatched roof and porch. The sand had been raked around it so that there was no driftwood or debris.

The man sat on the porch. He reclined in a deck chair, a book across his lap. He had a narrow face and protruding ears. He adjusted his black sunglasses to look at me.

He wore blue shorts, a blue silk shirt, and leather sandals. On his head was a large straw hat. There was a puckered quality about his small mouth which made him appear spiteful.

He didn't move from his chair. He held his glasses and stared.

"Jackson LeJohn," I said and held out my hand.

"Be as brief as possible," he said. He wouldn't shake my hand.

"I'm after information on Paul Elgin. You used to be his employer."

"Why should I give you information?" He had a toneless voice, hardly more than a whisper, yet in a room full of people he would be heard.

"I've been sent by my church."

His puckered mouth smiled slightly. The young Negro stood close behind him.

"And you're after character references?"

"You might say."

He laughed quietly, as if he were saving his throat. He leaned forward and swung his small feet down from the deck chair.

"A character reference for Paul Elgin," he said. He touched his chest. "I can tell you he's one of the biggest characters I've ever known, but I doubt that's what you want." He stopped laughing and eyed me. "I was about to have a drink. I won't if it offends your religious sensibilities."

"It won't."

"Perhaps you'll join me."

"Sure."

"I'm relieved you're not a Puritan," he said. "Though few of your denomination fail to be tainted by a certain grimness and fondness for doom."

He lifted his small hand and let it drop. The young Negro went inside. He crossed to a bamboo bar and began mixing something in a pitcher.

Bonnert gestured to a deck chair alongside his. I sat down, removed my hat, and lifted up my feet. He closed his book.

"Of course it had to happen," he said. He leaned into the chair. The back of it tilted his straw hat over his eyes. He drew up his feet and crossed his ankles.

"What had to happen?" I asked.

"You can't beat nature," he said and adjusted his straw hat. He had no tan. His skin was fair, almost anemic. "You may baffle her a moment, but when you dam her in one channel, she bursts out another."

He turned his head to examine me.

"Are you thinking of hiring Mr. Elgin?" he asked.

"We're thinking of firing him," I said.

Bonnert laughed, delighted. He swept off his straw hat. He was completely bald. He waved a hand on which was a gold signet ring.

"Did you ever hear of anything more ridiculous in your life than

177

Smooth's becoming a preacher?" He laughed and sailed his straw hat across the porch to a canvas chair.

The young Negro brought us drinks on a bamboo tray. The glasses were frosted. A twist of lime floated among the crushed ice. I reluctantly lifted mine. I didn't like my liquor fancied.

Yet the taste wasn't bad. It was rum, but not sugary the way I expected. As he sipped, Bonnert watched me.

"My own creation," he said. "Subtle, don't you think?"

"It's different," I said. I'd never thought of a drink being subtle.

"A circumspect answer," he said. He leaned back in his chair and crossed his pale ankles. "Now as to character references for Smooth—negative character references you might say. First let me state that whatever happened had to be. For years I've been expecting to pick up a newspaper and see that he was in trouble." He turned to me. "What's he done? No, don't tell me. You don't have to. I know the general area of his trouble because I studied him. It has to be women. Or a woman. Am I right?"

"You're right."

"Of course," he said and smiled. "He was never meant to be a minister. He attempted to go against his blood—as I told him."

Bonnert nodded. The young Negro had gone back into the cabin. I glanced at the line of breakers. The tide was moving in. The breeze rattled thatch on the roof.

"I was the first to see what he was," Bonnert said. He waved his hand. He wore the gold signet ring on his little finger, and the ring had a black stone in it. "I was a senior at college. He was a great lumbering rube carrying a tin suitcase. Honestly, a tin suitcase. You would have believed he was created by the Drama department—a caricature of a hick."

I thought of the farm, of the burned-out flat country and the red dirt. I imagined Paul walking into Dusty Cross and leaving on the bus he had to flag down. He would have been dressed in his one good suit, wearing his one pair of Sunday shoes.

"I stood in the doorway of his dormitory room to look at him," Bonnert said. He tapped his empty glass against the arm of his chair. The Negro glided onto the porch carrying a frosted pitcher. "I really looked to see hayseed on the floor." Bonnert held out his glass. "Then Smooth—though that wasn't his name yet—turned to me. He was still holding the tin suitcase as if it were a book satchel. He smiled. When I saw that smile I knew he was pure gold."

I shook my head when the Negro offered to fill my glass.

"He had the smile of the innocent," Bonnert said. "He was pure, trusting, and virginal. He was money in the bank."

"Money for whom?" I asked.

"For the person or agency who harnessed him," Bonnert answered. He spoke impatiently, as if he didn't want to be interrupted. "I assume you know that for some years my family had owned a distillery—among other things."

I nodded. He sipped his drink, set it on a bamboo table, and drew a silver cigarette case from his shirt pocket. He opened the case and offered it to me. I declined. He tapped his cigarette against the case five times, very precisely. The Negro stepped forward with a light, shielding the match from the ocean breeze.

"There's very little difference among liquors," Bonnert said. He exhaled smoke. He held the cigarette in the exact center of his mouth. "Between rotgut and the most expensive Scotch there's no more than a few cents a gallon in costs. When you go to your store, you're just as well off buying the cheapest brands, the kinds with sweet peas and cupids on the label."

He turned the cigarette in his small fingers.

"Success in the liquor business is a matter of selling. You have to get your product into bars and stores. Taste is inconsequential. The most important item is to have male beauties on the road to romance the goods."

He liked the sound of his own voice. He tasted his words as he spoke them.

"I saw that Smooth Elgin was going to be one of the great male beauties. Even when he was a hayseed I saw it. He couldn't speak a sentence that didn't sound as if he'd learned it in the barnyard.

In that tin suitcase his mother had packed him long johns and red galluses."

Bonnert snickered. He put out his cigarette carefully, as if he didn't wish to mess the ashtray.

"He wasn't dumb. He wanted to get ahead, and he could adapt. That's all I needed to play Pygmalion. He listened to what I told him. He learned how to speak good English, pick the right fork, and wear clothes. There were times I couldn't teach him·fast enough."

Bonnert again tapped his empty glass against the chair arm. The young Negro moved in silently with the pitcher.

"From the first, girls wanted him," Bonnert said. "They sensed his . . . vitality. They wrote notes and telephoned him at the dormitory. Some were seniors and drove by for him in their fathers' shiny cars. He seemed so naive, so trusting, that they were astonished to realize he had seduced them."

Bonnert tittered. His small red mouth drew in as if he were chewing a grape. "The fascinating part is I never knew a girl who had bad feelings about Smooth. He used women, but with a gentle proficiency that made them ask about him years later, after he'd thrown them over. There was no bitterness, no recrimination. 'How's Smooth?' they inquired longingly. 'Is he getting along all right? Tell him to call the next time he's in town.'"

I thought of Flo Legere and how she too had remained faithful.

"He was a magnificent football player," Bonnert went on. "He didn't like to play. In spite of his size, he was never rough. He would have rather swum for the college. He learned in a farm pond and had a very unorthodox style, but he shot through the water like a torpedo. He was all coiled back muscles and power."

Bonnert lifted his glass toward the ocean. Far out, where the green water faded into darkness, porpoises arched through swells.

"He didn't drive into the line or smash people," Bonnert said. "Rather he used delicacy, if in football such a word isn't a contradiction. Because of his size, he didn't appear fast, yet when tacklers reached out for him he left them clutching air. Watching him move made one aware of the glory of the human body, and all the fairies in the stadium, as well as the ladies, screamed with the joy of it."

Again he tittered. He stopped abruptly. The young Negro had stepped forward and touched his wrist. Bonnert frowned.

"Fish," Bonnert said. "With a light salad and some Rhenish."

The Negro backed off and moved around us to the steps. His feet crunched on the sand.

"Lon," Bonnert called. The Negro slowed. Bonnert turned to me. "Perhaps you'll dine with me, Mr. LeJohn."

I didn't want to. I didn't care for the man. I had, however, no choice until I'd learned all he knew about Paul.

"You're kind," I said.

Bonnert flicked his fingers as if shooing a fly. The young Negro continued on toward the house. Bonnert prodded at his stomach.

"I have to be careful of my weight," he said. "On a small man, fat is truly repulsive." He reached for his drink. "When I was a boy, I was so skinny I used to hate swimming. I didn't want anybody to see my pipestem legs. Vanity, vanity, all is vanity. Now I fight blubber."

He swung forward and let his sandaled feet drop to the floor.

"Let's go to the house," he said. "I'll have Lon bring in your car and you can freshen up."

He got his straw hat and set it squarely on his bald head. I followed him across the sand. A sea gull watched us from a dune.

[31]

The house was cool and dim. The walls were painted a pale blue and on the floors were blue carpets. Oil paintings hung in every room—nightmarish abstracts ablaze with color.

Over a fireplace set with driftwood was a portrait—of a beautiful young matron in a silver gown. She was small, petite, and her shoulders were bare except for thin straps of her dress. She sat on grass, and her skirt spread around her like a puddle. A lock of her platinum hair was blown back by wind.

"My sister," Bonnert said and smiled fondly at the picture. She resembled him slightly. "Perhaps she'll visit us tonight, though I'm never sure when she'll come."

He showed me into a bathroom on the first floor and said he would be waiting topside. Even in the bathroom there were paintings. I washed my hands with scented soap.

I climbed blue carpeted steps. A shelf ran along the wall, and on it were dozens of bottles—ambers, dark reds, yellows. They reflected light from a window on the landing.

A screen door opened to a sun deck surrounded by a white railing. On the deck was a white table, a yellow-fringed umbrella, and four aluminum chairs. Bonnert sat at the table. He was still drinking.

"Help yourself," he said, indicating the glass pitcher on the table. "Or you can have a highball if you prefer."

"I'm fine."

He smiled as I sat.

"You look like a man who's had a bout or two with liquor. Am I right?"

"You're right," I said. I thought of Kitt.

"I usually am," he said. "If that statement sounds immodest, I can plead only the truth. I have a very high intelligence. Tests out to almost the genius category. Very little ability, however, with the brush. I expect you agree."

I hadn't considered that he'd painted the pictures in the house, and I didn't know how to answer him. He went on talking without waiting for me.

"I almost convinced myself I was good. The human capacity for self-deception is limitless." He laughed and rubbed his small chin. "Or why else would a golden one like Smooth become a preaching man?"

He poured from the pitcher into the glass. His face was flushed. He stared at the ocean which grew dark with the setting sun. That darkness had different shades, and the breaking waves flashed white. Gulls wheeled around the beach cabin.

"Smooth had great ability," Bonnert said. "Truly he was a gifted man, one of the golden people destined for the high life and silken thigh. He was born to seize love and glory. Like a moth he became enamored of the flame—in this case a flame of spirituality that sizzled him."

Bonnert waved his hand slowly as he talked. The gold ring with the black stone caught the last light.

"He was often confused," Bonnert said. "One afternoon in college I found him attempting to read Rilke under a pecan tree—as if Smooth could ever understand such a complex poet. I pulled the book from his hand and told him to go find a lonely coed."

The young Negro came out with a plate of hors d'oeuvres. Bonnert told him to bring the binoculars.

"The women Smooth loved," he said. "He needed an accountant to keep his assignations straight. The girls couldn't stop touching him. They were constantly rubbing themselves against him. He was a stallion among mares."

The Negro brought the binoculars. Bonnert raised them to his eyes and then handed them to me. He pointed. Far out a cruise ship glittered with lights.

"I was his best friend, yet he deceived me too," Bonnert said. "I was a skinny little mutt of an intellectual. I did, however, have the advantage of money. I owned a convertible and lived in a town apartment. I had a servant and a cook.

"My Babs was like a toy doll. She had blond hair she wore long and a boyish figure. Her mouth was a rosebud. I was crazy about her. I took her home and introduced her to my father."

His expression changed, not all at once, but in pieces—first the eyes, then his mouth and cheeks. For a moment he looked hateful.

"We were at a fraternity picnic," he said. "I was on the serving line and Babs helped me. She wore a blue shirt, blue shorts, and white tennis shoes. After everybody had their plates, I directed cleanup operations. I told her to walk down to the lake and that I'd join her later.

"It was dark when I got away. I walked along the edge of the lake looking for her. I carried a flashlight but didn't turn it on because it was the love hour and couples lay on blankets in the sand and grass. A few were swimming. I heard them splashing in the water.

"I was afraid I'd passed her in the dark. I walked along calling her name softly. 'Babs, Babs?' I followed a path under pines. A jut of land was awash. I crossed it. Moored to the other side was a boathouse. I stepped aboard and stood in the doorway. It was black inside. I switched on my flashlight.

"In the slot was a Chris-Craft runabout, and on the leather seat of the cockpit were Babs and Smooth. He was humping her. He had her spraddled on the leather seat. They didn't even stop. 'Get the hell out, Bunny!' Smooth called to me."

Bonnert laughed, but he held his glass as if he would crush it. He set the glass carefully on the white table.

"Of course I was shaken for a while," he said. "My ego had been pricked, if you'll forgive the pun. I have, however, always believed in rationality. I told myself it was not Smooth's fault and it was not Babs'. There was no more use blaming them than blaming the law of gravity."

His features relaxed, and he reached for a cigarette. The Negro appeared in the doorway.

"You can serve now," Bonnert told him.

We ate on the sun deck. Bonnert was particular about what he put into his prim mouth. He examined each piece of pompano as if it might have dirt on it. He made me think of a coon washing crawfish in a stream.

"So now Smooth's in trouble," he said, chewing. "It had to be because he stopped listening to his genes. He was a golden stud meant to service the silken mares. As soon as he went against his nature, trouble was inevitable."

He dabbed at his mouth with a heavy linen napkin. The Negro again came to the door.

"Buddy's on the radio," he said.

"We don't have telephones, thank God," Bonnert explained as he pushed back his chair. "Friends, and there are precious few of those, call by wireless."

He left me. I cleaned my plate. The ocean breeze flapped the tassels on the yellow umbrella. The tide was coming in, and the ground vibrated with the impact of waves. Far out, a buoy blinked. I heard the faint, mournful sound of a bell.

Bonnert returned and sat at his place. He pulled his chair closer to the table with petulant jerks.

"I can't stand disorder," he said. "The least a person can do is plan his life so it's not sloppy."

From the tray he plucked a small silver bell and shook it. The Negro came out. Bonnert told him to clear away the table and bring coffee.

"A friend was supposed to visit me tonight," Bonnert said. "It's the only reason I flew down this weekend. Now he's canceled. A very careless person I'm afraid."

He sighed and sipped his coffee.

"What about your sister?" I asked, thinking of the painting of the pretty girl in the silver dress over the fireplace.

"My sister? As I told you, it's impossible to tell when she'll come." He smiled. "She's rather an enigma."

He rang the silver bell and asked for brandy.

"I've spent a lot of time thinking how a person should live his life," Bonnert said. He rolled the snifter between his small palms, and his ring clicked against the glass. "I've come to a very simple conclusion. A man should strive to discover his own nature. Then he should saddle and ride it as he would a wild horse. The great mistake is to attempt to change what you are."

He nodded as if agreeing with himself.

"Smooth's difficulties arise from the fact he wouldn't be content with what he is. He could have remained with the company and be making thirty-five thousand a year, plus an expense account. When he became spiritual, you might say he flushed his life."

The buoy flashed in the dark, and there was a slight phosphorescence on the water. Bonnert lighted a cigarette. His face appeared yellow, Oriental, in the flare of the match. The mournful sound of the bell crossed the water.

"I tried to dissuade him," Bonnert said. "I tried to show him he was going wrong. He was confused because he had an accident in which a young girl was killed. Do you know about that?"

"Yes."

"It caused him to lose his nerve. He asked for a leave from the company, which we were glad to grant, but then he went home, and his sister got hold of him. She jabbed her hooks into him when he was confused and frightened. Religious hooks. It was a damn shame."

Bonnert shook his head and clucked his tongue.

"Is it a choir girl?" he asked. "The woman Smooth's involved with?"

"Not quite."

"I thought perhaps it was one of the young ladies who sit so angelic in the choir loft. He used to like them young. He had a yen for my sister."

The glow of his cigarette spread across his face. His eyes were almost closed.

"A married woman then?" he asked. "A pillar of the church?"

I didn't answer, and he smiled.

"There are only so many possibilities," he said. "Poor Smooth. It probably wasn't his fault. He always attracts them. They twisted off their wedding rings and stuck them in their pocketbooks. Even innocent little country girls with cotton stockings and Woolworth girdles scratched on his door. He was too kind to refuse."

"It was his fault," I said.

"Oh?" Bonnert asked. "You're telling me he forced his attention where it wasn't wanted?"

"Yes."

"I'm surprised. It was never his style to use muscle—with the exception of one." He considered. "Perhaps it's his age. The years bring the paunch and thinning hair. And all that bogus spirituality would frustrate the great animal vitality he has—the sexual perfume the mares winded. It's sad, very sad, because they all loved him once, even my little sister, who yet remembers him fondly."

He clucked, shook his head, and sighed. On the beach a dog barked, just loud enough to be heard in a lull of waves. Then, carried on the breeze, was a woman's laughter.

"The lovers come up here," Bonnert said. "They block my road. I thought I'd be able to get away from people, but you never escape the lovers. They make nests among the dunes. If you went out with a flashlight, you'd flush them like partridges."

His speech had thickened, and he was slightly tilted in his chair. His eyes were almost closed.

"Thanks for your help," I said, standing.

"You're not leaving?" he asked, also standing. He pushed unsteadily at the table.

"I have a long drive."

"I won't allow it at this time of night. You can remain here."

I was very tired. It was easier to stay.

He rang his silver bell for the Negro and told him to bring my bag from the car. Bonnert then led me to a bedroom on the upstairs front of the house. He wound open louvered windows, and sea air swept into the room.

On the walls were more of his abstract paintings. The large bed had a bookshelf at the head of it. At the foot was a TV set. There were several photographs of his sister.

"Is there anything else you need?" Bonnert asked. The Negro

had brought my suitcase and opened it on a luggage rack. Bonnert was weaving but solicitous of me.

"No thanks," I said and thought I ought to like him. He was being more hospitable to me than I would have been to him.

When he closed the door, I undressed, brushed my teeth, and turned out the lights. I sank to the bed. The tide was still rising, and the ocean pounded as if it were going to break into the room. I tried to sort out the information I'd received from Bonnert, but I was too weary. Before I rolled over I was asleep.

When I woke, the room glowed. I thought it must be the moon. I turned my face to the window. I sensed rather than saw movement in the doorway. I sat up quickly.

It was Bonnert's sister, the one in the painting and photographs, and she had on the silver dress. I realized the glow wasn't the moon, but an indirect source in the ceiling. She shimmered in light.

She was small, dainty, and she walked slowly to the middle of the room. Her feet were bright with silver slippers. Her shoulders were bare, and on her cheek was a beauty mark. Her platinum hair was long and curled under.

I believed she didn't know I was here. She had come in late and either didn't want to bother Bonnert or couldn't wake him. When she visited, this was probably her room.

To warn her, I coughed. She stopped and looked toward the bed but was not alarmed. Instead she put a hand on a hip and smiled. She walked toward the bed, her hips turning slowly, her chest thrust out. I couldn't move.

She reached the bed and smiled down at me. I smelled her perfume and heard the faint rustling of her dress. She bent a knee. It touched the bed. One hip dropped lower than the other. She leaned toward me and lifted a hand to hold her breasts. Hardly moving her small red mouth, she spoke in a whisper.

"Are you lonely like me?"

I stared, unable to answer. She sat carefully on the bed. Her platinum hair swung over a cheek. She still held a hand at her breasts.

She reached the other hand toward me. My eyes widened. On the little finger was a gold signet ring with a black stone in it.

As I twisted away, I saw a red fingernail that had not been pasted on exactly right. A heavy layer of powder covered a coarseness of face. The platinum hair was not centered. I pushed out from the far side of the bed.

"What is it?" she asked, smiling. She crossed her legs and adjusted the silver dress over her knees.

"What are you?" I asked. I was backing across the room.

"Come here and find out." She patted the cover.

I shook my head. She pouted and then began to laugh, at first softly, but gradually more loudly, more highly-pitched, until the laughter became shrill.

She stood, walked to the door using small steps, and turned. She put her hands on her hips, and in the soft glow she again looked beautiful.

"You'd think I'd learn to leave country jakes alone," Bonnert said, in his own voice. He went out, his silver heels tapping against the polished floor.

I dressed quickly, threw things into my suitcase, and hurried from the house. I thought somebody might try to stop me, but I saw no one and the gate was unlocked.

I shoved it open, started my car, and drove down the narrow road. Shells banged against the frame as if I were being shot at. My headlights swept shadows off dunes.

When I reached the paved road, I turned inland. I drove twenty miles before I slowed. In a small lumber town which had a silver water tank floating above it I found a tourist court and a bed.

I'd gotten what I came for. I had enough.

Book Three

[32]

The church officers came to my house. The afternoon was fiery, and heat seeped into shade. The roof was so hot that birds wouldn't walk on it.

Harvey Boyle arrived first, driving his pickup truck, in the back of which were watermelons. He wore his work clothes—khakis and a canvas hat with a green visor sewn into the brim. He sat on my porch and swatted flies.

Wayland Counts was next. He'd just closed the bank, and his fingers were tinged with green from the money and stock certificates he'd handled.

"Do we have to meet in the afternoons?" he asked. With his handkerchief, he dusted his black-and-white shoes.

"Time's time," Harvey said. "Day or night."

Archie LeBuck arrived in his chauffeured car. He wore a white linen suit and a white hat. He carried his black cane.

Sutter came last. He was rumpled, and his eyes watered. He limped onto the porch. His hand was a corpse's. He slid into a chair as if punctured.

I began to talk. I heard the drone of my own voice as if I too were a listener. I told them everything I'd learned since our last meeting. I went into detail about the death of Clinton's daughter and about Bunny Bonnert.

They watched me. Their faces grew astonished and indignant. Harvey's hands lay still, though flies crawled over them.

When I finished, I wet my lips, leaned back in my chair, and waited. Archie poked his cane against his shoe. Wayland dried

193

sweat on his face. Sutter was mournful. Harvey spat over the railing.

"You think that Paul and Bonnert, that they—?" Archie asked, unable to put the question into words.

"Bonnert hinted at it two or three times," I said.

"Goddamn," Harvey said and again spat. "Excuse me for cussing in a church meeting."

"Can there be any doubt now?" Wayland asked. He was angry. "Do we or do we not know what has to be done?"

We stood and went to our cars. We drove in line to the church. Our faces were solemn, and people watching from the curb must have believed we were part of a funeral procession.

We parked under the sticky maples and went to the study. Paul wasn't in. The others waited in the garden while I walked to the manse. I knocked on the screen door.

One of his daughters answered. She had washed her hair and had a towel wrapped around it.

"Where's your father?" I asked.

"This is his tennis day," she said.

I thanked her, walked back to the garden, and told the others to wait.

I drove to the park. Paul was by himself, hitting the ball against a weathered backboard. I pulled up to the rusty fence and honked my horn. He caught the ball, smiled, and waved. He put his racket down and opened the gate.

"Bring your racket," I called to him.

"I have a game."

"You'll have to cancel it."

He went back for his racket. He wore shorts, and his strong, heavy legs were hairy and slightly bowed. I thought of what he'd done with Bonnert. I wondered how many others there were.

"Pete and I are playing for the world championship," Paul said as he approached my car.

"Leave him a note. We have a meeting."

"Right now?"

"The officers are waiting at the church."

I handed him my pencil and tore a strip from a map. He used the hood of my car to write to Pete. Paul fixed the note to the gate, jamming the paper onto a piece of wire.

I backed my car around. Paul, however, didn't hurry. He crossed through weeds to a faucet and cupped his hands under it for a drink. He then strolled to his old Dodge, tossed his racket into the back seat, and wiped his face before getting in himself.

I returned to the church. The others stood around and sat on the stone bench in the garden. They sought shade under the drooping apple tree.

"Where is he?" Wayland asked, hot and angry.

"He could be on the way," I answered. I was attempting to control my own feelings.

"Could?" Archie asked. He tapped his cane against the baked ground. "Could?"

"If it suits him," I said.

We shifted from one foot to the other and fanned ourselves with our hats.

His car rattled up the street. The Dodge sounded as if it were dropping nuts and bolts along the way. The engine wheezed and clanked. We stood facing the entrance to the garden. We heard the car door open and close.

When Paul entered, he acted as if it were a social occasion. He shook hands and smiled. He squeezed arms. He wouldn't see how we stepped away from him.

"How've you been?" he kept asking.

We didn't want to touch him, but he wouldn't let us escape. He lay his hands on our shoulders or prodded us in the small of our backs. His laughter was loud.

He opened the study and stood aside. He was sweaty, his dark, thinning hair stuck in wet ringlets against his forehead. We walked past him like a jury.

He left the door open and circled around his desk. He gathered chairs.

"Sit down, sit down," he said. "I'm a poor minister with hungry children, but I have enough chairs for my officers to rest their bones."

We sat on the edge of the chairs. He went back around his desk and pushed at his sweaty hair. His T-shirt stuck to his skin. Black hairs on his chest showed through. I thought of the silver dress.

Paul sat at the desk. He put his hands behind his head and grinned at us. On the bookshelf beyond him the golden trophy of the Greek Athlete glittered in the hot light from a window.

"Why don't we start a little air-conditioning campaign right here and now," Paul said. "It would bring more people to church in summer, and that in turn would pay for the unit—a fact that'd make Wayland happy."

Wayland twitched. As treasurer, he'd never been pleased with the reckless way Paul handled money.

"It would be nice to be happy," Wayland said and glanced at us.

"We could make our church not only a spiritual oasis, but a bodily one as well," Paul said, enthusiastic now. "We'd offer evening services and compete with the drive-in movie. I'd like to hear one of you make a motion that we put on a drive for funds."

"Paul," I said.

"At least let's get estimates," he said, refusing to hear me.

"Paul," I said a second time.

"Yes, Jack," he said, pushing at his hair. His blue eyes swept across our faces. He grinned. "You sure look gloomy." He scratched his chest. "I'd like to know what there is to be so gloomy about. Sure it's sizzling hot, and the tobacco resembles stinkweed, but we're all healthy and have food in the cupboard. Each of you has a roof over his head and clothes for his children. None of us suffers from a deadly disease or—"

"Stop it," Harvey said. "We didn't come for a sermon."

"A sermon might not be a bad idea," Paul said, throwing words up as if he could hide himself in them. "If I believed it'd get the church air conditioning, I'd preach here and now."

"You're not going to need air conditioning," Wayland said. "At least not around here."

"Well, it's true I can get along without it," Paul said. "People have got along without it for hundreds of years. But I don't believe God has anything against our being comfortable when we worship Him."

He was talking too loud, and his voice was strident.

"Paul," I said, my hands jerking against my legs.

"I'm listening," he said and laughed. "I know you're trying to cut in, but why don't we see whether or not we can collect the money here and now. If each of you'd pledge a hundred and fifty dollars of tax-deductible money, we'd get the ball rolling." He reached for a pencil and brought a yellow legal tablet from the drawer. "Who'll be first to have his name down?"

"That's enough," I said.

"I'd like you to think of this as an opportunity," Paul said, ignoring me. "What about you, Archie? Let me put down your name."

"No," Archie answered. He sat erect, his patrician hands on his cane, his face set in judgment.

"Surely a hundred and fifty dollars is not too much," Paul said. "All of you can afford such a piddling amount. But if it'll make you more fervent, I'll lower the ante to a hundred. Just to get the ball rolling."

"Will you shut up?" I said.

He stared at me, put down the pencil, and leaned back in his chair.

"I'll have to let Jack talk I guess," he said. "I haven't given up on the air conditioning, though, I'll warn you of that. I'll get you when you're weak." He laughed, but his eyes shifted at us like a man who sees knives.

"This is an official meeting of the Board of Officers," I told him.

"Then somebody has to take minutes," Paul said. He slid his pencil and yellow legal pad toward Wayland.

"You sure you want minutes?" Wayland asked me.

"The *Book of Church Order* states you have to take minutes at any meeting of the Board of Officers," Paul said.

"You don't want it," Archie said.

"Why don't I?" Paul asked, smiling.

"We came to ask you to leave," Harvey said.

Paul didn't say anything. He sat still. He then shifted in his chair and shuffled his feet. His big hand drummed on the green blotter. He turned his head to look at each of us.

"Well," he said. Slowly he pulled his hands across the desk and let them fall into his lap.

"You'll get severance pay," I said.

"Your generosity overwhelms me," Paul said.

"Talking like that doesn't help anything," Archie said.

"You misunderstand the tone," Paul said. "It's awe. Apparently you've figured out everything, and I'm interested in knowing what else you've done to my life."

"We're not studying your life," Harvey said. "We want to keep mess out of our church."

"Why?" Paul asked. "The church was born on mess. It's not supposed to be antiseptic."

"You're lucky you haven't been shot," Wayland said.

"I don't feel lucky."

"Why don't you make this easy on all of us and leave gracefully?" I asked.

"Now let's see if I understand right," Paul said. He sat forward. "You want me to pack up my wife and children and slip away into the night."

"With pay," Wayland said.

"What am I supposed to do then? My action will be taken as an admission of guilt, and I'll never be able to find another pulpit."

"I hope the hell you won't find another pulpit," Harvey said. Ordinarily he was a kind, considerate man, but now anger reddened his face.

"I have no intention of sacrificing myself for your convenience," Paul said, staring at Harvey.

"Sacrifice is the wrong word," Wayland said. "To sacrifice you'd have to be not guilty."

"No one is not guilty," Paul said, swinging to Wayland.

"Will you tell him?" Wayland asked me.

He had the pencil pressed against the legal tablet on his desk. The point snapped. Sutter jerked in his chair.

"By all means tell me," Paul said.

"You don't want it," I told him.

"But I do."

"All right," I said. I had no wish to club him. If he would allow me to, I'd still spare him the worst. "Item one: Were you drinking the night Caroline Gaines picked you up in her car to ride you home?"

"Did she tell you I was?"

"He's doing the asking," Wayland said.

"I'd like to know what she told you," Paul insisted.

"She says you had Scotch."

Paul watched me. He too was angry, and the anger firmed his flesh.

"There's nothing in church articles that forbids a minister to have a drink," he said.

"Is that an admission?" Archie asked.

"I had a drink," Paul admitted. He kept his head high. "It's the first time in many years."

"Well, we got that out, didn't we?" Wayland asked.

"Wait a second," Paul said, resenting Wayland. "I wasn't trying to hide my drinking. Rather it's my feeling that it isn't any more of your business when I have one than it is of my business when you do."

Paul was staring at Wayland, and Wayland squirmed. He'd once been a heavy weekend drinker. He'd started as soon as the bank closed and increased his intake up through Sunday night. On Mondays he'd looked as if he'd been bled.

"Question number two," I said, breaking in to keep Paul and Wayland from going at each other. "Why did you go into Caroline's house?"

"She asked me in," Paul answered. "I don't like these questions."

"We can see why," Harvey said.

"I don't mind answering questions man to man," Paul said. "I do object to being grilled."

"The rest of us will keep quiet and let Jack do the talking," Archie said. He nodded at me. Coming from Archie, it was a command.

"It seems unusual you'd go in the house," I said to Paul. "You knew Lou was out of town."

"Whether I knew or not, there's no reason for me not to go in after she invited me."

He was stubborn. He had his squarish chin out as if he dared me to hit it.

"Do you want to give us an explanation of what happened in the house?" I asked.

"Why ask when you're so sure you know?" he said. His hand was clenched on the desk.

"Your attitude isn't helping," Archie said. He tapped the cane against the floor.

"Helping what?" Paul asked. "I don't feel it's part of my job to help you stomp me."

Archie sat erect. Not many men dared talk back to him like that. Nor would he suffer it from them. His face became rocklike.

"You've already made up your minds about me," Paul said, looking at each of us. "You're here to cook me."

"We have made up our minds," I said. "We found good reasons for doing so. I suggest you leave it there."

"I don't want to leave it there. It's my life you're trying to ruin." His blue eyes were bright. "How come my accuser isn't here?"

"She wouldn't come without Lou, and you wouldn't want to be in the same room with him," Wayland said.

Paul thumped his fists against the desk, bowed his head, and closed his eyes—not like a man praying but like one fighting to restrain himself from violence.

"What is it you want me to tell you?" he asked, his voice almost a whisper.

"Are you officially denying Caroline Gaines' charges against you?" I asked.

"Yes," he said and opened his eyes.

"Why did you go into her house?"

"I told you she invited me."

"You don't think it's unusual for a minister to go into an empty house with a married woman and drink her husband's Scotch?"

"In some countries it's considered civilized to have a drink, even for ministers."

"We're not talking about some countries."

"Other men are allowed relaxation from the pressure of work," he said. "I had a drink, but I wasn't drunk."

"Then what did you do?"

"Do?"

"I want the sequence of events. You had a drink. Were you sitting down?"

"Why do it this way?" Wayland asked me. "Use what you have."

"Be quiet," Archie told Wayland.

"We were sitting on the screened-in porch near the pool."

"Doing what?" I asked. I'd been on that porch. In the summer the underwater lights of the pool gave the shrubbery an eerie green cast.

"We talked," Paul said.

"After the talk?"

He hesitated. He pulled his hands toward him. His blue eyes darted in the direction of the door as if he were thinking of escape.

"She got up and left," he said. "When she came back, she'd changed her clothes."

"I don't like what you're saying," Wayland told him.

None of us did. A woman changed her clothes in a situation like that for structural reasons. We thought of the old line, Excuse me while I get into something more comfortable.

"Do you want me to answer questions or don't you?" Paul shot back at Wayland.

"You grabbed her," Wayland said.

"I never grabbed her."

"You're denying you touched her?" I asked.

"There's a big difference between grabbing and touching." He rubbed his face, and we heard the rasp of his skin. "Of course I touched her. They didn't geld me at the seminary. Maybe they should have so you could have eunuchs for your pulpits."

His dark hair was caked against his sweaty forehead. He held to the desk as if to steady himself.

"Then you admit you . . . handled her," I said.

"I'm a man. You have no right to expect more of me than you expect from yourselves. Suppose you'd been in my place."

I tried to imagine myself on that porch. She would have been perfumed and coolly beautiful. I thought of the eerie pool lights on her and her silken ladylike legs. If the conditions were right, any man would have been aroused.

"That sounds like an admission," I said.

"Think what you like."

"There's only one thing we can think unless you tell us differently," Sutter said.

We hadn't expected him to speak, and his voice surprised us. I frowned. I was ready to put the lid on Paul. Sutter kept lifting that lid.

"I'll tell you this," Paul said, facing Sutter. "Before I knew Lou was in the house, I was backing away from her."

We shifted impatiently. I remembered the bite on her neck. In Paul's grasp Caroline would have been as small as a child. He wouldn't have backed off. He would have rooted.

"That isn't what she claims," Sutter said.

We glared. We wanted him to shut up and let us finish it.

"I'm not talking for her," Paul answered. "I'm telling you I was backing away."

"I suppose you weren't tempted," Sutter said, and for the first time he too looked as if he disbelieved.

"I was tempted. Any of you ought to be able to understand that. But I conquered that temptation and was backing off."

Even Sutter was growing angry. Paul was blaming it on Caroline. They looked at me. Their eyes directed me to use the filth I had.

"Tell us about the girl," I said.

"What girl?" Paul asked, surprised.

"The nineteen-year old you killed."

He flinched as if I'd laid a lash across him. His big hands reached for each other in his lap.

"You must have gone to lots of trouble to dig that up on me," he said.

"Right much trouble," I said.

"You want me to defend myself?"

"I don't think you can defend yourself."

He put his hands flat on his desk, palms down, and looked at them. Slowly he raised his eyes.

"That happened in another life," he said.

We waited for more, but he sat passively—as if the explanation should satisfy us.

"Is that all you're going to tell us about killing a girl?" I asked.

"I was once a corrupt man," he said. "I've never denied it. You've heard me say it from the pulpit."

It was a recurring theme in his sermons—that man was incapable of good without God, that man could not even conceive what good was without the notion being put into his head by God.

"There's a pattern," I said. "You were used to women. Smooth was your name. Big Smooth. But now your hair's thin, and you're getting fat. You sucked up some Scotch, and you thought you could play the great lover all over again."

Outside, locusts whirred in dusty trees. A truck banged up the hot street.

"You've done quite a research job on me," Paul said, looking at his hands as he flopped them on his desk.

"There's more if I need it," I said. I would still hold back the last if he would allow it.

"I'm trying to figure out a way to answer you."

"Give us your resignation," I said.

"Wait a minute," he said. He pushed hair off his brow. "I admit to doing lots of bad things in my life, terrible things, but it wasn't me, not the me that's sitting before you now. It was another man who just happened to be named Paul Elgin."

"Caroline Gaines wasn't with the other Paul Elgin."

"I told you I was backing off," he said. "What more can I do?"

Again they glanced at me. I was ready. I wanted to use it on him now.

"I talked to one of your friends," I said.

"Who?" Paul asked. His face shone with sweat.

"From your other life," I said. "He owns a villa on the seashore. He has a beautiful sister in a silver dress."

Muscle and bone shrank in him.

"You did a remarkable hatchet job on me with these men," he said. His voice was husky.

"Your resignation," I said.

He struck the desk with his palms and nodded.

"You found plenty of garbage," he said. "You found muck and stink. I admit it. I gladly admit it. But I say to you it's a part of my life that is no longer connected to me."

Right in front of us he was aging.

"I sold hooch," he said. "To understand me, you have to live that life. In the line of duty I stayed plastered three and four days at a time. It was a kind of sickness. People passed in and out of my vision as if I were underwater. They weren't real. Nothing had any reality or focus."

He leaned across his desk and allowed his head to droop.

"Bunny Bonnert was just one more experience, just one more meaningless experience in an existence I had no control over—a lost life, sinful and terrible, a profanation."

He raised his head.

"That life has nothing to do with me now. If you believe your own religion, you must accept the fact that thieves, whores, and murderers can be saved."

"Did you rape the girl too?" I asked. It was a brutal question, but I wanted to skewer him.

Again he flinched. He wiped the back of his arm across his mouth.

"In years she was young," Paul said. "In depravity she was nearly as advanced as I was. You wouldn't believe a girl nineteen could learn so much depravity. We were alike, two of a kind, and I loved her for her corruption. Had she lived I would have married her. We understood there could be nobody else for us because nobody lived as degenerately."

I remembered the small picture of his daughter Clinton had showed me, painted on ivory, the girl appearing innocent and mistily beautiful.

"I loved her, and I heard her die," Paul said. "I was less than a foot from her and couldn't reach her because my arms were broken. I lay in that wrecked car and heard the blood drip out of her. She held her fingers to my face and tried to comfort me, and she was the one dying."

His light blue eyes became wet, and he pushed at his nose with the back of his hand.

"After she was gone and I got out of the hospital, I saw nothing but skeletons," he said. "I'd be sitting in a dining room with a beautiful living woman, and I'd see right through to her bones. The people at tables around us would shed their skins, and the food they ate dropped between their ribs. I'd put my hands over my eyes and see the bones in my fingers. I was haunted by death."

For an instant I felt myself feeling sorry for him. I had lived with too much death. In the horror of his face as he stared into the pit, I saw my own.

"Nobody can live in a world of skeletons," he said. "I fed on corpses, and when people saw me they turned the other way. For weeks I didn't leave my apartment. It and I grew filthy. I tried to starve myself, but I had too much fat to live on.

"Finally, like a gut-shot animal dragging itself, I went home to North Carolina. I lay on the bed to die. I think I would have except for my sister. She cared for me as if I were a baby. She cleaned me, fed me, and dressed me. She got me on my feet and fixed a chair for me on the porch."

Paul wiped the sweat from his eyelids. He let his heavy hand slide down his face and across his chest.

"As I grew stronger, I began to work around the farm," he said. "I planted, patched the barn, and strung fence. I went at it in a kind of daze. I wouldn't let myself think. I drove myself to exhaustion so the bed would receive me without dreams."

He rubbed an arm. He cleared his throat and looked past us to the open door and burned garden. A truck was passing.

"A thing happened," he said. "I was mowing hay and stopped to rest. I put my back against the rough bark of a tree. I heard a voice behind me. I got up to look and nobody was there. I sat down. The voice came a second time, and it cut into me. I fell to my knees shivering and felt the old part of me drop away like a husk. Across eternity came the hand of the Lord."

We sat very quietly in our chairs. My back ached from wood pressing into it. We couldn't move until Wayland broke free of the words. He shifted his feet and raised his chin as if his collar were too tight.

"What were you drinking?" Wayland asked.

"I was drunk all right but not with liquor," Paul said. "I was suddenly drunk with hope. I was ten times higher than I'd ever been on hooch."

"You could have deceived yourself," Archie said, not mean like

206

Wayland. We expected Wayland to talk mean because he belonged to Lou, but in Archie's blood ran the old genes.

"I could have," Paul admitted, nodding. "I've asked myself about it a thousand times. I can say only that I don't believe God deceives."

"The Devil does," Harvey said.

"The Devil deceives in the direction of sacrilege and a weakening of faith," Paul said.

"Isn't that what's going on in this church?" Harvey asked. "You think what you've done has strengthened anybody's faith?"

Paul sat straighter. He pushed at his sweaty hair. He looked at each of us, and when he spoke, his voice was polite, and stubborn.

"I've been as honest with you as I can," he said. "I've let you open me up and put your fingers inside. I think it's enough."

"Wait outside," I told him.

[33]

He stood and walked into the scorched garden. He sat on the stone bench under the apple tree. I shut the door on him.

"Let's get this over quick," Wayland said, tapping his pencil against Paul's desk.

"A man's career is involved," Sutter said. "We shouldn't put him in the grave without a few words."

"What words are left?" Archie asked politely.

"I don't like doing anything too fast," Sutter said.

"You're trying to find a way to make it easy on him," Wayland said. "It can't be done."

We all watched Sutter. He was sunk in the chair. He held to the leather arms as if they were keeping him from going under.

"Why doesn't he act guilty?" Sutter asked us. "Somebody tell me that."

"'Act' is the right word," Wayland said.

"But he admitted everything we charged him with—except the part about Caroline."

"That's the only thing we couldn't prove," Harvey said.

"I can't see that it's been proved either side," Sutter said. "She's claiming one thing, and he another."

"You can't take his word over hers," Wayland said, excited. "God, you can look at her and see she's been hurt."

For a moment we sat silently in the hot room which smelled of books and dust. A truck thundered down the street, its engine roaring and shaking the windows. Through one of those windows I saw Paul on the stone bench. He sat motionless, his big hands cupped over his knees.

"We have to ask ourselves what we're concerned with here," Sutter said. "I'm assuming it's justice."

"We're concerned with a lot more than justice," Wayland said. "You know it, and I know it."

"What is there more than justice?" Sutter asked, staring back at Wayland.

"There's Lou Gaines who's our friend."

Again we sat silently. We eyed Sutter.

"Go on and vote then," he said. "Don't pay any attention to me."

"He never really came to grips with Caroline," Archie said thoughtfully. "He talked about everything else openly."

"He's guilty," Wayland said. He pointed toward the garden. "It all fits with his background. He was lushing it up, believed he could help himself to a little, and got caught."

"He claims he was backing away," Sutter said.

"Of course he claims it, but can you accept it? She was screaming, and her blouse was torn."

"If there's any doubt, Lou ought to have the benefit of it, not him," Harvey said, gesturing toward the garden.

"Absolutely," Wayland said. "I call for the question."

"We don't have a question yet," I said. "We don't have a motion."

"I'll make it," Wayland said. "I move that this board release the minister."

"Second," Harvey said.

"You heard the motion," I said. "Any further discussion?"

"I'm puzzled by a few points in the case," Archie said. "But I'm going to vote to dismiss him."

"There's no reason any of us have to have a bad conscience," Wayland said.

We looked at Sutter. He acted as if he weren't listening.

"You heard the motion," I said. "Those in favor say aye."

"Aye," Wayland, Harvey, and Archie said.

"Not everybody voted," Wayland said. "I think it ought to be unanimous."

"It's unanimous enough," Sutter said.

"The motion carries," I told Wayland. "That's all you need to write down."

I walked to the door and opened it. Paul was still on the stone bench. I motioned him in. He hitched up his shorts and crossed toward me with long, heavy strides.

"You look like the executioner," he said as he passed me.

I closed the door. Paul walked around his desk and held to the back of his chair.

"You realize you've put us in a very uncomfortable and embarrassing position," Wayland said, not waiting for me.

Paul watched, his tenseness showing only in the way he gripped the chair.

"By your actions you've hurt this church and caused wounds that will require years to heal," Wayland said.

Sutter glanced at me. Wayland had no business making a speech.

"I'll take it from here," I said to Wayland. He flushed. I spoke to Paul. "The Board of Officers has voted to release you."

"You're kicking me out," he said. He leaned on his hands. He straightened and squared his shoulders. "No."

"No what?" I asked.

"I won't leave."

Wayland and Harvey turned to me. I tried to remember passages from the *Book of Church Order*.

"You're being very foolish," Archie said, not harshly, not threatening, but as one might counsel a son.

"I didn't put on the cloth lightly," Paul said. "I won't take it off lightly either."

"We're not changing our vote," I said.

"This board can't make me leave," Paul said. "Only the congregation can do that."

He was technically correct. A minister always had the right of appeal to the congregation. It was an action, however, no minister in my memory had taken. A meeting was like putting mess on the radio.

"You don't want that," Archie said. "Believe me you don't."

"I don't want it," Paul said. He had his feet planted, and stubbornness muscled his face. "But I'll take it before I leave."

"You're a cockster," Wayland said. "Just a fancy, preaching cockster."

Paul turned slowly to face Wayland. Paul seemed to become furious little by little—first his hands, then his arms, his chest, and his face. He grew with anger. He moved around the desk after Wayland. Frightened, Wayland backed off.

"That's enough!" Archie said.

Paul stopped himself. He held to the edge of his desk and pulled himself back to it. A smile bent through the iron of his face.

"Brother Counts, I forgive you your stupidity," he said.

Wayland's mouth opened, and he looked around for help, but none of us wanted to help him.

"We're cutting off your pay," Wayland sputtered. "You're not getting another cent out of us."

"And you're not driving me out," Paul said.

"Then we might as well leave," Archie said. He stood and went out the door. Harvey, Wayland, and I followed. I glanced back at Paul. He still held to the desk.

I walked through the dusty garden. The sun struck hot on my skin. Another truck roared down the street. The trucks were carrying cucumbers to market and were being detoured from the highway because of pavement repair. Jackhammers banged into cement.

I went to my car. As I opened the door, Sutter caught up with me. I slid into the seat. The hot covers burned through my clothes.

"We tried," Sutter said. "If he wants to be stubborn, it's his funeral. I'm washing my hands."

We saw it develop on the street in front of us. The dirty truck, top-heavy with crates, came up behind us. The red convertible, driven by Mary Dupuis, a college girl on her way to the country club, turned out of a drive. She wore a yellow bathing suit and had tied a yellow scarf around her hair.

The truck driver, a Negro in a billed cap, blew his horn. His tires smoked and squealed. Mary jerked her steering wheel and speeded up to get out of the way. Her car fishtailed drunkenly. The skidding truck hit it on the rear fender.

Mary froze at the wheel, her foot still on her accelerator. The red convertible jumped the curb, its wheels shrieking. It slid across the grass of Bo Carter's house. The tires threw up clods of turf.

The small boy, five or six years old, stood in the yard. He wore a plastic space helmet and carried a wooden sword. He didn't move. The red convertible spun into him and covered him.

I was yelling, but Sutter acted before I could. He ran across the street on his scrawny legs. I pounded after him, the pavement hot under my feet. Mary Dupuis was weeping in her car. She had her hands over her face.

"Oh no!" she said. "No!"

Sutter dropped to his belly and looked under the convertible. The boy was a bloody bundle. His head and ears oozed blood. His mashed hand still touched the wooden sword.

"Call a wrecker!" Sutter yelled at me as he wiggled under the car. "We have to get weight off him."

I turned toward the house. Alma Carter, the boy's mother, was running out. She was screaming. A neighbor caught at her to hold her back.

Somebody pushed me aside roughly. I stumbled and turned. It was Paul.

He ran to the car and knelt to look under it, his hands splayed against the burned grass.

"Call a wrecker!" I shouted toward people who stood on porches.

"No time!" Paul yelled. He was wild—hair in his face, grease on his T-shirt. He stood, spread his feet, and hooked his big hands under the chrome bumper. He lifted.

The car came up, but the tires were still on the ground. I ran to help him. Alma Carter screamed. Through it all the jackhammer pounded.

Paul and I were lifting. Men and women ran to us and surrounded the convertible. They grabbed fenders, door handles, headlights, but it was Paul—his eyes closed, his shoulder hunched —who did it. He got on his hands and knees under the bumper and raised his body. Muscles pulled in the back of his neck, and sweat rolled from bulging veins in his temples. The tires quivered and swung off the ground.

"I got him!" Sutter shouted. "He's free!"

Paul and the rest of us held the car up until Sutter brought the Carter boy out—slowly in order not to bend him. Sutter cradled his arms like a mother.

We let the convertible down with a bending of our knees and a release of our breaths. Paul sat on the ground.

We heard a siren and saw a flashing red light. Women were gathered around Alma Carter. They held and shielded her. Mary Dupuis, weeping, her hair in her face, was being led away.

Sutter worked a stretcher under the Carter boy. Easily, lightly, the ambulance driver and a policeman carried it. Sutter scurried along beside them. They lifted the stretcher into the ambulance. Sutter climbed in. They shut the doors.

The Negro truck driver, his cap in his hand, stood under a maple tree looking frightened and as if he might flee. Alma Carter wailed.

I turned and saw Paul walking back toward the church. I watched him go, his feet heavy, his gait shambling, his head hung forward. He shone with sweat.

He turned into the garden. I stood a moment before I realized my hand was raised toward him.

[34]

Shaken, I drove to the store. I went in the back way and rested in the shadows. I heard my heart beating. I wiped my face with my handkerchief.

I walked to the front of the store. Injun stood on his box before the cash register. He wore a clean white shirt, a black bowtie, and a starched linen jacket. From the jacket pocket half a dozen pens and pencils stuck up. Over his cuffs were celluloid sleeve protectors. His light hair was plastered down, and the crease was so perfect it looked as if it'd been axed into his scalp.

I went to my office and sat. I was still trembling. I heard Injun walk up behind me and stand in the doorway. I turned to him.

He stood shy and proud—like the time he caught the eight-pound bass out of the river.

"How's business?" I asked. I dried the palms of my hands.

He walked to the cash register, climbed on his box, and punched the NO SALE button. The drawer clanged out. He pointed inside.

I stood and crossed to it. The bins were full to the top with neat stacks of bills and coins.

"You better make a deposit," I said.

"I was fixing to."

"You ought to do it every day."

"I do do it every day."

I stared at him. He was smiling.

"These are a day's receipts?"

"Yes, sir."

I looked toward the front of the store. A sign was taped to a window. I walked outside. SALE, crudely lettered in red paint, blazed across cardboard.

"What's on sale?" I asked. I inspected shelves, afraid he might be letting goods go too cheaply.

"Everything," he said.

Before I could question him further, two women entered the store. Injun hurried to wait on them.

I sat in my office. I lifted the telephone and called the hospital. The lady at the reception desk said the Carter child was in surgery.

I listened to Injun wait on the two women. He was polite and helpful. He was almost servile. He sold an electric iron, wrapped it, and held the door open for the women to leave.

"How can everything be on sale?" I asked him.

"I didn't change the prices," he said. He smiled.

"You can't have a sale unless you change the prices," I told him.

"Down at the Progress Store they do," he argued. "They may have one little old screwdriver on sale, but they act as if everything is."

"They don't know any better down there," I said, and even as I sat in my chair I heard the hillbilly music thumping into the street.

Injun backed off. I'd spoken more roughly than I intended. He was scared of me. I'd never meant to do that to him. I tried to soften my voice.

"If we're going to have a sale, everything has to be cheaper," I said. "That's the honest way. Now go take down the sign."

His shoulders pulled in, his eyes down, he walked to the front of the store and climbed into the window to tear the sign off the glass. I felt guilty. He was trying to please me, and I'd jumped him.

I went to the cash register and took out four five-dollar bills. I called him to me. He edged up as if he thought I was going to hit him. I counted the money into his small hand.

"You been doing good work," I told him. "You been doing a man's job, and I'm proud of you."

He took the money, but he didn't appear convinced. A lick of his tow hair had worked loose from the grease on his head. His small face was like Kitt's, and for an instant it was as if she were there—as if she were reaching out and touching my arm, urging me to go to Injun and at least put my hand on his shoulder, to kneel down maybe, to hug him.

Injun, however, turned away to go to the front of the store. I went to my office. He stayed wide of me the rest of the afternoon, and I never did put my hand on his shoulder.

[35]

Before locking up, I dialed Val. Miss Minnie answered and called her. I heard Val come down the steps.

"Have dinner with me," I said.

"Where?" she asked guardedly.

"Lynchburg."

"Lynchburg's okay. I just don't want to ever see another tree."

I drove home, dressed, and telephoned the hospital a second

215

time. The woman at the desk told me the Carter boy was out of surgery and having a transfusion.

I left Injun with Aunt Delia and drove to Val's. She was ready. She wore a pale blue dress and a pair of white gloves. Her dress brushed my clothes as she walked beside me to the car.

"Did he really lift the convertible?" she asked as I drove through the town.

I nodded. I'd been trying not to think of him.

Val picked at her gloves. Her hands lay across her thighs.

"Miss Minnie says he's been fired."

"He has."

"What happens next?"

"He's threatening to go to the congregation."

"Will he?" She had turned to me.

"I hope when he considers, he'll see it can't help."

Picking at her white gloves, she was silent a moment.

"It was a fine thing he did, lifting the car."

"Let's make a deal and not talk about him," I said. I didn't want to see any more goodness in Paul.

She nodded and nibbled at her lower lip. We were out of town. I drove the highway toward Lynchburg and passed a truck full of cattle. Val made a face at the smell.

"Suppose there's something else?" she asked.

"About what?"

"About him."

"Let me make myself clear," I said. "I'm getting him out of my life."

She glanced at me but said nothing else.

We went to the Lynchburg Country Club where I'd held an out-of-town membership since the days I courted Kitt. In the dining room Val chose a table near the window so we could look out at the tennis courts. I had a bottle in a paper bag. The colored waiter served us setups.

"All the collecting you've done's been from one side," Val said.

216

She had taken off her gloves, and she dragged her red nails across the tablecloth, leaving furrows in it.

"What collecting?" I asked.

"About him. What about her?"

She meant Caroline. I put my drink down and reached for her hand.

"It couldn't be," I said. "Now please shut up."

"Why couldn't it be?" she asked, pulling her hand away.

"I've known her too long."

There had never been anything about Caroline. When she first came to town, we'd all been astonished that Lou had married such a beautiful woman and were slow to accept her. We waited for her to make mistakes. She never did.

"She's not a native," Val said. She frowned. "What do you really know."

"You're driving me into despair," I said.

She frowned and made furrows in the cloth. "I wonder how the Carter child is."

I stood and excused myself. I telephoned the hospital from the pay booth in the paneled grill. The woman at the hospital desk said there was no change in the child's condition.

I went back to the table and told Val. She looked out the window at the tennis players, but she didn't see them.

"If he lives, Paul saved his life and not the doctors," she said.

I drank and refused to speak. She tapped her red fingernails against a plastic ashtray.

"How can he be so good and bad at the same time?" she asked.

I put the glass to my mouth so no words could come out.

"They have such a terrible time of it," Val said. "Ministers do. They have a worse time than anybody."

"It would help if you remembered what he tried to do," I said, unable to hold the words.

"They're sort of like scapegoats," she said, ignoring me. "They take on our sins, and we destroy them."

I stood and walked around the table. I again sat down. I held her hand.

"You're my favorite person," I said. "But if you mention his name once more I'm going to become foul of mouth."

She pulled her hand away quickly and placed it in her lap. I signaled the waiter and without consulting her ordered lobsters. She drew her lips tight.

There were only a few people eating, and most of those were elderly. The silence of the dining room was funereal. I tried to converse with Val. I told her about Injun running the store. She wouldn't talk.

As soon as we finished eating, I got her out of there. It was growing dark. We walked by the pool. The pool was lighted from underwater, and wavy patterns swirled on her blue dress.

From a loudspeaker music played over a flagstone terrace. The tune was slow enough that I could dance to it. I lifted my arms to Val. She held herself as if she wore a cast.

"I'm sorry I was rude to you," I said. "I've been having a very difficult time lately. I need you to be friendly to me. Please don't punish me further."

She watched me out of dark eyes that caught slivers of light from the clubhouse. As if she clicked a switch, she softened and stepped in against me.

"I been henpecking him," she said.

We danced across the terrace, staying out of squares of light on the flagstones, moving instead through fringes of darkness. I touched my cheek to hers. She rolled hers against mine.

Her long, supple body bowed into me. She acted lovingly contrite. To my surprise passion rose out of my deadness. For the first time I really thought about seducing her. Yet I wanted her not so much to feed the stirring lust as to break through to her and establish a tie she couldn't easily loosen. I would then take her home, and she would rear my son for me.

Yet how did a fossil like me proceed to seduction? I had married Kitt as a young man, and I'd been faithful to her. Even in the

Army I'd been faithful. One summer in my drunken days I'd picked up a woman while staying at a Norfolk hotel. I had been unable to complete the act. She'd given me back my money.

"You're tense," Val said, speaking against my cheek. I felt her breath and smelled her perfume.

Another couple came out to dance, an elderly man and his white-haired wife. They moved gracefully on the checkerboard of lights. I kept us in shadows and waited until the elderly couple were at the other end of the terrace before I kissed Val. On my part it was a tentative move. She raised her hand to my neck and pulled my head down harder. I tightened my arms around her waist.

"That was a southern degenerate kind of kiss," she said, her lips brushing my cheek. "I need air."

"Wouldn't it be nice if we were alone for a little while," I said. My voice was scratchy. She could be in a loving mood, I thought. I might have just caught her right.

"I don't think we're destined to be alone," she answered. Another couple had come out to dance. They circled toward us.

"We could work at it," I said and kissed her a second time. She allowed it only an instant.

"Work at it how?" she asked. She touched her hair and stood very properly as the couple passed us.

"Suppose I found us a place," I said. The words scared me. Once they were out, we were no longer playing.

She drew away and eyed me. I was ready to laugh if I had to, to pretend I was joking.

"Lecher," she said, but what was more important she hadn't refused or become insulted. I figured her reaction was a sort of consent.

I held her hand and led her across the grass to the car. Her dress swished. She had to run to keep up with me. She started laughing.

"You're acting very frisky for a person whose blood's been thinned by inbreeding," she said.

I helped her into my car and drove quickly away from the club.

219

If what was happening was what I thought was happening, maintaining momentum was important. I pulled her to me. Her hip and leg touched mine.

There was a motel on the west side of town—brick cottages with petunias planted along the walks and in front of porches. To get to it seemed to take hours. I hit every stoplight. I got behind a truck and cursed. She was amused. I didn't care as long as she laughed her way into bed.

"You're rather excited," she said. She put her ear against my chest. "I feel your heart bumping."

"It's sending a message," I said. "I hope you can read it."

"I'm not sure I should."

Ahead I saw the neon sign in front of the motel. The VACANCY light was on. I slowed, turned into the drive, and cut off the engine. The car coasted to a stop in front of the office.

"What are you doing?" she asked. She drew away from me and blinked. She smoothed her hair.

"I'm finding us a little place to be alone," I said.

I left the car. I walked fast toward the office. I didn't want to give her a chance to call me back. Each time a foot struck the ground, shock went up through my leg. As I got farther from my car, I said to myself, It's possible.

When I reached the brick building, my hand was shaky and felt strangely light lifting to the handle of the screen door.

I walked into the office, which was at one end of a small restaurant and souvenir shop. Truck drivers sat at a counter. Above a mirror was a line of wood slabs which had been painted with pictures of Robert E. Lee and shellacked over.

At the cash register stood a short, hairless man. He was egg-shaped and held his pants up by suspenders. He smiled like a mouse nibbling cheese.

"I'd like a cabin," I said.

"Just you?" he asked. He reached to a shelf behind the cash register for a registration card. He handed me a ball-paint pen.

"And my wife," I said. My voice didn't waver, and I allowed

my eyes no swerve. The man still smiled the cheese nibble, but his rodent-like eyes became shiny and alert.

"Don't she want to see the cabin?" he asked. He pulled back the card.

"We know they're nice," I said.

"You stayed here before?" he asked. At the counter several of the truck drivers had turned on their stools to watch.

"My wife says anybody who takes such good care of petunias has to run a clean motel," I said. I would have walked out and tried to find another place, but I was afraid of frightening Val and losing the momentum.

"I planted those petunias," he said and slowly slid the card to me.

With a trembling hand, I wrote Mr. and Mrs. Everett Bentley, 804 Tulip Street, Richmond. He watched.

I pushed the card back to him. He put on glasses and read it carefully.

"You forgot your license number," he said.

I'd seen the line for the license number, but I'd hoped to avoid using it. I opened my wallet to look at my registration card. I held it so the rodent couldn't see my real name.

"You don't stay much in motels," he said as I wrote the license number on the registration card.

"My wife and I are on vacation."

"People who travel know their license numbers," he said. "That'll be nine dollars."

I counted out the money, and he rang it up on the cash register. He turned to a board on which keys hung from brass hooks. He selected a key, but instead of putting it into my hand he walked to the screen door and opened it for me. As I crossed to the door, I was aware of truckmen watching.

"Drive your car around to number six," the rodent said. He started away from me. He had a waddling gait—like a man lifting his feet out of mud.

"I can do it," I said. "Just give me the key."

"I'll turn on the lights," he said.

I was scared he'd spook Val. I went to my car. She sat erect. She was smoking. I slid in beside her and started the engine.

"You're really doing this?" she asked.

I didn't answer because I was obviously doing it. I drove around the circle to the cabin. The man stood on the porch and motioned for me to pull my car into the slot beside the cabin.

"Do you think I'm going in there?" Val asked as I opened the door on my side. I pulled the door to quickly.

"Don't cause a scene now," I told her. I glanced at the man. He was motioning us to come on.

"What do you think I am?" she asked. She pushed her skirt down and crossed her arms.

"I've already paid," I said. "If you want to, we'll just go in and sit a minute, but don't make me look crazy in front of the man."

She turned her head and stared at me.

"But do you really want me to go in there?" she asked.

"I want and need you to go in there," I answered.

The man had stepped off the porch and was crossing toward us. I pushed open the door and went around to her side to help her out. I held Val's arm firmly.

"Mrs. Bentley," the man said and shook hands with her. Val glanced at me and let him pump her hand. "Very pleased to have you here. I'll help with your baggage."

"We'll unpack later," I said. I felt Val's fright through her elbow. She would have gone for the car had I not held her.

"No charge for carrying bags," the man said, his bright rodent eyes glittering in the light from the porch.

"We'd like to relax a minute before we face that," I said. Pressuring Val with my hip, I moved her past him toward the cabin door.

He came in after us. He showed us the closet, the towels, and the shower. He explained we could have food sent from the restaurant. He opened drawers of the bureau. As he talked, he watched us.

I was holding to Val. She stood stiffly in the center of the room, and he circled around us talking. I let go of her to try to get him out the door. He hung back.

"You people churchy?" he asked. "There's a revival down the road. Got a powerful preaching man from the mountains."

"We may wash up and go later," I said, trying to move him through the door.

"Let me show you how to use the air conditioner," he said.

"I've used an air conditioner before," I said and stood in front of him so he couldn't get to it.

He smiled the cheese nibble, winked, and backed away.

"If you want anything, just call," he said.

"We will," I said and leaned my weight against the door. He was squeezed out but not before a last curious look at Val.

She still stood in the middle of the room. She held her pocketbook to her stomach. I locked the door and crossed to her. I tried to put my arms around her. She pushed free as if distracted.

She turned to examine the room. There were yellow plastic chairs, a blond dressing table with an oval mirror, and a big bed with a yellow cover. At the foot of the bed was the TV set.

"I can't believe this," she said. She kept turning. "How'd you get me to do this?"

"You felt sorry for me," I said and slipped my arms around her from behind.

"He's suspicious," she said, wiggling away from me.

"He's just nosy."

"Suppose he comes back."

"Why would he?"

"Or suppose he calls the police. Don't the police sometimes raid these places?"

"He wouldn't call the police," I said. "Not a sweet little rodent like him."

But she was making me nervous. I imagined police knocking down the door and arresting us. I thought of the news reaching

Black Leaf. She'd lose her job, and I might just as well close my business. Then there would be the shame for Injun.

"Well, I don't like this," she said and her face became rubbery—as if she might cry.

"I like you," I told her and again put my arms around her waist. She was trembling. I nosed through her clean black hair and kissed her neck. I rubbed her back. I felt her soften a little under my hands. I groped for the zipper on the side of her blue dress and worked it down.

"What are you doing?" she asked, jerking away.

"I'm trying to be suave," I said.

"Well, stop it," she said and walked away from me. She zipped up her dress.

"Would you tell me how I'm supposed to seduce you if you won't let me touch you?" I asked.

I must have appeared pretty silly to her because she smiled and began to laugh. She pointed at me.

"You're not exactly the world's smoothest man in the boudoir."

"I may not be smooth, but I'm sincere." Smooth, I thought. Smooth.

She laughed, crossed demurely to me, and put her head on my shoulder.

"Poor Jackson," she said and sighed. "Long-suffering he is. What does Jackson want me to do?"

"He wants you to take off your dress," I said and thought how quickly they could change from iron maiden to kitten.

"Right here?" she asked. She stepped back and raised her palms. "Like a stripper?"

"You go in the bathroom," I said. "I'll cut down the lights."

I crossed to a lamp and switched it off. She watched me.

"You really want me to?" she asked. "I mean honest?"

"I might attack you if you don't," I said, which was about as big a lie as I'd ever told. In spite of her youth and prettiness, my passion had withered. I was nervous, and I sensed Kitt in the room, standing in a corner, her expression disapproving.

"All right," Val said, determined and brave. She walked into the bathroom. The light silhouetted her figure. "For you."

She turned her back, reached for the zipper, and lifted the dress to pull it over her head.

There was a knock on the front door. Val jerked down her dress and cringed.

"I told you!" she whispered. "It's the police."

"Don't get excited," I said, but I was alarmed. "Stay in the bathroom."

She peeked out through a crack. I switched on lights, straightened my tie, and crossed to the door. I unlocked it slowly.

"Hello, hello," the rodent said. "I forgot to show you about the TV. The fine tuning's tricky."

"We don't watch much TV," I said, guarding the door to keep him from pushing in.

"It's unusual for people not to watch TV," he said. He was trying to see around me into the room. His head swung from side to side. "It's practically miraculous." He grinned. "You haven't unpacked yet."

"We're cooling off."

"You don't have the air conditioner on."

"It hurts my sinuses."

"Maybe you'd like to order dinner. My wife's the cook. She also makes pies—pecan, brown sugar, vinegar."

"We've eaten and had dessert too."

"Check-out time is two o'clock," he said. "We have to clean up the rooms."

"We'll be leaving early," I said.

"Don't forget to turn in your key."

"We won't," I said and shut the door on him. I locked it, crossed to the bathroom, and tapped on the door.

"It's all right," I said. "You can come out."

Val opened the door half an inch. I saw her dark eye.

"He was checking on us," she said.

"Well, he didn't find anything."

225

"He might be telephoning the vice squad right now."

"I don't think this town's big enough to have a vice squad."

"Well, they have some sort of squad."

"You're a coward."

"I am not," she said and opened the door a little wider.

"Prove it," I said.

I went around the room cutting off lights. She stuck her head out and watched me. I removed my coat. She pulled back and closed the bathroom door.

I took off my tie and shirt. I sat on the bed to unlace my shoes. I folded my pants over a chair. I stood in the darkness and waited. I heard nothing from the bathroom.

Even in the dark I saw Kitt. She sat at the dressing table and waggled a finger at me. She chided me. I wanted to speak out, to tell her this wasn't whoring but an attempt by an aging man, to hold and have a little life. It would provide a mother for her son.

"You ought to approve of a girl like Val," I told Kitt.

"What?" Val asked from the bathroom.

"Nothing," I called.

I heard the click of the light switch, and the sound of the door opening. In the darkness I saw the milkiness of Val as she moved slowly and silently. She wore her slip. She held herself as if cold.

"What am I supposed to do now?" she asked. "Flop on the bed like a strumpet?"

I crossed to her and reached for her hand. Gently I pulled her to my side. I felt the softness of a warm arm and the silkiness of her slip. We walked to the bed. I put my arm around her waist. We sat down together.

As I leaned toward her to kiss her, there was a knock at the door. She jumped up and ran to the bathroom. I grabbed for my clothes. I put a foot into the wrong shoe.

The knocking was louder. I dressed and turned on lights. I thrust my arms into my coat. I stumbled to the door. I ran my hand over my hair. I unlocked the door.

The rodent was there. He held a small tray with a pitcher and two glasses on it.

"Mom thought you'd like some ice tea on a hot night like this," he said. "Mint ice tea. No charge."

I stared at him. My hand fluttered on the doorknob.

"She learned it from her grandmother who came from Knoxville," he said. "Grows mint right outside our kitchen door."

He shoved forward with the tray. I was forced to reach for it.

"It's very kind of you," I said.

"We want our guests to come back."

"We're turning in," I said. "We appreciate the tea, but we'd like not to be disturbed."

"You turning in without unpacking your bags?" he asked.

"We've got a bag in here. You just didn't see it."

"You do?" He tried to peek around me. I kept him blocked. "You must have sneaked out."

"I don't have to sneak out to get a bag."

"I meant you must have done it when I wasn't looking."

"Good night," I said and shut the door.

I locked it, carried the tray to the night table by the bed, and crossed to the bathroom.

She opened the door. She was fully dressed.

"He's spying on us," she said.

"Mom sent us some mint tea."

"In order to spy." She drew back. "He may be peeping in the windows."

I went around the room and adjusted all the blinds.

"He can't see in," I said. I switched out lights. "Would you kindly assume the state of dishabille you were in."

"I'm very jumpy," she said. "Why don't we do this some other time?"

"Now," I said, because I realized if this moment passed, we'd never again find it.

Reluctantly, she backed into the bathroom and shut the door. I removed my clothes down to my underwear and paced in the dark. I wondered whether seduction was so complicated for the great lovers of the world. I didn't understand how they kept their passion hot through the complex mechanics of preparation.

Moreover, Kitt was still in the room. She sat on a plastic chair and clucked her tongue at me.

"I'm doing it for Injun," I said.

"What?" Val called from the bathroom.

"I was clearing my throat."

Val opened the bathroom door. Again I went to her and led her to the bed. I rubbed her back above the slip. Her skin was warm. We sat. Very gently but firmly I pushed her onto her back. I lowered my head to kiss her.

"Jackson," she said.

"What?"

"Tell me about your wife."

"For God's sake!" I said and sat up. I glanced behind me. Kitt stood smiling in the center of the room.

"But you've never told me anything about her," Val said. She sat up.

"Now's not exactly the ideal time," I said. I frowned at Kitt. She had put the thought in Val's mind.

"Did you love her?"

"Of course I loved her. Now please shut up."

"Why don't you want to talk about her?"

"It's too painful," I said. I believed I heard Kitt giggle.

"Poor thing," Val said.

I took advantage of her pity to press her down on the bed and slid my hand across her stomach. I kissed her neck and chin. I worked toward her mouth.

"Jackson," she said.

"What?"

"May I have a glass of that mint tea?"

I groaned.

"The lobster made me thirsty," she said.

In the dark I poured her a glass of tea. She sat on the edge of the bed to drink it. When she finished, I set the glass on the tray.

"Is there anything else?" I asked.

"Don't sound so mean."

I put an arm around her waist and slid my hand down her stomach and along her thigh. I tried to raise her slip. I felt her stiffen and resist. I stood her and attempted to pull the slip over her head.

"What are you doing?" she asked.

"I'd appreciate it if you'd cooperate a little."

I had the slip halfway off her. Her arms were raised, and she stood knock-kneed in her stockings and girdle. Her face was covered by her slip. Something was snagged.

There was a knock on the door. She whimpered and stumbled about. Blinded by the slip, she felt for the bathroom. I thrashed around for my clothes. On the porch somebody turned the knob and pushed against the door.

I hit my shin on the foot of the bed. I moaned and hopped across the room. As I turned on lights, I heard a key being inserted into the lock. The little rodent had called the vice squad. Frantically I dressed.

The door shook. Cautiously I opened it. A tall, elderly man blinked at me. He still had his hand on the key. With the other hand he held a small dog. He looked astonished.

"What are you doing in my cabin?" he asked. "And where's my wife?"

"This isn't your cabin, and I don't know about your wife."

"Don't tell me this isn't my cabin," he said. His false teeth clicked with anger. "Bess!" he called. "Bess!"

"Sh-h-h," I said. "Look at your key."

Indignantly he pulled the key from the lock, held it up to catch the light, and read the number on the diamond-shaped celluloid slab. The number was that of the cabin next door. He smiled and did a little back step.

"I'm terribly sorry," he said. "I've never had an adequate sense of direction."

"Good night," I said and shut the door. I stood against it. I wiped my brow.

Val peeped out from the bathroom. She was again dressed.

"I'm wearing my clothes out putting them on and taking them off," she said. Her face was strained.

"Let's try one more time," I said.

"I don't think you really want to."

"Will you stop saying that?"

She sighed and closed the door. I switched off the lights and stripped down to my underwear. Kitt sat at the blond dressing table and grinned wickedly at me.

When Val came out, I led her quickly to the bed, put my arms around her, and moved her sideways. We fell to the bed and bounced on the mattress. I tried to put on a show of being passionate. I breathed steam, twisted, entwined, and gasped. All the while I knew Kitt stood above me and shook her finger.

I tried too enthusiastically. As we wrestled on the bed, I felt space at my back. I had to let go of Val or I'd have dragged her with me. I slammed to the floor. For a moment I was stunned. I lay on my back, my arms and legs in the air.

Val switched on the lamp. She peered over the bed at me. She started laughing.

"Lover," she said and tee-heed.

"I don't see the humor," I said. I sat up and rubbed the small of my back.

"You'll be black and blue in the morning." She laughed. In a corner of the room Kitt covered her mouth.

I felt skinny and abject. I wanted to roll under the bed. Wearily I pulled myself up. I sat beside Val. Before I could make a move, she captured both my hands in hers.

"It isn't going to work," she said. She was smiling, and her dark eyes were wet from laughing.

"Why not?" I asked, though I knew.

230

"Because you're nice," she said, and she sat there patting my hands. She reached to the night table for mint tea. She held the glass to my lips. I felt like an old man being ministered to.

"And you're sort of puritanical," she said. "You wouldn't really have approved."

It wasn't that I was puritanical. But how could I explain to her about Kitt who sat smug and pleased at the dressing table?

"So let's go home," Val said. She kissed my cheek.

"It's embarrassing," I said. "Think of what this does to my self-esteem."

"You're a very nice man."

"I don't want to be a very nice man."

"Well, you are anyway." She put her head on my shoulder. "Now let's get dressed."

"First thing you know we'll end up calling each other good friends," I said.

We sat holding hands and sipping mint tea. She again kissed my cheek, stood, and walked into the bathroom. I watched her shadow on the wall.

I put on my clothes. Val came out touching at her black hair. She straightened the bed. I left the key in the door. Holding each other around the waist, we went to my car.

As I backed, I saw Kitt on the porch of the cabin. She waved and blew a kiss.

[36]

I drove to Black Leaf and walked Val to her door. We were too tired even to sit on the swing. She touched my hand and walked inside.

I went home. Moonlight lay pale on the hot dusty land. When

I reached the house, all was dark except for a single light in the upstairs hallway. Bugs pinged against the screen.

Injun was asleep, lying naked and sprawled on his bed. Beside him was his flashlight and his bone-handled bowie knife. His store clothes were hung over a chair. The button eyes of a stuffed owl glowed yellow on top of a dresser.

I walked to my room. Propped against my pillow was a note on lined notebook paper. The scrawl was Injun's. It read, "Call Doc Sutter."

I didn't call him. I was worn out, and whatever he wanted could wait until tomorrow.

I did telephone the hospital. The lady at the desk told me the Carter boy was alive but in a coma.

I lay on my bed. I felt older than usual. As a lover I was a real bust. God, I'd probably lost her for good. I went to sleep thinking of her and the young doctor hurrying up the aisle with people throwing roses and rice at them.

In the morning I woke to smell bacon. I padded downstairs to find Injun cooking breakfast. He had my plate on the table. He was a good boy, and I should have somehow made him know I believed it.

"You're some cook," I said.

"I had to fix mine anyway."

I stared at him. He wore his white shirt, his bow tie, and his dark trousers. He didn't know how to accept kindness. That was my fault. I'd been so busy with my own private sadness that I hadn't anything left over for him.

"We ought to have a little talk," I said.

"About what?" he asked. He turned from the stove. His eyes were wide and innocent. He didn't realize I'd been neglecting him. Maybe he believed all fathers were sonsofbitches like me.

"Just a little father-son talk. You probably have some things on your mind."

"I been thinking of a real sale at the store."

232

"I'm not talking about the store."

"I don't get you," he said, puzzled.

He stood waiting for me to say something, but the words wouldn't form in my mouth.

"You're doing a good job," I said and turned away.

We went down to the store together. I told myself I'd talk to him later in the day, but the closer he drew to the cash register, the more he changed. He shucked off the boy and prowled for customers.

I wanted to say to him it was important he remain a boy, but he was too busy selling. There was always somebody in the store, and the phone rang. Trucks came with deliveries. I couldn't make him stand still.

I called the hospital. The lady at the desk told me the Carter child had spent a quiet night and had opened his eyes. The prognosis, she said, had improved.

I began to write checks for the invoices piled up on my desk. The front door opened and closed. I heard Sutter speak to Injun. Sutter walked to my office. The cuffs of his gray suit dragged the floor at his heels.

"You didn't call me," he said.

"You'll probably find it hard to believe, but sometimes I get tired of you."

"I'm not exactly enthusiastic about coming over here in the heat of the morning."

"The trouble with doctors is you're spoiled. A few years ago you wouldn't have been invited into the best homes."

"I'm not invited into the best homes now," he said. He sat in the chair by my desk and patted his face with his handkerchief. He eyed me. "You act as if I'm going to operate on you."

"You've been operating on me ever since you got me into this mess."

"It's a fact," he said and sighed. "Paul's really going to the congregation. He's going to lay it all out where everybody can see."

233

"He'll be sorry." I was through thinking about Paul. I had closed him out. I savored the bitterness of Val.

"You and I been priding ourselves on being fair," Sutter said. "We been telling ourselves we did our duty."

"I have," I said.

"You've done some," Sutter said. "You couldn't help it. It's in your blood to want to do right."

"You're greasing me."

"You saw him," Sutter said. "You saw him come tearing across that lawn, set himself, and lift that red convertible. You saw his muscles bunch until they looked as if they'd pop through his skin. No bastard did that."

I wanted to pound on the wall. I needed to be free. I thought of Val whom I should have made love to and maybe would have if I weren't drained by Paul.

"I believe in letting the past lie," Sutter said. "He may have been pure bastard once, but that don't mean now."

"I thought you believed in patterns."

"I also believe in regeneration and redemption." He dabbed at his face. "It's remarkable how stupid we've been. We don't know hardly anything."

"We know more than enough."

"About him, yes. Not about her."

I closed my eyes. Val had talked the same way last night. I thought of Caroline—contained, untouchable.

"Lou brought her to town," Sutter said. "All we really know is what she told us."

"I'm not listening."

"You ever met any of her kin?"

"I don't want to meet any of her kin."

"She never goes to visit anybody. You'd think she'd have some kin down in South Carolina, her being from such an old family and all."

"You're forcing it."

"You'd think she'd have a sister or cousin drop by her house to say howdy, but I never heard of it."

"It doesn't mean a thing," I said. "Some people are loners." I thought that even when she was with Lou or her daughters, she looked alone.

"But everybody's got somebody," Sutter argued. He wiped his lips with the wad of handkerchief. "And southern people are friendly and visit."

"I'm not friendly and I don't visit."

"You're excluding a certain young schoolteacher," he said.

"I'm not hearing you," I said, turning away from him.

"Now suppose Caroline don't want to see somebody for a reason. What sort of reason would that be?"

"Come off it."

Sutter again sighed. He looked out the doorway to see where Injun was and lowered his voice.

"I been searching for a connection," he said. "I been lying awake trying to find it."

Slowly I turned back to him.

"He played football down there," Sutter said. "They might have known each other previously."

Silent at the implication, I stared at him.

"It ought to be checked out," he said.

"I have a store to run," I said finally. "Find somebody else."

"Who?"

"Wayland."

"You know better. Wayland's blind."

Wayland was blind, but I was thinking what would I do with it if I did find something about Caroline. I'd just as soon hold a viper.

"No," I said and stood.

"Shame," Sutter said.

"You can't come in here and talk to me like that in my own store," I said. I walked out of the office.

235

He came after me, his eyes rheumy, his expression mournful. I went into the storeroom and stood among iron stoves I'd never been able to sell. I heard Sutter wait out there a moment. His steps to the door were slow. It opened and closed. When I looked, he was gone.

[37]

He had, however, put the burden on me. I carried it around with me the rest of the day as I helped Injun run the store. After we locked up and went home, I fixed dinner while he fed the dogs. Later I sat on the porch and was gnawed by what Sutter had suggested.

The telephone rang. I didn't answer it. I was afraid Sutter was still tracking me. I told myself I ought to get Injun and take him fishing on the river. I felt too tired.

I thought of calling Val. I wouldn't know what to say to her. I was ashamed of last night. She wouldn't understand about Kitt. Val would just consider me bumbling and inadequate.

I propped my feet on the railing and smoked. I waited for some coolness to come in, some movement of the soggy air, but the night was so still not even a tree toad croaked.

I heard a car on the highway turn at my road. I watched the headlights shine on the loblollies. The car came so slowly and rattled so noisily that I believed it was Sutter again. I went into the house. I would not answer the door for him.

The car nosed up my drive as if unsure which way to proceed. A rabbit hopped unhurriedly away from the headlights. The car circled in the wrong direction, hesitated, and backed. It stopped in front of my porch. I stood away from my screen door.

"Mr. LeJohn?" a woman's voice called. She sounded apologetic.

I walked onto my porch and down the steps. A shadowy figure had opened the car door. She put a foot to the ground. It was Helen Elgin. She looked as if she meant to flee if I were displeased.

"Do you have a minute?" she asked and pushed at the loose strand of brown hair that fell against her temple. "I promise I'll hurry."

Though I felt like running out into the deep darkness of the pines, I had to ask her in. I walked with her to the steps and held her tense elbow as we went up to the porch. I seated her on the swing. I sat on a wicker chair. A light from the hall, stained pink from a painted globe, touched her face and made her seem to glow from within.

She was distraught. She kept pushing at her hair. She wore a plain, sexless cotton dress. Her rough hands moved in her lap, changing position in a gentle, silent slapjack.

"I realize it's late," she said, her voice so soft, so whispery, I leaned toward her. "I telephoned but nobody answered."

She pushed her low-heeled, old-woman shoes against the porch and caused the swing to move slightly.

"I know I shouldn't thrust myself on you like this." She looked at her hands. "I hope you realize it's difficult for me."

She was beat down and broken even before Paul got into trouble. The reason wasn't her children. Rather, it was the women working on her, women of the congregation, who felt they owned her just as they owned the rugs in the church and could criticize her for what she wore, the way she kept the manse, and the number of times she conceived. She was their meat.

"I'll be as brief as I can," she said, her hands continuing to top each other in her lap. Her squat, ugly shoes tapped the floor. "First let me say Paul doesn't know I'm here."

Maybe, I thought. Some men would use their wives.

"I just had to talk to you," she said. "He won't tell me things. He thinks it worries me if he puts his troubles on me, but it worries me more not knowing."

237

Her face moved in and out of the pink light.

"I need to know where we stand," she said. Her hands rubbed each other.

"Stand?" I asked.

"In the church here," she said, and her toes tapped the floor. She swung in and out of the pink light.

"We've asked Paul to leave," I said. There was no way to make it soft.

"Ah," she said and swallowed. Her hands became still. "He's a good man. I know my husband, and he's a good man."

"We voted."

"Then you made a mistake." Her eyes reflected the light. "No husband can fool his wife."

I understood she had to stick up for him. I just hoped she wouldn't break down and cause a scene.

"You all don't know how hard he works for this congregation," she said. "He's worked until he reeled, but he never showed it to anybody except me."

She swung in and out of the pink light.

"You're lucky to have him," she said. "For the little bit of money you pay him, he's giving everything for you."

It was the first time I'd ever seen her show temper. Her lips were small, and her hands wrenched at each other. Then, as if repentant, she lowered her eyes, and her hands quieted.

"You believe everything Caroline Gaines says. Why do you take her word over a man sworn to serve God?"

"There's evidence," I answered, being drawn into it against my will.

"What evidence?"

"I'm not free to discuss it."

"People can make evidence."

"We know that."

"You can't blame him for his past," she said.

"What about his past?" I asked.

"He was a terrible man once, Mr. LeJohn, but that's done, and if you keep on you'll destroy him."

There was nothing I could answer. We sat in the dark, she swinging in and out of the light. Time stretched between us. In the distance a dog barked.

"You must be very sure," she said.

"We're as sure as we can be."

"Do you think I'd be able to come here if he did that awful thing?" she asked. Her hands climbed on top of each other, and her eyes flashed in the pink light. She leaned toward me. "What about Caroline Gaines? She wears tight dresses and flaunts her body. A woman who does that is asking for men."

I wouldn't speak for Caroline. I was not a court.

"She walks down the street slick and perfumed," Helen said. "She's the one you should go to."

I shifted forward as if to stand.

"She knows how to handle you," Helen said. "She shows a leg and bats her eyes and men fall over themselves trying to wait on her."

Helen put her feet down hard and stopped swinging.

"Let me tell you something," she said. "It would be a terrible thing for you to be wrong about a man of God. It would be one of the worst things anybody could do. Therefore you must be very certain."

She pushed up slowly from the swing. She looked so worn and used I held out a hand to her and helped her down the steps. I opened the door of her car.

She had difficulty starting the engine of the old Dodge. I leaned into the window to adjust the choke. She smelled of soap. The engine fired, and oily blue fumes rolled up from the rusted exhaust.

"Thank you for listening to me," she said.

She was crying.

" 'The way of the just man is sweet in the sight of the Lord,' " she said.

She gunned the engine, sending up more blue fumes, and drove off cautiously. I watched her car move slowly down the driveway and slide into blackness under the pines.

I went upstairs, undressed, and lay on my bed. I was sticky with sweat. I clenched my eyes, but finally I had to stand and walk through the dark hallway to the telephone. I dialed Sutter's number.

The telephone rang nine times before he answered it.

"Damn you," I told him.

"I've been waiting for you to call," he said. "Since she's a member of the gentry, surely somebody down there will remember."

[38]

So I was on the road again, this time driving to South Carolina. My tires sizzled on the black highway that lay soft as a serpent in the yellow sun. Heat withered the land. Streams had stopped flowing, crops were burned and bent, and cattle hung their heads in fields of blanched stubble.

I had a flat before I reached the college town. The tire blew on a road so straight that it seemed to lead off the world itself. Rubber thumped softly against asphalt.

I pulled onto a sandy shoulder and rolled up my sleeves. While I worked, cars shot past me and flapped the sweaty shirt on my back.

By the time I reached the college town, I was half sick with heat. I found an old hotel—a red brick building with cupolas and gables. On the steps of the veranda were stone urns with nothing growing out of them. Pigeons circled, and their wings sounded heavy on the acrid air.

"There's a breeze at night," the clerk said, explaining the ab-

240

sence of air conditioning. He was a young man in a rumpled cream-colored suit. His pearl tie had a spot of catchup on it.

A colored boy carried my bag to my room and opened the two windows. The room was furnished with a black table, black dresser, and a black bed. There was an oval rug which had once had a flower design, but the design had been walked out years before. In the bathroom was an old-fashioned light fixture that hung down from the ceiling on an electric cord. The globe had dead bugs in it. I tipped the colored boy fifty cents.

"I want lots of ice," I told him.

I turned on the bathtub, and water gurgled out slowly. At first it was rusty. I peeled off my clothes and lay in the tub. I mixed a drink, sat in the tub, and swished water over my legs and stomach.

As soon as I dried myself, I was again sweaty and weak. I had a second drink. I stood in the room and drooped like the stunted corn. Somewhere in the town a bell rang. I looked out a window and saw pigeons swooping to burned grass.

I tried to think about Caroline. It was easy enough for Sutter to say somebody would remember her, but I had to have a start. At this hour the college offices would be closed. I rattled my ice and crossed to the thin directory under the black telephone.

Her maiden name was Van Meissen, and if she were from around here, she ought to have family. I ran my finger down the names, fast the first time, more slowly the second. There were no Van Meissens.

Of course she could have just attended the college. It was a small, prestige school which drew its students from wealthy families, many of them in the North. Perhaps she was from the eastern part of the state. I'd imagined her living near the coast, a place of salty rivers, Spanish moss, crinolines, and white mansions.

I dressed, carried my coat over my arm, and rode downstairs on the shaky elevator. At the desk I stopped to talk to the clerk, who was reading a newspaper spread over the switchboard.

"Dining room open?" I asked. Through a glass door covered by gauzy curtains I saw tables.

"We close summers," he said. "When the market opens, we do."

"I need a place to eat."

"Try the Rice House across the street." He was looking at me, but he turned a page of the newspaper.

"Do you happen to know any Van Meissens around here?" I asked.

"Who?"

"Van Meissen. It's supposed to be an old name in this state."

As he thought, he rubbed his nose. The tip of it bent as if made of rubber. "Know some Meskins," he said. "Charley and Alfred Meskins run the Planters Warehouse."

"Van Meissen," I said a third time.

"I don't know Van."

I thanked him and thought I wasn't destined to have anything easy.

I walked out of the hotel and down the steps between the stone urns. I crossed the street to the Rice House. Over the doorway was a neon sign of a Creole chef wearing a large mushroom-shaped hat. He winked and motioned one in with a spoon.

The restaurant was cool and smelled of fish frying. I sat in a booth. A girl in a blue uniform brought me a menu. She had black hair, olive skin, and very red lips. She tapped her pencil languidly against her order pad.

"Just salad and iced tea," I said. I thought of the tea Val and I'd had at the motel. "No mint."

The waitress crossed to the counter where her boyfriend sat— a muscular young man with brown arms that swelled against his tight white shirt. As she gave the order to the cook, she leaned against the young man with proprietary intimacy.

"Do you know anybody named Van Meissen?" I asked when she brought my tea.

She eyed me suspiciously, sure I was trying to pick her up. Her boyfriend frowned. His red hair was thin on the sides and high in the center.

"Van Meissen," I said. "An old name around here."

"No," she said and started away.

"You never heard of it?" I called after her. She stopped, turned, and watched me.

"I been living around here all my life and never have," she said and returned to the protection of her boyfriend. They glanced at me and talked.

I told myself it didn't mean anything that neither she nor the hotel clerk knew the Van Meissens. They would not read the social columns. In the morning I'd go to the college where even if there were no records on Caroline, surely somebody would be familiar with the name.

I ate my limp salad, drank my tea, and left a tip for the waitress. I wanted to look around the town, but it was too hot. I crossed to the hotel and sat in the lobby. An electric fan moved air over dusty palm plants.

Several men sat reading and talking in old leather chairs. Their voices were so southern, they made mine sound Yankeefied. One of the men was a tractor parts salesman. He was red-faced, and his belly thrust against his thick belt.

"They take cheap labor and cheap steel and knock together shoddy you wouldn't want to plow a three-legged mule with," he said angrily. "Now I sell quality products, and I swear we ought to have some protection in this country for first-class merchandise. In the long run it's in the farmers' interest."

I moved from chair to chair until I was closer. At first I didn't speak. I sat and listened so they'd have a chance to look me over. When they rubbed their eyes and stretched their legs, I introduced myself.

"Any of you gents heard of a family around here by the name of Van Meissen?" I asked.

"Mason?" they asked, staring at me.

"Meissen. M-e-i-s-s-e-n."

They glanced at each other and shook their heads.

"No," they agreed. "Not in these parts."

"I never heard of it," the tractor salesman said. "And I travel up dog paths."

Before I went to my room, I stopped at the desk to buy a magazine. The night clerk was a woman, graying and smiling sweetly. I asked her about the Van Meissens.

"I'm not a native," she said. "I come from Crabcreek."

"Where's that?" I asked.

"Down the road about twenty-five miles."

"And you're not a native?"

"Different county," she said.

[39]

I went to my room and sat on the bed. Pigeons walked the tin roof and gutters. The bell was ringing. I stripped to my shorts, switched out the lights, and waited for the breeze to come. It never did.

I wrestled sleep. The heat would wake me, and I'd go to the bathroom to wash my face, neck, arms, and chest. I'd then sit on the bed until I was so tired I'd topple over.

At dawn I was dressed and downstairs. Nobody was in the lobby. I walked through the town. Palm trees drooped motionless in front of the white courthouse. I heard the bell. It was part of the clock in the courthouse steeple. I stopped at the bus station for toast and coffee.

At nine o'clock exactly I drove to the college at the west edge of town. I passed plantation-style fraternity houses. Students, appearing gentlemanly in coats and ties, rocked on verandas.

I parked in shade and followed signs to the Registrar's Office.

His secretary was just sitting at her desk. She showed me in immediately.

The registrar was young, hardly thirty, and in the brightly lighted, air-conditioned room, he acted competent and precise.

"I appreciate your problem," he said. He adjusted a line of yellow pencils on his desk. "I'm afraid, however, we don't make our files public."

"I'm not asking you to do anything wrong," I argued. "Just help me locate the family."

He was thoughtful as he squared his calender with the base of his fluorescent lamp.

"I can't see any real harm in it," he said. "Give me a minute."

He left me sitting in front of his desk. I stood and looked out the clean windows at the campus. There were live oak trees and brick colonial buildings. A few students moved about, careful to stick to the shade.

The registrar came back. As he sat, he jerked at creases in his pants.

"My secretary's going through the index," he said. "It'll only take a few seconds."

While we waited, he asked where I was from. He told me he had an uncle in Norfolk. A buzzer sounded. He picked up the telephone.

"You double-checked it?" he asked.

He put down the telephone and shook his head.

"Nothing."

"Not a single one?" I asked.

"Nary," he answered and smiled to let me know he realized he was using a country word.

Out the window I saw a silver convertible drive by. Young men and women were waving their hands and laughing, but I couldn't hear them in the vacuum of the office.

"And you're not familiar with the name?" I asked.

"I'm from Tennessee."

"Where would you go if you needed to find a family?" I asked.

245

If I could only have talked to Lou Gaines—but that was impossible. He would never forgive my checking on Caroline.

"Born around here?" the registrar asked.

"I'm not certain."

"Well," he said and rubbed his nose thoughtfully. "Try the courthouse. They might have a birth certificate on record."

I thanked him, shook his hand, and crossed to the door. I turned.

"You ever hear of Paul Elgin?" I asked.

He stood. He walked me through his secretary's office and out into the corridor. On the walls were colored photographs. One, enlarged to the size of a portrait, was of Paul. He was in his uniform and had one knee on the ground. He held a football. He was young and strong, with outcroppings of muscles in his arms and face. His black hair was thick and tangled. His light blue eyes were shiny. His teeth were square and bright. He felt his power. If a man could be called beautiful, he was.

"He's the only super star we ever had," the registrar told me. "People still ask about him. Handsome brute, eh?"

"Yes," I said. "You know anything about him?"

"Just what's in the record books. He was obviously before my time."

He smiled, proud of his youth and success, a man still untouched by the aches of age and a knowledge of death.

[40]

I drove back to town and parked behind the courthouse. From the shadowy barred windows of the jail I heard voices, but no faces peered out.

In the courthouse I followed signs to the second floor and

entered the Clerk's Office. At a counter stood a pretty young brunette with a pencil in her mouth. She leafed through a ledger.

"We might and we might not," she said after I told her what I wanted. "There's a Bureau of Vital Statistics at Columbia. A person can have his birth certificate registered here, but he doesn't have to."

"Would you look for me?"

"I'm not supposed to do the looking," she said, indicating the shelves of large brown ledgers.

"I'd be glad to pay you."

"I wasn't hinting about that," she said. She smiled. "And I don't mind doing the looking."

She lifted down ledgers and went through them. She went into another room where I heard her open drawers and file cabinets. I sat on a wooden bench and smoked a cigarette. In the heat I felt sleepy.

"Sorry," the girl said when she came back. She lifted her palms and shook her head.

"Were there any Van Meissens?" I asked.

"I found none. It doesn't necessarily mean anything. As I told you, a person doesn't have to be registered here."

"What about real-estate transactions?"

"It would take days to go through the deed books," she said and her expression was wary—as if I might ask her to do it.

Behind her was a door with CLERK painted on it in black letters. I looked at it.

"Would you like to talk to Mr. Braxton?"

"If he could spare me a minute."

She went to the door, tapped on it, and entered. I heard her talking. She came back and opened a gate in the counter for me. She led me into the office.

Mr. Braxton stood from his desk. He was a tall, elderly man as white as cotton. His skin seemed to have no pigment. Even his fingernails appeared white—like a leper's.

247

"Offhand I can't recall," he said. He pursed his lips. "Van Meissen?"

"Most names would come through this office, wouldn't they?" I asked.

"Well, a lot of names certainly do come through here, and I pride myself on knowing them. Still, I can't recall a Van Meissen."

"I had an idea they were landed gentry."

"You sure they're from Barefoot County?"

"I'm not sure of anything."

"I'd of heard of them if they were from Barefoot."

I thanked him and his pretty secretary and left the courthouse. I walked up the street. I thought of going home. I stopped in a drugstore and drank a Big Orange.

I went toward the hotel. Heat rose from the sidewalk and stung my face and eyes. As I passed a ten-cent store, the hot oily smell of popcorn wrenched my stomach.

At the corner was a brick building with a lawyer's shingle hanging on it. I walked past it, turned back, and climbed the scuffed brown steps. I followed signs tacked along a hallway until I reached a glass door with the name McPeak painted on it in gold letters. I pushed open the door.

McPeak was talking on the telephone but waved me in. He was a tanned, rotund man with a pipe in his teeth. He put down the telephone and came into the outer office for me. He slapped my shoulder as if he'd known me all my life.

"Yes, sir, yes, sir, yes, sir," he said, leading me into his office. "Mr. Jackson LeJohn from Virginia. How come you're in our fine town, Mr. LeJohn?"

He seated me, and I told him, but he didn't seem to be listening. Instead he loaded his bulldog pipe. He scraped the bowl before tamping in tobacco. He tested the draw.

"You're asking for information only?" he said, his face half teeth as he gripped his pipe in them. He struck a match.

"I'm trying to find the family."

"What'd they do to you?"

"They didn't do anything to me."

"What'd you do to them?"

"I've never met them."

"What you want them for?"

"I want to talk with them," I said, feeling as if I were on the witness stand.

"About a legal problem?"

"About a personal matter."

"Ah," he said and grinned around the pipe. "It involves a woman. Tell me I'm right."

"You're right."

"I knew it," he said and sucked the pipe. "I can always discern when it involves a woman." He puffed. "Want to confide in me?"

"Have you heard of people called Van Meissen?"

"What's the name again?"

"Van Meissen."

"No, sir," he said. He puffed. "I can tell you I don't know that name."

"If you were me, where would you look?"

"Try the courthouse," he said.

"I did."

"Did you speak to the sheriff?"

"This family isn't in trouble—at least it isn't as far as I know."

"The sheriff is an elected official. He makes it his business to keep in touch with voters."

"Thanks," I said and stood.

"No charge," he said.

I went down to the street and walked behind the courthouse to the jail. As I passed barred windows, I heard a discordant note strummed on a guitar.

The sheriff's office was in the basement. Just inside the door was a squad room where a deputy read a copy of *Life* magazine. A teletype clicked. Until I spoke, the deputy didn't glance at me.

"Is the sheriff here?" I asked.

The deputy continued to read but pointed down the corridor.

I walked on concrete floor until I reached an office where a radio played hillbilly music. I thought of the Progress Store. The sheriff, a large young man in a khaki uniform and cowboy boots, was talking to a Negro. The Negro wore a dark suit which was spotted and torn. He held his hat.

"We're tired of picking you up," the sheriff said. "You tell us where you get your moon and we'll fix it so you can't buy no more."

"I'm not tired of living yet," the Negro said. On his suit were beggar lice.

"We'll protect you," the sheriff said. He wore his golden cowboy hat pushed back on his head.

"You can't protect me in the dark," the Negro said and looked around him as if he thought it might be night pretty quick.

"One of these days we'll have to send you to a place where the moon never shines," the sheriff said. "Skedaddle and don't bother me nomore."

The Negro hurried on tiptoes down the corridor.

The sheriff removed his hat and plopped it on his desk. Along the left side of his scalp was a scar two or three inches long. His sandy hair was combed over the scar.

"He gets mooned and lies around in the ditches," the sheriff said, propping his feet on a drawer. "Never hurt anybody in his life, but the ladies complain. Can't have citizens lying around in the ditches." He pointed to a chair in front of his desk. "Come sit awhile and tell me what I can do for you."

His green eyes, clear and hard, moved over me carefully. His smile meant nothing. It was part of his uniform—like his badge or the big pearl-handled pistol that clunked against his chair.

I sat and asked him about the Van Meissens. With a jackknife he poked at the sole of a boot. The boots were black and inlaid with white leather diamonds.

"Could be before my time," he said, frowning. "But I surely ain't heard of a Van Meissen." He scratched the back of his neck with the knife. "Ash!" he hollered at the door.

The deputy who'd been sitting in the squad room came up the corridor. He still held the copy of *Life*.

"You ever hear of a Van Meissen?" the sheriff asked.

"A family," I explained.

The deputy's mouth sucked in as if he were chewing the information like a gumdrop.

"There's Vaughans in the south end," he said.

"Van," I said. "V-a-n."

The deputy stared at me. He shook his head as if he didn't want to disturb his neck.

"Nope," he said.

"Sorry we can't fix you up," the sheriff said.

"You're no sorrier than I am." I thought of the long hot drive to Black Leaf.

"In a squeeze, huh?" the sheriff asked. He ran his fingers over the scar on his scalp, adjusting the hair to it.

"Steamrollered."

He lifted his boots off the drawer and let them bang to the floor.

"There might be a fellow who can help," he said. He reached for his hat. "My father was sheriff forty years. If Van Meissens lived here, he'd know."

We walked out of the courthouse basement.

"He's sometimes difficult to talk to," the sheriff said. He flicked lint off the arm of his khaki uniform. "He's been poorly lately. If he acts peculiar, don't pay no attention."

He drove me in his police car. A metal rack between us held tear gas grenades and a riot gun. We went several miles past the college, turned right on a dirt road, and stopped at the edge of a ten-acre field which had a small, white boxlike house in the exact center of it. There were no trees or shrubbery.

We left the car and walked toward the house. The grass was dusty and dry under our feet. Two large dogs, German shepherds, raced toward us. They circled and snarled. The sheriff talked quietly.

"My father has some ideas," the sheriff told me as we moved slowly toward the house. The dogs still circled. "He believes hoods are after him. He won't have trees here because he's afraid hoods'll use them to hide behind and slip up on him."

The dogs sniffed at us, bared their teeth, and snapped at our heels. I stayed close to the sheriff.

"Don't come no nearer!" a voice shouted from the house.

We stopped. The dogs growled.

"Now, Daddy," the sheriff said. He winked at me.

"Root them feet to the ground," the voice ordered. "You searched him?"

"He don't need to be searched."

"You go over him or back off."

Apologetically, the sheriff turned to me.

"Don't pay no attention," he whispered as he ran his hands lightly over my pockets and down the outside and up the inside of my legs. He stood and again faced the house. "He's clean."

"Under his arms!" the voice commanded.

The sheriff patted me along my ribs.

"Nothing," the sheriff called toward the house.

"Come up slow," the voice said.

We walked to the steps. Growling, the dogs moved beside us. We climbed the stoop. The sheriff stopped me from stepping on the mat.

"He's got an alarm bell under there," the sheriff explained.

"You quit telling where I got my alarms," the voice said. "Now I have to change it. I sometimes think you want to see me dead. Isaac, get on out there."

A colored boy in shorts appeared and unlocked the storm door. The door had strips of steel across the screen. There were half a dozen locks. The colored boy was shirtless and shoeless. He was blackshiny with sweat. He held the door open. The sheriff urged me in.

"Stand right there!" the voice commanded as soon as I had one foot in the house. A strong light flashed into my eyes. I raised a hand to shield them. I couldn't see beyond the light.

"Where you from, mister?" the voice asked.

"He's from Virginia, Daddy," the sheriff answered.

"You don't have to do his talking, do you? He's got a tongue, don't he?"

"Yes, sir," I said.

"You know Red Randal?" the voice asked.

"No."

"Pat Angle?"

"No."

"I put them all away. They could've sent you to get me."

"I'll vouch for him," the sheriff said.

"What does a baby face like you know?" the voice asked angrily. "All you ever learned is to shake hands and smile at the ladies. Red Randal killed three men."

"I looked this fellow over good," the sheriff said.

"You don't know how to look anybody over. You ain't even learned how to jissom good yet."

I was still shielding my eyes. The colored boy, Isaac, held the door. The sheriff's expression was patient.

"Daddy, you're not being polite," he said.

"I'm alive because I ain't polite."

"Am I supposed to keep holding the door?" Isaac asked.

"You hold it if I tell you to hold it," the voice said. "I pay you to hold it, and you stand there and hold it all day if I tell you to."

Isaac rolled his eyes upward and exhaled.

"I'm surrounded by bastards who want me dead."

"Now, Daddy," the sheriff said.

"Shut up. You from Virginia, you can come in a little, but if you move sudden I'll shoot your pecker off."

I wasn't anxious to budge. The sheriff touched me gently from behind. I took two steps. The strong light was still aimed at my face.

"Stop!" the voice said.

The light snapped off. For a moment I was unable to focus. The old man seemed to rise from the red dusk of my eyes. He sat in a wheelchair, hunched forward as if he'd spring. He was wrinkled and hulking. A fly buzzed around his bald head.

In one hand he held an outsized flashlight and in the other a horse pistol. The horse pistol was aimed at me. His meaty face was pulled in at the mouth as if his lips held a curse.

He wore dark pants and a white shirt buttoned at the collar. His swollen feet were thrust into a pair of leather slippers which had been slit to allow his toes to wiggle free. Under his weight the tubular steel wheelchair appeared frail.

"State your business," he ordered me. His skin was venous, but in spite of the heat he had no sweat on him. The horse pistol was aimed at my navel. His hand did not shake.

"I told him you might be able to answer a few questions," the sheriff said. He stood at my shoulder.

"Let him mouth it," the old man said, flicking the horse pistol impatiently.

"I'm after information about a family," I said.

"Why should I give you information when I never seen you before? The Butcher brothers could have sent you to stick a knife in my belly."

"He don't have a knife," the sheriff said.

"You didn't look in his shoes," the old man said, his expression crafty. "He could have a blade lying along the sole of his foot."

"Now, Daddy, you're not going to do that to him."

"Take them off," the old man said, jabbing the horse pistol in my direction.

Leaning my back against the wall, I removed my shoes and socks. The old man watched me closely. He snapped on the flashlight, peered at my feet, and grunted. He spun in the wheelchair and thrust himself down the hall.

I put on my socks and shoes. The sheriff and I walked after his father. At the end of the hall we turned into a darkened room.

On nails driven into plaster hung rifles, pistols, and shotguns. The old man was at the window peeking out a drawn blind.

"Rest yourself," the sheriff said. He indicated a chair, the only one in the room. There was no other furniture. A TV set was on the floor.

"I didn't ask him to sit," the old man protested. He released the blind, and it slapped against the window.

"A man comes out here in the heat of the day and you cuss at him and don't offer him no ice water," the sheriff said. "Some hospitality."

The old man's petulance and suspicion turned to remorse. He sank into his wheelchair. His arms hung down alongside the aluminum wheels. The horse pistol lay across his lap.

"I seen too much," he said. "I lived with the law, and men are waiting to get me for it." Again he peeked through the blind. "They're out there loading up."

"Nobody's out there, Daddy," the sheriff said. He leaned against the doorframe.

"Don't tell me what is and isn't!" the old man shouted. His shiny veined hand curled around the horse pistol. "There's men who swore before God to take my blood."

"Bring some ice water," the sheriff told the colored boy Isaac. Isaac started down the hall.

"Wait a minute," the old man said. "He's my boy and he gets the ice water when I tell him to. I pay his wages, and I got that right." The old man glared at his son. He then turned to Isaac. "Get the water."

Isaac brought it in a large pitcher painted with yellow flowers. Ice clinked. He had a stack of Dixie cups. In the close heat of the house, the water was thick and sweet on the tongue.

The old man watched me drink. From his shirt pocket he pulled a pair of glasses with steel frames. He put them on to examine me.

"You're no lawman," he said. "I can smell a lawman."

"He just wants some information," the sheriff said.

"How you know he ain't trying to memorize the layout and carry it to Red Randal?" the old man asked. "Then Red could come sneaking up during the night." His old hand moved to the horse pistol. "Not that it'd do him any good. I got alarms nobody can find but me."

He nodded and looked sly. Sweat filled and ran down creases of my body. In appeal I glanced at the sheriff.

"Talk to him, Daddy," the sheriff said.

"How can I talk to him when I don't know what he wants?" the old man asked and peeked through the blind.

"He's inquiring about a family," the sheriff said.

"The Van Meissens," I said.

"I told him if anybody knew, you would," the sheriff said.

The old man squinted and frowned. He squinched up his nose. He shook his head.

"Nobody by that name ever lived around here."

Again I thought of the hot drive to Black Leaf. Sutter and I should have tried to find some sort of record on Caroline there— her Social Security number maybe or perhaps information through the Credit Bureau. At any rate, I gave up.

In front of the house was an explosion. The old man shouted and threw himself out of the wheelchair to the floor. Involuntarily the rest of us squatted, including Isaac with the pitcher.

We heard the sound of a truck coasting down a grade. We looked at each other.

"Come on, Daddy," the sheriff said. He helped his father back into the wheelchair.

"They could've killed me," the old man said. "They could've bought a surplus bazooka and stood over there in the woods to pop at me. I have to get more trees removed."

"You cut all the trees off your land," the sheriff said.

"Then I'll buy me some more land. I got to be ready for Red."

He was frightened. He shook so violently the wheelchair rattled. The horse pistol thumped against his leg.

"I've seen the murder in the soul of man," he said. "Once you've seen that you can never live in peace again. Man's soul is black and it stinks of death." He sniffled, and the horse pistol thumped against his lap. "I've seen it."

"The Van Meissens, Daddy," the sheriff reminded him. "You never heard of them?"

"I was in public office for forty years," the old man flared. "I know every rut and hollow in this county. There was nobody by that name even among the niggers."

Isaac, standing by, didn't flinch. Maybe he'd taught himself not to hear the word.

"Perhaps in some other part of the state," I said. "They were supposed to be prominent."

"Ha!" the old man said. "I've known eight governors well enough to shake their hands. I've known attorney generals, committeemen, and congressmen. Anybody prominent I had to know. There were no Van Meissens."

He peeked out the window. I thanked him and indicated to the sheriff I was ready to go. We started from the room.

Behind us, the old man snickered. The sound was wheezy and turned into a cackle. I eyed the sheriff. He shrugged.

"I just had a thought," the old man said.

"What, Daddy?"

"Prominent were they, the Van Meissens?"

"Supposed to be," I said.

The old man looked canny—as if he were going to horse trade.

"Meissen," he said and cackled. He worked his tongue in his mouth. "Mice."

"Huh?" the sheriff asked.

"Meissen and mice," the old man said. "Mices we used to call them."

"Who?" I asked.

"There was a family of them around here in the thirties," the old man said. "The father tarred roofs and cleaned furnaces. He named all his sons after millionaires. There was a John D. Rockefeller Mice, a J. P. Morgan Mice, and a Henry Ford Mice." He cackled. "They weren't exactly prominent."

"Speak it out, Daddy," the sheriff said.

"The father's name," the old man said. As he laughed, air fluted his nose. The laughter had a different quality about it. It sounded like the response to a dirty joke.

"What about the father's name?" I asked.

"He was Commodore Vanderbilt Mice," the old man said. He laughed tears and rubbed his eyes. "We called him Vanderbilt—and Van."

"Van Mice," I said. Not Caroline, I thought.

"He was flushed out of Tennessee by the TVA," the old man said. "A bunch of Tennessee sodbusters came up here with government money and swarmed over the county like hungry termites." He laughed. "Commodore Vanderbilt Mice. A name like that had to come from Tennessee."

I shook my head. Impossible to think of the elegant, untouchable Caroline as kin to a bearded, sweat-soured hillbilly.

"Commodore Vanderbilt Mice wasn't even a good sodbuster," the old sheriff said. "He lost his hog farm and lived in what we called the Hardtime Tract south of town." He cackled. "We always made a point of standing upwind of him."

"Did he have a daughter?" I asked.

The old man looked hard at me. He turned to the colored boy. "Get on out of here, Isaac."

Carrying the pitcher, the colored boy left. The old sheriff winked and lowered his voice. His face became lewd.

"Out of horse manure pretty flowers do grow. The fraternity boys nailed them red shoes to the powder room door."

Book Four

[41]

I left South Carolina in the late afternoon. I hadn't eaten anything since breakfast, and as I drove I was numb. I became a part
of the shimmering heat and the hiss of my tires on the hot black
road.

I carried words which had dropped from the sly, salacious
mouth of the old man. He'd been precise in details, but my mind
short-circuited the pictures. I kept shaking my head as if arguing
with somebody in the car.

I didn't reach my house until almost three in the morning. I
sat at the kitchen table, too tired to climb steps. Red ants trailed
across the checkered linoleum and up to the sink. I felt I'd been
on a jag.

Using the railing, I pulled myself up stairs. I fell face down on
the bed. I never turned over.

Sun woke me. I took off my clothes, washed, and dressed.
Before eight o'clock I was in town. I squinted against the sun. As
I drove to the manse, I was shaky in the stomach.

I went up the walk where dandelions grew in cracks and
knocked on the door.

Paul answered my knock. He wore a T-shirt, rolled-up khaki
pants, and no shoes. He hadn't yet shaved, and beard darkened
his face.

"Let's go to your study," I said.

He put on tennis shoes, and we walked across the grass. The
sun had already burned away the morning wetness. We went
through the garden. He held the study door open for me.

Sun reflected on the golden trophy. I thought of the picture I'd seen of Paul at the college—young, powerful, heroic. This morning he appeared soft and aging.

"You're acting pretty mysterious," he said. He rubbed at the sleep in his eyes.

"I won't be mysterious long," I said. "I've been to South Carolina."

"Hope you had a pleasant trip." He sat on the old sofa.

"I was studying genealogy," I said. "Particularly of a family named Mice. Ever hear of them?"

His light blue eyes swerved from mine. For an instant he couldn't find words. I remembered the old man cackling.

"Who?" Paul asked, his voice quiet.

"Mice," I said, the delighted lewdness of the old man still beating in my head—him talking about the father, Vanderbilt, Commodore Vanderbilt Mice who had lived in an unpainted board-and-batten house and spawned urchins out of a humpback wife. "Rosy Mice."

"What makes you think I know anyone by that name?" Paul asked, giving me not an answer but an evasion.

"You're a lying minister," I said, remembering what the old man had told me—how the flower that grew out of the manure pile had walked down the streets of the college town in a cheap cotton dress and high-heel shoes. Before she was fifteen, she'd had grown men gawking as she passed. She'd smelled of orange blossom perfume and swung her hips so freely that the dress twitched across her back. The men gaped and thought of dipping into her—like a pot of jam.

"You don't own me," Paul said, pushing up from the sofa. He stood taller than I. "I belong to myself."

"I wish I'd never heard of you," I said. I thought of the young girl working at a drugstore counter. The college boys leaned over to look down the front of her white uniform when she bent to the coolers to scoop ice cream.

"It would be less than Christian for me to say the feeling's

mutual," Paul said. "But God I'm fed up with the bunch of you."
He clenched his hands.

"I'm giving you a chance to tell the truth," I said.

"What do you know about truth?" he asked, contemptuous of me. He crossed to the desk.

"For once try straight talk," I said, following him. I thought of young Rosy Mice. Of course she would have gone out with college boys. They would have been drawn to her like hummingbirds to the mimosa. They wouldn't have picked her up openly but met her in the alley behind the drugstore and driven her to fire trails and fraternity houses. It'd just been a matter of time, the old man said. From the very first, everybody knew it was just a matter of time.

"What are you charging me with?" Paul asked, turning on me.

"You went out with her," I said, though I had no proof of that. I had to forge the link.

"What good will it do?" he asked. He shook his head. "Go back to your store."

"How many times you all been together since you came to town?" I asked.

"We've never been together." He moved away from me.

"You were together the night you tried to lay her."

"Quit jumping on me," he said. He bumped into his desk.

"You were having a big time that night," I said. "Except Caroline never expected Lou to come home. She got scared. She panicked and threw you to Lou to save herself."

"I don't know what you're talking about," he said. He slid around the desk and backed away from me.

"She was your girl before you came here," I said.

"No!"

"Why do you keep lying?"

"You're so smart, you figure it," he said.

"I have figured it."

"Then why talk to me?"

"It might save your hide."

263

"I haven't asked you to save my hide."

"You better ask somebody."

"Not yet," he said.

I stood by the desk. I couldn't understand why he kept protecting Caroline.

"I won't plead with you," I said. "I'm sick of you."

"I'm not holding you here." He walked to the door and opened it for me.

Furious, I went out. In the garden I turned back. He was about to shut the door. I walked to it and pushed it.

"For old times' sake you thought you could help yourself to a little," I said. "But you got caught, and now she's throwing you to the buzzards."

"That's the thing," he said softly, not to me really, but to himself. His expression was puzzled. "Why?"

"Why what?" I asked quickly.

"Is she doing this to me?"

"Don't you know?"

Instead of answering, he tried to close the study door. I pressed my palms against it.

"If there are things you don't understand, why not talk to her?" I asked.

"I've tried," he said. "She won't come to the telephone."

With uxorious Lou guarding her, perhaps she had no opportunity to get at Paul and discuss—what? I didn't know. Maybe they were both lying. Or perhaps there was no truth.

"Suppose I arrange a meeting," I said. "Will you come?"

"Yes."

I left him at the door and walked under shrilling locusts out of the garden.

42

Injun stood just inside the front door. He waited for customers. He smiled at me. I walked past him to my office.

I dialed slowly, putting off the completion of the call as long as I could.

"Gaines' residence," Lucy, the colored maid, said.

Lowering my voice, I asked for Mrs. Gaines. I didn't want to identify myself, but Lucy would have none of it.

"Who's speaking, please?"

I gave my name, allowing my voice to slide into its normal register. Suppose, I thought, just suppose Lou were at home and had answered the phone. I would have had no excuse to be calling.

"I'll see whether she can come," Lucy said, not quite so condescending now, but still superior. She was the maid of the richest family in the county. She rode home in a Cadillac.

I heard her walk away from the phone. Above me the old clock ticked as if it would stop of weariness. I brushed a fly off my knee. When I heard Caroline's voice, I kicked the door shut.

"Yes?" she said. She sounded as if she were speaking from a high place. "Jack?"

"It's important I see you a few minutes," I said.

I sensed her hesitation.

"As you can imagine, I'm rather involved these days."

"I wouldn't be bothering you unless it was important."

"You're welcome here."

"I don't want to come there," I said. There was not only the chance of interruption by Lou, but also the fact I might need her and Paul to confront one another. Moreover I intended to take her away from the security of her own house. "Can you drive to my place?"

Again she hesitated. I pictured her covering the phone with the palm of her long cool hand and glancing over her shoulder.

"I'm not certain that would be discreet," she said and laughed just once in her precise voice.

"If you can suggest someplace else, fine, but I have to see you," I insisted.

"If I come, I won't be able to get away until after dinner."

"I appreciate your cooperation."

"You're talking like a policeman," she said and hung up.

I telephoned Paul. He was still in his study.

"I think she's coming," I told him. "You stick close to your telephone tonight in case I need you."

"Don't call the manse," he said. "It might alarm Helen."

"Just stay close," I said and hung up.

I spent the rest of the day cleaning up my desk and helping Injun. Not that he needed much help. He jumped to wait on customers, and he had learned to sweet-talk them like the salesmen down at the Progress Store. He bowed to ladies, which was all right except he was oily about it. I would have said something, but I had too much Caroline and Paul on my mind.

After we locked up, I took him to the hotel for dinner and sent him to the movie, which was open only twice a week and for sale.

I drove home and waited on my porch. If Caroline came, I figured it wouldn't be until dark when there was less chance of her being seen. I smoked and watched shadows stretch across the scorched land.

I heard her car turn in. At least I thought it was her car until it drew closer. It was no baby-blue Cadillac, but the old Dodge. The Dodge bucked and spewed blue smoke. Paul was behind the wheel.

"I don't want you here now," I said. I glanced at the highway, afraid Caroline would turn in and catch him.

"You'll need me," he said. He wore his black preaching suit.

"Why can't you do as you're told?" I asked angrily. Sending him back was too dangerous. If he passed Caroline, he would spook her. I ordered him to park his car at the side of the house where she couldn't see it.

I led him hurriedly up the front steps. He walked heavily. I took him to a guest bedroom on the second floor. It was far enough away from the parlor that he wouldn't be able to hear.

"Don't come out until I call you," I told him. "If I call you."

I closed the door before he could answer and went downstairs to the porch. I paced from railing to railing. By nine I was sure she wasn't coming.

As I opened the screen door to go in the house, I heard a car moving fast down the highway. It turned in, and the tires squealed.

She came in as if racing. Dust billowed behind the Cadillac. It slid to a stop.

I went down the steps to open the door for her. She swung her legs out of the air-conditioned coolness, her perfume sweet on the night. No matter how many times I saw her, I was always startled at the precision of her beauty. I thought of silk touching that body. I also thought of red shoes nailed to a door.

"Thanks for coming," I said. I helped her out and started her toward the steps.

"Do we have to go in?" she asked. She balanced herself on her high heels. She wore a pale green dress and a pair of white gloves.

"If we don't, the bugs'll get us," I told her and touched her elbow.

We went up to the porch and inside to the parlor. The room was furnished with pieces that had belonged to my grandparents —needlepoint upholstery, a claw-foot table, and a tasseled lamp. The fireplace brass was tarnished.

I offered her a red velvet straight-back chair which had tips of brass on the legs. She sat on the edge of it and jerked at her gloves. Her shoes matched her dress, and her dress a small hat. I thought of plumed hats in the court of Charles II.

"I don't have much time," she said, slapping her gloves into a palm. She glanced at a diamond watch around her wrist. In spite of face powder, she appeared pale. She sat with her shoulders back. Her blond hair was perfectly in place.

"I don't know how to start," I said. Her green dress had a high collar. I thought of Paul's teeth marks.

"Try the beginning," she said curtly. She slapped her gloves against her palm. "I don't like being here without my husband."

"I realize that, and all I want is to ask a couple of questions," I said. She made questions seem ridiculous.

"Just get to it," she said and again looked at the diamond watch. I found myself attempting to imagine her disheveled by the act of love.

"Would you like a cigarette?" I asked, standing to offer her my pack.

"Jack!" she said, the word a warning. She crossed her legs and adjusted her dress at her knees. Diamonds flashed on her fingers. Her nails were a bright red and matched her lips.

"All right," I said. I fidgeted in my chair. "What I want to know is whether or not you knew Paul Elgin before."

"Before what?" she asked. My question hadn't surprised her. She didn't flinch or even blink.

"Before you came to Black Leaf."

She stared. She was very still. She sat on the red velvet chair with her knees toward the fireplace and her torso half turned to me.

"What makes you ask?"

"It's an answer I very much need at the moment." I felt her dominating me. I had to be careful or she would have me apologizing.

"Did he tell you I knew him?"

"No."

"What did he tell you?" she asked.

"Nothing."

She frowned, opened her pocketbook, and drew out a cigarette which she tapped against the tan leather. I hurried to light it for her. As I stood above her, I again smelled perfume.

"Then how'd you get the idea I knew him before he came to Black Leaf?" she asked.

"I made a trip," I said. "To South Carolina."

I saw a gathering of muscles. She had the cigarette at her lips, and it trembled just once.

"To snoop on me?" she asked, her gray eyes bright.

"Yes."

"What do you think Lou would do if he knew you were snooping on me?" she asked. Nothing had given way in her.

"I hope he won't know."

"Why should I protect you?" Her eyes were catlike. "Why should I do anything for you?"

"Because I'm not against you."

She watched me, drew on her cigarette, and shifted her weight. She rearranged the white gloves.

"All right, you went south to check on me," she said. "What am I supposed to do—scream and faint?"

"Did you know him?" I asked gently.

She stood and crossed to my fireplace. She never merely walked. She threw her ladylike legs forward aggressively. She held her shoulders proudly. I thought of red shoes and plumed hats.

"I don't have to tell you," she said.

"I realize that."

She faced me.

"Then why should I?"

"For two reasons. First, I want to be on your side. Second, I don't want to have to reveal what I was told in Carolina."

"And what was that?" she asked. Contemptuous, she threw her cigarette into the fireplace.

"You don't want to hear."

"I very much want to hear," she said. She slapped her gloves against her thigh.

"I was looking for your kin," I said. Her haughtiness made me doubt. It didn't seem possible any connection could exist between what the old sheriff had told me in South Carolina and this contained, highbred woman.

"And?"

"I found no Van Meissens."

I saw a tiny crack of fear break into the cold, powdered perfection of her face.

"I could walk out right now," she said. She crossed to the door. "You have no proof."

"There was a man from Tennessee," I said. I wanted to lower my eyes. "Commodore Vanderbilt Mice. He had a beautiful daughter."

She tottered as if I'd pushed her. Her hands twisted the gloves. Her throat muscles bulged as if she were screaming silently.

"I pulled myself up," she said hoarsely. She held to the doorframe. "I could have ended in the gutter."

I knew that. I'd thought of what she should have turned into after allowing college boys to take her out. They would have driven her in their fathers' cars to dark, fetid places. Yet she had risen from that slime to stand before me proud and beautiful.

"I grew up in filth and stink," she said. "I had to fight off my own brothers." She bit into the words and paced. Her heels hit the floor angrily and the impact flowed through the pine boards. "I refuse to be judged by you." She cracked her gloves against her thighs. "I'm not ashamed of pulling myself up."

"The last thing I'm trying to do is shame you," I said.

"Oh, you're a lamb—a sweet, innocent lamb."

She crossed her arms and paced in front of me—her gray eyes narrowed.

"I'm not begging you," she said. "I'm a fighter. I'll fight you and anybody."

She was fierce. I imagined her coming at me with those red nails like claws.

"I don't want to fight you," I said.

"You want to help him and ruin me," she said and gestured toward town as if she could reach across miles to the manse and touch Paul.

"I'll help you if you give me a chance," I said. I thought of Paul sitting upstairs in the bedroom.

"Then get rid of him," she said. "Get him out."

"I want to, but there are still questions."

"What questions?"

"About your past."

"There's nothing mysterious about my past. I was poor, I worked hard, and I found myself a fine husband. If I lied to him about what I came from, if I bought an oil portrait of a colonel at an auction and claimed he was my kin, they were good lies."

"And Paul?" I asked.

She stopped pacing and looked at me hard.

"I don't trust you," she said. "I don't have to trust you." She started to leave, walking proudly.

"I'll have to tell the church officers what I heard down there," I said as she reached the screen door.

"Tell them." She pushed open the door.

"Not just about being poor, but also about a young girl at a drugstore counter who used to slip through windows to go out with college boys."

It was as if I'd run her through. She drew in her shoulders and let the screen door close slowly. She turned on me.

"You sonofabitch," she said, not loudly, hardly even a whisper, but the word was like a hot bullet coming from her small, red mouth.

As she crossed toward me, I backed into the parlor.

"There was no one to help me," she said. She spoke through clenched teeth. "There was never anyone to help."

I could guess. Her beauty would have drawn them, not only the college boys, but also the men who cruised and knew about motels and cabins on lakes. I thought of the intense male pressure, never relenting, thrusting at her before she had a chance.

"I didn't want to end up like my mother," she said, still coming at me. I retreated slowly. "My mother was a brood animal."

I backed around the sofa as she came—hard, intense, furious.

"I went to a dance," Caroline said. She nodded. "With one of the college boys. I spent all my money on a white dress and golden slippers. In the ballroom other girls wouldn't speak to me. They treated me as if I were infected."

As she talked, I put parts together. To attract college men, she would have allowed them to dance close to her. Later, there would have been further payment—hot writhings in darkness.

"I was fifteen years old," she said. "I was in love with a boy. He'd been very anxious to take me out. We had a date. The next afternoon I met him on the street. I just wanted to be in love with him, but he looked at me as if I were dirty."

A lot of men would have used her—fed her sweet wine until she was addled and had their lay. Then they would have been afraid because she was jailbait. They would have crossed streets to keep from meeting her. They would have refused to answer her telephone calls. Christ, and she'd been only fifteen.

"If I was dirty, men made me that way," she said. "They wanted me dirty."

She followed me as I backed away. Her red lips were twisted as if she would spit on me.

"Did Paul take you out?" I asked.

She understood what I was really asking—had he been one of those who made her dirty.

"Go to hell," she said. "You've had all you're getting from me."

Again she started away. I didn't want to be a sonofabitch. In a way I loved her. But I had to use the words for her sake.

"What about the dancing?" I asked.

The words stopped her. She faltered.

"Dancing?"

"On the bar," I said.

The old sheriff—his voice cackling, his eyes alight. She was very drunk, he'd said, Rosy Mice was, and the fraternity boys lifted her to the bar. She danced for them. They held up their hands to keep her from falling. They shouted for her to take it off, and she dropped clothes to them. I imagined her pale adolescent body bumping and grinding while a piano thumped and the brothers howled. She kicked off her shoes, her red pumps, and her escort nailed them to the door as a trophy—like the silver cups and gilded footballs in the glass display case.

"I'm not talking to you," Caroline said. Her lips were a wound in her powdered face. She kept shaking her head.

"You haven't told me the most important part," I said. God, I didn't want to. She would have left. I had to be the sonofabitch.

"No more," she said, walking into the hall. "No more."

"The part about why you left South Carolina," I said.

She bent and raised a hand. I watched her break. I saw that fine spirit crumble.

"I'm sure you know the answer to that too," she said. She bowed her head. "You have answers to everything."

I felt filthy and ashamed. What I was doing with her was worse than what the fraternity boys had done in their white-columned house—at the Fancy Dress Ball where they were cavaliers in the court of Charles II and wore boots, sabers, and plumed hats as they waited in line for her in the upstairs hallway while she lay sprawled and uncomprehending on a cot of a darkened room.

I'd broken her. She walked slowly to the red velvet chair. She sat, and her hands fell lifeless into her lap.

"Why don't you shoot me?" she whispered without looking up. "If you want to kill me, just get a gun and shoot."

She didn't cry. That would have been better. She was beyond crying.

273

43

I moved to her and reached for her hand. I felt defeat in it. I squeezed in an attempt to transfer some of my strength to her. She raised her face.

"Let me help you," I said. "Tell me the truth."

Her gray eyes lifted only a moment. Again she bowed her head. I held her hand.

"The truth is simple," she said, her voice small. "A lot of fine, upstanding people have betrayed me."

"Him too?" I asked.

"No, not him. I thought he was a nice one. I really believed Paul was nice, and I loved him, though he never knew it. He came into the drugstore and was polite. He didn't looked down my dress or leave notes on napkins. I went to all the football games to see him, and in the fraternity houses I'd watch the door for him. Once I had too much to drink and—" She stopped, gathered herself, and withdrew her hand from mine. "He drove me home and was a gentleman."

One nice man in the crowd, I thought, or so she believed at the tender age of fifteen when she was already being passed around.

"I wanted to go out with him," she said. Her hands worked, wadding the white gloves. "He never asked me. He had all sorts of girls after him. He was polite, but he never had time for me."

Her head bowed, she wadded the gloves.

"I had to leave," she said. "The court decided that."

"Yes."

"They sent me to a Female House of Correction. I could have become anything in that place, but I fought. I never stopped fighting. When I got out, the war was on. I'd been taught to type, and the director was able to find me a job in Washington—at the Navy Department."

"You met Lou," I said. I backed away from her and sat on the sofa.

"Not at first," she said. She balled her gloves. "At first I had nothing to do with men. I'd had enough of them. I lived in a small room and hid. I wore no make-up. I cut my hair short and bound my breasts. I wanted to be so ugly men wouldn't think of me."

She couldn't have made herself ugly, I thought, not with the shape of that body which even in despair was exciting.

"Lou came later," she said and raised her face slightly. Her long hands continued to wad the gloves. "He'd been wounded and assigned office duty. He hated it. He was ashamed of sitting at a desk while other men were at sea."

She raised her face, but her eyes remained down.

"He wasn't like the others," she said. "He didn't carouse or look at women's legs. He was hurt and used a cane. When he had to speak to me about some office matter, he acted embarrassed."

Lou had always been like that. With his money and position, he could have dated even Richmond girls, but he'd never believed any of them liked him for himself. While the rest of us went to dancing school, he'd studied accounting.

"He was so shy I didn't realize he wanted to go out with me," Caroline said. "Then one Sunday evening I met him at church. I was often at church. I was trying to put my life together."

She wadded and twisted the gloves.

"He was on the steps after a Sunday night service. He'd followed me. He took off his hat and asked to walk me home. I was afraid. I was sure he would be like the others. Yet he was hurt too and had to lean on his cane. I felt sorry for him because I knew about hurt."

She raised her gray eyes and looked beyond me.

"We walked two blocks to the building where I lived. He was careful to stay on the proper side of me. We climbed the steps

275

to the door. Here it comes, I thought, but he just shook my hand very formally and didn't try to come in."

Memory softened her face, and for a moment her hands were still.

"It was so innocent," she said. "He opened doors for me and held my coat. We went to baseball games and ate peanuts. He was always protective. He tried to shield me from wind. I didn't know a man could be so good."

For an instant she smiled, but her hands again kneaded the gloves.

"I was astonished when he asked me to marry him. He got down on his knees in the old-fashioned way. I couldn't answer him. I was afraid again, yet I was also tired of living alone and of fighting. I wanted peace. He made it seem possible."

She frowned and watched her hands twist the gloves.

"I didn't know he was rich. He never acted it. He always counted his change and was careful never to tip more than ten percent. He told me he worked in a plant, not owned it. I believed we would be ordinary people and safe."

She flattened the gloves, and I was thinking ahead of her—how it must have been for her when she found who Lou was. The marriage automatically set her on top of Black Leaf's social spire. She who a few years previously had been white trash was now society.

"I was terrified," she said. Fear drew her features to thinness. "I was frightened my English would give me away. I had to think through every sentence before I spoke. I couldn't let people come close to me."

We'd believed she was snooty. The ladies had thought she was putting on airs and flaunting her aristocratic background.

"I had to work," she said. "I read etiquette books and studied fashion magazines. I learned to decorate, set a table, and choose wine. There were a million traps I had to avoid. All the women were ready to tear me apart."

Her hands twisted the gloves.

"Each night when I went to bed, I wanted to cry, but I couldn't because I also had to hide from Lou. There was no one to talk to or ask advice of. I fought it out alone, and I made it."

She raised her face, and pride flowed back into her.

"I fooled you," she said. "I fooled all of you. You believed I was a lady."

Her shoulders squared, and her head was high. For a moment she again felt the power of being Mrs. Lou Gaines.

"Yet I never got over being terrified," she said. "There was never an instant I felt really safe. I was afraid of talking in my sleep and giving something away. One Saturday afternoon I was downtown shopping. I had my daughters with me. It was just before Christmas, and carols were playing. We waited at the corner for a traffic light to change. Also waiting for the light was a cattle truck and trailer. It was mud-splotched and smelly. I looked at the cab of the truck and almost died."

She stared past me, her face pale, her gray eyes large.

"The driver was one of my brothers," she said. "His name was Earl, and I hadn't seen him for seventeen years. He was dirty, needed a shave, and wore a denim jacket with stains on it. He was watching me. I almost fainted."

Her hands were motionless on her gloves.

"Then the light changed, and he drove on. My daughters felt my shaking hands and were looking up at me. I began to laugh. People turned to look. I couldn't stop laughing. He didn't know me. He was just gawking at a pretty woman standing on a street corner. I wanted to sing."

She spread the gloves across her knees.

"For the first time I felt a little safe. If I could fool my own kin, who would challenge me? I began to believe I was no longer the same person. I really had changed. Rosy Mice was dead. I was Mrs. Caroline Van Meissen Gaines."

She sat poised and aristocratic on the velvet chair, her ankles crossed, her hands settled in her lap. She could have been serving tea.

"Until Paul came to town," she said. Her hands twisted the gloves, and her eyes faltered. "I had no warning. Nobody called him Paul when I'd known him. He was always Smooth, Big Smooth, and certainly he would never have become a preacher."

I heard a creak of the steps. I glanced at the hall. Paul was on the stairs, halfway down. He held to the railing. Slowly he lifted a finger to his mouth. I scowled at him and would have motioned him back up the steps, but I was afraid Caroline might raise her eyes and see.

"I went to church with Lou the first Sunday Paul was in town," she said. "When I saw who it was in the pulpit, I almost vomited. Lou thought I was having a chill and wanted to take me home."

I glanced into the hall. Paul was still on the steps. I jerked my head to send him back up. He moved down slowly.

"I tried to brass it out," Caroline said. "After the service, I walked right up to him and shook his hand. He was confused. He thought he knew me, but he wasn't sure. He couldn't make the connection."

It was hot in the parlor, but she hugged herself as if cold. Her head was bowed. Paul came down another step.

"He was trying to place me," Caroline said. "Whenever he saw me, he tried to fit the pieces. I began to hope maybe I'd be able to fool him too. At least I hoped it until the afternoon we dedicated the new addition to the Sunday school. I caught him eyeing me, and I saw he knew. He never said anything, but he knew."

She hugged herself. Her voice was a monotone. I looked toward the hall. Paul was at the bottom of the steps.

"Do you know what it was like for me?" she asked, not raising her head. "I kept waiting for him to say something. I knew he could ruin me. I'd go into the bathroom, lock the door, and shake. I was afraid to leave the house."

Paul was just outside the parlor doorway. A board creaked. Caroline raised her face and saw him. She looked at me as if I'd sold her out.

I crossed to Paul and tried to block him. He pushed me aside easily and stepped into the room.

"I never told anybody," he said. "Not even Helen."

Caroline stood slowly. Her hands pulled against her waist. She was bloodless.

"He wasn't supposed to be here," I explained to her. Again I got in front of Paul.

"I didn't tell," Paul said, moving past me. "Because you weren't the same person. You weren't Rosy Mice."

"What are you doing to me?" she asked. She raised a hand as if to keep him off.

"I admired you," he said. "I know what it takes to change."

She watched him and shook her head.

"I'd changed too," he argued. "We were allies in change."

"Quit blaming me," she said, backing away from him.

"I'm not blaming anybody."

"Oh yes," she said, nodding. "You want me to take the blame."

"Why'd you have to stop your car that night?" he asked. "I never wanted you to stop for me."

"I had to find out what you were going to do about me."

"I wasn't going to do anything."

"I had to know," she said. "When I saw you walking by the river, it was a chance to have you alone. So I stopped."

"I never told anybody. I never would have."

"You wanted me."

"No!"

"Don't act innocent. You were Big Smooth, and I felt you wanting me."

"Any man would want you."

"I felt it when you walked into a room," she said. "You'd hardly look at me, but you were thinking of me."

"You're a beautiful woman. I didn't stop being a man."

"I had to find out," she said. "I had to do something even if it meant giving myself."

"Don't put that on me," Paul said.

"Oh yes," she said, nodding. "With my fear what was one more man? I was willing to trade."

"You misunderstood," he said. He sweated.

"You bit my neck and tongued me."

"But I stopped," he said. "I could have done more."

"Yes, you could've," she said, her voice intense with hate. She held her gloves as if she'd slash them across his face.

"I was backing away," he said. "Before I knew Lou was in the house, I was backing."

"You wiped me off," she said. She brushed her fingers across her mouth. "You were remembering Rosy and where she came from, and you wiped me off as if I were filth."

"No!" Paul answered. "You got it wrong."

"I couldn't stand it," she said. "You had no right to disgust. I screamed."

She was breathing hard. The skin of her powdered face stretched taut and pale.

"It wasn't you," Paul said, closing his eyes. His voice was a moan. "I wasn't thinking of you."

"I don't believe you," she said. Sweat soaked through her make-up, and her temples glistened.

"Listen," Paul said. "It was me I was disgusted at, and it was me I was wiping off. I was ashamed for what I was doing to you."

"You're lying."

"I saw myself."

"You're trying to confuse me," she said, edging away from him. "You're making it up to confuse me."

"I swear I'm not."

"Oh Christ!" she said. She put her fingers to her eyes as if she were dizzy.

"I couldn't be disgusted at you," he said. He crossed to her. "I respect you too much."

"Don't," she said. She held out a hand to keep him off.

"It's the truth."

"What am I supposed to do?" she asked him.

"I don't know," he answered.

"You know." She became angry. "You want me to ruin myself."

"I don't want anybody ruined."

"But that's what you expect me to do—to tell them it was my fault."

"I'm not asking you anything."

"You want me to save you, and I can't unless I ruin myself."

"You could go to Lou," Paul said. "A word from him and charges would be dropped."

"No," she said. "I'd have to tell him too much. He thinks I'm pure. He wouldn't be able to understand."

Paul held to the back of a chair.

"What am I supposed to do?" he asked.

"I can't worry about you," she told him, shaking her head. "I have my daughters."

"I have children too."

"You're a man and can make another life. It'll be over for me."

"This is the only life I could lead."

They stared at each other.

"No," she said, her face slack and glazed with sweat. "I won't die for you."

She ran out.

[44]

Her feet tapped fast against the boards of my porch steps. She was in her Cadillac and gone before I reached the yard. Dust settled silently.

Paul stood on the porch and looked after her. The sound of the car faded toward town. He leaned on the railing.

"It appears we've reached the end of the road," he said.

"You going to leave?" I asked. I sat on the bottom step and lit a cigarette. My hands were shaky. I looked out across my land. Moonlight lay on ashen fields.

"No," he said.

"No?"

"There's the congregational meeting," he said.

"You'll have to give her to them," I told him.

"Maybe not." He clasped his hands.

"You won't have a chance otherwise." I was still shaking.

He came down the steps and sat beside me. He ran his hand through his hair.

"I might have a chance if you help me."

"Help you how?"

"You know the truth."

"I won't talk against her."

"I'm not asking that, but at the congregational meeting you could sit with me in the pulpit. You don't have to speak, but I'd like you with me."

I threw my cigarette onto the gravel drive. The cigarette sparked and lay burning. Joining him in the pulpit would be the same as my proclaiming him innocent and Caroline guilty.

"You don't mind asking a whole lot, do you?" I said.

"You're a responsible man. How does your conscience give you a choice?"

"I lost my conscience when I killed my first man."

"I won't accept that."

"You're not innocent," I said. He may not have bedded Caroline, or intended to, but his maleness was part of what happened.

"I am of the charge."

"A piss-poor technicality."

"You won't sit with me in the pulpit?"

"No."

"My thanks."

"For three reasons I won't. First it would indicate I approve of you, which I definitely don't. Secondly it would be a charge against Caroline. Thirdly I don't turn my back on friends."

"You're turning it on me and my family."

"You're just passing through."

"What about truth?" he asked.

"I don't know where truth starts and stops," I said. "But if I did, all the truth in the world isn't as meaningful to me as close flesh and blood."

"I need you badly," Paul said.

"Why don't you just go?" I asked angrily. "Just get out and leave us alone."

"I won't run."

"I'm going to bed," I told him. I went up the steps.

"I had hopes for you, Jackson," he said. He stood and crossed the dry, crackling grass to his Dodge.

I was inside before he drove away.

Book Five

[45]

The congregational meeting was set for two o'clock Friday afternoon. Old men were talking about it in front of the courthouse and post office. Ladies were on the telephones. In the drugstore, filling stations, and the bank, people bent toward one another and shifted their eyes as if they suspected somebody might be sneaking up on them. You could feel expectancy in the bricks and stones of the town.

I found my *Book of Church Order,* presented to me when I was first installed and ordained an officer. The book was on a shelf of the kitchen cabinet, and a bottle of vanilla had made a circle on the faded blue cover. I thumbed through the pages until I reached the section on Impeachment. It was at the end of the book as if to hide it.

Procedure to be followed is that of any congregational meeting. The senior officer will preside, or if he is not available, other officers in rank of their seniority, with the reservation that at any meeting three officers must be present.

I carried the book with me to the store. The pavement was hot. Injun was already at work. His light hair was slicked down with tonic. He was selling a woman wallpaper, and he used a fast spiel patterned after the redcoats at the Progress Store.

"This paper won't clash with nothing," Injun said, stripping down a roll. "It's a universal color developed by the company to mesh even with such shades as beige and chartreuse."

I shut the door of my office and sat at my desk. I listened to the clock. It was ten minutes after eight. I wanted some kind of miracle to happen which would save both Caroline and Paul.

Somebody came in the store. His footsteps were too quick for a customer's. I opened my door to look out. Speaking to Injun was a stoop-shouldered young man who wore dark glasses and a sport shirt. Injun pointed toward my office. The man came on back.

"Buddy Hicks," he said, his hand out to me. "From the Richmond *Southern American.*"

I pulled my hand away quickly. I'd been hoping we might be able to get by without newspapers.

"They tell me you're the presiding officer at the meeting," Hicks said. He leaned against the door and took a pad and pencil from his shirt pocket.

"That's my misfortune," I said.

"Jackson LeJohn. I try to spell the names right." He smiled. "I'd like to sit in on the deliberations."

"It's not up to me," I said. I intended to work against him. There had to be some place where newspapers couldn't set off fireworks.

"Who then?" Hicks asked. He tapped his pencil against the pad. He was thirty or so. In spite of the heat, he twitched with energy.

"The church officers."

"You're the chairman, aren't you? Give me a ruling."

"I'll be frank with you, Mr. Hicks. I'm going to suggest to the other officers that the press be kept on the street."

"You going to kick us out if we come in?" he asked. He put the pencil and pad in his shirt pocket. He removed his sunglasses and cleaned them with a handkerchief. In the shadows of my office, his eyes seemed without pupils.

"The ushers will escort you out," I said, though I wasn't sure they could.

"A very Christian act," he said. He put on his sunglasses, turned, and walked from the store.

I picked up my telephone and dialed Archie LeBuck.

"The buzzards are here," I told him.

"I been expecting them."

"They want in the church."

"I'll put extra ushers at the door."

I hung up. Over my head the clock ticked. The air was heavy and hot. It felt like fuzz against my skin. I had the sensation I was being watched. I spun in my chair. Injun was behind me.

"What about me?" he asked.

"What about you?"

"Do I get to close up the store and go to the church?"

So even the children wanted to be in on the preacher-roasting —as if it were a double feature with cartoons.

"You think they're going to hawk peanuts and popcorn?" I asked angrily.

"Skeeter's going," Injun argued, backing off. Skeeter was one of his river-rat friends. "There won't be anybody here to sell to."

"Skeeter might be going, but he's not getting in," I said.

I called Archie and told him to instruct the ushers not to allow anybody under twenty-one to enter the church. Archie said he already had given the order. I turned in my chair. Injun was at the front of the store.

"You can stay here and dust the stock," I called to him.

I spent the rest of the morning studying the Impeachment section of the *Book of Church Order*, searching for a loophole, some fine print that would let us out. I found nothing.

Though I wasn't hungry, at noon I walked down the street toward the hotel. People treated me as if I were a celebrity. They smiled and waved across the street. I could have been a halfback in the big game.

I considered the vine-grown hotel a refuge. The street could be raucous with hillbilly music from the Progress Store, but inside the old brick building the air was of the past—the same that Lee and Grant had breathed on the way to Appomattox, though filtered uncountable times since through the shiny leaves of magnolias in the garden.

I was one of the few businessmen who still ate at the hotel. Most people were in a hurry and went to the Southside Tavern which had a stainless-steel kitchen, pretty waitresses, and air conditioning. But at the hotel the tables were set with linen so thick you could hardly bend your napkin, and the silver was so heavy your wrist ached holding it. Each table had an old-fashioned cut-glass carafe on it, and the water inside looked yellowed. Sunlight came through tall dusty windows, past mangy curtains— light somehow benign and touched with gentleness.

All the green rocking chairs on the porch were occupied, not with guests of the hotel, but with old men who came each day to sit, hoist their feet to the railing, and speak legends. They splattered the dried-up strip of flower bed between the hotel and the sidewalk with dark heavy blobs of tobacco juice.

"Jackson," they said, eyeing me as I passed.

"Gentlemen," I answered.

I walked through the lobby, which had shined brass spittoons, and stood at the entrance to the dining room. Rickety fans squeaked on the ceiling but stirred no coolness in the old air. Nor was the dining room a refuge today. Most of the tables had people at them—people I didn't recognize. They looked at me as if I had no right to enter.

I sat in a back corner, near the kitchen door, and ordered a salad from Terry, a colored waiter in a white coat and black bow tie who'd served me here when I was a boy. He'd been big then, husky, but age had shrunk him, and he now appeared sick, and tragic, though he could still carry a loaded tray around a corner at a forty-five-degree angle and never spill a drop of soup.

I resented the people who had come to town for the preacher-roasting. I saw Hicks, the newsman, at what must have been a table of reporters. They talked and glanced my way. I wanted to tell them to go down to the Southside Tavern with its neon and nickelodeon where they belonged.

I ate quickly, but before I could leave the table Baxter Hopkins caught me. He saw me from the lobby and came toward my table. Baxter, a man in his late fifties, had retired almost as soon as he was born. His father had left him a thousand acres of good bottom land, and Baxter had been selling it off a chunk a year ever since. He was stringing the land out so it would last him the rest of his life. He lived in a fine old house which was falling apart and had bees in the attic. Honey ran down the walls.

"Service is kind of slow around here today," he complained as he slipped into a chair. He poured himself a glass of water from the carafe. He wasn't going to buy anything, but he could still complain. He wore a salt-and-pepper suit that had belonged to his father. The jacket had a belt at the back. Baxter never came to town unless there was an election, a big preaching, or something free.

"Excuse me," I said and stood. I didn't want to talk now. I felt in my pocket for money.

"Wait a second," Baxter said. He'd shaved but hadn't got all the gray stubble off his chin and cheek. He smelled of sweat. He clutched my arm. "You run him out, hear?"

"Sh-h-h," I said, moving away from the table. He came after me. I hurried so that he couldn't put on a show for the reporters. But Baxter talked loud enough so they heard us from the lobby.

"I can still boil tar and notch a rail," he said. "And I got me a good blacksnake whip."

The newsmen were stretching their necks to watch us. I walked quickly past the tassels and converted gas fixtures of the lobby. I pushed open the screen door. Flies circled to come back. Men sitting in the green rocking chairs stopped their chewing and turned to look as Baxter kept talking.

"Give him a little tar bath and a fast ride on the notch," Baxter said. "That'll teach him where to keep his pecker."

The men in the rocking chairs were solemn—as if they were judges being pled to.

"I'm late," I said and again pulled away from Baxter.

"Think of the harm he's done," Baxter said. He was still after me and grabbed at my arm. "Think of the young minds he's poisoned."

"You don't know what you're talking about," I said, at the corner now.

"Don't I?" he hollered. People turned on the streets to look. His face puffed with his words. "You're telling me I don't know? Why listen, I know what my ears hear and my eyes see. I surely know the difference between a preaching man and a whore-monger."

His eyes were bloodshot, and the stink of a person living alone in dirt for too long came from inside and outside him. I crossed the street, half-running to escape him.

"Ball him!" Baxter yelled after me. "And I got the knife!"

[46]

When I reached my store, I hurried inside and stood in the shadows of the back room. Injun sought me out. He handed me a slip of paper.

"You had a call."

The number was written on the paper in big blocked figures. The church's telephone. I walked to my office and dialed.

"The place is almost full already," Wayland said. "They're parked up and down side streets."

"What do you want me to do?"

"I thought you ought to know," Wayland said and hung up.

My clock on the wall ticked toward one. I walked to the front of the store. Through the window I watched people move up the street. Their steps were quick and purposeful.

Amos Elliot came into the store. He was a tobacco buyer, a bulky, shambling man with oily jaws. He wore his Sunday suit and hat. He smoked a cigar.

"How long you figure this meeting'll take?" he asked. Elliot was a hard-drinking, rutting man who'd broken his wife to humility. He never went to church, but he was going today. He had a flower in his buttonhole.

"It beats football, don't it?" I asked. I turned my back on him and walked toward my office.

"You mad at me about something?" he called.

"I'm mad at everybody."

"Sorry," he said. He left and slammed the door.

I had to go the the church. First I went to the storeroom, removed my shirt, and washed myself. By the time I put my shirt back on, I was again sweaty.

I picked up the *Book of Church Order* and left the store. I didn't drive. From what Wayland had said, there'd be no place to park. Besides maybe I'd become lucky and break a leg on the way. Injun stood at the window and watched me plod the hot, dusty pavement.

Stores were emptying and closing. The owners, members or not, were going to the roasting. Men and women hurried past me. Only the Negroes seemed the same. They watched from strips of shade.

Before I was in sight of the church steeple, I passed cars parked solid on both sides of the street. It was a bigger crowd than Billy Sunday had drawn when he came to preach during the thirties and wrestled the Devil to three falls in the aisle.

In front of the church was a green panel truck with a TV camera on it. People stood on the sidewalks, the grass, and the steps.

They gathered in clusters. They watched the TV crew making preparations. Young men wearing sport shirts attached cables and tested equipment.

People saw me and whispered. They stood aside to let me through. They nodded, their faces resolute. I touched my hat to ladies.

I went up the steps, which were crowded with people jostling toward the door. Ushers held them back. A reporter was trying to get past Haynes, who owned the laundry.

"I'm the same denomination," the reporter said. "In Richmond I belong to the same church."

"You go to church in Richmond then because this is an intra-congregational matter," Haynes answered. His hair was messed.

People packed the vestibule. Deacons and ushers stood against them, guarding the sanctuary. Eddy Paulette held up his hands like a traffic policeman, and Macon Johns used his elbows as prods.

Many people were from other churches in town—Baptists, Methodists, a few Lutherans. They had come for the free show and refused to leave.

Just inside the sanctuary, Miss Minnie, Val's landlady, was arguing with Burnette, another deacon. Minne's flowered hat had been knocked askew.

"They're sitting in my pew," she complained. She was speaking of a family named Lassiter who were Episcopalians. "They have no right to be sitting in my pew."

"Nobody owns church pews," Burnette answered. A harried, nervous man, he ran the co-op.

"My family's been sitting in that pew for generations," Miss Minnie said. She shook her funeral-home fan in Burnette's face. "They have left their spirits there."

"Well, those spirits are being sat on by Episcopalians," Burnette said.

I moved down the center aisle of the church. The light was colored lavender by stained-glass windows. The pews were filled.

294

So were the balconies and choir loft. Ushers were setting up metal chairs.

There were no flowers on the altar table, and the big Bible had been removed from the pulpit. The front of the church thus appeared as bare and threatening as a courtroom.

Saunders, a deacon, touched me on the shoulder. He was a young man, an electrical contractor.

"They want to stand around the walls," he said, indicating the crowd at the sanctuary entrance. "Shall I allow it?"

"How can you stop it?"

Saunders went back up the aisle. I was looking for Jefferson Stokes, our clerk. He was in his pew, near the front. He held his hat on his lap as if afraid somebody might step on it.

"Do you have the minutes?" I asked him.

Instead of answering, he lifted his hat. Under it was a black notebook and two sharpened yellow pencils.

"I'll call on you first," I said.

"I would expect you to," he answered. Jefferson, a teller, a prissy, precise bachelor, wiped off the silver when he went into restaurants. He believed microbes were after him.

I looked at my watch. It wasn't quite two o'clock. People watched me and shifted in anticipation. "He's about to start," a woman said. The words swept back through the pews like wind. They blew through the vestibule and out to the steps and street. The crowd pushed against ushers and deacons.

"It's not time yet," I said loudly. I held up my hands. The crowd gave back a little.

Archie LeBuck passed. He called instructions to ushers. He held his cane as if he would slash out.

"You seen our preacher?" he asked.

"I wish I'd never seen him," I said. "But I'll look."

I edged toward the door which led from the sanctuary to the Sunday-school section of the building. Claude Watkins was there. He had the door locked and held the brass key.

"What about our preacher?" I asked.

"I don't know," Claude said. He was a dairyman, and he stood with his legs spread, as if he'd fight if he had to. "I'm just trying to keep people from crashing the door."

He unlocked it for me. I went through and walked along the sunny corridor, bright with crayon drawings. There were crooked houses with smiling doorways. Children had small bodies and great heads. In one drawing a little girl stood under a black tree and cried tears as big as bricks. They splashed on the purple grass at her feet.

A man walked toward me. He wore a sleeveless white shirt which had pulled from his plump waist. Across his shoulder was the leather strap of a camera bag.

"Mr. Elgin?" he asked.

"Newsmen aren't allowed in here," I said.

"I'm a photographer."

"You'll have to wait outside." I moved toward a door at the rear of the building.

"Are you the reverend?" he asked. He brought a camera out of the bag.

"I'm a church officer," I said. I pushed open the door and held it for him.

"You can't put a lid on this," he said.

"Please get out."

He shrugged and walked past me. I shut the door and locked it. He bent forward to peer at me through the glass.

I went back up the corridor to the study, where I knocked. There was no answer. I opened the door. Paul and Helen sat on the sofa. Their heads were bowed, their eyes shut. They held hands. After the crush of the church, the study was dim and peaceful.

They withdrew their hands and opened their eyes.

"It is time?" Helen asked. She wore a dark dress with a white collar. Her shoes were low-heeled, schoolteacherish.

"You have a minute," I said. She was trying to look brave and serene but fright cracked her face.

"I'm leaving anyway." She stood, touched her brown hair, and lay fingers on Paul's shoulder. For an instant they looked at each other. She then turned, smiled weakly, and left. She smelled faintly of cologne.

"Is she coming to the meeting?" I asked Paul.

"She was reared to let men handle affairs," he said. He stood and walked to his coat which hung from the back of a chair. He rolled down his sleeves. Hair was thick and black along his arms. "When I met her, she'd never voted. It took me three years to get her to register."

I was relieved she wasn't coming and would be spared hurt.

"What about you?" I asked.

"Me?" He reached for his coat.

"I assume you'll speak," I said.

"I have to speak." He adjusted his coat and collected papers from his desk. "You can't keep a minister from speaking." He ran his hand over his hair. "What's the procedure?"

"I call the meeting to order. Jefferson reads the minutes. We go through committees. Then it's open."

He nodded and shuffled papers. He should be more afraid, I thought. He's going to let them have Caroline.

"What'll you say?" I asked.

"I don't know exactly." His eyes avoided mine. "I made a few notes I probably won't use." He put papers in his Bible. "Maybe something will occur to me."

"Don't give them Caroline," I said.

He frowned.

"I've protected her," he said. "Who could have done more for her than I have?"

"I think that means you'll throw her to them."

"If I can, I'll shield her," he said angrily. "But I have my family and work to think of."

I couldn't argue. I had no right to argue.

"I'll be back for you." I went out.

[47]

I walked along the corridor and knocked on the door into the sanctuary. Claude let me through. The sanctuary was hot with people—all glazed with lavender light from the stained-glass windows.

Bodies bumped one another. Ushers attempted to keep space open in the aisles. I had to twist and push to get through. More people were surging in from the front.

"We'll have to shut the doors," Archie said. His bow tie was crooked.

I looked across heads to the street where the TV truck was parked. On top the truck a man swung his camera as if it were a gun. An interviewer holding a stick microphone moved among the crowd.

"Has Lou come?" I asked. I glanced at his pew. It was the one place in the sanctuary where there was an empty seat.

"Not yet," Archie said.

I saw Val with her young doctor. She looked scrubbed and pretty in a white suit. I didn't have time to be resentful.

Sutter was at the rear of the church. He stood slumped against the wall. He fanned himself with his hat.

"Is Lou coming?" I asked.

"You know he's coming," Sutter said.

There was a ballooning of the crowd at the door. Ushers called out and spread a path. Lou walked in. He looked tired. His normally ruddy face was pale, and his skin sagged as if his skeleton had grown smaller. The corners of his shirt collar were turned up. His red hair was messed.

I crossed to the front door. Deacons and ushers were pushing against the crowd.

"You ready?" I asked Lou.

"I'm ready," he said, his eyes accusing.

"Lock them," I said to the ushers.

"We're trying to," Archie said, his palms against a door.

I went down the center aisle to the sanctuary. Claude let me through. I walked to the study. As I raised my hand to knock, the door opened quickly—as if Paul had been standing and waiting on the other side.

"I was coming," he said.

He stepped out and closed the door. In his left hand he carried his Bible. We walked the corridor. The sound of our feet drummed. We reached the door into the sanctuary. He fingered the knob.

"Touch it," he said to me.

I put my hand on the knob. You could feel vibrations from the crowd.

"Each Sunday before I preach, I stop here and try to understand their mood," he said. Again he put his hand on the knob. "Today they're lynchers."

"If you don't want to go in, I can announce it," I told him.

He shook his head, ran his hand over his graying black hair, and adjusted his tie. I knocked on the door. Claude opened it and stepped back.

I went in first. As soon as people saw Paul they quieted. Their faces hardened. I wanted to reach out and soften their expression as a sculptor might change pieces of clay.

Paul moved away from me and went up the steps to the pulpit. Behind the pulpit were the three massive oak chairs, like thrones, and he sat in the center one. I crossed in front of the pulpit to the altar table. I knocked my knuckles against the wood.

"The congregation will come to order," I said. I looked back over the crowd. The doors were closed. I paused to allow people to settle. "I'll ask the clerk to read the minutes of our last meeting."

Jefferson rose and walked toward me. He stood on the other side of the altar table, adjusted his glasses, and opened the black notebook. In a whining voice, he read an account of the spring elections, the plans for vacation Bible school, and the announcement of the receipt of a second water cooler in the Sunday-school building—a gift of Lou Gaines.

People turned to look at Lou. They were thinking how much he'd contributed to the church. He had pledged twenty thousand dollars to the rebuilding after the fire and had taken time off from the plant to come daily and supervise the construction. He was always giving, not only money, but rugs, baptismal fonts, collection plates, even a cushion for Miss Bonner, the organist. If what Lou had given were taken away, we'd have no church, and people were remembering it.

"Are there any additions or corrections to the minutes?" I asked. "Hearing none, I'll consider them approved."

Jefferson nodded and made a note in the black book. Saunders brought us two folding wooden chairs. Jefferson sat and put his book on the altar table. According to procedure, reports from committees were next. He formed the word "finance" with his thin, prim mouth.

"Is there a report from the Finance Committee?" I asked.

Wayland Counts stood. Dapper in a light gabardine suit, he spoke softly.

"Mr. Moderator, isn't it possible to dispense with the normal order of business and get on to the reason for this meeting?"

I turned to Jefferson. He was the parliamentarian as well as the clerk. He leafed through the *Book of Church Order*.

"This is a special kind of meeting," Wayland said. "People are hot and crowded in here uncomfortably."

"Mr. Moderator, I think it's proper to dispense with normal procedure at this meeting if the deviation is put in the form of a motion and duly recorded in the minutes," Jefferson said.

"I so move," Wayland said.

"Second it," Buster Perry said. He was our Ford dealer.

"I'd like to ask a question," Billy Mosby said. Billy was a young attorney just a year out of law school. He saw legal entanglements everywhere. "Suppose the determination of this meeting is appealed. Could a procedural change be grounds for invalidation?"

"Mr. Parliamentarian?" I asked Jefferson and at the same time glanced at Paul who sat with his hands on the arms of the oak chair, his Bible in his lap. He appeared alert and friendly.

"As I interpret the *Book of Church Order*, the membership has a right to dispense with normal procedure of business if the meeting is one in excess of the required quarterly meetings," Jefferson said. "Which, of course, this meeting is."

"That answers my question and thank you." Billy Mosby sat down.

"If there's no further discussion, I'll call for a show of hands from those who favor the motion that we dispense with the normal order of procedure," I said.

The air whooshed with the thrusting of hands.

"The clerk will record the motion as passed," I said to Jefferson. Not sure what I should do next, I looked at him.

"Just announce it's open," he whispered. "It's up to them to bring charges."

"This meeting is open," I said. "Anybody who wants the floor may have it by gaining recognition from the chair."

People stirred and shifted their eyes toward Lou. Before he could rise, a hand went up in front of him. It belonged to Miss Abbey Abbot, our town librarian. She was deaf.

She stood and held to the rear of a pew. She wore a black straw hat and a nosegay of pansies. People were confused. They stared at her, unable to believe she was going to lead the attack.

"Yes, Miss Abbey," I said. "You have the floor."

"I have what?" she asked, leaning toward me. She cupped a hand to an ear.

"The floor," I said, raising my voice. "You may speak."

"Oh yes," she said, nodding and blinking, her eyes outsized behind thick glasses. She cleared her throat. "Now what about the water fountain. The children need a fountain."

There were groans. People shook their heads and whispered it was just like her. She had once frightened a visiting minister by standing in the middle of his sermon, she believing he was giving the benediction.

"The fountain's been taken care of," I told her.

"We ought to have plenty of water for our children," she said and scowled as if she thought somebody might disagree.

"We do, Miss Abbey," I shouted.

"What's that?" she asked, the hand cupped to the ear.

People around her called to her and tried to explain. She was startled and confused.

"It's been taken care of," I shouted.

"Oh," she said. "Well, it's about time. Our children have to have water."

She sat and settled her hands in her lap. She nodded around her as if she'd set the matter straight once and for all.

"The floor's open," I said. Let it come and be over with quickly, I thought. I looked toward Lou, but Wayland Counts stood.

"I'd like to ask the chair whether the minister ought to be in here," Wayland said.

Now I was confused. I glanced at Jefferson. Methodically he thumbed through the *Book of Church Order*. I became aware of movement on the pulpit. Paul had his hand up.

"I'd like to say respectfully that as minister I'm also a member of this congregation," Paul said. "Therefore I have every right to be here."

"You shouldn't be able to sit up there and intimidate us," Wayland said. "And certainly you shouldn't be in the pulpit at a time like this."

People nodded.

"I'll leave the pulpit," he said.

Holding his Bible, he walked down the three steps. He had no

302

chair, and he stood to the left of me. I offered him my chair, but he didn't sit.

"He's a full member of the congregation," Jefferson whispered to me.

"The pastor is a member of the congregation and has a right to attend the meeting," I said. "The floor's open."

Wayland sat. Lou Gaines stood. People quieted. He looked angry, sick, battered.

"I'm asking this congregation to do me the courtesy of finishing this business quick," Lou said. He was hoarse.

People whispered and nodded.

"Wait a second if you don't mind," Billy Mosby said. He was again caught up in legalistics. "We can't vote unless he's been charged."

"You know what I'm charging him with," Lou said.

"But it has to go on the record," Billy said. He received a lot of business from Lou and was certainly on Lou's side, yet his loyalty to the beautiful maze of the law was even stronger.

"That's correct," Jefferson said. "There ought to be a charge to put in the minutes."

"All right," Lou said. He looked as if he wanted to shout and was holding his mouth small to keep his voice controlled. "If I have to parade it out in front of everybody, I'll do it. I'm charging the minister of this church with assaulting my wife. I'm charging him with invading my home and attempting rape. Is that clear enough for the record?"

The congregation shifted and talked. It was as if a wave rolled through them. I held up my hands for quiet and glanced at Paul. He stood with his arms at his side. He was colored red by sunlight passing through a stained-glass window on the west side of the church—a stylized scene of Christ multiplying fish and loaves.

"Now you know the charge," Lou said. "I'd like to vote."

The congregation shared his outrage. They looked hatefully at Paul. He backed up a little. His legs touched the dais. He could retreat no farther.

"I'd like to ask one more question before we vote," Wayland said. "Shouldn't the minister leave while we vote?"

"Since he's a member of the congregation, I assume he has a vote," I said.

"But charges have been made," Wayland said. "He now stands before the bar, so to speak."

"May I say a word?" Paul asked me.

I nodded.

"In any court the accused has a right to present a case. We wouldn't want to violate that principle of justice in this church."

"You can have your say at the proper time," Wayland said. "But we ought to be able to discuss this without you looking sanctimonious up there."

"I am not attempting to be sanctimonious," Paul said. "I merely want to be present when I'm talked about."

"I'm putting it in the form of a motion," Wayland said.

"You can't put it in the form of a motion when there's no precedent for it," Paul said.

He looked at Jefferson. Jefferson adjusted his glasses and leafed through the book. He nodded.

"Why does everybody have to be so formal?" Harvey Boyle asked. His white shirt had the sheen of newness on it, and his black tie was knotted tight against his Adam's apple. He looked at Paul. "We just can't talk about you in front of you. I suggest you take a notion to wait in your study."

"I'm taking no notions," Paul said. The mulishness firmed his face.

"We can have a show of hands to find out what we want, can't we?" Wayland asked.

"Mr. Parliamentarian?" I asked Jefferson.

"The congregation can show its hands anytime it wants," Jefferson said.

"Will the members of the congregation who'd like the preacher to step outside a moment show their hands," Wayland said.

"It has to come from the chair," Jefferson said.

"Show your hands," I told them. I felt ashamed for Wayland. He was toadying to Lou, and everybody knew it.

People put their hands up. There was easily a majority, though not all the congregation favored Paul's leaving. Sutter and Archie LeBuck didn't. Neither did Val.

"You see what they want," I said, turning to Paul. "You can't be made to leave."

"All right," Paul said. "I want to be reasonable." He walked to the door which led from the sanctuary to the Sunday school. "I'll be given a chance, won't I?"

"You will," I said.

Claude unlocked the door, and Paul went out.

[48]

I faced the congregation.

"The floor's open," I said.

"Mr. Chairman," a lady's voice said from the rear of the church. It was a trembling voice—soft and frightened like a little girl. I recognized Aunt Delia, her who never visited town because she had been seared by her marriage to a musician and had become as frightened of people as a doe.

She stood in the last pew, small, full of fear, holding her hands. Her wispy white hair was tucked under a dark felt hat, and her yellowed blouse was fastened at her neck by an opal brooch as big as a chestnut.

"I think this is a tragic affair," she said. Tremolo shook her words. "It will hurt our church and our community. It will hurt us."

She had been broken so badly through intensity of passion

305

for her vagabond husband that she became all sensitivity for the pain of others. She suffered suffering.

"I hope everybody concerned will deport himself with decorum," she said. It was taking great courage for her to speak. Her frail body quivered. "We wouldn't want anybody ever to say we had failed to be decorous."

There were people in the church who'd never heard her speak, and they stared. She couldn't endure their eyes. She wanted to say more, but the eyes melted her. She looked around apologetically and sat down. She bowed her head.

Lou stood and gentled his voice as best he could.

"Miss Delia, try to think of me and my wife, will you?" His voice drew people's faces away from Aunt Delia to himself. "There was nothing decorous about what happened to my wife. It was ugly and vicious. Now, I'm trying to be fair to everybody, but it's very difficult when I think of what he did to Caroline, and I'd appreciate it if you all would do me the courtesy of voting."

For Lou, it was humility. People were touched. They faced me, ready to do what he wanted. I glanced at Jefferson.

"I'm not sure of the motion," Jefferson said.

"Mr. Chairman," Billy Mosby said as he stood, "why put this thing in terms which are reprehensible to us all. Let's practice a little euphony. Mr. Chairman, I move that our congregation withdraw its support of our minister, that we cease to pay his salary, and that we request him to vacate the manse. As part of the same motion I also move that a pulpit committee be formed to seek out a new minister."

Billy Mosby sat down.

"Is there a second?" I asked.

"I second it," Gerald Emory said. Gerald, a widower, sold Oliver farm equipment.

"Discussion," I said.

"We've discussed it plenty in one way or another," Wayland said. He spoke without waiting to be recognized. "I call for the question."

"You can't call for the question yet. We promised the preacher he'd have his say."

"We don't owe him a thing," Wayland said.

"We're going to let him speak," Archie LeBuck said, cutting off Wayland, who glared.

"Are we ready to call him back?" I asked the congregation.

They talked among themselves. I nodded at Claude. He went through the door.

As we waited for Paul, people fanned themselves. Their faces were slick with sweat. Men loosened their ties. Women dabbed at their foreheads and necks with dainty handkerchiefs.

Claude returned and stood aside for Paul to cross the floor toward me. He walked with a heavy-footed stride. He had washed his face while he was out, and he looked cool and contained. He squinted at me questioningly, his blue eyes defensive under his thick brows.

"There's a motion on the floor that your salary and support be stopped and that a pulpit committee be formed to find another minister," I explained. "You have the right of discussion."

He rubbed his palms and lifted his jaw to loosen his neck in his collar. His eyes swept across the congregation like a man judging the worth and temper of a horse. He squared his shoulders.

"It's my hope that we can talk together like reasonable men," he said.

"Do you call what you've done reasonable?" Birdwell asked. Birdwell had a pug face. He owned a garage and did welding.

"What I've done?" Paul said. He moved a few steps up the center aisle toward Birdwell. "Who knows what one man does and doesn't?"

"We know about you," Birdwell said. He was embarrassed about speaking out and fidgeted in his seat.

"You may think you know," Paul said. "You see the outside of me and the way I walk. But you don't see the inside. You don't see my will, my hope, and my intentions."

He modulated his voice to a rich baritone.

307

"Many things may not appear reasonable that are," he said. "Look at the prophets. Certainly they didn't appear reasonable when they forsook their families and homes to take issue with the opinions of their day. Who would have called Moses or Isaiah or John the Baptist reasonable men?"

"How can you mention yourself in that company?" Wayland asked.

"Don't misunderstand me," Paul said quickly. "I'm not comparing myself to them. I'm just saying that in their own time they were misunderstood. Men quick to judge wanted to put them to death."

He moved a little farther up the aisle.

"The point is, don't judge me too hurriedly. Try to remember that I've tried in this community. If I've fallen short, remember the dilemma of being a Christian is that our creed asks more than we can give. Ours is a religion of failure because God asks of us what we cannot possibly do. Like Sisyphus and his eternal stone, we push against our vices only to stumble, fall, and be crushed by our imperfections."

He was selling now. His voice was silk, and his eyes moved over the people.

"We are advised to turn the other cheek. Who among us can do it? We are told if a man asks for our cloak, to give him our shirt also. We are admonished to love our neighbors, but who can love the man next door whose dog digs up our shrubbery and who won't mend his part of the fence? Yet we try. Brothers in sin, it's all we can do."

He was attempting to save himself and Caroline by throwing up a fog of words. His voice was deep and convincing. In spite of themselves, people were interested. They set their feet to resist him. Mistrust showed on their faces like blooms uncurling.

"I know what you think," Paul said. "You believe a man of the cloth has to be different from other people—that he has to be better. But a minister is made of flesh and blood. Like all men he is prey to mortality and corruption."

"Does he have a right to preach a sermon?" Wayland asked, standing. "This is supposed to be a discussion of a motion."

"He has a right to his say," I said.

"I don't think you ought to let him carry on in here any way he wants."

"You haven't been recognized by the chair," I said. "Mr. Elgin has the floor."

Wayland sat. He was furious.

"I don't mean to sound sanctimonious," Paul said. He moved slowly up the center aisle so he could talk to the people in the rear. "But what is living all about? I put it to you that we are here to learn contempt for the flesh. Daily we see decay, loss, pain, and death. In suffering we reach out our hand, and God takes that hand and leads us from the realm of flesh into the country of the soul."

He came back down the aisle.

"Yet no man escapes his flesh entirely. Like Sisyphus', our journey is a series of climbing up and falling down. We are all rolling that stone up the mountain, losing our footing, and being crushed. In this life we never get to the top of the mountain."

His words were soft now. He spoke as if whispering into each of our ears. There was a soothing rhythm which took hold of one. The hardness of faces grew less angular.

"I'm a man," Paul said. He touched his arm as if examining himself. "I'm a minister, but most of all I'm a man. If I've caused division here and suffering, it was not my intent. Certainly I repent my wrong. Why can't we just leave it like that? Why can't you just give me your forgiveness and let's all go home? Say to yourself, 'He's a man, and he needs my help as I have needed help.'"

Lou stood. His hands flapped against the back of the pew.

"These words," he said. He threw an arm in front of him as if to clear away a web that held him. "Does anybody remember what we're talking about? Not some . . . slight indiscretion. He tried to rape my wife."

Lou's rebuke stung people. They sat straighter and shuffled their feet. They were ashamed they had been listening to Paul.

"The despair of the world is the breach between fact and appearance," Paul said. He was speaking directly to Lou. I understood it was a warning.

"You're using words to set up a smoke screen," Lou charged. "I'm not letting people forget what happened in my house."

"No smoke screen," Paul said. "Please, Lou. If you want me to, I'll abase myself here before you and everyone, but then let it drop."

"No," Lou said. He swung around to speak to the congregation. "How long you going to listen to him?" Lou's face shone, and his words writhed in his mouth before coming out. His freckled hands worked against the pew top. "I want to vote on the motion."

"It could be your great opportunity," Paul said. He held a hand toward Lou. "For you above all, it could be a great display of faith."

"You're crazy," Lou said.

Paul lowered his hand. Slowly he backed off. He pushed at his rebellious hair. He gathered his forces for another try at it.

"I want everybody to understand what's involved here," he said. "It's not merely my leaving this church. I'll do that. I'll pack up and go."

The people watched him, wary. Lou was still standing, his expression caught between puzzlement and fury.

"It's not even that your censure of me will stop my preaching," Paul said. "That'll hurt me terribly, but it's not the worst thing."

He waited a moment to build suspense.

"The worst thing is what's going to happen to each of you," he said. "I stand here before you and ask you to forgive me. If you refuse, you hurt me, but more than me you hurt yourselves. You mock the very faith you profess to defend."

Again he moved up the aisle. His light blue eyes sought out uncertainty and irresolution.

"Do you think any of you deserves to be forgiven?" he asked.

310

"Our faith says each of us is flawed and unable of himself to do any good."

"Words again," Lou said and slapped the back of the pew.

"What is the greatest sin in the world?" Paul asked. "It's not pride, lust, covetousness, or murder. The worst sin, the most damning, is to turn your back on a person who has come to you for forgiveness."

Paul didn't give Lou a chance to speak. Instead he talked fast, pacing quickly up and down the aisle, his hands circling and moving out.

"It isn't as if you don't know me," Paul said. "I didn't just blow into town and try to rob a bank. You've watched me for years, and you've seen the work, the hard work, I've done. You remember the sickness and death I've been through with you. You should think of the times you came to me for help, and I gave it."

There were few among us he'd not touched, and as he talked people remembered suffering, accidents, funerals. They thought of him lifting the red convertible off the Carter child. Even Lou was beholden through a younger sister who'd died by inches, taken by multiple sclerosis. Paul had sat with her a dozen nights and laid his palm on her forehead to ease her cry.

"I ask you to treat me as I would treat one of you who came to me in trouble," Paul said. "And if you won't show kindness and mercy to me, how can you ever ask them for yourself? And you'll need kindness and mercy one day. All men do."

Paul rushed on before Lou could speak, and his voice was deep, rich, and intense. In spite of themselves, people bent forward to listen.

"I'd like to read to you from Isaiah," Paul said, opening his Bible. He had the place marked. " 'All flesh is grass, and all its beauty is like the flower of the field. The grass withers, and the flower fades when the breath of the Lord blows upon it. Surely the people is grass. The grass withers, and the flower fades, but the word of our God will stand forever.' "

Paul turned, his eyes seeking out believers.

"What is the word of God?" he asked. "There's nothing complicated about it. It was spoken off the cross. It is the most common, the most majestic, the most abused, and the most glorious word in the dictionary. That word, my brothers, is love."

He stood still, and for a moment he had them. I thought that after all he might be able to do it—that he might be able to save himself without giving them Caroline. They were caught. Their expressions were rapt.

[49]

Lou was first to shake himself free. He was standing, and his hands grasped the back of the pew. He jerked his head around. His lips twisted.

"That was very pretty," he said. "If we're not careful, he'll be making us feel we're in the wrong. We'll be the guilty ones."

"Everyone's guilty," Paul said, speaking quietly. He watched Lou.

"You listen a while," Lou said angrily. "Mr. Chairman, if I have the floor, you keep him from talking."

Paul nodded and backed toward the pulpit. A spectrum of color from the stained-glass windows fanned his face. A strand of his hair lay against his brow.

"I've lived in this town all my life," Lou said. "I was born here, and I'll die here. My people are buried outside this church. It's the same ground I'll lie in."

He turned as he talked.

"You all know me," he said. "You knew my people. I've put my word on the line with you a hundred times."

He wasn't the speaker Paul was. Lou's voice was jarring, and his pronunciation slurred. But belief and sincerity came through strong. People listened and acted as if he'd caught them doing something unlawful.

"I want you to understand," Lou said. "In all the tangle of words, don't forget what the reason is we're here. Let's get it straight. If you don't censure him, then you censure me, my wife, and what I've stood for in this town. Let's put it so you all can see it. You'll be calling me and my wife liars."

He turned slowly and nodded at them.

"So make up your minds what you're going to do," Lou said. "Get clear on who you're voting for and against." He faced Paul. "And if you want to go around forgiving everybody, drive up to the state prison and ask the warden to let off the rapists and murderers. Turn them loose and be so forgiving you fix it so they can burn, rape, and kill all over again. Then maybe what happened to me and my wife will happen to you, and you can be really forgiving."

He'd finished speaking, but he didn't sit immediately. He kept turning, and his eyes moved along the rows. People were cut down before his glance—as if his eyes were a blade swinging through grain.

Paul was alarmed. He pushed at his hair. The lavender light from the window made his sweat appear oily.

"Those are powerful words," he said. He took a step up the aisle. "They're so powerful I'm thinking we ought to all put ourselves in the prison. We're made of the same dust and spittle. We're all full of corruption. We ought to take no chances on goodness but lock up the whole human race."

He was using his rich voice to try to rally the congregation to him, but they sat motionless, their faces fixed. They belonged to Lou. Paul saw it. He wiped sweat from his chin.

"It's gotten cold in here," he said. "It's so hot everybody's shriveling, but I feel a cold wind. It's wind coming off hardened hearts."

He smiled, but they didn't respond. They were stones sitting in the pews. I watched him become afraid.

313

"Cold," he said and hugged himself as if he were in a blizzard. "A real snowstorm's blowing through our church in the middle of August. Who'd believe it?"

Unmoved they waited. Paul glanced at me as if there were something I could do. I lowered my eyes.

"It's become so quiet," he said. "Somebody passing out there on the street would think this church's empty it's so quiet in here. And cold."

His shoulders were hunched, and his big hands twitched at his sides. He moved up the aisle.

"I used to have lots of friends here," he said. "Why, I couldn't walk down the street without getting a sore palm from shaking hands. And I've gone weeks without eating at home I've had so many invitations to dinner."

They watched with unblinking eyes.

"I've been fishing with a lot of you," he said. "And I hit a home run over the high-school fence. I used to get warm in the middle of the winter thinking how many friends I had. Yet I tell you I'm feeling cold now."

He laughed artificially—a frightened laugh which was more like a cry.

"Doesn't anybody here have a kind word to say about me?" he asked. He paced the aisle. "Can't anybody remember anything good I've done?"

They sat planted and unyielding.

"I'm not asking anybody to stand and praise me," Paul said. "If one or two of you would just remember how you thought of me earlier in the summer. You liked me then. I haven't changed. I'm the same man."

He moved across the front of the church and looked into faces.

"Think of yourselves," Paul said. "We're heirs to imperfect flesh. Being human involves weakness and stumbling."

He'd lost his timing and certainty. Now his voice sounded loud and harsh.

"Can any of you remember a time you called me and I didn't come?" he asked, casting out desperately. He moved up the center aisle. "What about you, James?" He'd singled out James Vaden, a farmer who'd been stung by hundreds of bees. Paul had rubbed butter over him and carried him to the hospital. Now James sat small in the pew.

"Or you, Edgar?" Paul asked Edgar Pickett who believing the malignancy in his bowels couldn't be cured had shot himself in the chest and would have finally succeeded in dying had not Paul and Helen nursed him, never leaving him alone, until Paul could arrange for the cobalt treatment at Duke. Now Edgar wouldn't look at Paul.

"Or you, Sam," Paul said. Sam Basset lost his job at the chenille plant and went on a three-year toot. Paul took up a collection to send him away to a health farm. Paul also sweet-talked the telephone company into giving Sam a job in the business office. Now Sam pulled at his ear and kept his eyes down.

"Won't anybody stand up and name just one good thing I've done since I came to Black Leaf?" Paul asked. He whirled in the aisle. Fear was sticky on him.

"I'm saying please," he said. "I'm begging."

He came down the aisle to me. He wanted me to save him—to throw them Caroline. I wouldn't look at him. I saw only his black shoes and the lower part of his heavy legs. I heard him breathing. He kept standing in front of me.

Finally he moved away, up the center aisle again. He seemed uncertain which way to go. His voice became sarcastic, bitter.

"So everybody's forgotten me," he said. "All anybody wants to remember is the bad. I hope when each of you needs help—and you will, you will—that you find more generosity than I have here. I hope when you become lonely, sick, and afraid, you remember what you did here to me."

He moved up and down the aisle. People watched him come apart.

"I'm a man lost in the darkness," he said. "I need a hand to reach out to me. I need some pure human kindness. Surely somebody I've helped in their bad days will reach out to me."

He stopped and turned as if he'd lost his sense of direction.

"All right," he said. He sounded angry. "You all are so stiff-necked and righteous, but you don't know everything."

He came down the aisle and stood in front of me a third time. "Question Jackson LeJohn here," he said. "He can tell you things."

I didn't look up. His feet passed in front of me.

He said. "I'm asking for my life."

Again he turned. He wiped his face. His voice became an accusation. He was girding himself to give them Caroline.

"You're so righteous," he said bitterly.

He prowled the aisles.

"You swell with righteousness, and you're so fat you're about to pop. You need a shock to wipe the smugness off your pious faces."

People were resentful but puzzled. They glanced from him to me and back to him. Even Lou was unsure. He sat forward and scowled.

"I'm not without resources," Paul said, nodding. "I have a right to save my life. I have a responsiblity to think of my family. And it'd do this righteous congregation good to know how wrong it can be."

He walked faster up and down aisles. He slapped the knuckles of one hand into the palm of the other.

"Let's go back to beginnings," he said. "Let's go back to a long time ago—before any of you heard of me or another person who's involved here at this time."

He kept nodding and slapping his knuckles into his palm.

"Nobody believes me," he said. "Nobody here's even willing to give mercy. You want me to be guilty. You want to enjoy squashing me."

He prowled a side aisle. People rolled their eyes to watch.

"Well, I'm not letting you squash me," he said. "I'm going to tell you a little story that goes back to my college days. You won't be so stiff-necked and righteous after you understand it's about a person you think is perfect—so perfect that everything automatically has to be my fault."

He nodded and smiled like a man baring his teeth to bite.

"Here we go," he said, pacing. "Here are the facts of the matter. A long, long time ago when I was in college I met a young woman by the name of Rosy."

"No!" I said, standing. People gaped at me.

"Why not?" he asked, prowling toward me. "Just tell me why not."

I was sitting down.

"I have a right to save myself," he said to me.

There was noise on the other side of the front door. The noise sounded like the sea. Ushers hurried to the door and twisted the large brass handles. Outside, people surged and raised their voices.

Archie LeBuck shouted orders. The congregation stood. For a moment I couldn't see what it was. I heard a gasp. I saw black around paleness. Caroline's face floated in the crowd.

She wore a black suit and a large black hat which shaded her face. She looked like death. On each side of her she held a young, sun-tanned daughter. The daughters wore pink dresses that belled around their thin, girlish legs. The dresses were pinched in at the waist by bows. The girls were clean, their blond hair brushed shiny. Frightened, they pressed against their mother's thighs. They were about to weep.

Lou sidled from his pew and hurried to Caroline. He touched her arm and reached protectively to his daughters. He stood in front of them as if to hide them from Paul.

"You shouldn't have come," Lou said. "You shouldn't have brought them here."

People watched Caroline.

Her mouth was open slightly, and her pale face strained. She stared at Paul. Her gray eyes pleaded. She teetered. She would have fallen had not Lou caught her. The little girls started crying.

Paul backed away as if from fire. He shook his head. He saw the truth in the flesh. If he saved himself, or a part of himself, he would have to ruin other human beings. He would have to offer them up.

Still shaking his head, he backed off. He bumped into a pew but continued to back until he reached the altar table. He was lost. He turned in a half circle. His sweaty face was slack. He looked as if he wanted to ask questions but could find no one to speak to.

He moved along in front of the pews. His legs were shaky. He steadied himself by leaning to the marble baptismal font. He blinked as if blinded.

"Take me home," Caroline said to Lou. Her shoulders sloped, and she wept. "God, haven't I had enough?"

Her head bowed. Her daughters—their small, clean faces wet and frightened—clutched at her legs and looked up at her. Lou drew her toward the doors.

"I hope you're happy," he said to us. His voice trembled and was husky. "I hope all of you are happy at humiliating my wife, my children, and me."

The doors opened. Ushers gathered around Caroline, Lou, and their daughters. Shielded from the crowd, they left. Cameras flashed. Cries rose from reporters.

Paul stood at the front of the church. He was unsteady, drunken, on his feet. His face was dazed. He backed away.

Claude unlocked the door which led to the Sunday school. Paul backed through. He raised his right palm like a man expecting somebody to drop a coin into it.

[50]

After Paul left, we voted. Jefferson cut up neat slips of notebook paper for ballots. Deacons passed them out.

"What should we write on them?" Jesse Ingram, the postmaster, asked.

"If you favor the motion to stop support of the minister and to form a pulpit committee, you vote yes," I said.

People bent over, positioning the ballots on their knees, pocketbooks, and hymnals. They folded their ballots. Some of the slips were folded so many times they were hardly as big as stamps. Deacons collected the ballots in hats and brought them to the altar table.

The deacons did the counting and whispered the results to Jefferson. Jefferson wrote down the totals and handed the paper to me. There were pitifully few "No's."

"The motion carries," I said. "Is there any other business to come before this congregational meeting?"

They shuffled their feet. They were tired, satiated, and they wanted to go home.

"I declare this meeting adjourned," I said.

I turned quickly away from people and left the church by the door into the Sunday school. I walked to the study.

Paul and Helen were waiting. He had taken off his coat and tie. He sat in his desk chair. Helen stood behind him and massaged his lumpy shoulders. When I entered, her hands stilled.

"I'm sorry," I said. The shades were lowered against the sun, but a shaft of light glittered on the golden trophy of the Greek athlete.

"Was it even close?" Paul asked. He was limp under Helen's hands.

"You had some support."

"It's nice not everybody abandoned me," he said. It was an accusation, but without intensity. Helen's hands moved on his shoulders.

"Is there anything you want me to do?" I asked.

"You've done a whole lot," he said, allowing his body to slump in the chair.

"Stop," Helen said, chiding him. She still watched me.

"If you need money, I have a little," I said.

"If I need money," he said and let his head loll against Helen.

319

He laughed. "Well, I need it. We have twenty-eight dollars in the bank. So since I have to move and find a new life for me and my family, I think you can safely assume we need it."

I walked to his desk, opened my wallet, and took out a check. I wrote it for a hundred and fifty dollars. That was a lot of money for me, how much he'd never know. I left the check on the desk.

"Blood money," he said. "You feel guilty."

"Don't, Paul," Helen told him. She massaged his shoulders.

"Maybe," I said. "But the money spends the same way no matter how I feel."

Ugly words formed in his mouth and distorted his lips. The words would have come out had not Helen stopped them. Her hands tightened on his shoulders, and her nails dug in. He sighed, patted her hand, and leaned across the desk to pick up the check.

"I'll accept your money," he said. "I have no choice."

"And thank you," Helen said to me.

"It's deductible of course," he said. He couldn't let go of me.

"I won't deduct it," I told him and moved toward the door. "Is there anything else I can do?"

"That's the famous line," he said. "They always ask that to the man they shit on."

"Paul!" Helen said.

"It's a living fact," he said.

"He'll be better tomorrow," she explained to me.

"I'll be wonderful tomorrow," he said.

Wearily he let himself sink in the chair. He closed his eyes.

Book Six

Though I felt like getting drunk, I didn't. I went home and sat on my porch. I looked over my burnt fields to where the sun was a red wound above the dusty pines. I sat in the hot glare because I didn't want to escape my pain.

At six Injun came home on his bicycle. He carried the day's receipts in a canvas moneybag. I fixed him supper, and to keep from having to talk to him I walked around the house and down to the spring. Cool water oozed out of moss. I patted the coolness against my flushed face.

I couldn't get preachers off my mind. I had this feeling that all over the world they were being chased from pulpits and devoured. It was a kind of slow crucifixion where they took our sins on themselves and then went not to a wooden cross with honest nails but to the daily serving up of their spirits as congregations dipped into and fed on them.

I walked around until dark. Mosquitoes searched me out. I listlessly slapped at them. I thought of preachers sitting in manses, waiting behind those flimsy walls to be eaten alive.

When I returned to the house, Injun was at the desk in his room posting ledgers from the store. He wore a green eyeshade and looked like a gnome as he bent his nose close to the page.

"You'll ruin your eyes," I told him absently.

"I'm almost finished," he said, raising his face to squint at me. "I heard downtown Mr. Elgin's leaving."

Injun tried to hold his small face impassive, but there was delight there—in the pulling of his mouth and the ferret brightness of his eyes. Even in a child, I thought. I wanted to grab him and shake him. I wanted to yell at him that he ought not batten on anybody's misery. But I didn't because we were all born with the rottenness in us, and Injun couldn't be blamed for being human.

I told him good night, went to my bedroom, and undressed. I lay on the big bed that had belonged to my father and two of my grandfathers. It was the bed where Kitt and I had slept and loved. It was the bed where she had died, and my hand moved across the sheet as if it might feel her.

I seemed to become aged right there on the bed. It was as if my muscles were softening and my skin shrinking. I felt wrinkles groove my body. My backbone drew up on me. I wanted to whine. Oh I needed my Kitt.

I stood and walked barefoot downstairs to the kitchen. In the dark I sat at the table and listened to bugs ping against the screens. I heard bullfrogs in the slough, uh-rumping and maybe praying to the frog god of rain. Through black pines, heat lightning flashed silently.

Injun came down, carrying his flashlight and wondering what I was doing sitting in the dark. He stood in the doorway, his skinny legs poking down below the pajamas which were a foot too short for him. I'd have to buy him some new ones.

"You all right?" he asked. His little face was worried.

"Go to bed," I told him.

He turned, went to the steps, and then came back to the kitchen.

"I'm going to put on a bicycle sale," he said. "I'll call it a pre-schooler and cut prices on bikes. We'll make our profit by charging a higher markup on accessories."

"Sure," I said, not listening to him.

"We could have some advertising."

"Don't talk to me about it now," I said impatiently.

He went on back up the steps.

I sat in the dark until three o'clock. My dogs started barking, and I padded to the back porch. In the moonlight I saw a stray hound ghosting across the yard.

I grabbed for my shotgun, jammed two high-brass number fours into the breeches, and leveled the barrel at the dog who had stopped. His tail was down, and his puny rump was drawn in. He looked in my direction. It would have been an easy kill, but I slowly lowered the shotgun. Let him live, I thought. Let all poor bastards in this world live.

[52]

In the morning I drove to the manse. The moving van was already there, backed up to the gate in the picket fence. Children were helping load by carrying out toys.

Helen was on the front porch. She had a pink kerchief wrapped around her brown hair. She was packing a cardboard box with linens.

"Can you use an extra hand?" I asked.

"I expect you want to see Paul," she said. She was sweating and had a smear of dust on her cheek. Two colored men came out with a black table. She stepped aside for them and pushed at her hair as if distracted.

"I'll be glad to help here."

"You're very kind, but the men can do it. They have their own system."

"Where is he?"

"At the church."

Children were marching in and out, carrying toys and games. Each of them let the screen door slam. The children weren't hurt, not yet. They tried to act serious, but they were excited about moving.

A little blonde walked out. She wore only her underwear. She held a small plastic horse with a red bridle. She carried it to the colored man on the truck.

I stood by helplessly. Helen went inside. I put on my hat and walked toward the church. The grass was brown. In the distance I heard a siren, and even the sound was hot.

I went into the church by the front door. Yesterday the sanctuary had been charged with intense people, but now the pews were empty and silent. Lavender light fell on the carpets. The spot where Paul had stood to make his final plea was just a place along the unmarked aisle. Christ in stained glass was forever serenely multiplying bread and fish.

I walked through the door to the Sunday-school building and along the sunny corridor. All the crayon drawings were still pinned up. Pasted to a window was a paper strip of yellow tulips. Lucas, our sexton, had not swept. The floor and sills were dusty.

I found Paul kneeling before shelves in his study. He was removing books and packing them in cardboard boxes. He wore shorts and tennis shoes, but no shirt. The black hair on his chest glistened with sweat.

He glanced at me and continued packing.

"You come to pick my bones?" he asked.

"No."

He shook his head and closed his eyes as if he couldn't believe what was happening to him. His big hands reached for a clutch of books.

"Most of these aren't mine," he said. "Other preachers left them in passing through. And I'll leave one or two of my own to make my mark." He smiled tight. "Not that I haven't."

I took off my coat, draped it over a chair, and rolled up my sleeves. I knelt beside him.

"Hand them to me and I'll pack," I said.

"You're certain you're not afraid of becoming contaminated?"

"I'm not afraid."

"The neighbors are watching. They know you're here."

326

"Just hand me some books."

He nodded and lifted books to me. We filled two boxes. He cleared his throat.

"I was rough on you yesterday," he said.

"That's okay," I said, fitting books into the box.

"I'm not entirely sorry, but I'm trying to be. Helen's helping me try."

"I've forgotten it."

"I don't want you to forget it."

He stared at me.

"Okay," I said.

"I had no right to expect you to do the dirty work. It was unreasonable and unjust of me."

He handed me another book. We filled a third box.

"Give me a day or two and perhaps I'll honestly be able not to dislike you," he said.

I helped him carry boxes of books from the manse to the moving van. As we worked, I saw that people were watching. Ladies peeked from behind curtains or came out onto porches of their houses. Men driving past in their cars eyed me.

When Paul and I finished the books, we packed things from his desk. Most of the furniture stayed in the study as did the pictures on the walls—those fading prints of the Last Supper and the Colosseum. They would serve the next minister who came.

Paul and I went to the kitchen and drank water from the tap. He leaned against the sink.

"You have guts, Jackson," he said. "Why, you might catch some sort of germ from me and go around philandering women."

"Not at my age."

"The ladies will lock their doors when they see you coming," he said and put the jelly glass he'd drunk from into the sink. He faced me. "One of the things I regret about what's happened here is that you and I didn't become better friends."

"Maybe we can go fishing one day," I said. I didn't believe it. I would never see him again, but even if it were possible, I would never become close to him. He was God-bitten, and his journey was along a lonely road I could not walk.

"That's a nice thing for you to say, Jackson. You're really a staunch fellow."

We finished packing. Doing so wasn't difficult. The Elgins owned pitifully little of their own. Not even the icebox belonged to them. They were kind of spiritual Okies, and the old Dodge resembled one of those rattling sway-backed cars that had fled the Dust Bowl. We tied bags on top and to the bumpers. The children were inside, fighting for positions by the windows.

"Where you headed?" I asked him as we carried out suitcases. I didn't really want to know. I intended to free myself of this man who'd caused me so much trouble and shame.

"We'll stay with my sister until I find another pulpit," he said.

I looked at him. He would never see another pulpit—at least not in this communion.

"They can't keep a preaching man down," he said, understanding my expression. He laughed. "I can always find a soapbox somewhere. There are dark places and jungles. I'll know."

I imagined his big body dirty and insect torn. I thought of him lifting that great, rich voice to natives—they astonished at the message that a god could die.

We went back to the manse for the last of the bags and put them in the trunk. One of the girls carried out the golden trophy of the Greek athlete straining for the laurel. The gold plating had worn off in spots, and base metal shone through. Paul stuck the trophy behind the treadless spare tire.

Helen was making sandwiches in the kitchen. The children, anxious to leave, carried their sandwiches to the car. She filled a thermos with milk. Her brown hair wouldn't stay in place, and she pushed at it vaguely, hopelessly.

Paul and I couldn't get the car trunk down. We tried repacking it, but still it wouldn't close. We fastened it to the bumper with a piece of clothesline.

The old Dodge was so loaded it sunk around its wheels. Paul started the engine. Oily blue smoke shot out of the rusted exhaust. The smoke moved sluggishly in the hot, dusty air. The car shook as if it'd settle to the concrete and expire.

I helped Helen in. She had her arms full of bundles. People up and down the street were watching openly.

Helen turned back toward the manse, and I believed she would cry. She did not. She touched her nose, sat erect, and stared straight ahead.

"Jackson," Paul said.

He was in the car, behind the wheel, and he stuck his hand out to me.

There was ugliness, I thought, always ugliness, but under the muck was, perhaps, goodness too—at least a mustard seed of it.

I shook his hand and stepped away. Helen sat unblinking. The children bounced on the back seat. Paul waved.

The old Dodge bucked. The rear was so low it resembled a bootlegger's car. The exhaust spewed blue smoke. It didn't seem possible they could make it twenty yards down the street, but on the car went, rattling and bucking.

I heard singing—Paul, Helen, and the sweet voices of children: *Protect us, Lord, when the bitter winds blow, Love us, Lord, when we suffer here below, Extend thy hand, Lord, in the dark of this night, Lead us, Lord, to the balm of thy light.*

The old Dodge turned the corner slowly. Blue smoke hung on the hot air, and they were gone behind the sere drooping arms of a weeping willow.

[53]

It was after three o'clock. I went home, took a bath, and put on a clean shirt. I opened my metal lock box. I drove to Miss Minnie's to see Val.

Miss Minnie wasn't in her wicker chair under the scrollwork

of the porch, but her knitting bag lay on a chair, the wooden needles sticking out. I knocked on the screen door. Nobody answered. I turned to the street. Val's car, the blue Volkswagen, was parked in front of the house. The car was shaded by an oak. I rang the bell, opened the screen door, and stuck my head inside.

"Val?" I called.

I heard somebody upstairs. Val came to the head of the steps. She had on yellow shorts, a yellow shirt, and white tennis shoes.

"Are they gone?" she asked.

"They left a while ago."

"I believed him," she said. "And I cried most of the night."

She looked as if she would cry now. She came down the steps slowly, her hand on the railing. She took my arm, and we walked into the parlor. She was young and modern against the Victorian furniture—the settee with dainty feet, the lace of chair arms, the painting of Miss Minnie's stern father in an oval butternut frame. Val's tan legs mocked the squat black table and the tiled fireplace. Her perfume taunted ghosts who lived in the house.

"You men should have done something," Val said. "You shouldn't let it end this way."

"We tried," I told her.

We sat on the settee, but she rose and paced around me.

"I believed him," Val said. "I voted for him."

She paced, her footsteps silent on the carpet. She came and sat beside me. She folded her hands between her knees.

"People here destroyed him," she said. "They wanted to believe the worst." She fidgeted. "Miss Minnie's been gloating on the phone." She bit her lip. "I hate them."

"There's no difference in people here," I said.

"That's the terrible thing. That's the worst thing of all."

We sat a moment without talking. Miss Minnie's father watched disapprovingly from his frame.

"God he spoke well in front of that bunch," Val said and sniffled. "They came to slice him up, but he almost pulled it out."

She unclasped her hands and settled them on her knees. "May I have a cigarette?"

I gave her a cigarette and lighted it for her. She was so young, alive, and full of protest. I felt like the old man of the mountain.

"Think of me," I said. My throat was tight. I sensed Kitt in the room.

"Think what of you?" Val asked. She turned her knees toward me.

"I want you to marry me," I said.

I reached into my pocket for the old-fashion ring. It had belonged to my great-grandmother and had her initials cut into the gold. I took Val's hand and fitted the ring onto her finger. Her finger was too large, and the ring stuck halfway down.

"I'm honored," she said. She stared at me with dark, solemn eyes.

"I hope that means you accept," I said, feeling Kitt beside me on the settee.

"I can't," Val said. She held up her hand and looked at the ring. Her lips trembled.

"If you won't marry me, you can't keep the ring," I said, trying to speak lightly but wanting to close my eyes and lie down for a long sleep.

"Indian giver," she said and started crying. She still held her hand up and didn't wipe at the tears.

"That's me," I said. I was very tight in the chest. "I'm an unreasonable person who expects the girl who wears his great-grandmother's ring to love him."

She slid off the ring, reached for my hand, and pressed the ring into my palm. She balled my hand into a fist. Then she did the nicest thing. She kissed my knuckles.

"You know I can't," she said.

"Do I?"

"You belong to your wife. You'd always be comparing me with her. I don't want to live in bigamy."

How could they know so much about a man? I'd hardly ever

331

mentioned Kitt to her, but Val knew. Maybe like me she felt Kitt there with us—small, lovely, a sad girl who had laughed for me. I expected Kitt to be laughing at my foolishness now, but I felt her touch my back, and there was kindness in her hand.

"If it's any comfort, I think you're a fine person," Val said.

"It's not much comfort."

She was still crying, not loudly, hardly even changing her breathing, but tears tracked her face and fell on her yellow shorts, making spots on them. I was tempted to do something dramatic like stomping out or throwing the ring into the river, but then Kitt would surely have laughed.

"You're not going to marry that good-looking dog of a doctor, are you?" I asked.

She sniffled and shook her head.

"I'm going away," she told me. "I've asked them to let me out of my contract."

She boohooed, and her face became rubbery. She leaned toward me. Her eyelashes were wet. She pressed her face against my chest.

"Where to?" I asked. I took out a handkerchief and dabbed at her face.

"Back to college," she said. "Syracuse." She reached for my handkerchief and blew her nose. "I'll ask you up for a dance."

"I'll have to find my raccoon coat," I said. I'd never owned one, but Kitt had been able to play the banjo.

"Write to me," she said. She sat straight and handed me my handkerchief. "Promise me that."

"It'll be a pleasure."

With our arms around each other's waist, we walked to the front door. I should have stayed around to help her pack, but I didn't want to watch her drive away too. So I kissed her lightly, like a brother, and very bravely pushed open the screen door and walked down the brick walk.

I told myself I was lucky. For a few months I'd had something pretty close to the love of a fine young girl. She liked me enough to cry over me. And I still had Kitt. I would always have Kitt.

I drove to the store. I left my car in the alley at the rear. I was hardly able to get past the piles of excelsior and crates which had been left for the town trash truck. Even before I opened the back door, I knew something was wrong.

First it was music which throbbed and thumped through the old brick building. The walls seemed to flap. Voices howled above the twanging of metallic guitars—*Up in the sassafras, dreaming about you.*

I pushed the door open a crack. The screeching and wailing shoved me like a hand. It is, I thought, the end of the world.

I stole through the storeroom and peeked into the front. Bicycles were everywhere. They jammed the aisles and reared on counters. They hung from hooks on the ceiling, dangling from silver plastic cord. Bicycles spun slowly and chrome glittered in red spotlights.

Plastered to the front display windows were great tulip-shaped posters—yellow, orange, red—with the word SALE on them. Over the front door was a metal loudspeaker, blasting the music into the street. Voices shrieked against the crashing of steel guitars. *I miss your sweet lips and your honied hair too.*

Customers jostled each other in the aisles. Injun hurried among them. They examined bicycles, fingered price tags, and blew electric horns. His hair was slicked down. He wore a red jacket and rang up sales on the cash register as if playing it in time to the music. He had a pencil behind each ear.

"What in the name of God!" I shouted.

Customers stared at me. Injun, his fingers still on cash register keys, stopped his spiel to a young girl wearing sunglasses. He drew in as if the cash register would protect him.

I hurried to the front of the store and tried to choke the loudspeaker. I pulled the thing from its hook and strangled it. It felt alive in my hands. Voices continued to howl. I grabbed the speaker cord and trailed it to the counter. I found the turntable. I lifted the arm and jerked off the record.

I tried to break the record. I beat it on the counter and threw it on the floor. I hit it with a hoe handle and stomped it.

"Get that red coat off!" I shouted at Injun.

I kicked the record under a counter and climbed into the display window where I began ripping down the big colored tulips. The paper twisted around me.

"We're making a killing," Injun protested.

"We're closed!" I yelled at the customers. "Get out!"

"But I want to buy Wayne a bicycle," a big woman said. She was smoking a cigarette and held Wayne by the hand. He was a fat little boy who gaped at me.

"We don't have any bicycles," I told her. "Everybody out!"

People backed away. I was still ripping paper off the windows. I balled it and threw it across the room. It snaked over counters and rustled to the floor.

On the sidewalk a crowd gathered to look in at me. I jumped to the floor and pulled down the blinds on the glass doors.

"Closed!" I shouted at people.

I tore away more of the red, orange, and yellow tulips. Injun watched warily. He had the red coat off.

"You make me ashamed," I said and threw a wad of paper at him. He ducked behind a counter.

"If we don't move these bicycles now, we'll have them all winter," he said.

"I was running this store before you had bat brains," I said. "So was my father and grandfather. And if we can't have dignity here, then by God we'll go out of business."

When I'd ripped off all the paper tulips, I washed windows and scraped the sticky spots with a razor blade. Outside, the crowd grew. I ordered Injun to sweep up paper and take down the bicycles hanging from the ceiling.

"We're not Progress Store redcoats," I told him. I yelled it. I was out of breath and wild-eyed. "We're LeJohns, and our people been living in this town for almost two hundred years. We'll go to the poorhouse before we whore to make money."

Each time I passed him he cringed. As I became calmer, I started to feel guilt. Because if he didn't know any better than to whore himself, it was my fault. I failed to teach him. And he was whoring to please me.

"Dignity," I said. I switched out lights. "I'm going to make you find the word in the dictionary and write out the meaning a hundred times with both hands. Now get to the car."

We left through the storeroom. He sat hunched in the back seat. I drove from the alley and town. I turned onto the highway.

The land was cooked, and dust lay on it thick as fur. I braked for the red road under the pines. I drove down to the river. Weeds beat against the car frame. I stopped behind my swaybacked cabin.

I opened the rear door of the car and took hold of Injun by his skinny arm. I walked fast to the river. I jerked off his bow tie and threw it to the ground. I spun him down on the grass and pulled off his shoes and socks. He was so scared he was limp. I felt his heart thumping as I shucked him out of his shirt and pants. He was toadstool pale, and his little bones poked against his skin.

I stooped to the river for a heavy handful of oozy black mud. I balled it and flung it at him. The mud splattered his pale, blue-tinged skin. He was splotched and astonished.

"You may think you're a hotshot salesman, but you're still a boy," I told him, stooping for more mud. "You don't have much time to keep being a boy, so you better live it right up to the last minute."

I let him have it with more mud. He was too shocked to move. I dumped mud on his head and slapped it against his bony shoulders. I caught him by his wrist and foot, spun with him, and arched him out into the river.

The water brought him alive. He came up sputtering and cussing beautifully. "Why damn!" he said. "Why damnittohell!" His voice was music, and I thought if I did nothing else, I'd see he got all his boyhood.

He surface-dived, his puny rump mooning under the green water. He came thrashing up with a handful of mud which he slung at me. I danced away and began stripping off my clothes. He flailed mud at me. I hurled clothes over my head and ran into the river. A blob of warm mud splattered against my chest. Injun giggled and swam for the other bank.

I dived under and thrashed after him. I caught him in the middle of the river. I ducked him. He grabbed my ankle and pulled me under. We were both laughing and swallowing water.

We eased onto our backs, kicked lazily, and lolled in the sun. We spouted water, which glittered in coils and splashed on our bellies.

I swam to the bank and lay on the grass. I turned my head upriver. Shadows gathered on the water. I grew sad remembering.

I stood, walked to the end of my rickety dock, and sat to dangle my feet in the warm water. I watched my fine, coltish son who lay with his skinny arms spread on the water as if sleeping. He turned onto his stomach. He dipped his face into the river and bubbled. He lazed to his back, raised his legs, and sunk slowly. He rose spouting water.

I looked up the shadowy river. The land was parched and dying, but the darkening water flowed gently, whispering against the willows, the dock, and me.

I bit down on my sadness. I thought that even pain had goodness. A dead man couldn't suffer. To grieve, a man had to be alive and to care about something.